Wizard
in the
Woods

Jeffrey Poole

Jeffrey Poole's Epic Fantasy Books
Bakkian Chronicles:
The Prophecy

Insurrection

Amulet of Aria

Disneyland Debacle (short story)

Winter Wonderland (short story)

Tales of Lentari
Lost City

Something Wyverian This Way Comes

A Portal for Your Thoughts

Thoughts for a Portal

Wizard in the Woods

Close Encounters of the Magical Kind

The Hunt for Red Oskorlisk (short story)

May the Fang be With You (Pirates trilogy #1)

The Hammer is Strong with This One (Pirates #2)

These are Not the Stones You're Looking For (Pirates #3)

Blast from the Past

Dragons of Andela
Harness the Fire

Strike the Spark

Clear the Water

Mysteries by J.M. Poole
The Corgi Case Files Series
18 delightful cozy mystery novels featuring corgi sleuths, Sherlock and Watson

WIZARD IN THE WOODS

Tales of Lentari, Book 5

JEFFREY POOLE

Secret Staircase Books

Wizard in the Woods
Published by Secret Staircase Books, an imprint of
Columbine Publishing Group, LLC
PO Box 416, Angel Fire, NM 87710

Book layout and design by Secret Staircase Books
First Secret Staircase paperback edition: July, 2023
First Secret Staircase e-book edition: July, 2023

* * *

Publisher's Cataloging-in-Publication Data

Poole, Jeffrey
Wizard in the Woods / by Jeffrey Poole.
p. cm.
ISBN 978-1649141446 (paperback)
ISBN 978-1649141453 (e-book)

1. Lentari (Fictitious location)—Fiction. 2. Epic fantasy fiction
3. Dragons and mythical creatures—Fiction. 4. Time travel—Fiction.
I. Title

Tales of Lentari : Book 5.
Wizard in the Woods
Poole, Jeffrey, Tales of Lentari epic fantasy series.

BISAC : FICTION / Fantasy/Epic.

813/.54

For Giliane —

Words cannot begin to describe how fortunate I am to find you by my side each and every day.

Love you always & forever!

J.

Acknowledgments

Once more I am preparing to publish a book and as always, I am incredibly thankful for a small but elite group of people.

First and foremost, I have to express my profound appreciation for my wife, Giliane. She's my primary proofer who has the uncanny ability to spot gaping plot holes who then, bless her heart, has the amazing ability to suggest changes/fixes for the aforementioned plot holes. Also, I have to thank my Posse, who willingly took time out of their busy lives to help an indie author clean up his manuscript before presenting it to the world. My betas for this title are: Diane, Jamie, Scott, Kristen, Jason, Linda, Caroline, Lawrence, and Tanner. Then, I have my Secret Staircase Books beta readers, who are Susan Gross, Sandra Anderson, and Paula Webb. You guys are the best! You all have my eternal thanks!

The last person I need to thank is YOU. You, the reader, have kept the series alive when I was more than ready to end it to move on to other things. I've had an absolute blast writing more stories about Lentari and will continue to do so as long as I can. Thank you very much for helping to support an indie author! You guys & gals rock!

J.

Table of Contents

Prologue

Dark clouds of jet-black smoke billowed steadily up on the northern horizon. Just as the ominous smoke had begun to dissipate, more roars echoed loudly throughout the still forest. Flashes of bright orange light illuminated the surrounding countryside, followed almost immediately by more of the black smoke curling up into the air.

Several dozen villagers were chatting nervously amongst themselves, pointing at the uncomfortably close wall of smoke. Many had climbed onto their roofs and were dumping bucket after bucket of water on the tops of their thatched cottages in the hopes that the impending fires would spare their homes.

A large, middle-aged, barrel-chested man appeared astride a horse. Both he and the white stallion were out of breath. A moment later, a dozen more riders appeared by his side. They were the voluntary village militia, and from the looks of their less-than-stellar appearance, had been hastily assembled without adequate time to don their gear. The lead rider pointed angrily at the northern horizon.

"What the blazes are you people doing? Do you not see the approaching fires? Forget about your homes. They can be rebuilt. Your families are more important. Get them and yourselves to safety. Now!"

One villager, a gaunt older fellow in his late sixties, stubbornly crossed his arms over his chest and glared at the deputies from his position on the roof. "I'm not abandoning my home for one lousy fire, constable!" He emptied his bucket of water onto his roof and moved back toward the ladder propped up against his house. He descended only long enough to refill the pail before he returned to the roof. "Three generations of my family have lived in this house. I won't turn my back on everything that I—"

"I don't have time for this," the constable irritably snapped. He looked over at two of his deputies. "The next time he climbs down that ladder you'll see to it that he collects his things and leaves."

"If he doesn't?" one of his deputies asked, looking up at the angry homeowner who continued to glare at them as though they were nothing more than a band of filthy invaders.

"Then take him into custody. No home is worth losing a life."

The villager lobbed his bucket off the roof and angrily shook a fist in the constable's direction.

"Over my dead body am I gonna leave this here house!"

"Don't tempt me," the constable muttered. He turned to watch the great clouds of smoke drift closer. He heard a distant roar and another section of the horizon went up in flames. Another bout of angry black clouds rose up into an already darkening sky. "Blasted dragons are going to force us all out. Perhaps we should…"

He trailed off, noticing his men had begun violently shaking their heads.

"Don't even suggest it," one of his deputies told him in a wary voice. "There's no way we're gonna take on a dragon. We're only volunteers. Battling angry dragons was never part of the job description."

The constable scowled. A breeze had picked up, one that unfortunately came from the north. The dark clouds were being pushed closer, as were the fires. Three more distinct roars sounded in the distance. The constable groaned. This wasn't the work of a solitary dragon. There must be at least two wyverians out there now. He sighed. He hadn't signed up for this, either. He turned to look back at his deputy.

"Send word to the king."

Chapter 1 — A Momentous Day

That's a good girl. Bring it back, Peanut. Come on, if you want me to throw it you'll have to drop it. No, I didn't say we were going to play tug, did I? Now, drop it!"

A soggy, battered, fabric disc that had seen better days was reluctantly deposited at his feet. The young man tentatively stooped down to pick up the sodden toy. He ignored the numerous tiny rips and punctures the dog's teeth had wrought on the old toy and expertly spun the disc around on his finger. His canine companion was beside herself with anxious anticipation. Her piercing barks could be heard all across the countryside, even as far back as the northern gates to the city. He glanced over at a nearby copse of fruit trees and narrowed his eyes.

Watching from a distance of several hundred feet were four soldiers, each standing stiffly at attention, and each wearing a distinctive maroon tunic embroidered with gold thread in the shape of the Royal family's personal crest. These were the Javyn, his bodyguards. Each guard had been hand-picked by either the king or the commander and each one, Mikal dryly noted, had the personality of a slug.

The young prince sighed heavily. Even though his father insisted the soldiers were under orders to not interfere, Mikal knew that they were simply glorified babysitters. He turned to his left and snapped his wrist, sending the disc careening toward a row of sidah trees. Peanut took off amidst a chorus of joyous barks. In moments she had returned and was waiting by his feet. He bent down for yet another tug-of-war match with the dog and then flung the padded disc toward the mouth of the dragon cavern. The Welsh corgi bounded after the toy, eager to please him and anxious for the game to continue.

Peanut returned to his side and dropped the disc on the ground. Not before Mikal's feet but in front of her own two paws so the game could easily be switched back to a much more entertaining game of tug. Sensing her owner's duress, Peanut whined, reared up, and placed her two stumpy front legs on top of his.

"What's the matter, pretty girl? Are you bored, too? I know what you mean. Nothing ever happens here."

Peanut cocked her head, staring at him, as if to indicate her long-term memory was much better than his.

"Fine. Nothing happens here *anymore*. Is that better?"

Satisfied, the corgi dropped back down to all fours and snatched up her beloved disc. She settled into the soft grass and started adding more punctures and rips to the already tattered surface of the padded toy.

Mikal slowly looked around the countryside. His last bit of fun was listening to the astounding tale his former protectors had spun when they described going back in time, two years ago. Why hadn't he been the one to find that hidden portal? Why couldn't he have been the one to have all those glorious adventures?

At the time of their disappearance, he'd been studying. Always studying. Or perhaps sitting in on one of his father's many boring sessions with various nobles and court officials. Yes, he knew it was for the day when his father would pass him the crown, but everyone knew that day was nowhere in the foreseeable future. Why, then, did he have to be subjected to such mundane proceedings on a daily basis?

Lentari was a peaceful kingdom, Mikal knew. Ylani, the neighboring kingdom to the north, hadn't caused any problems since Shardwyn's son, Thaden, had persuaded the Ylanians to invade Lentari, unsuccessfully. Keeping the peace through communication was something his father had drilled into him at an early age. Make sure you're always in contact with your neighbors, his father had told him. Even in peacetime, it was prudent, according to his father, to maintain the bond of friendship.

Mikal thought about their neighbors to the south. Straosia. The wild lands to their immediate south were largely unexplored and sparsely populated. The king had sent an emissary to visit their Straosian neighbors late last year but they had returned almost immediately, citing poorly maintained roads and a lack of hospitality, not to mention a disturbing absence of vacancies at the few inns they could find.

They would try again, possibly in a few months, according to his father. While not overly concerned, Mikal knew the king would extend a helping hand if the Straosians would ask. But, more than likely, they would not. Perhaps he could ask his father to allow him to take an extended journey south to see if there might be anything he could do? After all, it was time he started accepting more responsibility, wasn't it?

Hearing some heavy breathing, Mikal glanced down and smiled. Peanut had fallen asleep on her back with all four of her paws sticking straight up.

"Come on, girl. Let's go home."

One of Peanut's eyes cracked open and studied him. The corgi refused to move until he had taken the first step back toward the castle. In a flash, the dog regained her feet and bolted after him with several inches of her tongue hanging out.

Peanut yipped excitedly at him from the other side of the castle's drawbridge, encouraging him to pick up the pace. As soon as the teenager stepped foot on the heavy wooden planks, she turned around and ran through the open doorway, expertly weaving between the many legs that were passing by.

"Peanut! Wait up!"

Mikal caught up to the playful corgi just in time to see her dash into the Great Hall. Horrified, and certain that his parents would not approve of the dog's presence while they were conducting their usual dour meetings, Mikal hurried to catch up. He came to a halt as he noticed Peanut had jumped up onto his mother's lap and was now snuggling against her chest.

"Oh, man," Mikal softly muttered.

His parents were in the middle of a meeting and it couldn't have been good. The seriousness of the situation sunk in as Commander Rhenyon, Captain Pheron, and Lieutenant Darius turned to regard him with grim expressions. Mikal plastered his best smile on his face and looked at Peanut. The corgi was sitting complacently on the queen's lap and was watching him, as though he alone were responsible for interrupting everyone in the room.

"Uh..."

Kri'Entu stared sullenly at him. "Son. Is something the matter?"

"I, er..."

Why wouldn't his mouth work? It wasn't as if he were there to admit his romantic interest in a certain girl from Capily, or to admit to bribing the dwarf keymaker to secretly create a portal key for him to visit her.

"Yes, Mikal. Is there something you need?" his father asked again.

"I, er, was wondering if perhaps I could make a journey to Straosia. Little is known about them, father. Perhaps I could—"

"A journey to Straosia will have to wait, son," his father gently told him, shaking his head. "There are more pressing matters right now than sanctioning an exploratory expedition."

"Like what?" He winced at the irritation in his own voice.

Kri'Entu's face became even more solemn than it had been. "That which does not concern you, my son."

"Father, perhaps if I..." Mikal trailed off, noticing his

father's darkening eyes.

His mother came to his rescue. She quietly rose from her throne and gently placed the corgi onto the ground.

"I will leave you to your discussion, my love," Ny'Callé calmly announced. "Mikal, come with me." A look of gratitude briefly appeared on the king's face.

Kri'Entu nodded. "Thank you."

Within moments the king had returned to whatever quiet discussion he had been having prior to Peanut's sudden appearance.

"But there's nothing to do," Mikal grumped, plopping himself onto one of the plush chairs inside his mother's private reading room. "It's the same thing day in and day out. You and father sit in the Great Hall while I study in the Archives. I'm tired of studying, Mother. I'm eighteen years old now! Isn't there *something* I can do? Something worthwhile?"

His mother was silent, studying him.

"Why wouldn't Father let me go south? So little is known about Straosia. What if they're in trouble? Wouldn't it be prudent to send a Lentarian representative to offer help?'

His mother was softly stroking Peanut's fur as the corgi snoozed on her lap.

"Straosia is the least of our concerns right now," his mother softly told him.

"So it doesn't rank that high on the totem pole. I get it. It's still important to try, isn't it?"

"What is a 'totem pole'?" his mother asked, confused.

"I'm sorry. It's a saying I've picked up from Steve. It refers to priorities. Straosia isn't a priority. I know that. You know that. However, it's still something Father thinks about."

"How can you be so certain?"

Mikal was silent.

"You're not certain, are you?" Callé guessed, gazing at her son's face.

Mikal slowly shook his head. "It was an educated guess."

"Mmm-hmm. You're bored, aren't you?"

"Aye, I am. You have to help me, Mother. Ask Father to

give me something to do. I've earned that right, don't you think?"

The door to his mother's chamber suddenly opened. His father strode in, smiled warmly at the queen, then eyed Mikal. The king closed the door and took the seat next to his.

"I'm sorry for intruding earlier, Father," Mikal told him, after a minute or two of uncomfortable silence had passed. "I was playing with Peanut. She ran into the Great Hall before I could stop her."

"You were playing," his father repeated, using a strangely neutral tone. His father eyed him in silence for another few seconds before he finally smiled. "I would have thought you'd be tired of playing by now."

Mikal jerked up straight in his chair. His face reddened.

"The look on your face pleases me, son. I assume you've been discussing your restlessness with your mother?"

"I, uh…"

"We will have to work on your public speaking skills," his father dryly observed. He reached up to take off his crown and set it on a nearby table. "Let me ask you a question, son."

"Uh, sure. What?"

"What has taken you so long?"

Mikal's brow wrinkled. "Huh? What do you mean?"

"I have been waiting a long time to see if you were ready to start accepting responsibility worthy of your status as prince."

"You have? Father, why didn't you say something? I have wanted to do something worthwhile for quite some time."

"Like running off to explore Straosia?" his father asked with a smile.

Mikal shrugged. "I still say it's something we need to do."

Kri'Entu nodded. "I agree, only there are more pressing things to deal with right now." The king leveled a gaze at him, causing him to squirm in his seat. "I needed you to *want* to accept the responsibility *and* ask for it."

Mikal nodded and cleared his throat. "Very well. Father, I hereby announce that I am ready to act on behalf of the crown."

Kri'Entu reached for his crown. "We'd better make

this formal." He placed the golden circlet back on his head. "Very well. The crown acknowledges that you've requested a mission with responsibility. I have one to give to you."

"You do?" Mikal asked, incredulous. The look of shock on his mother's face was something he wasn't going to forget anytime soon.

"You do?" Ny'Callé repeated.

"That's what I was discussing with Commander Rhenyon and the others. It would seem we have a situation brewing up north."

Mikal grinned. "Dragons!"

Kri'Entu frowned. "You don't have to look *that* happy. The dragons are our allies, aye. However, something has caused several of our wyverian allies to go on a rampage. Several fires have been started. The Dragon Lord has kindly extinguished the fires for us and offered his apology for causing the residents of Verdayn so much distress."

"What would you need me to do?" Mikal asked in a small voice. Now that he was faced with his first mission on behalf of the kingdom, he couldn't help but feel daunted by the involvement of the dragons.

"Kahvel assures me that he has his subjects under his control and will launch an investigation as to what happened. However, I would like to conduct our own investigation. You, my son, will be my emissary."

Mikal's eyes widened.

"You want me to find out why the dragons started a fire? They're dragons! Isn't that what they do?"

"Not without permission from the Dragon Lord. Kahvel assures me they did not. In fact, both dragons have denied any involvement even though they were witnessed by human and dragon alike. Something doesn't feel right. I need you to get to the bottom of this. Will you accept this mission?"

Mikal stood and solemnly bowed. "I will, Father."

"I will get you the portal key to Verdayn," his father told him. "Unless Maelnar made one for you as well when he crafted your Capily key?"

All the color drained out of Mikal's face. "I ... er ... uh…"

"We'll talk about that later. I am supposed to send a representative to meet with Verdayn's constable later today. May I suggest you start there?"

"Yes, Father."

"Take Peanut with you. She is restless. She could do with the exercise."

"I will, Father."

* * *

"There isn't much to tell. One minute all is well and the next minute dragons are on the rampage. What more clarification do you need, Your Highness?"

"Were the dragons hunting?" Mikal asked, staring hard at the constable and feeling his anger rise. Peanut was lying at his feet and resting her head between her forelegs. "Were they fighting something? Were they fighting each other? Constable, for all we know the dragons could have been honing their targeting skills and an errant shot started those fires."

Constable Brekon didn't bother to hide his irritation. He rose from his chair and sat on the corner of his desk closest to Mikal, presumably to look intimidating. He folded his beefy arms across his chest and scowled. "Look, Your Highness, everyone knows you're fond of all things wyverian, but don't let that cloud your judgment. I know what the people told me. It happened exactly as I said. You're wasting your time here."

Mikal's posture stiffened. "You will do well to remember who you're addressing, constable. If you find your position to be that much of an inconvenience and you'd rather draw conclusions from secondhand information rather than conducting your own investigation, just say so. The list of suitable constables is something that I am privy to, and let me assure you the list is long and extensive. Have I made myself clear?"

The constable's face noticeably reddened and his gaze temporarily dropped to the floor. "My apologies ... Your Highness."

Mikal's eyes narrowed. He had noticed the constable's

delay in adding his title after the forced apology. Mikal came to a decision, slowly walked around the desk, and sat down in the constable's chair.

"That will be all, Constable Brekon. You are dismissed."

Brekon was on his feet in a flash. His eyes practically dared him to stay seated.

"What do you think you are doing, Your Highness? You don't have the authority to dismiss me."

Mikal kept his face neutral. "As a duly designated representative of the crown, I must disagree with you, Constable. Fear not. You haven't lost your job. Yet. I haven't decided what I'm going to do with you. I assume you enjoy your duties?"

Thick cords emerged on Brekon's neck as he glowered at Mikal. After a few seconds he slowly nodded.

"May I give you a piece of advice?" Mikal coolly asked.

The constable nodded again.

"Show me you deserve to sit in this seat. So far you have failed to do so, and don't think for a moment that I won't have you replaced. However, I don't want to do that if I don't have to. You don't like me? I don't care, Constable. What I do care about is the welfare of this village. I care about our people. Do you?"

"Permission to speak freely, Your Highness."

Mikal's mouth turned upwards in the beginnings of a smile. "Granted."

"I know full well why you're here."

Mikal sat back in the chair and clasped his hands in his lap. "Enlighten me, constable."

"You're a spoiled rich boy who has always gotten what he wanted. You're the prince. I get it. However, just because you're the prince doesn't mean you're the right person to be sent up here. The dragons live nearby. You know this and I know this. At least two dragons lost their damn minds and started a fire that came close to destroying the village. *My* village, Your Highness. I ask the king for help and I get a boy who is trying to become a man. I'm sorry we got off on the wrong foot, Your Highness, but I need someone else. I need someone to believe me."

"Your point is taken," Mikal conceded, keeping his expression and his voice neutral. "Your opinion is that I shouldn't have come up here and instead my father should have sent somebody more experienced in these matters, is that it?"

A smug look appeared on Brekon's square face. "Aye. That is my opinion."

Mikal nodded. "Excellent. It's a good thing that neither my father nor I care about that opinion, Constable. My father sent me here. I will be conducting an investigation on behalf of the crown. You will assist me in whatever way that I need, is that clear?"

Brekon gritted his teeth and was silent as he studied the prince.

"This isn't open for negotiation, Constable. Either you will agree or you will be replaced by one who does. Which will it be? I grow tired of your impertinence. I'll have you know my father would have replaced you ten minutes ago."

"Very well," the constable softly grumbled.

"I'm sorry, what was that? Please speak up."

"I said, 'very well'," the constable repeated, only marginally louder. "My men and I will be at your disposal. Ask what you will."

"Thank you. Please be seated and we can begin."

The constable hesitantly sank down into the seat closest to him. Brekon cast a quick look at Peanut, who was eyeing him as though she would bite him at the slightest sign of trouble.

"Call off your pet," Brekon mumbled.

Mikal, about ready to pull out several sheets of blank parchment, hesitated, glancing back at the constable. He kept his irritation from showing on his face.

"Your Highness," the constable grudgingly began, "please call off your dog."

Mikal smiled. "Peanut, *off*. Leave him be. For now."

Her snarl disappeared. However, Peanut's ears were still lying flat and she stared, unblinking, indicating Brekon had yet to be invited to join the corgi's pack of humans.

"Now," Mikal began, as he spread the papers on the

constable's desk and reached for the quill and ink that were sitting nearby. "Has this happened before?"

"No."

"Do you know of anyone who was in the area when these dragons went on the attack?"

"No."

"Has anyone witnessed any other obscure wyverian behaviors that bore repeating to someone else?"

Brekon's mouth opened, ready to give an immediate 'no' when he realized the question was legitimate and worthy of an honest answer. The constable paused as he thought about the question.

"Not that I am aware of."

"Are there any other behaviors, non-wyverian in nature, which you or any of your deputies have witnessed?"

Again, Brekon hesitated. The scratching of the quill pen paused as Mikal looked up.

"Constable? Have you something to say?"

"I personally haven't, no, but I do remember one of my deputies, Bresk I think, mentioning something a few days ago. Something about a string of burglaries."

Mikal blinked with surprise. "Did you not file a report?"

Brekon's face colored with shame.

Mikal rose from his position behind the constable's desk. "Let's do this, constable. I'll give you some time to find that missing report while I visit the attack area. I'll also give you time to question your men to see if there are any correlating facts." Mikal turned to look out the window directly behind the desk. "There are only a few hours left before sunset. We will meet again tomorrow to discuss our next move."

For the first time Mikal felt a sense of gratitude coming from the constable. The hard lines around Brekon's face appeared to soften. A little.

"Very well. I will have everything you have requested ready for your perusal, Your Highness."

"Perfect. I'll let you know when I'm ready. Peanut, come."

* * *

Half an hour later Mikal emerged from the forest and looked out across the grass-covered valley floor. Far off in the north, visible as a thin blue line, was Lake Raehón. The majority of the dragons, Mikal knew, lived in the mountains directly ringing the valley and the lake. He also knew dragons were experts at camouflaging themselves, so it was possible that he could be standing directly before a wyverian and not even know it. Thankfully a peace treaty existed between humans and wyverians, and he didn't have anything to fear from a dragon should he come face to face with one.

Nevertheless, the last thing he wanted was to meet a strange dragon up close while he had Peanut with him. Knowing the feisty little canine, Mikal was certain the dog wouldn't hesitate to jump out in front of an adversary regardless of their size. He gripped Peanut's leash tightly in his fist and stepped out into the bright sunlight on the valley floor.

His gaze was automatically drawn to his left. A huge swath of charred land revealed the blackened husks of hundreds of trees and burnt grasslands. The charred, brittle vegetation crunched loudly under his feet. Remembering that Peanut was with him and would undoubtedly end up hurting her paws if she tried to follow, Mikal moved to the edge of the scorch marks and slowly walked along its border, keeping Peanut well away from the blackened ground.

The two of them approached the first row of burnt trees. Peanut edged close to a charred remnant of a tree and gave it a few cursory sniffs. Disinterested, the dog turned to Mikal.

"We're here looking for clues," Mikal told the dog. "Something set these dragons off. It's up to us to find out why."

Peanut's ears suddenly perked straight up. She lifted her head as high as she was able and looked around the valley.

"What is it, girl? What do you smell?"

She pulled at the leash.

"What are you doing? We came from that way and there was nothing. We want to check out the damage, remember?"

Peanut whined, pulling on her leash. She wanted to go back the other way.

"Peanut, if you go to the bathroom, I just can't leave it

there. I don't have a baggie. You had better not do what I think you have to do."

The corgi pulled him over to a large mound of rocks, guided him to the base of them, and whined. Then she pulled forward a few inches more, just enough to give the closest rock a lick.

Mikal stared at her as though she had lost her mind. "What's gotten in to you, Peanut? You're licking rocks now? Don't be a goofball."

Peanut sat in the soft grass before the rocks and gave a playful bark. Before Mikal could shush her, the rock pile began to shimmer. Mikal backed away, picked up Peanut, and retreated a dozen steps before the rocks completely disappeared and an immense form began unfolding itself from its curled-up position.

It was a dragon, a luxurious dark green color that had a hint of a golden glow around the scales. Mikal's eyes widened. He knew that dragon. He had met her before. In fact, so had Peanut, except the last time he had seen this particular dragon she had been a quarter of the size she was now.

Peanut barked and adopted her playful stance, waiting for acknowledgment from her former playmate.

"What have we here?" The dragon spoke and stretched her wings before folding them flat against her body. She lowered her enormous head until she was staring straight at the two of them.

Mikal cleared his throat. "Hello, Pravara. Do you remember me? We've met once before."

Pravara took a step closer and inhaled. "Ah. The young human. I do remember you."

Mikal pointed at Peanut. "Do you remember her? She certainly remembers you."

Peanut yipped loudly and maintained her pose. Her stumpy tail waggled back and forth with excitement.

Pravara smiled, showing that not only had she gained her adult size but a mouthful of long dagger-like fangs, too. "The creature from another world. I do remember you, small one. We played together."

Peanut gave a sharp piercing bark. The corgi had yet to

move from her playful crouch.

"What is she doing?" Pravara inquired. "What does she want?"

"I'd say she wants you to sniff noses with her. It's her way to say hello."

"Of course. Now I remember. Mother has sniffed noses with her before, hasn't she? Peanut. The name is Peanut, correct? Or is the species called 'peanut'? I do not remember."

Mikal chuckled. "It's Peanut. That's her name."

Pravara took a small step forward and touched her nose to Peanut's. The corgi finally bounded forward, barking excitedly, and then dropped straight to the ground to roll over onto her back, exposing her furry belly to the whole world.

Smiling, Mikal looked up at massive green dragon. "What are you doing here, Pravara?"

"The same as you, I would imagine," the dragon answered. She lifted her head and turned to look at the blackened forest. "My father wants to know what happened. Dragons did this. My father wants to know why."

"Do you know which dragons are responsible?" Mikal asked.

"Aye. Catrin and Jasmyre."

"Have you talked to them yet? Maybe they could tell you what was going through their heads when they did this."

"I spoke with each of them yesterday. Neither had any recollection of how they got here or what they did upon their arrival. I have been investigating the surroundings ever since. No matter how hard I try, I cannot see why this area was targeted. Was there a hidden purpose?" Pravara growled irritably. "Clearly someone better than I should be searching for clues. I think my father chose poorly when he picked me."

Mikal took in the extent of the damaged ground and burnt trees and whistled softly. "That must have been one heck of a fire. I don't think Steve could have put that one out."

Pravara's neck turned until she was looking down at him. "Tell me, young Mikal, is that why you are here? Is the human king looking for answers, too?"

"Don't call me young. I'm older than you are, remember?

By a number of years."

"Very well. My apologies. I meant no disrespect."

"It's okay. I get that all the time. I have been under the assumption that my parents don't take me seriously enough and then all of a sudden here I am, conducting an investigation on behalf of my father. I'm starting to doubt my father's decision to send me here, too."

"You, too?" Pravara asked, interested. She dropped her head back to the ground. "My father decided it was time I became an adult and tasked me with unraveling the mystery of why several of our brethren would jeopardize the peace we have with the humans."

"Nobody was hurt," Mikal pointed out. "We don't know for certain if the purpose of this fire was to hurt humans. If it was, don't you think they would have started the fire closer to Verdayn?"

"You have a point," Pravara admitted.

"We're both trying to solve the same mystery," Mikal told her, smiling. He had just thought of something that would make his father proud. "What do you say we work together? It sounds like we could each use the help. Besides, I'll bet both of our fathers would agree."

Pravara slowly nodded. "I see the logic in that decision. Very well. I agree. Where would you like to start?"

"Well," Mikal began, scratching the back of his head, "what have you learned so far?"

"There's nothing noteworthy about this locale," Pravara told him as she took a few steps back and started walking toward the center of the scorch marks.

Mikal scooped the corgi up and rested her against his shoulder. He gave the dog a few friendly pats before he started walking. Peanut whined and tried to get down.

"I'm sorry, Peanut. We have work to do. You'll hurt your paws on the burned ground. Just bear with me, okay?"

He looked over at Pravara and saw that the dragon was already standing in the center of the torched earth. Mikal's boots crunched noisily on the blackened vegetation as he joined Pravara. His companion looked over at him.

"I have searched the Collective. This is just an insignificant corner of the valley."

"Okay, so the location is irrelevant. What about the trees? Or the vegetation?"

Pravara glanced at the blackened remnants of several trees. "I see oak, pine, and birch. There are dozens of healthy specimens all around this valley. I fail to see why these trees would be targeted."

"How big of an area was burned?"

Pravara glanced east and slowly tracked her head to the right. "It's just a guess, but I would say at least five hundred meters."

"Five hundred meters," Mikal repeated. "What about the depth? How far did the fire burn inside the forest?"

Pravara approximated a shrug. "Unknown. I have not investigated inside the forest as it would be difficult for me to move around. As a young hatchling, I'd be able to do it but not like this. Do you believe this is information we need?"

Mikal nodded. "I'd like to know."

"Very well. I will investigate from the air." Pravara leapt straight up and snapped her wings open, mimicking her mother's technique.

He watched the dark green dragon fly back and forth overhead, inspecting the area. Several minutes later she returned to his side.

"The extent of damage inside the forest is minimal. No more than a hundred meters were burned. No more, no less."

"What, all the way across?"

"Aye. Why?"

"You're telling me that the area the fire burned looks like a perfect rectangle from the air? Since when does a fire burn so evenly?"

"I hadn't thought of that. Allow me to do a more thorough investigation."

Pravara returned to the air and circled slowly. Mikal shifted Peanut to his other shoulder and gave her a few friendly scratches behind her ears. He was rewarded with a goose bump-inducing lick on the back of his neck.

Mikal looked at the burned ground again. How could the dragons make a specific portion of the forest burn? Why would they? The only person he knew who could accomplish something like that was Steve. He and Sarah had attended his birthday party only last week and had since returned home. Besides, hadn't he heard his father say that Pravara's father, Kahvel the Dragon Lord, had put out the fires? Why hadn't the fires spread to the rest of the forest?

Mikal shook his head. There must be something he was missing. Pravara swooped in from high above and snapped her wings open to arrest her descent. She landed twenty meters outside of the burned grass and waited for Mikal to join her. As soon as he did so, Mikal lowered Peanut back to the ground and let her run around on her own. The playful dog looked up at Pravara and barked excitedly at the dragon. Pravara crouched low and swished her tail through the grass.

Once Peanut was running around in circles, chasing absolutely nothing, Pravara straightened and approached Mikal. "I found something you should know about."

Mikal's pulse quickened. "What? What did you find?"

"Upon closer inspection I can see that you were right. The fire burned a shape into the forest."

"A shape? What shape?"

Pravara extended a foreleg and used one of her talons to scratch a symbol onto the soft ground. She drew a rectangle with two interlocking diamonds in the center.

"How did you miss that before?" Mikal wanted to know.

"Those marks are only slightly lighter than the rest of the scorched earth. I had assumed they were mere discolorations. I know now they are not."

"It's a picture of two joined diamonds? What's that supposed to mean?"

Pravara shook her head. "Unknown."

Mikal stared at the symbol as a thought occurred to him. The dragons had placed it there for a reason. The symbol, while unknown to him, must have a purpose.

"What is it?" Pravara asked. "Your pulse has quickened and you are expelling more air than most humans need in order to survive."

"Pravara, this is a clue. It has to be. The problem is, what does it mean?"

"I would agree that the symbols are too specific to be random patterns. That is, unless there was a human structure that matched that shape and it resulted in the ground being marked as it is."

"Do you believe that?" he asked the dragon.

Pravara shook her head no. "I do not believe so."

"Neither do I. Hmm, you know what? I think I know what this might be."

"What?"

"A wizard's mark!"

Chapter 2 — The Rogue Resurfaces

A re you sure? Mikal, it could be from random striations in the surface rock. It could be vegetation that perhaps burned hotter than the rest. We don't know this was the work of a wizard."

"Pravara, you saw it for yourself. Do you think it to be coincidence we found two interlocking diamonds branded on the ground? Left by dragons?"

Pravara was silent, studying the scorched earth. "And if you are correct? What then?"

Mikal gave Peanut a few friendly pats on her head. "Then my father should be told. He'll want to know."

"It would be prudent to notify my father as well."

Mikal turned to look up at her with a skeptical look on his face.

Pravara, sensing she was being watched, glanced down at him. "What?"

"Are you sure you're younger than me? You sound like you're much older. It's hard to believe you're the same dragon that played with Peanut several years ago and consequently got me into a lot of trouble."

"Dragons mature far faster than humans," Pravara informed him. "I achieved my adult size last year after my last sloughing. As for you, are you at your adult size yet?"

Mikal looked down at himself. With his boots on he was nearly six feet tall. Not as tall as Steve, he thought bitterly, but still several inches taller than his father and six inches taller than his mother. His body was lean and fit, thanks to Steve's interest in a type of exercise called 'taekwondo' and Mikal's own desire to best him at it. Which, Mikal wryly thought, he had done on more than one occasion.

"I think I am done growing," he told the dragon. "At least my mother hopes I am. She still thinks of me as her baby boy."

Pravara grunted by way of acknowledgement.

"So, you need to tell your father what we found today, is that it? How long will it take you to fly home?"

"Why would I fly home?" Pravara asked, curious.

"You used the Collective, didn't you?"

Pravara's giant head nodded. "Aye."

"I wish we had something like that," Mikal muttered under his breath. "It would make things a lot easier."

"Humans cannot telepathically communicate with other humans," Pravara pointed out.

Mikal sighed. "I know, Pravara."

"Inform who you must," Pravara told him. "I will continue to investigate the environment to see if anything else can be learned."

"Shall we meet back here tomorrow morning?" Mikal asked, hopeful the dragon would want to resume their investigation together. "Then we'll be able to compare notes."

"Very well. Until then."

Pravara moved toward the closest corner of the large mark and brought her nose down to follow a scent. Mikal pulled the leash from his back pocket, clipped it to Peanut's collar, and headed back to Verdayn. He looked up, briefly wondering if his father would have given the soldiers tasked with keeping an eye on him the day off. But, seeing the four sets of eyes watching from a distance said otherwise.

"I'm heading back to the castle. See you guys there."

As expected, there wasn't any response.

* * *

"Let's go, Peanut. We can play later. We have a job to do."

Mikal made it three steps into the castle when his leash arm was yanked to a stop. The castle's portal room wasn't empty and Peanut felt it was her responsibility to make sure everyone received the corgi stamp of approval. She pulled Mikal over to a small group of kitchen staff who were having a meeting with the head chef.

The entire group ceased talking at Mikal's appearance. The head chef bowed while the rest of the staff dropped their gaze to the floor. Mikal nodded back. He gave the leash a couple of soft tugs to get the dog's attention and moved toward the exit. Determined to stay by his side, Peanut abandoned her attempts to greet every passerby and hurried to catch up. Servants and guards alike saw him coming and hurriedly stepped to the side.

Mikal stepped out into the Great Hall and almost collided with Commander Rhenyon. Peanut hesitated only long enough to cast a quick glance up at the commander. Rhenyon changed course and matched Mikal's pace, angling toward the Antechamber.

"Is the matter settled up north, Your Highness?" the commander casually inquired. "Was the fire an accident as the king believes?"

Mikal shook his head. "I don't think so. We found something I think my father should know about."

"Excellent. He and the queen are in... did you say 'we'? Did one of the Javyn help you with your investigation? I expressly forbade them from interfering with your activities."

Mikal finally paused and turned to look at the commander. "Commander, is their presence by your order or my father's?"

Rhenyon kept his face neutral. "Why do you ask, Your Highness?"

"I feel like I am still being treated like a child."

The commander stared at him silently for a few moments before he began walking again. Mikal automatically started walking, too.

"Both."

"You think I still need a personal guard?" Mikal demanded, incredulous. "I can best anyone with a sword except for maybe you. I can beat anyone in a fight thanks to Steve and Marshall."

"Marshall?" Rhenyon repeated, confused. "Who's Marshall? Is he a friend of Sir Steve's?"

"Aye. I haven't personally met him but Steve talks about Marshall Arts all the time. I think Marshall might have taught Steve all those fancy moves and he, in turn, taught them to me."

"You've bested me in hand-to-hand combat for several years now," Rhenyon admitted as he smiled. "Your Highness, please understand. You are the crown prince. Do you know what your father would do in order to get you back should you ever be abducted?"

Mikal sighed. "Probably anything."

"Exactly. For that reason alone, you must have protection at all times. It is no different for your father except his bodyguards number more."

"I have enough protection for this mission, thank you very much."

Rhenyon glanced over at him as they walked. "Oh? Please elucidate. And do not tell me you are referring to your canine companion, Your Highness. I've seen her with strangers. She'd lick a person to death before she'd be willing to take a bite."

"Says you," Mikal argued. "You've never seen her try to bite the bright red bug."

"What red bug?"

"It's a type of toy that lives in a pen," Mikal explained. "It... it's not important."

Mikal and Rhenyon approached the heavy, wooden double doors leading in to the Antechamber, private chamber and favorite room of the king. This chamber, Mikal knew, could repel all but the strongest jhorun. It was also where the king conducted closed-door meetings where he could rest assured no one would be able to eavesdrop.

The guards standing on either side of the chamber's entrance leapt to attention and hastily pulled the doors open. Rhenyon indicated Mikal was to enter first. The king was sitting in one of the plush armchairs by the hearth. He had an open book in one hand and a half empty tankard of ale in the other. Kri'Entu glanced up at his guests and nodded, then smiled sheepishly.

"Didn't Mother make you promise you'd stop drinking ale?" Mikal accused. "You must watch your health, Father. Too much ale isn't good for you."

Kri'Entu eyed his tankard before leveling a gaze at his son. "She doesn't need to know about this."

"Father, are you asking me to withhold information from my own mother? From your wife?"

His father's eyes narrowed suspiciously. "What do you want, son?"

"I don't know what you mean, Father."

"You haven't called me Father this many times in the last ten years. Again, I ask, what do you want? What is your price for your silence on this matter?"

Mikal finally smiled. "Get rid of my bodyguards. At least for the duration of this mission. Please, Father."

Both Rhenyon and the king frowned. Kri'Entu shook his head. "They are there for your safety. That is something that is non-negotiable I'm afraid. I travel with bodyguards, and so will you."

"What are you worried about?" Mikal asked, exasperated. "You already arranged with the Dragon Lord for my new companion, did you not?"

The king sat up in his chair, interested. Rhenyon sat in the chair closest to the king.

"I have not been in contact with Kahvel," his father contradicted. "Why would you suggest otherwise?"

"Do you mean to say you did not arrange to have a dragon meet me in their valley?"

His father again shook his head. "I did not. What dragon? Pryllan?"

"No. Pravara. She claimed her father asked her to launch an investigation of her own but I'm not sure I believe her."

"Believe her," his father told him. "I have not received any communiqués from the Dragon Lord aside from his acceptance of responsibility for the damage the fire caused. So, he has sent his offspring to conduct their own investigation, eh? How interesting."

"If you didn't send her then it's just a coincidence?" Mikal slowly smiled. "That makes me feel better."

"Why?" his father asked. "Do you think we're intentionally spying on you?"

His father smiled at him when Mikal refused to answer.

"Very well. I will make a deal with you." Kri'Entu held up the empty tankard. "Do not tell your mother about this, and I will call off your guards."

"Yes!" Mikal exclaimed, enthusiastically pumping a fist into the air.

"Provided you remain in contact with Pravara. I do not believe she will allow you to come to any harm."

Mikal's feeling of euphoria vanished in the blink of an eye. "What? That means I still have a babysitter. Father, I'm a grown man now. You said it yourself. Why must I always have someone looking out for me? I can take care of myself!"

"You are the crown prince. Either you will accept the presence of your Javyn or else you will agree to be Pravara's companion for the duration of this mission. I will not leave my only son unprotected."

Mikal hesitated, trying to think of a loophole that would allow him to travel alone.

"Final offer, son. What will it be?"

"Fine," Mikal grumped. "I will accompany Pravara."

The king nodded, pleased. "Excellent."

"What if Pravara goes somewhere I don't want to go?"

"The two of you are committed to solving this mystery. I'm sure you can work together. And, I'm sure Kahvel is telling Pravara the same thing right about now."

"You *have* been spying on us!" Mikal accused. "How else would you know she's talking with her father right now?"

"Believe it or not, it's an educated guess," the king jovially told him. "Now, would you care to tell me what you've learned?"

"I think, er, *we* think there may be a wizard involved."

Rhenyon coughed and sat up straighter in his chair. "Oh? What makes you say that, Your Highness?"

"Pravara checked out the destruction from the air. From up there she could see that there was a symbol burned onto the ground. From the ground it wasn't apparent."

The king's interest was piqued. "Oh? What symbol? What did it look like?"

Mikal rose from his chair and walked over to his father's desk. Peanut eyed his progress, but since he hadn't made any move toward the exit, she rested her head back on her front forelegs. Mikal took a blank sheet of parchment, and a quill, and recreated the symbol Pravara had scratched out on the ground. He handed the sheet to his father. Rhenyon leaned to his left so that he could see what was on the paper, too.

"Interlocking diamonds," the king softly murmured. "That's a very distinctive symbol. Are you sure they weren't some random marks that were already on the ground?"

I'm sure. Your father isn't very trusting, is he?

Mikal's eyes flew open and he gasped with alarm.

Concerned, his father leaned close. "What is it, son? What's the matter?"

"I just heard a voice in my head!"

Of course, you did. You heard mine, Mikal.

Pravara?

Aye.

What are you doing in my head?

Listening.

You mean you're eavesdropping?

That's one way to look at it.

"Would the owner of the voice be wyverian in nature?" Kri'Entu offhandedly asked.

Mikal nodded.

"Sir Steve communicates with Pryllan in much the same fashion. I didn't know you spoke with Pravara in this manner, too."

"That makes two of us," Mikal whispered. *This is really weird.*

Why? Because I can pick up your thoughts just as you can pick up mine?

Yes. Steve talks with your mother like this?

All the time. I wanted to try it out but I needed a human to talk to.

And you chose me?

Why not? Why wouldn't I choose you? You were there. Is there a reason why not?

No, of course not. You just took me by surprise, that's all.

Have you found anything out about the mark?

If you've been listening then you'll know that I haven't. My father doesn't really know much about wizards or their marks.

Who would?

Good question.

"Is Shardwyn busy today? I need to ask him about this mark."

"Shardwyn is away in Donlari at the moment," his father said. "It would seem several families have contracted some type of fever that the local healer has been unable to treat."

"Oh. Will he be back later today?"

"It all depends on how successful he is. He cannot treat an ailment until he knows what type of medicine he needs to administer."

"He should really talk to Lissa," Mikal said, more to himself. "She would be able to figure it out."

"I believe he already has."

Mikal slowly turned to his father; surprise etched all over his face. "Has what? Contacted Lissa? You're kidding."

"I am not kidding. His last message to me stated he was having difficulty. I suggested he contact your girlfriend and see if she'd be willing to help."

Mikal's face reddened. He gave his father a speculative look. "How much do you know about her?"

"I know that the two of you have been secretly seeing each other since Sir Steve and Lady Sarah returned from their trip through the time portal."

"You've known? All this time?"

Rhenyon chuckled. He slapped a friendly hand on Mikal's back. "Your Highness, this isn't my first day on the job. What do you expect when you sneak out of the castle in the middle of the night and trip on the rug in front of that display of armor?"

"I may have knocked over a piece or two but I caught them before they could fall. It wasn't that noisy."

"We take matters of security seriously," Kri'Entu said, keeping his face remarkably devoid of emotion. "Instead of confronting you as you were leaving it was decided to see where you were going."

"You followed me. I should have known."

"It's not important, son. She's a lovely girl who has a wonderfully intelligent mind."

"And hands down the best healer I have ever seen," Rhenyon added, drawing another gasp from Mikal.

"You've met her?"

"A few times," the commander admitted. "She's a lucky girl, Your Highness."

"Does everyone know about my love life?" Mikal demanded, growing angry. "Does Mother?"

Kri'Entu nodded. "Of course. Who do you think planted the suggestion you bribe Maelnar to make you a portal key? We couldn't have you traipsing about the kingdom in the middle of the night, nor would you ever be able to find a way to get inside my private vault. Your mother and I disagreed about whether or not you should have your own key but your mother assured me Lissa could be trusted. I am inclined to agree."

"Wait, you're giving me your blessing?"

The king cocked his head. "Are you saying you've proposed to this girl?"

"What? No! Of course not."

"Hmmm. Anyway, to answer your question, Shardwyn is indisposed. Hopefully not for too much longer."

Mikal nodded. "I'll head to the Archives. I can probably find what I need there."

"Now I have officially seen everything."

Mikal blinked his eyes a few times at his father. "Huh? What's that supposed to mean? Why did you say that?"

The king was proving quite adept at keeping any

expression off his face that day. Once more he pretended to be unaffected by his son's discomfort.

"Because I've never seen you willingly visit the Archives. Usually, you avoid it as though it was the worst dungeon imaginable."

"I have been to the Archives before," Mikal answered as he rose to his feet. "It's just past the Great Hall and down through the left corridor, am I right?"

Rhenyon snorted. "That would be the kitchen, Your Highness."

"I was kidding, Rhenyon."

"Of course, you were, Your Highness."

Mikal scowled. "I'm going to go now."

His father nodded. "Good luck with your research."

"If Shardwyn makes it back today, could you tell him I'm looking for him?"

"Of course."

The Archives were in the northern section of the castle and encompassed the entire wing. The first floor held the castle's extensive collection of books, catalogued and cross referenced by subject and author. Leaflets, essays, treatises, and hand written notebooks were found on the second floor. Historical documents, such as census reports, agricultural tallies, and weapon inventories were one floor down, in the large storage room the archivists affectionately nicknamed Purgatory.

Mikal walked through the large arched doorway and hesitated. The air in the room always smelled stale to him. However, as with most Archives, there were no windows. This room had to be protected from sunlight and inclement weather.

Mikal strode through the foyer and approached a large elliptical desk. It belonged to a woman Mikal knew well, for he had suffered through many of her classes. Watching mortar harden was way more entertaining than having to listen to Andra Alwyn prattle on and on in her boring monotone, about any variety of subjects. History, philosophy, mathematics, it did not matter. Anything she talked about made him instantly drowsy.

Andra was nearing eighty years old, had frilly white hair that stuck up in all directions, and wore the very same white floor length robe with purple butterflies embroidered all over it. She had a rimless set of spectacles perched on her long skinny nose and, as a result of years of scrunching her nose in an effort to prevent the spectacles from sliding off her face, looked as though she was always squinting. She also had a habit of talking to people who weren't in the room, so the phrase 'Absentminded Andra' had been coined a few decades ago. Mikal had yet to summon the courage to even *think* the words lest the ancient archivist be alerted.

Mikal eyed the fraying white robe and shook his head. He took a deep breath, cleared his throat, and stepped up to Andra's round desk, signifying he wanted help from the Archivist.

Right on cue, Andra looked up from an open tome of unfamiliar script and scrutinized him carefully. She clucked to herself and gently closed the book. She held out an expectant hand.

Mikal groaned and reached for a stack of small pieces of paper. He peeled off the top sheet, filled out his request, and handed it over. Andra briefly glanced at the sheet before returning her full attention to him.

Why has your heart rate accelerated again? Does this person disturb you?

Like you wouldn't believe, Mikal answered.

She appears to be a frail, harmless human female. How is it possible this person troubles you this much?

Pravara, be quiet.

I am quiet. I am not speaking. She cannot hear me.

You know what I mean. You're distracting me.

How so?

"Will you please shush?" Mikal whispered. He looked up and paled.

Andra Alwyn had, in a flash, risen from her chair and was now leaning on the counter, staring at him. Andra held up Mikal's note in one hand and waggled a finger at him.

She wasn't smiling. "Crown prince you may be," his former teacher began in her high quavering voice, "but you're still my pupil. You will show some respect to your elders. Are we clear?"

Mikal bit his lip and plastered a smile on his face. "Uh, sure, Ms. Alwyn."

Mollified, the archivist glanced at the paper to see what his request was. Her lips pursed as she thought about where to send him.

"There's no such book," Andra finally answered. "The closest approximation would be a series of observations Shardwyn's predecessor, Valtor, made on the subject nearly a full century ago. His notebook is amongst our collection. Would that suffice, Kre'Mikal?"

Mikal shrugged. "I really wasn't too sure where to start."

"Floor 2, rack 15, shelf C. I believe you'll find it about two-thirds of the way across the shelf from left to right. It's a small black leather notebook, if memory serves. Give me the leash. Canines are not allowed in the Archives."

Mikal reluctantly passed Peanut's leash to Andra. He squatted down to give the corgi a reassuring pat. "I'll be right back."

He straightened and looked back at Andra, shaking his head in amazement. Perhaps he had misjudged the canny archivist?

"Don't forget to say hello to Jamien for me."

Mikal had taken a step toward the heart of the Archives, when he turned back to Andra's curved desk. "I'm sorry? What was that?"

"Jamien. Be a dear and say hello to him for me. I haven't heard from him in several weeks and I'm beginning to worry."

"And Jamien is…?"

Andra answered him as though she thought he was a dullard. "The ghost that lives somewhere between racks ten and twenty."

"The ghost, huh? All right then. I'll let you know if I see him."

Humming merrily, Andra returned her attention to the book she had been reading when he arrived and was soon lost within its pages. Peanut gave him an imploring look as he walked away, urging him to hurry. Mikal chuckled to himself. Absentminded Andra, indeed. Maybe she ought to retire.

Why? Because you believe her to be senile?

Mikal jumped and almost clipped the side of a bookcase as he walked past.

Do you not have anything better to do?

As a matter of fact, no. I have completed my investigation and am waiting for your return.

It's been less than two hours! We agreed to reconvene tomorrow morning.

That is correct. Your powers of recollection do you credit.

That's a wicked sense of humor you have. I have work to do, Pravara. Are you planning on eavesdropping the entire time I'm here?

Of course. It is highly entertaining.

Most people would consider eavesdropping rude.

I'm a dragon. I eavesdrop. It's what I do.

Really?

Of course not. We should really work on your sarcasm skills.

You sounded just like Steve then.

My mother picked up the act of being sarcastic from him and I, in turn, have picked it up from my mother.

Oh, wonderful.

That was sarcasm. See? You're getting better.

Pravara?

Yes?

Be quiet.

For how long?

As long as I'm in here.

As you wish.

A few moments of silence passed.

Are you still there?

Of course.

You're not supposed to be talking.

Then stop asking me questions.

You're incorrigible.

He felt Pravara's chuckle as her mirth bubbled up inside

her. She was in a good mood. Either she enjoyed teasing him or she had some helpful information to pass along.

Or I could just be in a good mood.

I'm going to have to learn how to hide my thoughts from you.

Now he felt Pravara heaving with laughter.

I would love to see you try, Mikal.

You're saying I can't do it?

That is precisely what I am saying.

Oh, it's on, my friend. Before this mission is over, I will have managed to mask my thoughts from you.

Pravara laughed harder.

Nothing's impossible. I'm sure it can't be that hard to learn, can it?

Pravara continued to laugh.

You'll see. Now. Where should I start? This place is absolutely enormous.

Floor 2, rack 15, shelf C, about two-thirds of the way across the shelf from left to right.

So, you were listening to that too, huh? Fine. I'll find that notebook.

The notebook, unfortunately, while being extremely difficult to read, only briefly mentioned the marks some wizards chose to leave behind. Valtor went on to say that it was a foolish wizard, indeed, who openly identified their own private mark. The problem, Valtor explained, was once a wizard's mark was identified then additional wizards could be brought in to undo whatever spells the first wizard made, provided they wanted to take the time to figure out what spells had been used. Correctly identifying the spells, along with a properly identified wizard, was one of the very few methods of dealing with an out-of-control wizard.

Why, then, would this wizard sign his work? Perhaps it wasn't a wizard's mark after all.

I still think you're right, Pravara told him. **I think this is the mark of a wizard, albeit an arrogant one.**

We're no closer to determining who it is, Mikal pointed out.

True. You're in the Archives. Keep looking.

I wouldn't know where to look. And I really don't want to go back down to Andra to ask for more help. For that matter, I don't even know what help to ask for.

We're looking to unmask a wizard.

Thanks for the tip. However, I don't think they have a How to Identify a Wizard—For Dummies *book. I think we're on our own.*

Are you calling yourself a dummy?

It's a popular line of books back in the kingdom of Idaho. Sarah bought me one when they bought me a smartphone. It was the only way I could figure out how to use the blasted thing.

What is a smartphone?

Urgh. Don't get me started. It's just a device, that's all. I don't know why everyone on Steve's world has to have one in their hand at all times but they do. I'd much rather have a conversation face-to-face than on a machine.

Agreed.

Two hours later brought a welcome surprise. Shardwyn had returned, and he had brought his consultant with him.

"Mikal!" The shout echoed loudly in the room. Several patrons looked angrily up from their books and scowled at the interruption.

"Lissa! It's so good to see you!"

Lissa rushed to Mikal's side and gave him a hug. She looked around at the many cases full of books and sighed contentedly.

"I love the Archives. You are so lucky."

"Why?"

"You can come here whenever you want. You live right here with them. I envy you!"

Mikal grasped the girl's hands in his own. "You can come here whenever you want, too. Didn't my father give you full access when you asked?"

Lissa nodded. Her long brown hair, currently arranged in a thick braid, fell more than halfway down her back. She glanced down to see what Mikal had been reading. Her eyebrows shot up with surprise.

"You're reading about wizards?"

"Yeah. I think I found a wizard's mark and I'm trying to see if there might be some record of all known wizard marks. Maybe I can find a book, or a report, or a…"

"You won't find one, young master Mikal."

Mikal looked over at the tall thin man wearing robes of dark forest green. He smiled at the resident wizard and then closed the book he had been showing Lissa.

"What do you suggest, Shardwyn? How can I research this thing?"

"You say you found a wizard's mark, dear boy? Indeed! Let's go to my workshop. I'm sure I can find something that will help you there."

Mikal held out his arm and waited for Lissa to take it. Together they followed Shardwyn down the wide marble steps to the Archive's ground floor. Mikal pulled Lissa to a stop at the desk and then stared in abject horror at what he saw. Peanut was up on Andra's lap, sitting up as though she were rearing up on her haunches, and was snuggling up against the old woman's chest. Andra was crooning softly to the corgi as she stroked her new friend's furry belly.

"You've got to be kidding," Mikal muttered with disgust. Peanut's head lifted out of the crook of Andra's arm and studied him, as if to inquire about the nature of this interruption. "Let's go, furball. We have work to do."

Andra gently set the dog back on the floor and handed the leash back to Mikal. "That's a cute canine you have there. Any time you want to bring her by, you be sure to do so. Is that understood?"

"Yes, ma'am," Mikal automatically answered.

* * *

Lissa's eyes widened as the three of them entered Shardwyn's workshop. An acrid, pungent aroma was in the air, as if the quirky wizard had forgotten about a potion he had been brewing and had ended up burning it. Discolorations dotted the floor and even a few places on the walls. One wall, in fact, had every square inch colored bright neon pink.

Mikal looked the wall up and down and chuckled. "That's a new one on me. How long have you had a pink wall, Shardwyn?"

"What's that?" The wizard glanced over at the wall and shrugged. "Who can say? I think it might have been like that since I moved in here."

"No, it wasn't," Mikal murmured, softly enough that only

Lissa could hear him. She giggled.

Shardwyn cleared a space on his workbench and indicated the stools on either side of him. Once Mikal and Lissa were seated, Shardwyn turned to Mikal. "Now, what can you tell me about this mark? You say you're sure it's a wizard's mark?"

Mikal pulled out the sheet of paper where he had drawn the mark for his father.

"It looked like this. The burned ground was almost a perfect rectangle and there were clearly two interlocking diamonds in the center of it."

"How did this burn get there?" Shardwyn asked. He pulled a monocle from within his robes and pushed it into place over his right eye. He picked up the parchment and studied it closer.

"Dragons did it. The problem is, neither dragon says they can remember doing it. I do remember Steve telling me a couple of years ago that there was an instance of a dragon being possessed by a wizard and made to do things he ordinarily wouldn't have ever done."

Shardwyn's wrinkled face jerked up. He stared at Mikal for so long that the monocle popped loose and fell toward the scarred table that served as his workbench. Lissa caught it before it hit the hard surface.

"You're referring to the renegade wizard, aren't you? Are you thinking this is his mark, young Mikal?"

Mikal nodded. "I am."

"We have not had any signs of the renegade wizard for several years now," Shardwyn announced. "It was hoped, and believed, that he had simply moved on, or else passed away. Why would he want to resurface now? And then leave his mark for all to see?"

"Maybe he thought no one would be able to see it," Mikal suggested.

Tell them it can only be seen from the air.

"Pravara says the mark could only be seen from the air."

"More than one dragon made this burn, you say?" Shardwyn asked, stroking his stubbly chin. "Interlocking diamonds. Hmm."

"Is the mark familiar?" Mikal hopefully asked. "Do you

recognize it?"

"I am reminded of an occurrence several years ago. I think I might have seen this mark then."

"Really? Is there any way to tell for certain?"

Shardwyn nodded. "Aye. I just have to find my journal from two years ago."

Mikal groaned and slowly looked around Shardwyn's quarters. Stacks of books and mounds of clothes had been shoved into every available corner. Failed experiments and various mechanical apparatuses were perched precariously on the unstable stacks of books. Huge maps and tapestries covered large bulky items in the middle of the room. Where were they even supposed to start looking?

"Will you at least tell me that you know where it is?" Mikal asked, already knowing the answer was going to be negative.

Shardwyn turned and pointed back toward a smaller second room visible through an open doorway. It was even more cluttered than the main room.

"Oh, sure. It's probably back somewhere in there. Care to help me look?"

Mikal gave the wizard a dark look that said he'd rather jump in the moat with Bredo, the monstrous serpent, than willingly step foot in Shardwyn's personal bed chamber. Lissa held a finger to her lips and hooked her arm through his to pull him toward the room.

"We'd be delighted to help you search," she added brightly, smiling at the wizard.

"Well aren't you adorable? Thank you, young Lissa. I would greatly appreciate the help."

Mikal sighed. What had started out as a noble quest to investigate the mysterious happenings of two rogue dragons had now turned into a fruitless search for a missing book in Shardwyn's cluttered quarters. This was not what he had signed up for. He caught sight of Peanut sniffing around a large reflective object that had several colorful powders sprinkled over the surface.

"Watch it, Peanut. Do not get too close to that. We don't know what that stuff is."

Intent on seeing for herself what the strange smelling

substance was, Peanut thrust her nose down onto the surface to get a good sniff. However, as soon as contact was made, the tray, which had been balancing on a single stack of books, began teetering off balance. It started to slide forward, toward the curious dog, when Mikal caught the tray and prevent it from breaking. However, as soon as the tray jolted to a stop, the spilt powder on the surface slid forward, coming into contact with Peanut's nose.

The poor dog sneezed. Then she sneezed again. Peanut dropped to the ground and pawed at her nose a few times before turning to look up at her owner. Mikal burst out laughing. Peanut's snout was now the same shade of blue as the sky.

"Shardwyn? What kind of powder was on that tray by the window? Will it wash off?"

Shardwyn risked a glance up and saw the newly colorized corgi snout.

"Not to worry. It's a dash of powdered allon mixed with the pollen of a jansa tree. It's perfectly harmless. It'll wear off eventually."

"Do you hear that, Peanut? I told you to leave it alone. Now look at you. You have a blue nose!"

Anyone who claimed dogs were incapable of emotion has truly never owned a dog before, Mikal thought. The look Peanut gave him was one of utter disbelief and betrayal. Mikal chuckled again.

Shardwyn pulled a tightly rolled scroll from beneath a pile of soiled socks and started to unroll it when he accidentally dropped it on the ground. In a flash Peanut had darted in, grabbed the scroll, and tried to run. Amazingly enough, the wizard quickly grabbed an end of the scroll before Peanut could pull it out of his reach.

"Now, now, little Peanut, give me back my scroll. I do not think this is something you want."

Peanut playfully barked around her mouthful of scroll and gave three rapid reverse tugs in an attempt to claim ownership over the toy in her mouth. The ancient scroll, being nearly two centuries old, understandably began to crumble.

"What do we know about this other wizard?" Mikal asked,

gingerly lifting piles of discarded clothes to see what was beneath them. "After all this time we must know something, right? Peanut, *off*."

Peanut instantly released the soggy scroll, throwing Shardwyn off balance and stumbling backward. He tripped on a pair of his own boots and fell heavily onto his bed. He immediately sat up and dusted himself off. He placed the damaged scroll up onto a shelf already crammed with all manner of things.

"What we know is that he's quite intelligent," Shardwyn said as he hurriedly began removing his discarded things from the reach of the curious corgi. He grabbed an armful of clothes and tossed them onto his bed. "I have done a full census every six months in the hopes that something will turn up but it never does. I didn't think it was possible for a person to avoid detection by a census but there you have it."

"So, if he's smart enough to fool the census then what else is he capable of doing?" Lissa asked, as she combined two short stacks of books into one larger stack. "Umm, what are we looking for? What does your journal look like, Shardwyn?"

"My journals haven't been properly bound yet, I'm afraid. Right now it's just a gathering."

"What's a gathering?" Mikal quietly whispered to Lissa.

"It's a collection of pages that have probably already been stitched together but have yet to be bound to a cover."

"Correct!" Shardwyn beamed his appreciation at the young girl. He found a large bundle of papers, flipped through them, then tossed them up onto the bed. "We also know," the wizard announced as he continued to rifle through the many stacks of books in the room, "that he's powerful. He's demonstrated the ability to cast multiple types of spells. That, in itself, is a dangerous mix of power."

"I still don't understand how this wizard was able to fool your censuses," Lissa remarked. She had discovered a pile of laundry that the last ten cleaning girls must have missed because there were flies buzzing around the reeking pile of linen.

"I would have to concur," Shardwyn admitted, sitting

back on his haunches. He had just checked under his bed, spooking a family of mice. Six streaks of grey fur zipped across the floor and disappeared under a large storage cabinet. By the time Peanut trotted over to see what the disturbance was, the rodents were long gone.

"How do they work?" Mikal asked.

"How does what work?" Lissa wanted to know.

"The census. How can you be so sure the census should have found him?"

Shardwyn grunted, mumbled something, and thrust a hand into a large bin full of who knows what. After a few moments he pulled his arm out and held up a gold sphere the size of his clenched fist.

"This is a spent census. It's the one I just used three months ago. Up until I started searching for this wizard, I would have placed all my faith in this device. It had never failed me before. Now I can't seem to get the blasted thing to work properly."

Mikal took the golden sphere from Shardwyn's hand and held it up to his face. "How does it work?"

"Once properly activated, this sphere will travel over every square inch of the kingdom looking for signs of life. As soon as a human is detected then they are scanned, and a notation is entered into a book I have defined for the census as the journal. Name, age, jhorun, and address are all recorded for each person the census detects."

Mikal stared at the gold sphere. "How does it know it hasn't missed anyone? What if it's scanning Donlari, but you're presently in Avin? Wouldn't you be missed? So, when the census travels to Avin, and the villager from Donlari is on his way back home, how do you know that person won't be overlooked?"

"Because the census will leave a copy of itself at every location it goes to, which will continually scan to look for discrepancies in the data. If a person leaves or a visitor arrives it'll know. That's why the king always bans intervillage travel while a census is underway. Once the census is complete the copies are destroyed."

"How long does it take for a census to complete?"

"When the king gives enough notice to the people then most censuses can be completed in less than a week. Spontaneous censuses, like the ones I've been conducting for the past year, take longer as the people are on the move. I've had several take up to three months to finish."

Mikal cleared his throat. "Didn't you say you thought you had found him two years ago?"

"It was four years ago," Shardwyn corrected. He gave the two of them a sad smile. "I really thought I had found him."

"What happened?" Lissa wanted to know.

"It was the first unscheduled census I had ever done. The king wanted an immediate check of the entire kingdom. I can't say that I blame him. Another wizard had been living in Lentari, right under our noses, and I hadn't a clue. It was quite embarrassing, let me assure you. I launched the census and watched as the list began to grow. Two months later it was done. Everyone was accounted for. The census reported there were no inconsistencies, no tampering, and no foul play. We had him. I just knew we had him. Or so I thought.

"The census led me to Verdayn. There was a high concentration of jhorun coming from the village. I will say, young master Mikal, that I felt this validated my theory the wizard was nearby. I had called in the castle militia and the village constable. Even the king was standing by, eagerly awaiting news."

"What happened?" Mikal asked.

"I was led to a small cottage southwest of the village. A young family lived there. A mother, father, and young son were the only people living there. I tested them. You know what?"

"The tests came back negative," Mikal mouthed with Shardwyn.

Lissa hopped up on Shardwyn's unmade bed and sat cross-legged.

"What jhorun did the census find there?" she asked.

Shardwyn ran a withered hand through his short gray hair and sighed.

"Their jhorun was inconsequential. They tested negative for wizard-class jhorun. The father was a farmer. His jhorun allowed him to locate and purify water, thus allowing his crops to grow healthier and larger than most. And the mother's? Let me see." Shardwyn consulted his notes. "The mother's jhorun allowed her to persuade chopped wood to pull apart on its own rather than being split by an ax."

"You're right," Mikal agreed, nodding his head. "Those jhoruns aren't very strong. Could he have found a way to mask his jhorun from the census?"

Shardwyn shook his head. "No. No amount of deception or trickery could hide a jhorun's true nature from the census. At least not that I'm aware of."

"Could your census have malfunctioned?" Lissa asked.

Shardwyn shrugged and resumed his search for his missing journal. He opened a large blue trunk decorated with silver stars and sank both arms deep into its contents as he checked to see if the trunk contained any books. "While unlikely, dear girl, it was a possibility. This family was the only one identified by the census as having wizard class jhorun, yet each time I tested them the results were the same. I cannot explain it."

Lissa frowned. "You checked both the mother and the father. What about the child?"

Shardwyn extricated his arms from the trunk. His right hand was clutching a thick bundle of papers stitched together by a red cord.

"Ah! I knew it was here somewhere. What did you ask, dear girl? What about the child?"

"What was the child's jhorun?" Mikal asked. "Surely you tested him, too."

"Of course, of course." The wizard opened the bundle of papers and began skimming through them.

"Well?" Mikal prompted.

"Well, what?"

Mikal took a deep breath and gave Lissa an exasperated look.

"What can you tell us about the child?" Lissa asked. "You said you tested him. What was his name? What could he do?"

Shardwyn reached behind his back to pull a thick leather notebook toward him. He opened the census report and flipped to a bookmarked page about halfway through the report. After a few moments Shardwyn looked up, confused. He reread the passage about the family and then, muttering crossly, shelved the notebook and reached for another, presumably the results from a different census.

The three of them spent the next five minutes in silence as Shardwyn checked the results of each census so he could answer Lissa's question. One thing became disturbingly clear.

"You never checked the boy, did you?" Mikal guessed.

Shardwyn's shocked eyes looked up into Mikal's. "Your Highness, I cannot believe this has escaped my notice. I am at a loss for words."

Lissa slipped her arm through Mikal's.

"Could this child be the renegade wizard everyone is looking for?"

Shardwyn frowned. "He couldn't be. He's much too young. I'm told the rogue wizard demanded a king's ransom in gold and jewels from the zweigelans when he crafted the curse that almost brought down the dragons. What would a mere child do with that type of wealth? Wouldn't his parents have noticed? Besides, he also successfully switched the bodies of Sir Steve, Lady Sarah, and Pryllan. A child would not have been able to do that. The necessary spells would be much too complex for such a young brain."

"How old is this boy?" Mikal asked, growing excited that they might have finally learned the identity of Lentari's most wanted criminal. To think that it could be a simple child was too staggering to comprehend.

Shardwyn consulted the census report on his lap. "At the time of this census, he was twelve."

"Was that his age the first time he was mentioned?" Mikal asked, bewildered. "Why wouldn't he be tested for jhorun?"

Shardwyn pulled another notebook from a different stack of books. He flipped through the pages for a few minutes before he stopped and let out an exclamation of surprise.

"Aha! I see what happened. At the time of the first census, after the king ordered them done every six months until such time the wizard was revealed, the boy was nine years old. That's why. A child's jhorun won't be included on an official census until his tenth birthday. Since he wasn't on the original census, each following census overlooked him. It was a simple oversight, that's all."

"Why wait for their tenth birthday?" Lissa wanted to know. "What happens then?"

"Nothing really," Shardwyn admitted, shaking his head. "If that child is the wizard we're all looking for then he is probably the most powerful wizard this kingdom has seen since … well, since I was born I would imagine."

Mikal and Lissa eyed each other and tried not to smile.

"A wizard-class jhorun before the age of ten," Shardwyn mused. "That's remarkable."

"What age would he be now?" Mikal asked.

Shardwyn tapped the page he was looking at. "If these reports are true, and I have no reason to believe they wouldn't be, then he'd be turning sixteen this year."

"A fifteen-year-old wizard," Mikal breathed, amazed. "I cannot even begin to imagine what it would be like to have that much power. The only question I'd have now is, if this boy is the wizard, why has he been silent for two years? Why return now? What's happened?"

"Maybe he just wanted to take a break," Lissa suggested.

"What else is known about the family?" Mikal asked.

Deciding to give up the search for any mention of wizards and their distinctive marks, Shardwyn abandoned his journal and began to rifle through the large stack of notebooks in front of him. He selected the most recent census report.

"I never knew why I kept an eye on that family," Shardwyn informed them as he flipped through the pages of the report, "but I did. Maybe it was gut instinct? Perhaps I was having a premonition?"

"Perhaps you drank one too many tankards of ale," Mikal muttered. Lissa, who had slid her hand into Mikal's, gripped his hand tightly, threatening to dig her nails into his skin. Mikal groaned quietly and closed his mouth. Lissa loosened her grip.

"Here we are. Let's see. It looks as though the father disappeared. It's unclear what happened to him. The mother ended up moving in with her sister, who was living alone. The boy, too."

Mikal eyed his girlfriend. "How long ago was this?"

Shardwyn consulted the report. "Two years."

Lissa gasped. "And that's how long this wizard has been silent? No wonder he vanished. He was mourning his father."

Mikal rubbed his temples. "That's just great. I remember what I was like at that age. Trust me when I say that I wasn't the model child. This isn't going to be easy." Mikal caught sight of a smile forming on Lissa's face. "I know what you're thinking and I am not. I'm *not* moody. Do not suggest otherwise."

Lissa stifled a laugh. "No, of course not. Pssht. What could I have been thinking?"

Chapter 3 — A Break in the Case

The following morning Mikal awoke before sunrise, slipped out of bed, and dressed as silently as he was able. Peanut, who had been asleep on his bed, opened a single eye and studied him. Mikal slipped his personal copy of Capily's portal key into his pocket and turned to look back at his dog.

"You have to stay here, Peanut. I need to go get Lissa. We still have work to do back in Verdayn. *Stay.*"

The moment he stepped toward the door, Peanut was on her feet in a flash, and barking excitedly. Mikal silently cursed, scooped up the corgi in his arms, and wrapped his hand around her muzzle.

"Are you trying to get me into trouble? Shush! You need to stay here and you need to keep quiet, alright?"

Peanut whined. Her ears slowly lowered, realizing she wasn't invited on this excursion. Mikal saw the look of rejection on his dog's face and melted. "Fine. You win. You're coming with me."

In the blink of an eye, Peanut was a happy, energetic dog,

who eagerly squirmed in his arms. Mikal shook his head.

"I'm not putting you down. Not yet. You'll make too much noise. Come on. We need to get Lissa."

Half an hour later Mikal and his girlfriend were back in the castle, peering anxiously around each corner to make certain they wouldn't be seen.

"Why are we sneaking around like this, Mikal?" Lissa asked, confused. "You are going to tell your father, aren't you? He's the king. He deserves to know, don't you think?" Lissa was almost forced to break into a run. She caught up with Mikal and Peanut, just as they hesitated inside one of the many doorways leading into the Great Hall.

Mikal scowled. His father was getting an early start to his day. He was there, talking with Rhenyon. Neither man looked to be in a good mood. Mikal sighed. His father always seemed in a foul mood lately, as though he received bad news daily. He needed something to make him smile. A piece of good news, Mikal decided.

Being able to tell his father the identity of the rogue wizard definitely qualified. However, wouldn't it be better if he could say that he had *apprehended* the one who had troubled his family these last couple of years?

Peanut whined. She had spotted Mikal's father in the large room and wanted to go out and give her pack member a proper corgi greeting.

"Shush, Peanut. We'll be going shortly. We have to wait for my father to leave the area first."

"Why?" Lissa asked.

"Because if he sees me, he'll ask me for an update."

"But we have an update!" Lissa protested. "We shouldn't be trying to hide from him."

"Lissa, try to understand. I want to give him better news than a simple name. I want to be able to tell him that his wizarding troubles have been finally put to rest."

Lissa frowned. "That's just great. Mikal, I finally have something to talk to your father about. I'll be able to look at him without blushing like a school girl. Do you really want to take that away from me?"

Mikal nodded. "Thank you for understanding."

"I wasn't agreeing with you."

Mikal looked over at his girlfriend and saw that she was frowning. "Look, I'm sorry. Haven't you ever wanted to impress your father? That's all I'm trying to do here."

"By withholding information? Didn't you say this wizard was dangerous?"

Mikal shrugged and then nodded. "He can be. He hasn't been yet, though."

"But he could be," Lissa insisted. "I don't like this."

"Quiet! He and Rhenyon have gone to the Antechamber. This is our chance to get to the portal room. Let's go!"

"Did you just tell me to be quiet? You really don't know how to talk to women, do you?"

"You're just now figuring that out?"

Mikal stooped to pick up Peanut and then grabbed Lissa's hand. Together, the three of them made it across the chamber without being noticed. They ducked into the smaller portal room and quietly shut the door behind them.

Lissa surveyed the room and nodded. "Perfect. The last person to use this portal didn't put the tapestry back."

A twenty-foot-wide by eight-foot-tall tapestry was sitting in a large heap to the left of the portal. Ordinarily the tapestry would cover most of the wall they were facing, effectively hiding the portal from plain sight. Mikal sighed. It was a well-known fact around the castle that he was always forgetting to replace the tapestry on its holder whenever he used the portal. This was done on purpose. He didn't want to let anyone know he had been sneaking out several times a week to visit his girlfriend in Capily, so he had to maintain the ruse that he was a forgetful goofball.

Mikal reached inside one of his trouser pockets and felt the portal key Maelnar had made for him last winter. He frowned. His deception skills were clearly lacking, as his father knew all about the deal he had made with the dwarf keymaker. What else did his parents know about that he thought they didn't?

Lissa nudged him on the shoulder. "Stop scowling. If we're going to do this then we need to hurry up. It's only a matter of time before someone comes in here. And if your father revokes my access to the Archives then I'm never forgiving you."

Mikal reached inside his tunic and pulled on the leather cord around his neck. A second portal key appeared. This one, from his father, was a brilliant ruby red color, sparkling with hundreds of polished crystal facets. Holding the key in his right hand, he stepped aside to insert the key into the portal. As he moved through a sunbeam cast by one of the two arched windows, a myriad of bright reflected dots danced on everything in the room. Peanut was instantly on her feet. She barked enthusiastically as she spotted the numerous "bugs" that were now flying around.

"Quiet!" Mikal snapped. "They're nothing, Peanut. It's just the key. Keep it down!"

Lissa hurried to the closed door and held her ear up against the wood. "You'd better hurry," she urged. "I think I hear someone coming this way."

Mikal inserted the key into the portal's keyhole and twisted it clockwise. He retrieved Peanut's leash from the ground and then took Lissa by the hand. Together, the three of them stepped through the portal as soon as Verdayn's constable's office appeared. Moments later, the portal fuzzed out. Mikal turned to his girlfriend and clasped her hand tightly in his.

"You're worried about my father cutting off your access to the Archives? Don't be. He knows you're an aspiring healer, and a good one at that. My father would never do anything to hinder your education, so you'll never have to worry about losing access. Trust me, its fine. There are times I think he likes you more than me."

"Do you think your father would approve of my being up here? I don't want to get you into trouble, Mikal."

"You won't. Take Peanut's leash, will you? I don't want her wandering off. There are a lot of wild griffins around here and Peanut would be nothing more than a snack to them."

Lissa coiled Peanut's leash around her wrist and together they headed back toward the scene of the fire.

Welcome back. I was under the impression most humans refused to start the day until the sun did.

Mikal came to a sudden halt. Peanut turned to look back

at him and then up at Lissa, as if she expected the holder of the leash should inquire what the matter was.

Good morning, Pravara. We have news that couldn't wait. I believe we have identified the renegade wizard!

We? Is there someone with you?

You can't tell?

"What are you doing?" Lissa asked, dropping her voice to a whisper. "Are you all right?"

"I'm talking to Pravara. She knows I'm back."

"Ooooo, a dragon! You're talking to a real-life dragon? That's so exciting!"

Why would the act of talking to a dragon be considered exciting?

Mikal chuckled. "Great. Pravara heard you. She wants to know why talking to a dragon would be considered exciting. Let's do this properly, shall we? Pravara, this is Lissa, daughter of Fensham, of Capily. Lissa, this is Pravara, daughter of Pryllan, mate to Kahvel, Dragon Lord. Lissa, say something. Remember, Pravara can hear you."

Lissa's eyes widened. "I, um, er, hello."

Greetings, human female.

"Greetings, human female," Mikal relayed.

Have you come to aid us with this investigation?

Mikal repeated the question for Lissa.

"Um, I guess so. Is that okay?"

I have no objections. Is Mikal returning to the scene of the fire?

"Yes," Mikal said, answering his own question. "We'll be there shortly."

Excellent. My father says my previous interview with Catrin and Jasmyre was ineffective and I am to try again. Perhaps you could assist me? I would appreciate your presence there.

I suppose so, Pravara. Where would you like us to meet you? Back at the scene of the fire?

Aye. My father has instructed Catrin and Jasmyre to meet me here. Are you on your way?

We are now.

Mikal took Lissa's hand and guided her away from town.

Peanut trotted quietly alongside Lissa. The corgi's ears were pointed straight up and her head was quickly shifting about as a slew of interesting stimuli attracted her attention.

Excellent. Please make haste.

"She wants us to hurry."

Lissa glanced at Mikal. "Why?"

"Kahvel has sent two dragons to be interviewed again. Apparently, he thinks Pravara didn't do an adequate job last time. She has asked us to help."

Lissa smiled warmly at him. "Really? How sweet! Of course, we'll help her."

They followed the road north until they had passed the outskirts of the village. The gigantic pine trees seemed to rush in at them from all sides, threatening to swallow them up inside an endless sea of vibrant green foliage. The road narrowed to a single lane where two horses would be lucky if they could ride side-by-side. After another fifteen minutes it became a simple gravel path that had an occasional weed growing here and there.

"Where are we headed?" Lissa asked.

Mikal pointed north. "Just a little way up there the road will turn to the east. You'll be able to see Lake Raehón and its valley. That's where the fire happened. We're heading to the scene of the crime. Pravara should be waiting for us."

"I can't wait to meet a real live dragon," Lissa breathed with excitement.

"Well, you're going to meet not one, but three," Mikal reminded her. "Catrin and Jasmyre, the two dragons responsible for the damage, are on the way here, too."

Lissa came to a sudden stop. Peanut kept walking until she was forced to stop. Sensing this could be the start of a long conversation, Peanut promptly sat on the side of the pathway.

"Wait a moment. You're telling me that the two dragons that caused this fire are coming back here? Are you sure we should be doing this?"

"Doing what?"

"Going out to meet them. What if they go crazy again?"

"Pravara will be there. I'm sure she would warn us if she

thought things were about to become dangerous."

Indeed, I would.

"There, you see? She agrees."

"Is she speaking to you again?"

"That's right. In my head."

Twenty minutes later, Mikal was staring at the same burnt patch of ground from the previous day. Aside from a few patches of flattened prairie grass where Pravara must have been standing, the scene was relatively unchanged.

"There's more damage here than I imagined," Lissa observed, as she eyed the burned trees and scorched grass. "That must have been a substantial fire."

A large shadow fell over the ground. They turned around and looked up. Pravara was standing directly behind them. She lowered her long serpentine neck down until her head was resting on a section of unburned grass.

"You must be Lissa," Pravara observed. She gently inhaled.

Clutching Mikal's arm tightly in her own, Lissa nodded her head. "And you are Pravara? Daughter of the Dragon Lord?"

Pravara's huge head nodded. "I am."

"I'm pleased to meet you. I've never met a dragon before."

A distant roar caught everyone's attention. Peanut quietly woofed a warning. Pravara lifted her head off the ground and turned to face west.

"Jasmyre approaches."

Mikal could easily recall stories Steve and Sarah had told him over the years about how dragons could move about in extreme stealth, often masking their arrivals. He remembered Steve telling him about the time when Kahvel, Pravara's sire, escorted them north to find Maelnar, the dwarf keymaker. Kahvel surprised the men on more than one occasion, even out in the open.

Mikal eyed the large black dragon with silver blotches all over its body. It landed so hard its claws dug gouges into the earth as it tried to come to a stop. This dragon turned to look at Pravara, its nose lifted high into the air and, Mikal was sure, gave Pravara a scornful look.

"There's nothing I can tell you now that I didn't tell you before," the huge dragon rumbled. Its nostrils flared as it picked up unfamiliar scents. The black snout briefly oriented on Mikal and Lissa before turning back to Pravara. "Why am I here?"

A second dragon landed, much more elegantly than the first. It was smaller than the black dragon and even smaller than Pravara. It was solid blue with the exception of the tips of its wings, which were white. This one, Mikal decided, was female. Another young dragon, perhaps?

They are both female.

Oh. I thought the black one might have been a male.

No. Jasmyre is female. Do you see her markings?

What about them?

Only females can have three different colors on their scales.

Three? I see only two. Black and silver.

Note her wingtips. They are white, like Catrin's.

Oh. I didn't notice.

The blue dragon gave a noticeable cough. Pravara leveled a gaze at the newcomer.

"Catrin."

The sky-blue dragon nodded. She folded her wings against her back and regarded Pravara. "Why am I here? I thought we were done with this interrogation."

"As did I," Jasmyre grumbled.

"That makes three of us," Pravara confided. "However, my father believes there is more to learn here. Therefore, we will all revisit what has happened."

"Again?" Jasmyre groaned, which came out as a loud growl. "There's nothing to tell. I fell from the sky and woke up here, with the woods burning."

"That's precisely what happened to me," Catrin added. "I was hunting. I had located a stray bolger and was preparing to dive when I suddenly awoke on the ground and everything was burning."

"Where did you fall?" Mikal asked, curious.

Jasmyre's great black head swung over to stare at him. "Who are you, human? Why do you feel you may address me?"

"Humans are our allies," Pravara coldly informed her. "You will address them with the respect you'd expect to be given in return. To answer your question, this is Mikal, son of the human king. The female is his mate, Lissa."

Mikal choked. "Umm, she's not exactly my mate."

Lissa fixed him with a steely stare. She put her hands on her hips. "We are in a committed relationship, are we not? We have both agreed to not see other people. Does that not qualify us as being mates?"

Mikal's eyes widened. His felt as though his face was on fire. He didn't have to look around the clearing to know that three pairs of wyverian eyes were boring into the back of his skull. A small cough sounded from his right, indicating Lissa was waiting for him to respond. What was he supposed to say?

He desperately wanted to clarify to everyone present that he and Lissa were not married, only judging from the fire in Lissa's eyes, this wasn't the time or the place to attempt it. His expression softened as he looked into his girlfriend's deep hazel eyes. He really did care for the girl and it showed in everything he did. Lissa's eyes lost their fire and she smiled back at him. He was really smitten with her and she knew it.

"Aye, she's my mate."

"Why have you enlisted the help of the humans?" Jasmyre derisively asked. "Can you not figure this out yourself, Pravara?"

Mikal cringed. While he wasn't sure why Jasmyre would try to provoke his wyverian companion, he certainly didn't want to see anyone degrade her, either. He took a breath, ready to fire off an angry retort.

Be at ease, friend Mikal. I can handle this.

Mikal's mouth snapped closed.

Pravara took three steps and was suddenly nose-to-nose with the larger black dragon.

"Are you challenging my authority in this investigation, Jasmyre? Are you insinuating you have something to hide by this aggressive behavior? The Dragon Lord doesn't accept the answers you gave me yesterday. Therefore, I agreed to meet with you again. If you don't wish to discuss the matter with me, that's fine. You'll find yourself standing before the Dragon Lord, answering his questions. In front of everyone."

Twin plumes of smoke leaked out of Jasmyre's nostrils.

"What will it be?" Pravara continued. "You may choose to talk to me, and anyone else I deem worthy, such as my human companions here, or you may deal directly with my father. Personally, I think I am more reasonable, but I may be biased."

Lissa stifled a giggle and bit her lip.

"I will answer your questions," Jasmyre grudgingly agreed. "However, as I said before, I have no additional news to impart."

"You may start by answering Mikal's question. You said you fell from the sky. Where did you fall? Do you remember?"

The black and silver dragon cocked her head a few times struggling to remember the events that felled her from the sky. Her head rose skyward, looking around the area. Her snout pointed northwest. "It was that way."

Pravara looked over at Catrin. "And you? Do you remember where you were? I assume you fell, too?"

Catrin shook her head. "I apologize. I do not recall."

Mikal caught the giant black dragon's eyes as she continued to look around.

"Could you show us the exact spot?" Jasmyre growled, so Mikal hastily added, "It might help us."

"Very well. Follow me."

The black dragon turned about and headed north without bothering to see if she was being followed. The small group of dragons, humans, and canine walked along the forest's edge for nearly twenty minutes. Jasmyre was clearly content to walk in silence, and while Catrin didn't remember what had happened to her, she brought up the rear of their group.

"It happened here," Jasmyre announced, coming to a stop. "I remember I smelled humans nearby and knew I had to alter course. I saw those boulders over there and briefly wondered if a dwarf door might be concealed within. Then I felt a pain in my wings, as though I had overextended my abilities. The next thing I knew I was on the ground and a fire was blazing before my eyes. I cannot explain it."

Mikal looked around the quiet valley. A gentle breeze was blowing from the west, bringing scents of fresh pine trees and various aromatic shrubs. While he felt an overwhelming sense of peace envelope him, and he wanted to linger to appreciate the beauty of the forest, he knew that he had other matters to attend to. Three dragons, one corgi, and one girlfriend were staring intently at him.

"I don't see anything spectacular about this spot," Mikal admitted.

He squatted and scratched behind Peanut's ears. The dog instantly rolled over and presented her belly. Mikal had just given her a few scratches when the corgi twisted about and was on her feet. Her ears perked up, looking into the woods. She whined and pulled at her leash.

Everyone present, including all three dragons, immediately turned to look at the quiet forest.

"Wow, she made us all look," Mikal chuckled. He snapped his fingers a few times to get the dog's attention. When Peanut refused to turn around, Mikal again looked in the direction she was facing. "Does anyone see anything that way?"

Lissa shielded her eyes as she peered at the trees. "I don't see anything."

"Nor do I," Pravara admitted.

"Tsssk, tsssk," Jasmyre grunted. "You have much to learn, young Pravara. No, do not growl at me. I do not offer offense. I see that which you have missed."

Pravara returned her gaze to the west and stared silently at the trees.

"Do you see it yet?" Jasmyre asked, in a surprisingly gentle voice. "Look not at what is before you. Allow your eyes to unfocus and imagine what you're looking for lies behind the line of trees before you."

Pravara was silent, trying to follow Jasmyre's instructions. Mikal was shaking his head. "I only see trees. Why would unfocusing your eyes help a person to see something behind the trees?"

"You are not wyverian, human," Jasmyre impassively told him. "It does not matter if you unfocus your eyes, refocus them, and repeat the process as many times as you can. You will still only see what's before you."

Pravara huffed out a small cloud of smoke. Her eyes had widened with surprise.

Jasmyre grunted with approval. "Do you see it now?"

Long sinewy tendons rippled in Pravara's neck as she eagerly nodded her head. "Aye. I see a human establishment."

Mikal's head jerked up. "You do? How far away is it?"

Pravara was silent, studying what her developing vision was showing her. "Not far. Perhaps a quarter of the distance we walked to journey here."

Mikal looked back at the forest. "Well, that's not far at all. I think we should go check it out."

"Do you think it might be his house?" Lissa asked.

"That's what I'm thinking," Mikal admitted. He looked back at Jasmyre and Pravara. "Can either of you see any other houses in the area?"

Jasmyre's great black head slowly panned from the left to the right. After a moment she shook her head no. Pravara was quick to follow suit.

"It's too much of a coincidence," Mikal decided. "I'll wager we find that the house belongs to the boy's aunt."

Jasmyre looked back at Pryllan. "May I assume we are finished here?"

Pravara nodded. "You have been incredibly helpful. I won't forget it."

Jasmyre nodded once, spread her expansive wings, and took to the air. After a few moments of awkward silence, Catrin also bade them farewell and left. Pravara eyed the two of them.

"Will you investigate the house? I do not think it prudent if I were to appear before their door to see if they'd be willing to answer a few questions."

Mikal nodded. He took Lissa's hand. "We will. Stay close, in case we need you."

"I will be nearby. With your permission, I will mentally accompany you."

Mikal smiled at their large companion. "Deal."

The house was a simple, nondescript two-story dwelling.

It had been painted light blue and the trim around the windows had been left white. While Mikal could tell it was a house built in the older style favored by people from his father's time, the building had been well cared for. He could see that the thatch on the roof had been recently replaced. Probably within the last year or so. The windows were large rectangular openings that had their protective shutters open wide. Mikal also noticed there wasn't a single pane of glass anywhere on the house.

"What is it?" Lissa whispered. "You're frowning."

"The windows don't have any glass. I haven't seen a house without glass in quite awhile."

"Hey, glass is expensive. My house didn't have any glass windows until last year when the king increased my father's stipend."

"Oh. Uh, sorry."

"Not all of us are born into royalty, you know."

"Umm…"

Lissa giggled. "Mikal, I'm teasing you. Stop being so serious all the time."

Mikal cleared his throat, cast a look at Lissa, and then rapped his knuckles on the door three times.

Are you still with me?

Of course.

Here we go.

Go? Where are you going? You haven't spoken with the inhabitants yet.

It… never mind.

The door opened and a woman in her early forties appeared. She was wearing a discolored blue flannel dress that fell to within an inch of worn wooden floors. She had on a white apron, long since faded to a dull yellow. Tendrils of gray were just starting to sneak into her ash blonde hair, which had been pulled up into a bun. Something must have just made her laugh because her eyes were sparkling with merriment. She looked at the two of them and smiled.

"Good day to you. Are you lost? We don't get many visitors out here. We…" The woman trailed off as she stared at Mikal. Her eyes widened and she dropped to one knee. "By the stars! Kre'Mikal! You honor us with your presence! I had no idea you were in the area."

Mikal gently tapped the woman on her shoulder. "Please rise. You don't need to kneel in front of me. This is an informal visit."

The woman stood hesitantly and started twisting her apron into knots.

"What is your name?" Mikal asked. "You know who I am. This is Lissa, of Capily."

The woman looked at Lissa and curtsied. "Lady Lissa. It is an honor to meet you, too."

"Lady Lissa," Lissa quietly mouthed. Her face broke into a smile. "I can live with that." She looked at the older woman and curtsied back. "Hello. I'm pleased to meet you, too. What is your name?"

"A thousand apologies, Lady Lissa. My name is Adyna. I am at your service."

Peanut gave a friendly bark, as if she noticed she hadn't been introduced yet. Adyna instantly squatted down and gave Peanut a gentle stroke on her head. "And who do we have here?"

"This is Peanut," Mikal told her.

Adyna's face was alight with happiness. "A dog! How adorable! I haven't seen one in such a long time. Aren't you the prettiest thing?"

Peanut's head dropped low and her stump of a tail waggled back and forth with delight. She yipped excitedly at the woman.

"Who's there?" another voice called from somewhere within the house. "Dinna, who are you talking to? What was that noise?"

Adyna turned to her right and beckoned to someone they couldn't see. "Get over here. Right now! Hurry! There's someone you need to meet."

"We have guests?" the second voice asked. "How nice!"

Another woman appeared by Adyna's side. She was wearing a heavily faded green dress and an apron, whiter than Adyna's.

Mikal looked at the second woman's face and then back

at the first. The two of them had the same high cheekbones, the same rounded forehead, and the same dainty, if a tad elongated, nose. These two were undeniably related. Two sisters? Mikal's pulse quickened. The boy wizard they were looking for was supposed to be living with his mother and the mother's sister. This had to be the right place!

"Heavens above!" the second woman exclaimed. "Isn't that—?"

"Your Highness," Adyna interjected, interrupting her sister, "may I introduce my sister, Delythia. Del, this is Prince Mikal and the lovely Lady Lissa. Down there, gazing adoringly up at us, is Peanut, the prince's dog."

Delythia's eyes had widened and stayed that way.

"Kre'Mikal! We are humbled by your visit to our meager homestead. What may we do for you?"

"We wanted to know if there's a…"

Do not ask her if there is a young human wizard living there.

Mikal pretended to rub his temples. Lissa gave him a quizzical look.

We need to know if he's here, Pravara.

And if he is? Do you not think he'll want to remain anonymous?

What am I supposed to say?

You'd better say something. She's starting to think you are suffering from some type of medical ailment.

"We, uh, we were just in the area, and we, uh…"

Enhance your calm. If you're trying to appear indecisive then you're doing a marvelous job.

Easy for you to say. You're not the one standing in front of her. Listen, you think you can do better? Fine. Tell me what you want to say, word for word, and I'll repeat it.

Are you saying you want me to instruct you what to say?

Exactly. Let's see how well you do.

Very well. Here's what needs to be said. We're here investigating the fires that happened nearby.

"We're here to investigate the fires that happened nearby," Mikal relayed.

Adyna nodded. "That was a dreadful night. I wish those infernal dragons would keep their flames to themselves."

Mikal felt Pravara's irritation. **We suspect the dragons might have been bewitched.**

"We suspect the dragons might have become bewitched," Mikal told the two of them.

"Really?" Delythia exclaimed, holding a hand over her heart. "Who would want to bewitch a dragon? Why would they want to? Large, cumbersome creatures, if you ask me."

I wasn't.

"I wasn't," Mikal immediately repeated, then cringed.

Delythia blushed and dropped her gaze to the ground. "I'm terribly sorry, Your Highness. I'm just a peasant. You certainly don't want, or need, to hear what I think of the matter."

"What's the matter with you?" Lissa hissed quietly to him. "That was rude."

"That was my, uh, conscience," Mikal whispered back. "It was guiding me on what to say."

"Oh."

"Won't you please come in? Make yourself comfortable. Can I get you something to drink? We don't have much here but I will give you what I can."

"A glass of water would be fine for us," Mikal quickly told her.

"For both?" Delythia asked, raising an eyebrow. "How interesting."

Mikal had lost count how many times it felt as though his face had become engulfed in fire. Something told him this wouldn't be the last time today, either. A few moments passed before he felt he could look at his girlfriend.

"One glass would be fine," Lissa assured their hostesses. She glanced at Peanut, who had promptly settled down by their feet. The corgi's eyes were wide open and her ears were pointing straight up, an indicator that she knew she was in a strange environment and wasn't to let her guard down. "Perhaps a bowl of water for Peanut? I'm sure she's probably thirsty, too."

Adyna nodded. "Of course, of course. You two wait

here. I'll be right back."

Mikal took Lissa's hand and together, they sat on the couch.

Watch what you're thinking, Pravara. I keep repeating what you tell me, word for word.

My apologies. Ignorant humans annoy me.

Let's just get through this, okay?

Very well.

What now? I say we dispense with this façade and just ask her who else lives here.

All in good time. Now, repeat after me. Is everyone safe? Was anyone injured in the fire?

He repeated the questions.

"No, Your Highness. We are all safe."

Does anyone else live here besides the two of you?

"You said *we*," Mikal improvised. "Does anyone else live here besides you and your sister?"

"It's just the two of us," Delythia answered. "And my nephew."

Where is the nephew now?

"Where is the nephew now? Er, I mean, where is he now?"

My apologies. I did it again, didn't I?

Lissa gave him a concerned look.

"Gareth? He's outside somewhere. He spends most of his time outdoors lately."

"How old is he?" Mikal asked. "I do not recall seeing his age on the most recent census."

"My nephew is fifteen," Delythia answered. "His information wasn't reported to the last census? I'm sorry, Your Highness. I know I shouldn't cast negative thoughts, but that wizard is something else."

Surprised, and intrigued, Mikal and Lissa edged closer. "Oh? Are you referring to Shardwyn?"

"Aye."

"Would you care to tell me what your concerns are?"

"Do you know how many times he has been out here to ask his infernal questions? He wanted to know where my sister's husband was, what our jhoruns were, what type of work we do, and so on. Ordinarily I don't mind answering questions, especially when it's for the wellbeing of the kingdom, but when you've been asked the same questions on multiple occasions it becomes troublesome."

"I am truly sorry," Mikal said. "I will speak with my father about that. If you will tell me what you told Shardwyn then I will make certain the information is properly recorded."

Delythia smiled as she settled into one of the four chairs scattered around the living room. "Thank you. Now, let me ask you something, Your Highness. Why do you ask about my nephew? Has he done something wrong?"

Mikal smiled, realizing he had just thought of a perfect cover story to conceal his attempts to get more information.

"My father has started to entrust me with more responsibility. I have begun perusing the census reports. I researched this area when I found out I would be traveling here to begin my investigation. The census stated this house formerly had one resident but now has three. It also stated that your sister moved in not long ago."

"How did you even know my nephew lived here if he wasn't on the census?" Delythia asked somewhat suspiciously.

Mikal pointed at the dinner table. "There's a pair of boots over there. He may only be fifteen but those boots are way too large for either of you two. Therefore, a third person must live here, and judging by the size of those boots, the owner isn't quite an adult. There's also a pair of drogo dice on the table."

Delythia turned to look at the small wooden dice on the nearby table. She picked them up and studied them. "What type of dice did you say these were?"

"They're a type of dice made specifically for a game called 'drogo'. See the dragon head on the one and the sword on the other? It's a game of chance. It requires the players to act out whatever action scenes the dice directs them to. Girls don't generally play it."

"I've never heard of it," Lissa confessed.

"Nor have I," Delythia added.

"Gareth evidently has," Mikal told them both.

Delythia nodded her head. "Well, it's true, Your Highness.

All of it. Very impressive!"

Most impressive, indeed.

A smug smile appeared on Mikal's face. *Thanks!*

Lissa turned to look at him with an incredulous look on her face. "That is very impressive. How'd you do that?"

"Ask me again later, okay?"

Lissa nodded.

Adyna returned with a large tumbler filled with cold water for Mikal and Lissa to share and then set a shallow wooden bowl down on the ground. She filled it with water from a pitcher and watched as Peanut sank her entire snout down into the water. She'd pull out a few inches to lap a couple of times then she'd shove her nose back into the water. Once the dog was certain her snout was good and wet, she returned to her position by Lissa's feet, leaving a trail of water droplets the entire way.

"She really likes her water," Mikal tried to explain.

Delythia and Adyna both laughed.

Remain focused. What else can be learned about the boy?

"What else can you tell us about Gareth? What happened to his father?"

Adyna took a deep breath. "I knew you were going to ask about that. Shardwyn wouldn't stop pestering me about it."

"I'm truly sorry," Mikal gently told her. "Trust me, you'll only have to answer once."

"I appreciate that. Gareth's father disappeared two years ago. My son took his disappearance very hard. Gareth was already a quiet and shy boy. After his father vanished, he became moody, depressed. He wouldn't eat. He stopped going outside to do what he loved most, which was exploring. It was very hard on the boy. Truth be told, it broke my heart."

"As I'm sure it was as equally hard on you," Lissa softly added.

Adyna nodded. "It was. But, that's in the past. As much as I miss my husband, I have to realize that I have responsibilities here. I must raise and care for my son. That's what takes precedence now."

"Does Gareth make friends easily?" Mikal asked, after a

moment or two of silence. He had waited to see if Pravara had any other questions, but none were forthcoming.

"No," Adyna answered. "As I said, Gareth is a shy boy. He never has had many friends. In fact, the only friend I was ever aware of was someone whom I never met."

Mikal gave Lissa a quizzical look. What did that mean?

"I don't suppose you could explain?"

Adyna shrugged. "I never knew his name. Gareth talked about him all the time, though. There was some type of friendly competition going on and he was always looking for ways to best him."

"Best him in what?" Mikal asked.

"In whatever they were doing. He never really told me anything specific."

Mikal sat up straight as a thought occurred to him. "When was the last time Gareth talked to this friend?"

"It has been a while. Over two years ago."

"That's a long time to not speak to a friend, don't you think?" Mikal asked Adyna.

"They had a falling out. Something happened, which caused a fight. Gareth was angry. He refused to eat. He refused to talk to us."

"He retreated into his room and barely came out," his aunt added. "We were so worried about him. Adyna and Gareth came to live with me in the hopes that a change of scenery might be what was needed."

"Was it?" Lissa asked. "Was he all right once he moved here?"

Both Adyna and Delythia shook their heads.

"No," Adyna answered. "It took nearly a year and a half before Gareth showed some signs of returning to normal. He's still moody, but at least he gets out of that infernal room and goes outside."

"Do you have any idea when he'll be back?" Mikal asked, hoping his question didn't sound as eager as he thought it did. "I'd really like to meet him."

"It's hard to say," his mother admitted. "Sometimes he's home right after his lessons. Sometimes we don't see him until his supper has gone stone cold on the table."

"He left here about two hours ago," Delythia added. "I would imagine he shouldn't be gone too much longer."

Mikal rose to his feet, prompting Lissa to do the same. In a quick blur of motion Peanut was on her feet, too.

"Thank you for your time. You have been incredibly helpful."

"I can't wait to tell my son that Kre'Mikal himself was asking about him."

Uh, oh.

What is it?

His mother plans on telling him we were here.

That would be bad.

You think? How do I get her to not say anything?

Beg.

Beg? Are you serious?

Why not? It couldn't hurt to try.

My father is the king, Pravara. I cannot beg her to stay quiet.

I'm a wyverian, not a human. How would I know what would make the human female refrain from telling her offspring about your visit?

Great. Some help you are.

"Listen, when is Gareth's next birthday?"

"Next month," Adyna answered. "Why?"

Thinking fast, Mikal smiled. "What do you say we surprise him and perhaps give him a personalized tour of the castle for his birthday? Do you think he'd like that?"

"Why, that'd be wonderful!" Delythia exclaimed. "Gareth has talked about the castle. I'm sure he'd love to see it up close! Thank you, Your Highness!"

"We can't tip him off," Mikal warned, "so it'd be best to keep our visit today a secret, okay?"

Both women vigorously nodded their heads. "Absolutely! We won't say a word, will we, Del?"

"My lips are sealed, Dinna. Oh, Gareth is going to be so surprised!"

They bade the two women a fond farewell and headed back to the valley. Once the house had disappeared back into the forest Lissa turned to Mikal.

"Do you still think Gareth is the one we're looking for?"

"Without a doubt."

"You said I should ask you later about how you deduced Gareth lived there. Well, how did you know?"

"When I was living with Steve and Sarah in their world, they introduced me to all kinds of things. Movies, television, games, and books. One of my favorite books they introduced me to featured a man called Sherlock Holmes. This character had many adventures. Everyone wanted his advice because he had an uncanny ability to notice trivial details that most people overlooked. I've always wished I possessed those kinds of observational skills. I know I'll never be as good as that, but I am trying to observe everything I can. I saw the boots. They wouldn't fit either Adyna or Delythia. Then I saw the dice. It became clear to me that a third person lived there. More specifically, a young man."

Lissa clutched his arm tightly and beamed her approval at him. "I think I would like those stories."

"I'll ask Steve and Sarah to bring the books the next time I see them."

Peanut began barking and pulling at her leash. She had caught a whiff of something that excited her and she was eager to go check it out.

Pravara? Are you there?

Always.

Is Peanut barking at you?

Aye. You are close to my location.

She really wants to come see you. If I let go of the leash, will you keep an eye on her? In case she has smelled something else?

Of course.

"Okay, Peanut. Do you think you've found Pravara? Go get her!"

Those last three words electrified the corgi as nothing else would. She was practically bouncing in place and rearing up on her hind feet, attempting to pull free of Mikal's grasp. As soon as the leash dropped, Peanut was off like an orange and white lightning bolt. Mikal and Lissa emerged from the perimeter of the forest in time to see Peanut running circles around Pravara's enormous body. Pravara, in the meantime, quietly watched the small dog bounding joyfully through the thick grass.

They heard a loud squawk from somewhere close by. Peanut instantly changed course and bounded off, angling northwest. Pravara moved to step on the leash in an attempt to stop Peanut's sprint across the ground but missed. Mikal started running after her.

"Peanut! Stop! Off! Halt! Come back here you goofy furball! *Wait!*"

Nearly a hundred feet away, Peanut finally came to a stop. She turned to give them all a scolding look, as if to say it wasn't her fault they were so slow.

Mikal and Lissa were just passing by Pravara when everything changed. A long flat green spear suddenly skyrocketed past his head and shot high up into the air. Shocked, Mikal glanced around. More of the huge flat spears were everywhere. What were they? They almost looked like grass, but on a monstrous scale. Mikal stared up at the distant tips of the flat green spears and saw that the nearby trees had also exploded with growth. The treetops were now so high up that Mikal thought they were tickling the undersides of the soft fluffy clouds far above him.

"What—what just happened?" Lissa's shaky voice asked. She had fallen to the ground and was slowly rising to her feet. Her eyes widened, as she stared at the giant spear protruding from the ground right next to them.

"It's like all the plants have become enormous," Mikal reported, glancing around. His voice sounded muffled.

Lissa stared at the hefty flat blade and then up at the distant treetops.

"They haven't grown, Mikal. We've shrunk!"

Chapter 4 — Corgi Capers

Mikal stared at the surreal green forest that had seemingly sprouted up around him and Lissa. The spears were mere blades of grass? How tall were they now? Lissa, correctly guessing what Mikal was thinking, was ready with an answer.

"Three inches. I would say we are now about three inches tall. Mikal, what are we going to do?"

"Why would he shrink us?" Mikal wondered out loud. "How could that possibly benefit him?"

"How did he even know we were there?" Lissa asked, continuing to cast nervous glances in all directions.

Mikal scowled. "I'd say he must have returned home. I'll bet he was outside the window listening to every word we said. Do you remember? His mother told us Gareth had left a few hours ago and was due home soon."

"This is preposterous," a new voice chimed in.

Mikal and Lissa glanced over to see Pravara standing amongst the giant blades of grass. While still much larger than the two of them, Pravara could now barely see over the tips of the grass blades.

"What are you worried about?" Mikal asked their wyverian companion. "You're still way bigger than us."

"There has never been a wyverian as tiny as I am now," Pravara grumped. "Look at me! I am now the same size as your canine companion."

Mikal paled. What had happened to Peanut? Had she been shrunk, too?

"Peanut!" Mikal called out in as loud of a voice as he could muster. "Where are you, pretty girl? Come here! Come on, Peanut!"

A loud bark pierced the air. Mikal and Lissa clapped their hands over their ears. They heard a loud snuffling sound. The ground trembled and the blades of grass began swaying.

"You do realize we're small enough to be stepped on, don't you?" Lissa warned him.

Mikal nodded. "I know. I'm going to assume Peanut is now looking for us. Steve told me once that dogs have much better ears than we do. She heard us but can't find us."

Peanut yipped again. She was close.

"We're over here, Peanut!" Mikal called out. "Come on! Follow your nose!"

A huge orange and white snout appeared, capped by a tremendous black nose. Peanut's giant head pushed its way through the blades of grass and continued to home in on their location.

"Good girl, Peanut! You found us!"

Peanut eyed the tiny figures and cocked her head at them. Mikal had to laugh. He knew what she was thinking. They smelled like her humans and sounded like them but they didn't look like the humans she was familiar with. Peanut whined, edging closer to Mikal's tiny outstretched hand. She licked it, but ended up knocking Mikal completely off his feet and covering him in a layer of doggy drool.

"Ewww!" Mikal rolled to his feet and pushed the excess saliva off his arms and legs. "That's disgusting, Peanut. You be careful."

Peanut lowered herself onto the grass and looked expectantly at the two tiny figures, as though she was waiting for an explanation. The corgi cocked her head a second time and turned to her left. Pravara was less than a foot away, regarding the corgi with the same curiosity. Peanut waited a few moments, undecided whether she would accept the fact that her wyverian companion was now slightly smaller than she was.

"It's Pravara, Peanut," Mikal told the dog. "She's your friend. It's okay. You know her."

Peanut stretched out her neck and waited for Pravara to mimic her. They sniffed noses. Peanut let out a joyful bark and was ready to resume her exploration of the surrounding area. Her leash, Mikal noted, trailed off behind her and was easily wider than he was at the moment.

They all heard another loud screech. Lissa jumped and instantly flung herself into his arms. At any other time, Mikal would have appreciated the situation, but at this present moment, the significance of the screech presented a problem. Griffins. He nervously eyed their small group. Without Pravara's intimidating physique to protect them, they were in trouble. Especially if the griffins decided to attack.

"Were those griffins?" Lissa timidly asked.

"Aye, they were," Pravara agreed, looking nervously about. A dragon was easily more than a match for a single griffin, or possibly a dozen, but a miniature dragon had as much to be afraid of as her human companions.

"I think it's time to go," Mikal informed the others.

"Where?" Lissa asked. "How?"

More squawks and screeches sounded, alarmingly close.

"I can fly you to safety," Pravara told them, "but I am too small to aid your canine."

Mikal looked at Peanut, who returned his stare with wide unblinking eyes.

"I won't leave her here," Mikal vowed. "Whatever we do we have to do it together."

"I have called for assistance," Pravara told them, "but I do not think anyone will be able to get here in time."

A large shadow passed over their heads, causing everyone, including Peanut, to look up.

Mikal took Lissa's hand and ran toward Peanut.

"What are you doing?" Pravara wanted to know.

"We're going to ride Peanut out of here," Mikal decided.

"How do you plan on telling her which way to go?" Lissa asked, confused. "She isn't a horse. She doesn't have any reins."

Mikal pointed at Pravara. "That's where you come in," Mikal told their wyverian companion. "Peanut will chase you. She's done it before and she'll do it again. Fly low enough that she can see you and she'll be encouraged to pursue."

Pravara looked skyward. "And the griffins?"

Mikal turned to look at the forest. "We have the advantage. We're a lot smaller than they are. We can lose them once we reach the forest."

"Being this size is most certainly *not* an advantage," Pravara argued. "I am accustomed to flying at an altitude with no obstacles."

Lissa turned to look up at their dragon companion as she sprinted toward Mikal and Peanut.

"Pravara, you don't have a choice here, either. You're much too small to take on a griffin. Listen to those squawks! It sounds like there's an entire flock. You'd be done for if you tried flying out in the open."

"She's right," Mikal agreed. "As much as you don't like it, you have to keep fairly low to the ground."

Several larger dark shadows passed over them. Mikal reached Peanut's side. To him, Peanut was now the size of a dragon. She should easily be able to carry the two of them. He just had to be certain the corgi remained safe. He'd never forgive himself if something happened to his dog.

He grabbed a double fistful of Peanut's orange and white fur and pulled himself up until he was sitting at the base of her neck. He leaned over to his left and helped pull Lissa up. As soon as he felt her hands holding on to his hips, he urged the dog to run.

"Okay, Peanut. Follow Pravara!"

Peanut's head turned and was able to look at the two of them from over her shoulder. Her mouth opened and she panted contentedly. Her squat rear legs buckled and she plunked her butt onto the ground.

"No, Peanut! You must get up! You have to run! Hurry!"

Lissa twisted to look back at Pravara. Their wyverian companion had taken to the air and was vigorously flapping her wings in an effort to hover nearby. Even though the dragon looked as though she was close to fifty feet off the ground Mikal knew that in reality, it was only about ten. Pravara cast a worried glance behind her, saw several rapidly approaching specks, and decided it was time to go. At least half a dozen griffins were circling the area and it was only a matter of time before they were spotted.

One griffin shrieked a challenge. Pravara growled as Mikal cursed in disgust. They had been seen!

Pravara tucked her wings and dropped down. She snapped them open less than a foot above the sea of giant grass blades. Mikal patted Peanut's furry side and pointed up. The corgi's head lifted and she noticed Pravara's receding form.

"Go get her, Peanut!"

Peanut gave a playful bark and surged forward, nearly dislodging Mikal and Lissa both. His eyes shot wide open. It was all he could do to stay upright. A corgi might have some of the shortest legs in the canine world but never could it be said that they were slow or cumbersome. In a matter of seconds, the world had been reduced to a dizzying blur. Lissa screamed in terror and wrapped her arms around his waist in a desperate attempt to hold on.

It was, Mikal would think later, the ultimate thrill ride.

The corgi surged forward. The thick grass covering the valley floor was easily as high as the tips of Peanut's ears. She began bounding through the grass the way she ran through the snow back in Idaho. Mikal felt Lissa's arms tighten around his waist. He glanced over his right shoulder. Her eyes were closed and her face was pressed tightly against his back—not enjoying herself. He jumped when a loud screech sounded alarmingly close. Every time Peanut bounded, and her head cleared the tips of the grass, Mikal checked the skies for signs of pursuit.

He breathed a sigh of relief. It had been easier than he thought to lose the griffins in the tall grass. Mikal checked the sky again. Still no signs.

After the seventh or eighth bound he saw them. He heard one of the griffins give a loud squawk and within moments the six of them began angling their way. Once more they had been spotted. Mikal turned. There, in the distance, was where he figured they'd be able to lose the griffins once and for all. The trees grew so close to one another that it would make any airborne pursuit impossible.

"You're doing great, Peanut! Hang in there!"

At that moment the world went dark and the air became musty. Mikal quickly faced forward. He smiled. Peanut had come upon a long, hollowed-out log and elected to run through it instead of around it.

A piercing screech ripped through the air. A griffin had landed on the other end of the log and was now peering through the opposite end at them. It squawked again, this time its beak opened and closed several times in anticipation of what it thought would be an easy meal.

Uh, oh.

What is it?

We're in trouble. We're stuck in a log with a griffin waiting for us at the other end.

Can you turn around?

It's too tight in here. There's no room.

Lissa pointed back, the way they had come. "There's one on either end!"

I'm on my way.

What do you think you can do? It's just as dangerous for you. Stay where you are and stay hidden. Maybe they'll give up and go home.

Unlikely.

Don't try to help us, Pravara. I mean it. I don't want you getting hurt.

A noble sentiment. I reject it. Observe.

The griffin blocking their escape gave a deafening screech and the dangerous beak disappeared from sight. More squawks and trills, then another ear-shattering shriek.

At this size my blasts are non-lethal, but still effective. The griffin has retreated. Go now, while you can!

"Go on, Peanut!" Mikal urged. "Find Pravara! Go get her!"

Peanut emerged from the log and looked for Pravara. Mikal groaned. They were exposed, and if she didn't start running, they'd be sitting ducks.

Pravara's reptilian form appeared in the distance. It was all Peanut needed. Mikal felt Peanut's muscles ripple and contract as the dog eagerly surged forward in their risky game of follow-the-leader. The problem was, thanks to the increase in shrieks and squawks, Mikal knew the griffins had also renewed their pursuit.

The forest loomed closer. Peanut was finally able to run through the grass without bounding like a gazelle. Mikal urged the dog to run as fast as she could toward the safety of the trees.

He knew they were still being pursued, naturally, but he didn't know how close the griffins were until he felt, rather than saw, a large shadow pass over them.

Wow! They have to be close! I think I can smell them.

Aye, they are close. Four are pursuing.

I thought we'd lose them in the forest.

We aren't in the forest yet.

What? You're kidding.

I am not. I estimate less than a minute more.

Do you know where you're going?

No. I merely wish to elude.

We need a plan. They are way too close. Just get us inside the forest as quickly as possible.

Hmm, a moment, if you please.

Pravara's long neck turned about until she was looking back at the trailing griffins. Her jaws opened and she spit out a blast of fire. The ball of fire hurtled by the running corgi and slammed into the chest of a griffin who had just swooped low with its talons extended.

The shot, while significant, was nowhere close to being fatal. The griffin squawked angrily and abruptly veered off. Pravara fired three more shots, each one colliding with an advancing griffin. Each one, Mikal thankfully noted, did only minor damage, and had the effect of temporarily driving off the griffin.

Those were impressive shots. And both of you were moving, too.

How'd you get so good?

All dragons have impressive aim.

Pravara, you're flying forward, while facing backward. You hit four moving targets that were quite a distance from you. You're telling me all dragons could have made those shots?

Well, perhaps not.

What's your secret?

Practice. I've practiced my targeting skills ever since Steve worked with me to improve my aim.

Steve helped you with your aim? When did he do that?

It was when his mind was driven into my mother's body and hers was driven into Sarah's.

I do remember him telling me about that.

Ever since that day I have wanted to be the dragon with the best aim. I believe I have succeeded.

Oh. Watch out. The griffins return. They are clearly angry.

There's the forest. We're safe!

Pravara flew into the densely wooded forest and selected a fallen branch to alight upon, nearly a hundred feet inside the perimeter. Peanut, panting heavily, joined her and immediately sat down. Lissa released her death grip of Mikal's waist and patted Peanut's side.

"You're such a good girl, Peanut. Poor thing. She must be thirsty."

"I'll bet we all are," Mikal observed. He twisted around on Peanut's back to look back at the valley. What he saw made his blood run cold.

Four griffins had landed, folded their wings against their backs, and stepped into the dark forest. All of them were staring their way.

"You've got to be kidding me," Mikal crossly muttered. "Heads up, guys. We're not out of this yet. Pravara, you'd better get going!"

Pravara jerked her head up and growled at the advancing griffins.

"Peanut won't be able to keep up for much longer," Lissa advised them. "She's panting pretty heavily."

Mikal looked around the quiet forest. "We need a plan.

What are griffins afraid of?"

"Dragons," Pravara immediately answered.

"Just not tiny dragons," Mikal clarified. "That doesn't help us. What else?"

"Water," Pravara proffered.

Mikal and Lissa simultaneously turned to regard their large companion. "Water? Really?"

Pravara nodded. "They will swim if they have to. However, their feathers would take an inordinate amount of time to dry so a griffin will actively avoid swimming unless it absolutely has to. Therefore, we should seek out a body of water."

Mikal turned to regard the surrounding woods. "Where? Where are we supposed to find water in here?"

Pravara flew off, prompting Peanut to follow. **Unknown. We had better find some soon, though. Our adversaries are closing in.**

Mikal turned to look behind them. *They're getting closer! How can you remain so calm?*

Would you feel better if I were to panic?

Oh, please, would you?

Sarcasm?

You think?

Mikal felt Pravara chuckle. **We may still be able to lose them. Hold tight.**

Pravara kept low to the ground and selected the smallest openings she could find. She swooped under branches. Peanut followed. Pravara folded her wings flat against her back and touched down on the ground so that she could squeeze her way through a dense clump of bushes. Peanut, keeping low to the ground, followed.

Pravara spotted several fallen trees and instantly angled toward them. The second had fallen directly on the first, leaving a sizeable gap between the trunk and the ground. She flew under it just as she twisted her neck around to verify Peanut was still following.

She wasn't.

Pravara's wings snapped open. Where were they? Pravara doubled back and saw that the feisty little canine had been stymied by the first fallen tree.

Pravara growled with frustration. Peanut missed the gap between the huge root ball and the trunk of the next closest standing tree. Pravara looked back toward the open valley. Unfortunately, the griffins had caught up.

The first to arrive pounced. Peanut, having tons of experience dodging objects much larger than she was, darted to the left. The griffin ended up sinking its talons into the fallen tree. A second griffin arrived and it, too, attempted to pounce on the much smaller creature. However, much to its amazement, it was unable to land a solid bite as the foreign creature darted between its legs and was gone by the time the griffin lifted its leg to see where it had gone.

Peanut barked an invitation to keep the play going. The griffins turned to face Peanut and squawked their acceptance. A juvenile griffin pounced first and landed a bite. The problem was, Peanut had darted out of the way and the griffin had ended up biting one of its companions.

A loud screech erupted. The juvenile beat a hasty retreat as another took its place. This one, with no more experience than its predecessor, took several snaps at the rapidly moving canine. It landed not one but two bites. Unfortunately, it bit the same griffin that had been bitten before. The young griffin gave a tremulous squawk, which sounded more like a squeak, and began backing away from the adult that was now advancing on its companion.

With a squawk of rage, the wounded griffin launched its own attack, but this time it ignored Peanut and targeted the second juvenile. Both of the young griffins ended up fleeing, with the injured griffin in hot pursuit.

That left only one. The last griffin, who had been watching his companions depart, slowly turned back to Peanut. It shook its head and squawked a challenge.

"Damn," Mikal softly swore. "I was really hoping all of them would have left."

Pravara targeted the last griffin and shot off a blast. It looked as though Pravara's shot was going to strike the griffin's chest, but at the last minute, the griffin nimbly side-stepped to avoid the hit. It narrowed its eyes as it located

Pravara's small form.

The griffin puffed out its chest and squawked again. It bounded forward, intent on getting either a bite of corgi or dragon.

"Go, Peanut!" Mikal ordered, spurring her as though she was a horse. At that moment Pravara flew deeper into the forest. Peanut gave a few short barks and leapt after her.

Help is nearby, Pravara thought to him. **Three dragons are flying overhead.**

Wonderful news! We're saved!

Not yet. My brethren cannot safely enter the forest. We must either find a clearing or retreat back to the valley.

Not good. The griffins are still out there.

Agreed. I think we may be in luck.

Why?

I smell water.

You do? Good job, Pravara!

I must find it first. It could be nothing more than a puddle. I cannot tell while I am this size.

She crested a small hill, with Peanut trailing happily, and saw a very welcoming sight: a river, evidently one of the many tributaries feeding Lake Raehón. While tiny in size, from their vantage point this river looked as large as the mighty Zylan.

Something crashed through the forest behind them. The huge griffin appeared, only a hundred feet away. Its avian head jerked about, searching, and a few seconds later it had found them. It squawked angrily and sprinted toward them.

Mikal shouted, "We have to get into the water—now!"

Pravara flew to the water's edge, circling, waiting for Peanut. Peanut had other ideas. She shoved her nose into the water and began noisily lapping away.

"Peanut, get into the water!" Mikal urged. "Hurry!"

Thirsty, Peanut ignored him. Lissa released her grip on Mikal and turned to look up at Pravara.

"Peanut has been following you. Dive into the water so she'll follow."

"I don't want to get wet," Pravara promptly informed her.

"Neither do we," Mikal added, "but we don't have a

choice. Hurry, Pravara! The griffin is almost here!"

"I hope you realize the magnitude of the favor you owe me," Pravara grumped. She flew out over the water, tucked her wings, and dove straight down toward the river. She splashed into the water and quickly disappeared from sight.

Alerted by the splash, Peanut's head jerked up. She barked at the ripples.

"It's your turn!" Mikal told the dog. They only had a few second before it arrived. "Hurry! Go find Pravara!"

Peanut eyed the river and, after a second's hesitation, jumped in. Her long muscular body and short squat legs easily propelled them through the water. She steadily swam away from the shore.

Mikal and Lissa crawled up their mount's neck and were now stretched out on their bellies across Peanut's furry head. A loud indignant squawk got their attention. Peanut circled to see what the commotion was about.

The griffin had arrived at the shore and wasn't pleased about losing its prey. Again. It squawked irritably at them for twenty straight seconds before it eyed the nearby trees, unfolded its wings, and took to the air.

Mikal groaned. "We cannot catch a break, can we?"

Lissa turned to watch the griffin as it hovered by the water's edge. Many of the trees growing on the bank of the tiny river had spread their canopies out over the river. Apparently, the griffin was agitated enough to give it a try.

"What's it doing?"

"It's trying to decide if we're worth the effort of coming over here to retrieve us."

"Where's Pravara?"

Mikal turned to look back at the point where Pravara had splashed down into the water. The ripples had faded away, as had the bubbles. An uneasy knot formed in his stomach.

"Oh, man. I don't know. Let me try to mentally contact her."

Pravara? Are you there?

Silence. The knot got worse.

Pravara? Talk to me!

Mikal paled. Her gentle, but firm, voice was absent from

his head.

Lissa let out a shout of alarm. "Look out! It's coming for us!"

The griffin still wanted its hard-earned meal and was now flying out over the water, deftly dodging branches that were seemingly trying to pull it down. It extended its talons and dropped lower to scoop them from the water.

Lissa buried her face in Mikal's shoulder. Mikal closed his eyes. He couldn't see any way out of this.

As the griffin dropped the final few feet and prepared to snag its prey, the waters erupted straight up, as though some type of explosion had occurred beneath the surface. An impossibly gigantic, heavily muscled green scaled foreleg shot out and caught the griffin, seconds before it could grab Peanut.

The clouds of mist from the watery explosion finally cleared. Lissa gasped in shock. Mikal cheered. Pravara was sitting on her haunches in the middle of the river, so large that she had effectively created a dam. Many a tree lost branches and foliage as the full-sized dragon appeared. Water spilled over the river bank and threatened to flood the area.

The griffin angrily struggled. Those struggles ceased once Pravara brought her talons up to her face to scrutinize their adversary.

"Griffin. You antagonize the wyverian Collective, while threatening the life of the human prince, jeopardizing the human-griffin alliance. Do you wish to pursue this foolish line of thinking?"

The griffin ceased struggling and started squeaking like a tiny bird. Pravara brought the creature closer to her mouth. She used a talon from her other claw to idly pick a spot between two of her enormous fangs, as though something had become lodged between several of her teeth when, in fact, there wasn't.

"Are we going to have any more problems with you?" Pravara gently, but firmly, inquired.

Demonstrating its comprehension of human speech, the griffin quickly shook its head.

"Good. Be on your way."

As soon as the griffin was released it fled toward the north, back to the valley. Pravara stood on all fours and carefully stepped out of the river, scooping up the exhausted dog and carefully placing Peanut by the river's edge. Pravara returned her attention to her tiny companions and lowered her head to verify everyone was well.

"What happened?" Mikal wanted to know. "How did you get back to your original size? And why haven't we?"

"We thought you might have drowned," Lissa tearfully added, looking up at their gargantuan companion.

"It's the water," Pravara told them. "As soon as I entered the river I felt a tingling sensation on my scales. I scrubbed every last scale clean, thinking the wizard's spell could be undone that way. It worked."

Mikal slid down Peanut's wet fur and held out a hand in an open invitation for Lissa to join him. Together they walked to the water's edge, where Lissa bent to retrieve a large dull green piece of malleable material. She broke off a piece and handed it to Mikal.

"Here. Use this."

"What is it?"

"A piece of a dead freshwater sponge. Didn't you hear Pravara? She had to scrub every scale of hers before the enchantment was broken. We have to do the same."

"I, er…"

Lissa waded into the water and began scrubbing her arms and legs.

"What are you waiting for? Come on. It's not going to wash itself off your body. Unless you'd like me to do it for you?"

Mikal's face blushed bright red. He quickly waded into the water and started rinsing himself off.

"You embarrass way too easily," Lissa observed. "Why is that?"

Mikal mumbled something and quickly ducked his head under the water. Once he surfaced, he quickly faced the other way. Lissa had pulled her dress off and was busy scrubbing it.

"What are you doing?" Mikal hesitantly asked. "Why did you take your dress off?"

"Oh, stop being so prudish," Lissa scolded. "I have an undershirt on. Besides, we have to make sure everything is clean, otherwise we won't revert back to our normal size. I don't know about you but I'm tired of being this small."

There was a tremendous splash of water. Mikal turned to see Lissa's giant form erupt out of the water. The temperature of his face rose a few more degrees. She was only wearing her nightshirt and that left little to the imagination. He dropped his gaze back to the water.

"See? It's not enough we get ourselves clean," Lissa told him, unconcerned about her present state of attire. "Whatever he used on us must have gotten into our clothes, too."

She turned to look down at him. "Would you like some help?"

"No!" Mikal squeaked. "I can do this myself."

"Please hurry, would you? I'm tired and I'd like to get something to eat."

Mikal dropped down so that only his neck was above the water. He quickly took off his clothes and began scrubbing them so violently that the waters around him were churning.

"Make sure you get everything or else you'll be stuck that size," Lissa reminded him. Pravara had scraped several large rocks into a ring and picked up some of the recently broken tree branches. She easily broke the thick wood into smaller pieces and dropped them into her makeshift firepit. Pravara looked down at the tiny woodpile and spat a miniscule blast of fire at it. Moments later the fire was merrily crackling away. Lissa gratefully took a seat near the fire and held her wet dress up in an attempt to dry it as quickly as possible.

Peanut had chosen a prime spot, close to the fire's warmth and with a view of her unusual pack of companions. A few minutes later, their canine companion was on her back, with all four paws sticking straight up, snoring contentedly away. Only when Mikal emerged from the river, in his proper size, did Peanut crack an eye open. A second or two later it closed and she was snoring again. Mikal hurried over to the fire and sat on the opposite side, away from Lissa.

"Is there a reason you're not sitting next to me?" she asked, as she wrung out her dress for the second time. A few more drops of water fell to the ground.

"You're not wearing much," Mikal pointed out. "I don't think it'd be proper."

"We're not children," Lissa scolded. "We can certainly act like the adults we are supposed to be."

"I know," Mikal told her. "That's what frightens me."

"I frighten you?"

"That's not what I mean."

"Then what *do* you mean?" Lissa wanted to know. When Mikal didn't respond she casually walked around the fire and sat down next to him. She held her dress back up and continued her attempts to dry it.

"I never know what to say around you," Mikal lamely explained. "If this had something to do with matters of the court, then I could tell you whatever you needed to hear. But when it comes to matters of the heart, I don't know what to say. I like you, Lissa. A lot. I'm just scared I'll say something to drive you away."

Lissa nodded thoughtfully at him. "I understand. Your whole life revolves around the castle. And it should. You're the prince. I'm sure your parents have seen to it that you'll know everything in order to take over the crown someday."

Mikal nodded glumly. Lissa took his hand.

"Look at me, Mikal. Come on, look at me. I like you, too. I'm not going anywhere. I think what we have here is special. I want to help you. That's why I'm here. Whatever we do, we do it together. Agreed?"

"Aye."

"Relax. I won't bite you."

Mikal gave a grateful sigh.

"Not yet anyway," Lissa added.

Mikal's eyes shot open with surprise. Lissa giggled. "I'm teasing you. Seriously, you need to relax more."

"What do we do now?" Pravara wanted to know. "I think it is safe to say the wizard knows we are aware of his identity."

Mikal nodded. "I'll say. We need to find him, Pravara, as quickly as we can. I think it's time I tell my father what we have learned."

"Why?" Lissa asked. She reversed her hold on her damp

dress to give the other side a chance to dry out. She shook her head. "I mean, I know we need to tell him, but why now? What has changed your mind?"

"The stakes have changed," Mikal solemnly answered. "My father, and yours, too, Pravara, need to be told what happened here today."

Intrigued, Pravara dropped her head down to his level. "Why is that?"

"Because," Mikal slowly explained, "now our wizard friend has actively tried to kill us."

Chapter 5 — A New Era

Holding Lissa's hand tightly in one hand and Peanut's leash in the other, Mikal exited the portal room and entered the Great Hall. It was quiet and relatively empty. Mikal shrugged. He wasn't surprised. It was now well past evening and his parents would probably be in their private quarters by now.

"Are you sure you don't want to go home?" Mikal asked, turning to look at his girlfriend. "Your father is bound to be worried about you."

"I should certainly let my father know I'm alright," Lissa agreed. She gave him a soft smile. "But no, I don't think I need to go home to do that."

"Why?"

"Because he's already here."

"Your father is in the castle? What for?"

"He informed me this morning that he had to meet with the king. He didn't give me any specifics. All he could tell me was that the constables from every village were required to attend."

"That doesn't sound good," Mikal murmured. He turned to the closest guard who hurried over and bowed.

"Your Highness. How may I be of service?"

"Do you know if my parents are in their private quarters?"

The guard nodded. "The queen retired there an hour ago, but the king is in the Antechamber."

Mikal thanked the guard and automatically headed toward his father's enchanted private chamber. He approached the large double doors and was surprised to see it unguarded.

"Where are the guards?" Mikal wondered aloud. "I don't think I've ever seen these doors unguarded before."

Two soldiers came hurrying around the corner. One had a roll stuffed in his mouth while the other was taking a drink from a flagon. Both noticeably reddened when they saw him. The guard with the roll in his mouth forcibly spat it out, and it went straight toward a curious corgi.

"*Off*, Peanut," Mikal softly told her. He gave the two guards a neutral look.

"I swear to you, Kre'Mikal," the first guard quickly said, "that I have never abandoned my post before."

"Yet you just did," Mikal answered, crossing his arms over his chest.

The second guard took two steps forward then dropped to one knee. "This is my fault, Your Highness. If you're going to punish someone, please be sure it's only me. I was thirsty. The roast pork I ate must have been cured with too much salt. We decided to go to the kitchen for only a moment."

"Are you going to throw us in the dungeons?" the first guard fearfully asked. "Please don't be angry with us for sneaking to the kitchen. All the guards do it."

The second guard hissed with annoyance. Mikal narrowed his eyes, studying the two men. Both of them were barely older than he was.

"Do you have any idea what would happen if I inform Commander Rhenyon that his soldiers are intentionally abandoning their posts and leaving my parents unprotected? I assure you it wouldn't go over well."

Both guards let their eyes drop to the ground. "We were gone no more than ten seconds," the second guard sullenly told him.

"Whether it was ten seconds or ten minutes, it's plenty of time for an assassin to sneak in undetected. We're talking about your king and queen. Do you see where I am going with this?"

"We understand, Your Highness," the second guard said. His eyes, Mikal decided, had a look of regret about them. He knew that these two guards were sincerely embarrassed.

"Here's what we're going to do," Mikal told them. "This sneaking off to grab a bite to eat or something to drink ends right here, right now. Spread the word. I will be purposely dropping by, unannounced, at all times of the day and night. If I do not see whoever is on duty standing at that door then I will report this indiscretion directly to the commander. Do I make myself clear?"

Both guards snapped stiffly to attention. "Of course, Your Highness."

"Good. Now, is my father in there?"

The second guard nodded. "Aye. Would you care to enter?"

"I would."

The second guard rapped on the door three times then pulled it open, allowing Lissa and Mikal, leading Peanut on a leash, to enter. His father was sitting at his usual place behind his desk while three other men hovered nearby. Mikal recognized Rhenyon, commander of all the king's armies and his father's most trusted adviser. Mikal studied the other two. One had a shock of white hair atop his head and was easily older than anyone he had ever seen before. The fourth man, his back turned, wore the uniform of a soldier but ranking higher than an average guard. He stopped in mid-thought as the fourth man turned around. Mikal's face broke out in a smile as he recognized the friendly soldier.

"Captain Pheron! Hi!"

The tall captain, his face grim, his eyes as hard as steel, gave a curt nod in Mikal's direction. Kri'Entu gave a small cough. "Son, we are right in the middle of something. Can this wait?"

"I have some news for you, father."

His father's tired eyes locked onto his. "Is it important?"

Mikal nodded. "Aye. You need to hear this."

"Very well. Please wait outside or by the second hearth?"

Mikal looked over at the much smaller hearth on the far side of the room. "Of course."

The king looked at Lissa and nodded once. Mikal glanced at his girlfriend and saw that her face had again turned bright red.

"He's just my father," he whispered to her as he guided her over to the opposite side of the enchanted chamber. "Do you have to keep doing that?"

"I can't help it," Lissa whispered to him. "He's the king! He brings it out of me. If you had told me last year that I would be meeting the king and dating his son, I would have laughed in your face."

"And now that you are?" Mikal quietly asked as he took a seat next to the unlit hearth.

Lissa pointed at her red cheeks. "I don't think this will be going away any time soon."

"You're the expert healer. Isn't there something you can take for that?"

"There's no salve, potion, lotion, or elixir I can think of that will cure shyness."

"You're not shy," Mikal was quick to point out.

"Around him I am," Lissa argued. "Maybe once we're married I won't be."

Mikal's mouth fell open with shock. It was his turn for his face to turn beet red. He tried valiantly to come up with a classy retort; only high pitched squeaks came out. Lissa smiled triumphantly.

"Nothing makes a blushing person feel better than making another person blush." Lissa leaned forward and placed a cool hand on the side of his face. "Wow. I'm surprised your face hasn't caught fire. Your skin is hot!"

"Do you enjoy doing that to me?" Mikal hissed at her.

Lissa smiled innocently back at him. "Doing what?"

"You know what. Embarrassing me."

"Well, it is fun," Lissa decided. She paused for a few moments, as if trying to make up her mind. "Yes. I do. You're cute when you're all flushed."

Desperate to change the subject, Mikal looked back at his father's desk. All four men were looking dour and were wildly gesturing at one another. Mikal frowned. He wished he knew what they were talking about.

"They look upset," Lissa whispered quietly in his ear. "Do you know what they're talking about?"

"No," Mikal answered. "They're talking too softly to hear anything."

I can hear them. In fact, I can hear them using your own ears. It's a pity you can't.

Pravara?

Were you expecting someone else?

I wasn't expecting anyone. Are you eavesdropping again?

A bad habit, I admit. However, I can answer your question. Their jhorun conversation is much more interesting than yours.

They're talking about jhorun?

Aye.

Lissa nudged him in the ribs. "What's going on? Why did you go quiet?"

"Pravara. She can hear what they're saying."

"Really? That's amazing! What is it about?"

"Jhorun."

"Jhorun? That doesn't make any sense. Why would they be whispering? There's nothing about jhorun that needs to be kept secret."

They evidently disagree. It would seem there's a problem with the jhorun.

Mikal quietly relayed this to Lissa.

Lissa held Mikal's hand tightly in her own. "What's going on, Pravara? Tell us everything you hear."

They're talking about the human settlement on the western coast. Capily. The problem with the jhorun has spread throughout the entire village.

"Do they say what the problem is?" Mikal quietly asked, electing to speak his thoughts so that Lissa could follow along. "What's got them so worried?"

Pravara was silent as she listened to the hushed

conversation happening on the other side of the room. Mikal felt her grunt with surprise.

Jhorun is failing.

Mikal gasped with alarm. Lissa's grip on his hand tightened.

"Capily is your village. Have you noticed any problem with your jhorun?"

"Now that you mention it, I do seem to go through it faster than normal."

"That would definitely indicate a problem," Mikal decided.

You'd best keep your voices down. They heard your outbursts. Now they are wondering if you might have overheard their comments.

Mikal turned away from his father's desk and put a finger to his lips. "I don't think it would go over well with the dragons if they learned one of their own was eavesdropping on my father."

Definitely not, Pravara agreed. She was silent for a few more minutes. **They are alarmed. Quite a few dragons have noticed their jhorun has been declining in strength since the beginning of the year.**

Mikal relayed the information to Lissa. "They don't know how to fix it," he continued, using the same monotone. "They suspect it has to do with … something. Pravara, what was that word? I didn't catch it."

Athanaus.

"Right. Pravara says the word is Athanaus. They won't say much about it, and that's because they don't know much about it."

Lissa's brow furrowed. "I've heard that word before. I just can't remember where."

I am querying the Collective.

Mikal sent the dragon a silent suggestion to keep it discreet.

Sensing a lull in the conversation, Mikal looked over at his father's desk. The meeting seemed to be paused. Mikal slowly stood. His father's tired blue eyes shifted to his.

"Yes, son? I'm sorry to keep you waiting. Please come

over here. Gentlemen, you are dismissed."

Rhenyon and the two men turned to leave.

"No, wait!" Mikal rushed over to the desk. "I think you all need to hear this."

Surprised, Rhenyon returned to the king's desk. The commander clasped his hands behind his back and waited. Mikal motioned for Lissa to join him.

"We have identified the rogue wizard."

The king blinked with surprise and straightened in his chair. Rhenyon's eyebrows shot up and gave Mikal an appraising grin.

"How in the world did you do that?" his father demanded. "*When* did you do this?"

"You asked me to investigate the mysterious fire caused by the dragons up at Lake Raehón."

Not caused by the dragons. That young wizard is responsible.

Yeah, yeah, I know. I'm getting there.

His father nodded. "Aye, I remember. You're telling me that fire identified the wizard?"

"The burn was, in essence, a mark. The wizard used those dragons to burn his signature onto the ground."

"That was the mark you recreated and showed me," his father recalled.

"Aye. Shardwyn wasn't entirely convinced it was a mark but I knew it was. Then we checked the census reports and we figured out who it was."

"So, who is it?" Rhenyon asked, impatient.

"His name is Gareth," Mikal slowly answered. "And he's only fifteen years old."

"This wizard's a child?" the king stammered, rising to his feet. "These attacks have been happening for years now. Never has there been a wizard so young. Are you sure, son?"

"I'm sure. We found his house and spoke with his mother." Mikal noticed Lissa was trying to surreptitiously inch behind him. A twinkle of amusement appeared in his eye as he sensed an opportunity for a little bit of payback. "Isn't that right, Lissa?"

Lissa gasped as the king shifted his attention to her.

She struggled for a few moments to regain her calm so she wouldn't stammer in front of the king.

"Y-yes. That's right. We spoke with his mother and his aunt."

"Remarkable. Excellent work. Both of you. Where is this Gareth now? Did you see him?"

"No, we didn't, but he knows we know who he is."

"How can you be so certain?" his father inquired.

Mikal gave his father a recap of their adventures while miniaturized. As expected, it didn't go over well.

"This wizard, this *boy*... he tried to kill you?"

"Aye. He would have succeeded if it weren't for Pravara. She figured out that whatever had shrunk us might have been a potion of some sort."

"That was quick thinking, Your Highness," Rhenyon told him, giving him a congratulatory slap on the back. "Nicely done. And you, Lady Lissa. The prince couldn't have found a finer companion."

If Lissa's face wasn't red before it certainly was now. Her eyes darted from one castle official to the other before becoming affixed to the king's desk.

"Thank you for helping my son," the king gently told her. "I am not certain how you ended up in Verdayn, young Lissa, when I know you were aiding Shardwyn earlier in the day, but I will say that I am not surprised. I am sorry you went through such an ordeal. This wizard..."

"Gareth," Mikal helpfully supplied.

"Gareth. He unwisely chose to attack you two and also Pravara. I wonder what the Dragon Lord thinks about the matter. I can only imagine he will be as angry as I."

That would be an understatement.

Mikal smiled. Kri'Entu, who had been studying his son's face, also smiled. "Allow me to venture a guess. Pravara just said something to you."

Mikal nodded. "She said that would be an understatement."

"So Kahvel knows." The king sat back down into his chair and tapped his fingers on his desk. He looked at Mikal. "Pravara, what did he say?"

He wants this wizard found and neutralized, at all costs.

Mikal began relaying what Pravara was telling him.

"I couldn't agree more," the king answered.

He is also aware of Lissa's involvement with this investigation, Pravara continued. **He knows she is assisting the prince. He has no qualms about her presence.**

Mikal hesitated after he heard himself say the words. "Pravara, why would you say that? Did you say something to your father about her?"

No. However, she was concerned. I am allaying those concerns.

Mikal looked at Lissa. "You were worried about whether or not you should be helping?"

Lissa nodded. "I'm only supposed to be helping Shardwyn with the fever outbreak in Donlari. Now that I'm done, I really should be going home."

"Your father is here," the king casually told her. "I see no reason why you shouldn't be allowed to stay, too. I will assign temporary quarters for you while you are here helping my son."

Mikal stared at his father with shock. "What's going on? Why are you being so nice?"

His father gave him a cryptic smile. "Whatever do you mean? I thought I was being accommodating. Is that not the proper thing to do?"

"You're up to something," Mikal accused. "I'd like to know…" A strong wave of alarm rippled through him. He gasped and felt the hairs on the back of his neck jump straight up. He gave Lissa a worried look.

"What's the matter?" she quietly asked him. "Are you okay?"

"Something just spooked Pravara."

"Like what?"

"I don't know."

The Athanaus. I know what it is.

Mikal's eyes widened. *You do? What is it?*

You won't like what I have to say.

Mikal swallowed nervously. *Noted. What is it?*

It is a creature from the times of ancient legends. According to my father it has been imprisoned for many

centuries deep within the great western sea.

The western sea? Are you talking about the Erudian Ocean?

Aye.

You're telling me the Athanaus is some type of ancient monster? What is it? Why has it been imprisoned?

I asked my father those same questions. Then I had to explain to him how I knew of its existence. Consequently, I have been instructed to cease my eavesdropping.

Yet you still do it.

Bad habits are hard to break.

Mikal saw, in his peripheral vision, Captain Pheron open his mouth to ask a question but his father held up a hand, signaling quiet. His father must suspect he was once again talking with Pravara.

What can you tell me about this Athanaus creature?

The Athanaus feeds on jhorun, regardless whether it's from human, wyverian, or any other being.

Do you know what it looks like?

My father says it can take other forms, but will frequently be seen as a cloud of mist. Sometimes it takes the shape of various creatures.

You said this thing had been imprisoned, right?

Aye.

Who imprisoned it?

Unknown. Its incarceration predates the wyverians. My father is attempting to find out as we speak.

Mikal reeled in shock. Older than the wyverians? A hundred years was no more than a blink of an eye to a dragon; they had been around for thousands of years.

Much older than either you or I could imagine. Remember, I can still sense your thoughts.

Yeah, yeah. What do we do now?

You must inform your father that his suspicions are correct. Jhorun is in danger. An ancient creature that feeds on it has escaped and must be dealt with, lest all life as we know it change for the worse.

But that would mean I'd have to admit that we were eavesdropping. He isn't going to like that.

He must know, Mikal.

Mikal sighed and looked up at his father, who was staring back at him, expectantly. "Your suspicion about jhorun was correct, Father. It is disappearing."

"You *were* eavesdropping on us." Scorn filled the king's face.

"You are right to be worried. A creature that had been imprisoned has escaped. It…"

Recently escaped, Pravara interrupted.

"Umm, hold on a second."

How recently?

It is believed the Athanaus escaped its prison late last year and has been feeding ever since.

Got it. Thanks.

"It *recently* escaped. It apparently feeds on jhorun. That's why some people are reporting that their jhorun isn't as strong as it used to be. This monster—"

Athanaus.

Whatever.

"This Athanaus will keep draining jhorun until there's nothing left."

"Then what will happen?" Captain Pheron whispered.

It will move on until it finds another source. Presumably neighboring kingdoms.

Mikal relayed Pravara's answer.

"And we're first," Kri'Entu softly muttered.

"The Athanaus," Lissa quietly moaned. "That's where I've heard it."

Mikal turned to his girlfriend. "You've actually heard of this thing?"

"A week ago, had you asked, I would have said that I hadn't," Lissa admitted. "Thanks to your father, I get to spend a lot more time in the Archives than I would have ever dreamt possible.

"Why would you want to spend more time than necessary in the Archives?" Mikal asked, frowning.

"Believe it or not, Son," his father dryly answered, "there are people genuinely interested in conducting research on a great number of topics. Our Archives are equal to none. It is an honor to be granted access."

"To which I am eternally grateful," Lissa agreed. The king flashed her a smile, setting the poor girl's face aflame. "While researching phytochemical properties in local pontal last week I came across a book of folktales. One of them was about the Athanaus."

"Do you remember what it said?" the king gently asked her.

Lissa's brow furrowed, trying to think. "I only remember it being something about a supernatural water horse."

"A water horse?" Mikal chortled, earning him an instant disapproving frown from both his father and his girlfriend.

The king reached for a piece of paper on his desk and slid a bottle of ink closer. He hastily wrote several sentences, folded the piece of paper, and handed it to a guard. "Deliver that to Miss Andra in the Archives. She will fetch a book or two and give it to you. Return here once she does."

The guard bowed. "Aye, sir."

I have called for my father. He will initiate contact soon. He needs to know the humans are just as concerned as he is.

Good idea.

"Pravara has asked to speak with her father about this. She said that he needs to know we are just as concerned as they are."

The king sat back in his chair, stunned. "So, it's true."

"What's true?" Commander Rhenyon asked. "The existence of the Athanaus?"

The king leveled a gaze at Rhenyon. "Obviously. However, I was referring to the wyverians. I had heard rumors that dragons used jhorun but I passed it off as fanciful gossip."

It's no rumor. It is true. We use jhorun just as much as the humans. In fact, many would say we use it more.

Mikal passed along the dragon's thoughts.

"If the dragons rely on jhorun as much as Pravara suggests," the king began, "does that mean the Dragon Lord is planning some action? Mikal, would you please ask Pravara?"

"I will when she says her father has made contact with her."

The doors opened. The guard who had been sent to the archives held out a thin leather-bound book. The king nodded his thanks, took the proffered book, and began flipping through the pages.

"I never thought I'd consider a volume of bedtime stories as a credible source of information."

"Desperate times call for desperate measures," Rhenyon jovially remarked.

The king grunted. Nearly halfway through the thin book he stopped, leaned forward for a better look, and then thoughtfully tapped the page.

"Your memory is excellent, young Lissa. I have found the passage about the Athanaus."

"What does it say, Your Majesty?" Pheron wanted to know.

The king cleared his throat and began to speak.

The Athanaus was a creature that lived many years ago. It was a thriper, the last of its species.

Pheron raised a hand.

"Pardon me, Your Majesty, but a *thriper*? What's that?"

"Perhaps if I could finish then I could tell you."

Pheron's face flushed beet red. "My apologies, Your Majesty. Please continue."

The thriper was a wonder to behold. It was strong, powerful, and magnificent. It often appeared as a simple equine but the true nature of the creature could always be determined by looking at its mane. A thriper would have water dripping from its mane, regardless of how wet or dry it was. The skin was smooth to the touch, but cold. Cold as death.

Pheron cleared his throat. "This Athanaus creature is a simple horse? That's all? That's easy enough. We could send out—"

"We will do no such thing," the king snapped. He gave the tall captain a dark look. "That's twice you've interrupted me, Captain. May I continue now?"

"A thousand apologies," Pheron murmured, as his gaze dropped to the floor, but not before noticing the disapproving frown on Rhenyon's face.

The thriper was known to take other forms. It is said they could dissolve their bodies into mist and reform them into something else. A favored form was said to be a jet-black pony.

Mikal watched his father look up from the book. His father's eyes found his own. "Apparently thripers can also take the form of a young woman."

A deafening silence invaded the Antechamber. Every person in the room turned to look at Lissa, who tentatively took a few steps back.

"Don't look at me," Lissa sputtered. "I'm a girl, not a horse."

Rhenyon pointed at the book in front of the king. "Does it say in there if all thripers were to be considered a threat? Or were we lucky enough to get the only thriper that is dangerous?"

The king returned to the book. He continued to skim through the pages. Eventually he reached the end and shook his head. "It does not mention whether or not all thripers were considered evil. This one, the Athanaus, was, I'm sorry to say. According to this story, the Athanaus nearly wiped out all jhorun the last time it escaped."

"How long ago was that?" Mikal asked.

"It doesn't say. What it does say, though, is that it was driven into the sea and imprisoned. It also says it cannot be killed, only captured."

"How?" Mikal demanded. "How was it driven into the sea?"

His father sadly shook his head. "It doesn't say, son."

"It must fear something," Mikal decided. "We have to figure out what, and soon."

Mikal, I have my father's response. I will relay to you much the same way as you are relaying what I say to your father.

"It's Pravara. She's ready with Kahvel's answer," Mikal announced to the room. "She's going to relay to me exactly what he's saying, so I'll do the same for everyone here."

A few moments of silence passed, presumably as Kahvel relayed his message to Pravara.

Greetings, Kri'Entu. I should have thought about communicating like this long ago instead of relying on messengers.

"I agree," the king automatically responded. He briefly looked around the room before returning his gaze to Mikal. "Can he hear me?"

I cannot directly hear you but your words do reach me, through your offspring and then through mine.

"Excellent. I am told you are aware of the existence of the Athanaus."

I am.

"You are aware of what it can do?"

Aye, only because we asked our seafaring brethren. They reluctantly confirmed its existence and the location where it had been incarcerated.

"The sea dragons," Kri'Entu breathed, amazed. "So little is known about wyverians living under the sea. Sightings are incredibly rare."

They prefer to keep it that way.

"I understand. I am told you depend upon jhorun as much as we do. Is that true?"

We use it, although I disagree with your notion that we rely on it as much as you humans.

"Are you prepared to live without its influence?"

No.

"Do you have any idea what we should do?"

At this time, no. I would like to discuss the matter in detail, but not like this. I request a face-to-face meeting.

The king stared at his son as if he had misheard Kahvel's last message. "You wish to meet? In person? Where? When?"

The cavern you created will suffice. Myself and three others will be there tomorrow at sunrise.

Everyone turned to stare at the king in wonder. A visit from a single dragon was enough to spark conversations for months to come. Never had four wyverians visited a human settlement. Any human settlement.

"We look forward to your visit. Kahvel, I can't thank you enough for looking into the matter and proposing this meeting. Is there anything else you can think of that I ought to be doing?"

Aye. You can send three humans to our valley.

For the second time everyone in the room stared at Mikal in shock. The king cleared his throat. "Er, what was that? Could you repeat that, please?"

You and I will deal with the reemergence of this thriper. Our offspring have a dilemma of their own to solve, do they not? They are searching for someone, are they not?

The king nodded. "Aye. What of it?"

Send me three humans. I have three dragons here that have requested riders.

The entire room, Mikal included, gasped with astonishment.

"You're allowing the riders to return?" the king whispered, shocked. He stared at his son as though he was staring at Kahvel himself. "To what do we owe this honor?"

I have observed Pryllan and Steve for quite some time. He cares for her and protects her as she protects and cares for him. Three other wyverians have expressed interest in experiencing the benefits of having a rider. It occurs to me that Pravara and her rider, Mikal, could cover more area if there were more riders actively searching. If we...

"Wait," Mikal interjected, interrupting himself, "I haven't ridden Pravara. You're making me her rider?"

Aye, young human. I have silently observed the interactions between you and my daughter. I trust you. Pravara yearns for a rider. Who, then, should I allow as her rider? That would be you. This would make you the second known rider.

"And Lissa?"

And she can be the third, provided she rides Pravara alongside you. My daughter has no objections to this and neither do I.

Lissa swallowed nervously as all eyes found hers.

"Hey, we're dragon riders now," Mikal whispered to her as a wide smile formed. "That's so awesome! Isn't that cool?"

How soon will you be able to send three humans to me?

"I'm ready to go right now," Captain Pheron instantly announced, smiling sheepishly at the king, "provided I am one of the people chosen to accept this great honor."

The king smiled and inclined his head at the tall captain. "I have known of your fondness for the wyverians for quite some time, Captain. You are one of the three. I will leave the selection of the other two up to you. Do you have any idea who you will select?"

Pheron nodded. "Aye. Lieutenant Darius and Lieutenant Andreas."

"Excellent choices" Kri'Entu said, nodding his head in agreement. "Brief your men and be in the portal room before sunrise tomorrow."

Pheron bowed. "Aye, Your Majesty."

Once the captain departed the room the old noble, who up until now had refrained from saying anything, gave a hearty chuckle. "What I would give to be fifty years younger. I would volunteer in a heartbeat."

The king turned to the octogenarian and smiled.

"I know what you mean, Mister Kern. If I wasn't the king, and you weren't one of my advisors, then I'm sure we'd both be likely to volunteer. I know, Commander. You can close your mouth. It wouldn't be proper."

Rhenyon, about to lodge a formal protest, quickly closed his mouth and kept the smile from forming on his face. Kri'Entu turned to his son.

"Kahvel, are you still there?"

Aye.

Mikal confirmed that he was.

"If you're coming here tomorrow at sunrise, and I'm sending people to Verdayn so they can be in your valley at the same time, who is their point of contact?"

Rhamalli.

"Is he one of the dragons that will be participating in this endeavor?"

Aye. The other two are Selendran and Malthryp. Have your people in the valley, any part of the valley, by sunrise tomorrow. My dragons will find them.

"Understood. Thank you, Kahvel."

You give thanks? For what?

"For giving us the chance to prove ourselves as effective riders once more. I know it has been a long time since there have been officially sanctioned dragon riders."

Eight hundred forty-seven years, to be precise.

"We won't let you down," the king vowed.

See that you don't. Until tomorrow.

Mikal waited a few moments more to see if Pravara relayed anything else. When she failed to say anything, Mikal blinked his eyes a few times and looked at his father. "That was weird."

"Weird? Son, that was remarkable!" His father walked around his desk and grabbed his son's shoulders to give him a friendly shake. "There will be dragon riders again and we've been openly invited by the Dragon Lord himself! On top of which he has volunteered to work with us to solve this dilemma with the Athanaus. And that reminds me…" His father's expression darkened. "I have told you many times that it's considered rude to eavesdrop on a private conversation."

"It wasn't me!" Mikal protested. "It was Pravara! She's the one who said that she heard you using my ears."

O-ho! Tattle on me, will you?

Ummm…

Fear not. I am in a good mood. I have been given a rider. You.

I've been 'given' to you? What's that supposed to mean?

It means that you will be at my beck and call. A rider is responsible for the health and well-being of the dragon. If something becomes lodged in a fang, or if a talon needs to be filed then it will be up to the human to take care of it.

You're kidding.

Of course, I am. I am dependent upon no one.

What?! Why did you just do that to me? I thought I was going to have a nervous breakdown.

That was for tattling on me to your father.

Very well. I guess I deserved that. I'm sorry, Pravara.

You are forgiven. Until tomorrow.

"Did Pravara just chastise you?" his father mildly inquired.

Mikal sighed. "Aye. She accused me of tattling."

"Well, she was right to do so," his father told him.

"Did you want me to lie?" Mikal asked, incredulously. "Because that's what it sounds like you want me to do."

"She is your friend. Respect her as you expect her to respect you."

Shamed, Mikal dropped his gaze to the floor. "I'm sorry. I will, I promise."

"Good. Do not worry about the Athanaus. It is for me to deal with, not you. Kahvel and I, that is. Your task now is to find and apprehend this young wizard before he causes any more trouble. Will you do that for me?"

"I will. We'll find him. That's a promise."

"We?" his father repeated, raising an eyebrow. "I assume you are including young Lissa here?"

A hot flush started at the base of Lissa's neck and slowly crept upward.

"Aye. Her, too."

"And your canine? What of her?"

"Perhaps I could get mother to look after her for me?"

Kri'Entu shook his head. "She's your responsibility, son. It should be you who is looking after her, not your mother."

"Then she'll come with us," Mikal decided.

"The two of you will be on the back of a dragon," his father reminded him. "Do you really think it safe for her up there?"

Lissa brightened. "I have an idea. We can make sure she'll be safe. It might take a little time to get it ready."

"Get *what* ready?" Mikal wanted to know.

Kri'Entu watched, bemused, as the receding flush on his son's girlfriend reversed course and resumed its trek up her neck, over her face, and across her forehead.

"I, er, should be able to have it ready sometime tomorrow."

"Then I leave it up to you. It is late. I suggest the two of you turn in. We all have a busy day tomorrow."

* * *

The following day found them up before sunrise. Mikal

and Lissa had just finished their chedras in the Great Hall when she finally presented Mikal with her idea to keep Peanut safe. She held a lumpy piece of fabric out to him. Mikal took the gift and gave her a skeptical look.

"Do you really think this is going to work? It's a sack. You want me to put Peanut into the bag? Seriously?"

"She'll be fine. Look, I've sewn belts into each side of the sack, here and here. You slide them over each shoulder. This small strap here is the sternum belt. It connects the two shoulder straps together so there's no chance the sack will slip off your shoulders."

Mikal slid his arms into the straps and adjusted them for a comfortable fit. Once he was sure of the fit, he buckled the sternum straps together.

"You've turned this cinch sack into a backpack, is that it? Why not just get a backpack instead of going to all this trouble?"

In response, Lissa spun Mikal around and loosened the cinch keeping the sack closed. She picked up Peanut and slid her into place on his back. Then she gently pulled the string to close the sack until only Peanut's head was sticking through. Both of the corgi's ears were sticking straight up as she watched what Lissa was doing.

"Because a backpack doesn't have an adjustable opening," Lissa explained. "That's why. How's that feel?"

Mikal took a few steps in each direction and nodded. "Not bad, actually. I can obviously tell she's back there but I don't … wizards be damned!"

Mikal had come to a sudden halt and had shuddered.

Lissa was at his side in less than a second. "What? What is it?"

Mikal reached behind his shoulder and gave the corgi a tickle on her head. "Peanut just licked the back of my neck. I now have goose bumps running up and down my arms."

Lissa giggled and scratched the friendly corgi behind her ears. "Good job, Peanut. You keep him in line, okay?"

An hour later, they were looking at the quiet valley once

more. Streaks of burnt ember had appeared in the sky as the time neared for the sun to put in its appearance for the day. Mikal reached behind his back and gave Peanut a pat on the head. Turning, he saw the three soldiers who had accompanied him and Lissa. No one was talking. A case of the nerves?

Mikal eyed the scorched earth a final time before he looked up at the clouds. He didn't see Pravara anywhere. Maybe he was early? If so, then it'd be a first for him. He yawned. Truth be told, it was the earliest he had woken in as long as he could remember. The only way they had been able to make it back to the scene of the fire by sunrise was to be in the portal room at least a full hour before the sun would make its appearance.

He smiled as he remembered the activity level of the castle. When Mikal had arrived in the kitchen to claim some breakfast, he was surprised to see that the kitchen was fully staffed and bustling with activity. Then again, it made sense. Even though the Dragon Lord wouldn't be coming into the castle—there's no way his head could've fit through the gate—a visiting dignitary stipulated the castle would be in tip top shape, both inside and out.

The orchard had been pruned and spruced during the night, using nothing but torchlight to see. The castle's moat was cleaned and topped off, much to the delight of Bredo, resident moat monster. The drawbridge had been washed and the cobbled streets leading into the castle were swept clean by twenty volunteers. Shardwyn, secluded inside his tower north of the castle, was instructed to seal his front door and not come out until the dragons had left. There was no point in letting the dragons see that much clutter centralized in one area.

Never had Mikal been so glad in his entire life to say that he had work to do. There was no doubt in his mind that, had he not been on an important assignment, his parents would have drafted him into service. He'd be overseeing the housekeeping team detailing the castle's interior, knowing full well the Dragon Lord would never see it.

Having tired of looking at the familiar black scorch mark,

Mikal turned around to head back toward Lissa and the three soldiers. He was startled to see that he was looking straight into huge golden reptilian eyes. Pravara, true to her wyverian heritage, had snuck up on him and was lying down in the soft grass with her long supple neck stretched out straight ahead of her. Her head was also resting on the ground and she was staring, unblinking, straight at him.

"Your species isn't very observant," Pravara casually remarked. "You took way too much time in turning around. I can only assume you didn't notice my arrival?"

Mikal pointed at himself. "Does this look like the face of someone who knew they were about to be ambushed? I'm surprised I didn't faint. Why do dragons do that?"

"Do what?"

"Sneak up on people like that."

"I can't speak for other dragons," Pravara idly answered, "but I find it highly amusing."

Pheron, who had been conversing with the other two soldiers, cautiously approached. "How do you move with such stealth?"

Pravara's neck lifted. Her head swung around until she was facing the tall human officer. "When I don't wish to be heard, then I'm not."

"I heard something similar when we first met your father," Pheron told the young dragon. "He was just as helpful on that question."

"I told you they wouldn't notice," a new voice rumbled.

Mikal's head snapped up. He looked to his right.

Another dragon was sitting, complacently, in the grass as though it had nothing better to do with its time. This dragon was a dark ruby red color, had purple flanged wings, and was considerably larger than Pravara. Pravara nodded at the newcomer. "Rhamalli."

Rhamalli nodded in return. "Pravara."

"I am pleased to see you here," Pravara told the much larger dragon. "I know you have been pushing to lift the ban on riders for quite some time. Was it difficult to find two others who thought the same?"

"Not at all, if you must know. There is a growing

fascination for your mother and her rider. Other dragons want to try adopting a rider to see if they can recreate the success she has had."

The red dragon's nostrils flared open and they heard him take a deep breath, as though he had caught scent of something that piqued his interest. Mikal had to fight the urge to whirl around to see what was behind him. He looked at Lissa, who was already checking their surroundings to see what might have caught Rhamalli's attention.

Mikal hesitated as a thought occurred to him. "Is he legitimately looking at something or is he trying to fool us?"

Mikal felt Peanut grow tense and give a few warning woofs.

"You might want to look," Lissa murmured.

Mikal took a breath and turned around. Two more dragons were silently regarding them. The closest, smaller than Rhamalli and Pravara, was a solid brown color with streaks of white on its thick, muscular neck, and was watching them with a bemused expression. It lowered its head and opened its mouth, revealing some of the longest fangs Mikal had ever seen, some as long as Mikal's own arms. How could it close its mouth?

Standing behind the brown dragon was a fourth dragon. This one was slender and closely resembled the two-headed zweigelan dragons in appearance, except with one head. It was a burnished yellow color with small green patches all over it. Mikal learned that Malthryp, or Malth as he preferred to be called, was highly intelligent and had been meticulously studying each of them. Selendran, the brown dragon, also demonstrated a high level of intelligence but elected to keep quiet most of the time.

Introductions were made, new friendships were created, and, Mikal realized with a start, a new era had been born. The dragon riders had come again and he was thrilled to be included in their ranks! He was sure his parents were having a field day, knowing that their only son was now allowed to ride a dragon. Not just any dragon, but the daughter of the Dragon Lord himself!

Mikal watched the three soldiers hesitantly eye their

wyverian counterparts. Instead of choosing which dragons each of them wanted to ride, they honored the dragons even further by allowing their new wyverian friends to select which humans they wanted as riders. Rhamalli chose Pheron, while Malth chose Darius, leaving Selendran with Andreas.

Mikal helped Lissa climb onto Pravara's back. As soon as she was settled, he glanced back at the three new riders and their dragons. Each dragon was giving pointers to their humans about what to do, what not to do, how to initiate mental contact, and so on. Ten minutes later, all four dragons lifted from the ground and began their search.

CONSIDER THIS A TRAINING EXCERCISE, a different voice said in Mikal's head. **IT WILL TAKE US SOME TIME TO GET TO KNOW YOU HUMANS, AS FOR YOU TO KNOW US.**

Who was that? Mikal mentally asked. *I thought we couldn't hear any other voices other than our own.*

That was Rhamalli, Pravara's voice told him. **You're hearing his voice only because the Collective is presently active. My apologies. I shouldn't have left the connection open. As soon as I...**

WHAT ARE WE LOOKING FOR, PRAVARA? Rhamalli's voice interrupted.

Mikal, a moment, please. Rhamalli, you're looking for a young human.

HOW YOUNG?

Fifteen years of age. He's a wizard. If he sees you he'll more than likely do something to you, so you must be discreet. Observation only. Find him, but do not confront.

DO NOT CONFRONT? A SINGLE HUMAN BOY IS NOT A THREAT.

This one is, Pravara insisted. **Exercise extreme caution. He has the power to possess bodies, shift minds from one body to the other, and physically shrink us. The list probably doesn't end there. I personally don't want to find out what else he can do. Trust me when I say that you don't, either.**

THIS IS THE HUMAN RESPONSIBLE FOR

CAUSING CATRIN AND JASMYRE TO CREATE THAT FIRE?

Aye.

VERY WELL. WE WILL OBSERVE ONLY. WE WILL BE IN TOUCH.

Rhamalli's powerful thought faded as Pravara closed out her mental connection to the wyverian Collective.

"I do believe it is time to begin our search."

Mikal was confused. "Hasn't that been what we've been doing so far?"

"No. We've only been looking. Now we need to *search*."

"I don't understand."

"You will momentarily."

"What's that supposed to—oh, wow!"

Lissa leaned forward, sandwiching Peanut between the two of them, and rested her head on Mikal's shoulder. "What is it? Is everything alright?"

Mikal nodded, too overcome to speak.

His entire body flooded with warmth, almost as if he had jumped into a natural hot spring. The howl of the passing winds disappeared. He could now hear everything, from the chirps of nearby kytes to grunts of the other dragons, although out of visual range.

They were out of your normal visual range before, Pravara clarified, **but not anymore. Behold. There's Rhamalli, with his rider. Hmm. It looks as though Rhamalli's rider isn't enjoying himself.**

Mikal, sharing Pravara's impressive visual abilities, noticed that Captain Pheron's face had paled and was threatening to turn green.

It looks as though he doesn't like flying.

I would say he's about ready to soil Rhamalli's scales.

Sure enough, as Rhamalli's large body was buffeted by strong air currents, Pheron whipped his gold accented, custom ordered, and very expensive barbute, off his head and thrust it under his mouth. Pravara and Mikal looked away just as Pheron's breakfast made another appearance.

Poor Pheron. He's always dreamt of riding a dragon and what does he end up doing? Getting sick on their first flight together. That must be embarrassing.

I trust if you ever think you will soil my scales, you'll let me know so that we can descend?

Mikal chuckled. *You got it. The last thing I would want to do is puke all over you, too. Thankfully my stomach feels fine.*

A third voice appeared. *I wish I could say the same thing.*

Lissa? Is that you? Pravara, did you bring Lissa into the loop?

Aye. I thought it would be rude if we continue to converse without her.

Are you sharing your senses with her like you did with me?

No. A dragon will typically share their senses with one person and one person only.

The rider, Mikal guessed.

Correct.

Lissa? What do you think about all this?

I'm still getting used to it. Remind me to look for some zingiber root once we land. It will help battle my nausea.

I have a question for you, Pravara.

Go ahead, Mikal.

Did you know your father would bring back the riders?

Aye. He has broached the subject many times with my mother. My father is still impressed by the results of the Hunt from several years ago.

What hunt?

The Hunt is an annual competition amongst the wyverians to see who can capture an oskorlisk fang first, or else who might be lucky enough to ensnare a silver fang, found only in the jaws of a red oskorlisk.

I've heard this story before. Isn't that what Steve and your mother brought back after the Hunt? They had managed to not only find a red oskorlisk but also collected a fang, didn't they?

Aye. Many talented dragons were defeated by my mother and her rider. Rhamalli was one of them. He later confided to my father that he had already been considering making a formal request to be allowed to take on a rider. The results of the Hunt were all the validation he needed, so he volunteered. Many other dragons expressed interest, too.

Which dragons? Lissa's gentle thought spoke. *Can you tell us?*

Of course. There was Canilian, Falgoth, Sorahono, and Kaleth, to name a few. All were eager to try it out. I just hope they're not treating this as a passing fascination.

Back to our task, Mikal thought to Pravara. *How do we know who we're looking for? We've never seen this boy.*

An image of a tousle-headed, acne infested boy suddenly flashed through his mind. Surprised, Mikal turned to Lissa and she nodded in response to his unasked question.

Before you ask, I pulled the image from the mind of the boy's mother.

Isn't that considered rude? Mikal demanded.

Perhaps. She was thinking about her son for the entire duration you were in her house. The image was so strong that I am surprised you didn't pick up on it.

Did you already share that image with the Collective? Lissa asked. *Is that why the other dragons haven't asked this?*

Aye.

Dragons are amazing, Lissa decided.

Thank you.

The next hour found Pravara answering questions from both Lissa and Mikal as they searched. Lissa wanted to know all about the Collective, and how a dragon could access memories from another being. Pravara explained that anything noted by one's senses could be shared with others of her kind, and that included scents. Once she knew what this boy smelled like, she'd share the information.

I see something.

Mikal sat up straighter. *What? What do you see?*

I have located the missing boy.

You have? That's wonderful news! I'm glad we found him so quickly!

Where is he? Lissa asked, peering over each of Pravara's flanks. She tried to snuggle against Mikal's back but ended up getting her chin licked by Peanut, who had just awoken from her nap. *I don't know why I'm trying to look down. The ground is much too far away to see anything.*

Not for a dragon, Mikal contradicted. *I'm looking through her eyes right now. She has zoomed in on the ground and ... There he is, Pravara! Do you see him? He just ducked behind that large boulder. I think he knows we're watching him!*

The scene shifted from a group of large boulders and started skimming the surrounding landscape for a place to land. Their shared eyesight landed on a tiny glade that looked way too small to accommodate a full-sized dragon.

You can't fit in there, Mikal told her. *You're way too big.*

While not perfect, it will do, Pravara argued. **We must land as soon as possible before the boy disappears.**

Just be careful. I don't want you hurting yourself trying to land. There'd be no room for escape if something happened to us down there. I don't care how good you are. There's gonna be no taking off once you're on the ground. There just isn't enough room.

I understand. Cease your fretting. I will be fine.

'Cease my fretting'? I know you didn't just say that to me.

Be silent. Hold on. This will admittedly NOT be my best landing.

Pravara tucked her wings and rocketed through the tiny opening in the forest canopy. The tiny glade had space to snap her wings out to half of their potential, only marginally slowing her descent. She extended her talons and slammed into the forest floor so hard it snapped several trees off at the base. One evergreen crashed toward them, as the tree didn't have anywhere else to fall.

The dark green dragon caught the tree and easily snapped it in half, placing the broken tree on the ground next to them. Pravara bent her neck around to see for herself that her two human riders were uninjured.

We're good, Mikal told her. He cleared his throat a few times and switched to his normal speaking voice. "Well, that was unpleasant."

"That was scary," Lissa agreed. "I don't like dropping from the sky like that."

"It was necessary," Pravara reminded them. "Now, let us see where this boy has gone." The dragon fell silent and slowly scanned the surrounding trees. Mikal frowned as their dragon companion completed a three hundred sixty degree sweep of the area.

Mikal sighed. "Let me guess. You don't see him anywhere."

"I don't," Pravara agreed. "Could he have disguised himself?"

"Entirely possible. Gareth! Are you listening? We know who you are and we know you're out there. Tell us where you are so we can talk to you."

A cicada began buzzing loudly from a nearby tree. Then they heard a kyte start chirping. Then another. The rest of their flock joined in. The sounds and activity of the forest gradually returned to normal.

"Gareth, we just want to talk to you!" Lissa announced, raising her voice as much as possible without coming across as shouting. "Will you come out and talk to us?"

"I still see no other humans present," Pravara announced, causing both Mikal and Lissa to frown. "Is it possible that he…?"

The dragon trailed off as she detected movement where she had originally spotted the boy, behind a massive boulder. It began scraping across the ground, pushed by an unknown force. A second boulder, nearly as large as the first, also began moving toward them. Within moments a veritable slow-moving landside of boulders was closing in on them.

"I do not trust this," Pravara informed them. "You had best return to my back."

Mikal and Lissa hastily climbed into place on the dragon's back, watching, awestruck, as one of the larger boulders rolled up onto its neighbor. Another boulder did the same. More boulders began piling onto the stack of other rocks until a crude shape began to form. Mikal swallowed nervously. The crude outline was in the shape of a man. The huge rock creature took a thundering step forward.

"An earth elemental," Lissa whispered. She was both awed and cowed at the same time.

Mikal nervously eyed his friends. "I don't see Gareth anywhere. I think that little jerk just walked us into a trap."

Chapter 6 — Earth, Wind, & Fire

"Stay down!" the dragon instructed, charging forward, pushing through groves of trees so thick that she ended up snapping most of them off at the trunk. Pravara cast a worried glance behind her. The earth elemental was lumbering after her, crushing everything in its path as it built up speed. Five minutes ago, she had been easily able to stay in front of the rock monster, but as time progressed, she was shocked to see that something as large and unwieldy as the elemental was becoming more agile and nimble by the second.

"We're fine back here, Pravara!" Mikal shouted at her after he saw that she had just glanced back for the third time in as many minutes to see that they were safe. After their wyverian glanced back at them for the fourth time Mikal turned to point at the gaining rock creature. "We won't be if that thing catches up to us. Now move! Get us out of here!"

Pravara doubled her efforts. They were now crashing through the trees so fast that Mikal was afraid to even poke his head up to look around. Chunks of wood and debris whipped by them at an alarming rate. The last thing any of them needed was to have a piece of wood thicker than their arms become lodged anywhere it didn't belong.

Pravara lurched to the left and dove through a small opening in a wall of nearly a dozen trees. For a brief moment Mikal thought all had been lost as it felt like Pravara had become wedged in between the trees. He hurriedly glanced behind them and saw that the rock monster was almost upon them.

Pravara twisted to the left and then to the right, almost dislodging her two riders in the process. Mikal gripped the scale he was sitting on as tightly as he could, instructing Lissa to hold on as best as she could. They both heard Pravara roar with frustration. She was stuck! Of all the infernal luck!

The dragon's head whipped around and bit the tree, felling it with a single bite. She spat out a mouthful of wood and repeated the process for the tree on the right. Once she was free she grabbed the second fallen tree, jamming one end deep into the soft earth, levering it in place.

She didn't have long to wait for the rock creature to arrive.

The earth elemental rushed forward. Just before it could make contact, Pravara lifted the other end of the tree and made sure it was lined up with the elemental's head. The impact was so great that the tree practically exploded, becoming hundreds of thousands of tiny little wooden missiles. Pravara felt the splinters slam into her heavily armored body, but they had no more effect on her than a gentle buffeting wind.

The elemental's head was knocked off its body. The head, easily as large as both Lissa and Mikal combined, landed on the ground and rolled a few feet before coming to a stop near one of the stumps. The elemental ceased its relentless push forward and thrust its arms out in a blind attempt to locate its missing head.

Pravara growled with irritation. From the way the monster was stumbling away from them it would most certainly find what it was looking for. In fact, if it … She growled again. It just bumped into the stump where the head had come to a stop. The creature lifted its head high into the air and set it back onto its stone neck. After a few moments they all watched the stone head pivot in place until it was apparently facing in the right direction.

"That thing doesn't even have eyes," Mikal complained. "Look at it! How does it even know when it's facing forward?"

"Would you like me to ask?" Pravara dryly asked them.

Mikal shook his head. "Absolutely not. Get going! It's heading toward us again!"

Pravara continued her streak through the woods, glancing skyward, wistfully dreaming she could punch her way through the dense forest canopy and return to the open air.

"Hang in there, Pravara," Mikal tried to reassure her.

"We are close," Pravara confirmed. "Rhamalli and the other riders are outside the forest, waiting for us to reach the valley. Once we do, they will attack our sedimentary friend."

"That thing is almost as big as you are," Mikal reminded her. "It's made of solid stone. Do you think you and the others will be able to defeat it?"

Pravara snaked around a massive tree that even she wouldn't have been able to bite through. "Of course."

"And if you can't?" Mikal pressed. "What then?"

"The call will be issued for more dragons," Pravara told them. For the first time, Mikal thought she sounded like she was out of breath and tiring.

"Hang on," Pravara told them. "I will have to leap in order to gain enough velocity to punch through that line of trees. Are you ready?"

Mikal and Lissa clung tightly to each other. Peanut, sensing an exposed neck, twisted around in the sack and began licking Lissa's throat. "Peanut! Stop! Don't do that! It tickles!"

Pravara bunched her muscles, waited half a moment, blasted forward. Four trees instantly came uprooted while two others snapped in half like mere twigs. Bright sunshine blinded them. The valley lay open before them!

Rhamalli was standing before them and roared a challenge to the creature. Selendran moved to Rhamalli's right flank and issued his own challenge. Malth, being much smaller than the others, backed away from the fallen trees, ready to attack.

They heard the massive footfalls. They felt the earth tremble. Something was coming toward them and whatever that something was, it was big. The elemental appeared and didn't hesitate for a second, snapping trees as it moved onto the open grassland and once more advanced on Pravara. As for the other three dragons in the area, it ignored them.

Selendran fired first, belching a steady stream of fire at the elemental. The rocks and stones comprising the torso glowed red as its abdomen took the full brunt of the dragon's blast. Selendran paused and gulped air, to stoke his internal furnace to the maximum.

Rhamalli was next. He dug in his talons and snapped his wings together. A loud thunderclap echoed across the valley floor, and the blast of wind flattened over two dozen trees. The elemental was unaffected. It ignored Rhamalli and continued its advance on Pravara.

Malth waited for the elemental to clear the forest before he made his move. He slinked out from his hiding place to begin his attack while his rider, Darius, suggested possible targets, Malth darted between the elemental's boulder-legs and targeted the junction where they met. His blast of fire could have melted armor. The rock creature didn't flinch.

When it became apparent that Malth's attack had been just as ineffective as his companions, the long, sinewy dragon retreated to the safety of Rhamalli's side.

Pheron eyed the lieutenant from his place on Rhamalli's back. "Really? You thought you could hit it where it hurts the most?"

Darius shrugged. "Hey, you never know until you try. At least now we know."

"It's made of solid rock," Pheron pointed out. "I doubt very much that it has genitals, Lieutenant."

"We need to slow that thing down!" Mikal called out in a loud voice. "It was created by Gareth, the wizard we've been searching for. I'll bet he's nearby."

"Earth elementals don't need their creators to be nearby in order to function," Pheron argued. "That boy could be anywhere by now."

"I strongly doubt it," Mikal disagreed. "He's watching. He's angry at Lissa and me for figuring out who he is. Now he wants payback."

Lissa tapped him on the shoulder. "Did you see that?"

Mikal twisted in place to look at her. "Did I see what?"

"There's something metallic on the surface of the elemental's left foot. I just saw it."

"Pravara, take a look and tell us what you see."

"Malth," Pravara called. "You are in a position to see the creature's left leg. Do you see any marks on the backside of where its foot should be?"

They didn't hear a response but the thin yellow and green dragon circled behind the elemental and crouched low to the ground, slithering forward.

"Aye. There is a metallic rune set upon the boulder's surface. Is that significant?"

Mikal turned to look at his girlfriend after she gave a triumphant shout. "It's a sigil," Lissa explained to the three riders. "A mark of enchantment. It means it isn't a true elemental."

"Gareth," Mikal exclaimed. He was surprised, impressed, annoyed, and somewhat jealous of the fact that the boy wizard created a twenty-five-foot golem in the time it takes most people to put on their shoes.

He patted Pravara's side and slid down her heavily scaled abdomen. He waited a few moments for Lissa to join him.

"What are you doing?" She fearfully looked around the valley. The elemental, finally forced to deal with the other three dragons, was now actively engaging them by throwing whatever it could grab at them, including bits of itself.

Mikal pointed at two twisty, ethereal looking trees.

"Do you see those? They are pydagos trees."

Lissa shaded her eyes and studied the two misshapen trees. "I've seen them before. They don't have any medicinal uses that I'm familiar with. What about them?"

"They're one of the few trees that will actively try and protect itself if it senses danger. Swing at it with an ax, it will try to swat it away. It's more geared toward slapping away unwanted insects."

"Again, how does this help us?"

Mikal hurried over to the trunk of the closest pydagos tree. "Watch this."

He placed his hands on either side of the tree's trunk and concentrated. After a few moments he released the trunk and moved to the second tree to repeat the procedure. Ten seconds later Mikal sprinted back to Lissa's side. The two trees were now whipping their branches wildly through the air.

"I've enhanced them," Mikal told her. "I think I've persuaded them to attack any humungous rock creatures."

One of the trees lowered a branch to the ground and wrapped it around a stone the size of Mikal's head. It hurled the stone as if it had been launched from a sling. The stone whistled through the air and collided with the elemental's head.

The rock monster's head slid forward, threatening to fall from its neck. A quick poke by one of its bulky arms pushed the head back into place. It slowly turned around to address the newest threat.

Lissa's eyes grew wide. "Now what do we do? I think they only made it mad!"

Mikal leapt up and caught Pravara's attention. *Now's your chance! The thing has its back to you. Hit that sigil! Destroy it and you should destroy the creature!*

We melt that metal symbol and it'll destroy the creature?

Aye! Hurry!

Pravara relayed the instructions to the other three dragons. Rhamalli fired first, a barrage of fireballs, watching with satisfaction as most of them slammed into the elemental's left leg. Cracks appeared, but the huge boulder remained intact. Unfortunately, so did the sigil.

Selendran was waiting. As soon as the smoke cleared, the brown dragon threw his head back, took three massive gulps of air, and blasted forth an immense jet of fire, more than enough to melt the sigil.

The problem was, Selendran missed when the elemental stepped to the left to take a swing at the second tree.

The first pydagos tree, with most of its branches snapped off by the creature, was directly in the line of the incoming blast. In less than five seconds there was nothing left but ash.

All three dragons eyed the torched tree and then each other.

"I feel as though I should point out the tree's destruction wasn't my fault. It moved."

Malth was next. Slinking through the grass, he aimed a shot of fire. Unfortunately, with his smaller size, it wasn't enough to melt the wizard's sigil.

A blast of fire shot past Selendran and Rhamalli and slammed into the metal symbol. Less than a second later, another blast hit it. Then another. And another. All eyes turned to see Pravara, who had jumped into the air and was circling, watching the elemental, and firing off shot after shot. Not one of her blasts missed the target. Each time it moved, she lined up another shot.

Three more of Pravara's pinpoint blasts finally melted the mark. Tiny rivulets of molten metal dripped down the large boulder's smooth surface and fell onto the grass below, producing a tiny hiss every time a drop made contact with the ground. The creature took a final step and simply collapsed, as if a giant hammer had smashed the golem over the head. Thousands of pounds of solid stone thundered to the ground.

Rhamalli's head jerked up. His neck swung around until he was facing south and staring straight into the heart of the forest. He gave a loud growl. "Target acquired. I see the human boy."

Mikal pulled Lissa to her feet and looked up at Pravara just as she was touching back down.

"You see Gareth?" Mikal asked. "Where?"

"He's using jhorun to conceal himself," Rhamalli told him. "He is less than a hundred feet inside the forest staring straight at us. He appears to be angry."

"Well, we did just destroy his monster," Lissa stated matter-of-factly.

Selendran and Malth bared their fangs the moment they spotted the teen wizard crouching behind the trunk of an evergreen.

Pravara growled with frustration and turned beseechingly to Rhamalli. "I do not see him. Why is it I cannot see what you and the others clearly can?"

"Experienced wyverian eyes can penetrate practically any deception," Rhamalli answered. "I am much older than you, young Pravara. I have learned how to attune my eyes to that which cannot be seen."

"He's moving," Malth announced. "I do believe he knows he has been seen."

"Where's he heading?" Mikal asked. "Can anyone tell?"

"Southwest. Aye, he knows he has been seen. His gait has changed from a fast walk to a frenzied sprint."

Lissa stretched her back. "It sounds like he ... Mikal, what are you doing?"

Mikal had slid the pack off his back and held it out to Lissa. Peanut's ears perked up. Thinking she was about to be released from her confining prison, the corgi looked back at Mikal and uttered a short, low howl. Mikal was now sprinting toward the woods.

"Pravara! Stay with me. We cannot let him get away. Not again!"

Lissa held the pack out to Pravara and sprinted after Mikal.

Which way? Mikal thought to Pravara as he hurdled a small log.

Has Lissa caught up to you yet?

Aye. She's just behind me. Which way?

Angle more to your right. Do you see a break in the trees? Or the mound of rocks that is taller than you?

Mikal spotted the rocks farther to the right than he expected.

Those? Yeah, I see them. So, what happened? How is it you can see him now? Five seconds ago you couldn't.

He has let the jhorun drop. That's how I can see him.
Oh.

Run to those rocks. Hurry! The boy passed by those same rocks less than ten seconds ago. Maintain your pace and you should be able to catch up to him.

Where are the other dragons? Why aren't they helping?

Something strange is happening in the sky. Rhamalli has reported that the winds have increased tenfold. They

are no longer able to maintain their position.

Because the wind has grown stronger? I didn't think there was anything that could threaten a dragon in the sky.

It's not the fact that the wind is blowing, but *what* the wind is blowing. We dragons are strong, but if our wings are struck by a high-velocity object, thrown by this gale, then the damage could be fatal. My Lord has ordered Rhamalli, Senedran, and Malthryp to withdraw to a safe distance.

What about you?

What about me?

Do you have to leave?

No. I'm already on the ground. There is no danger to me. At least, not yet.

Couldn't the other dragons land nearby and help us?

They could if they would have thought of that sooner. By the time it was suggested, they had been pushed out of the vicinity. I believe, by the time they would reach us, this skirmish will be over.

Got it.

Back in the valley, Pravara felt the bag in her claw move and glanced down at it. Peanut was struggling to extricate herself and was slowly succeeding in wiggling her way out. As soon as she was free, she barked once, rushed to the edge of Pravara's open palm, and then peered anxiously up at her.

"Do you need to be set down?" Pravara asked the tiny creature. "If I let you down, you must remain by my side. I do not know when Mikal will be back."

Pravara lowered her claw until it was resting on the grass covered floor. Peanut jumped down from the dragon's claw and turned to look back at the dragon with a questioning look.

"We are waiting here," Pravara told the dog. She held up a single talon and peered intently at the small canine. "*Stay.*"

Peanut barked once and took off like a shot, disappearing into the woods in hot pursuit of her human.

Pravara looked at the claw she was holding up and growled. She had witnessed Mikal using the same exact gesture to Peanut when he had wanted the playful creature to remain in one spot. She had mimicked what she had seen and had given the dog the command Peanut clearly knew. Why hadn't the dog obeyed? Had she missed a step?

Your canine is now following you.

What? Pravara, you were supposed to hold on to her.

She wanted down.

Of course, she wanted down. She wanted to follow us. It's not safe for her in here!

I told her to stay. I did everything I have seen you do. It didn't work.

Clearly. Which way now?

What are you looking at?

There's a single tree rising higher than all the others. Directly to the left, er, my left, there's a small stream running north and south. I think it might be the same stream we were at before.

He appears to be headed back to his dwelling. He is constantly glancing over his shoulder to see if he is being followed. At the moment I would say he believes he has evaded capture.

Go left.

What?

You're about to be given a choice in which direction to run. Go left.

The trail Mikal and Lissa had been following terminated abruptly at a dense wall of thick green shrubs that were taller than he was. A quick check in either direction revealed that there was now a choice in which direction to go. He instantly turned left.

"Are you sure?" Lissa wheezed out. The poor girl was completely out of breath. The hair tie that she had been using had become lost and now her neatly braided brown tresses were swiftly unraveling. Every few seconds Lissa tucked strands of her hair back behind her ears in a futile attempt to keep her thick hair out of her face.

Mikal tapped the side of his head. "Pravara said 'left', so left it is."

What did you mean? Mikal asked the dragon. *Are they having problems with the riders already?*

Other than them constantly falling off in midflight, no.

Ah. It's just going to take some practice.

I agree.

If Gareth is heading home, is there any way for you to head him off?

There isn't enough room outside the dwelling for a confrontation, but based on the route he is taking to return home, there might be a chance of confronting him by the ravine. I believe I can beat him there, but only if I proceed in a straight line.

Will that be a problem?

There will be no time for stealth. He will definitely hear me coming.

If you think you can stop him from reaching his home then please do it.

I sense that you're tiring.

Aye. I hate running.

Has the little canine caught up yet?

No, but I can hear her.

That may pose a problem.

What? Why?

If you can hear her then perhaps the wizard can hear her, too?

And if he can? Are you saying he might try to do something to her?

He better not. I am fond of that little creature. Mikal. Seek shelter. Now!

What is it? Mikal's alarmed thought asked. *What's the matter?*

The trees. The trees are moving! They're swaying! I believe he is manipulating the air currents to try and slow us down. Seek cover!

Mikal ducked down near several scraggly bushes as the wind began picking up. He grasped the base of a bush with his left hand and stretched his right out behind him. As soon as he was holding Lissa's hand tightly in his own, he pulled her up to him and together they crouched low to the ground.

Several barks pierced the air. A few seconds later Peanut wiggled her way in between Mikal and Lissa's embrace. She gave each of them a welcoming lick across their cheeks and, comfortably sandwiched between her two humans, closed her eyes for a nap.

"Dogs," Mikal muttered. He looked into Lissa's frightened eyes. "Hold on! Pravara says the wind is going to get nastier than this!"

"Where's this coming from?" Lissa asked, raising her voice to a shout in order to be heard. "Is this from Gareth?"

Mikal nodded. "It has to be. He already used something similar to drive off the other dragons." He looked at the shrub he was holding and raised an eyebrow. He sent his jhorun down into the shrub to see about enhancing its very nature. Within moments the shrub's scrawny core had tripled in size. It rapidly thickened and spread out. As soon as the shrub had grown to shield size, he pulled his jhorun back. The shrub, now having quadrupled in size, easily blocked the vast majority of the howling wind.

Excellent thinking. Gareth is becoming increasingly frustrated. He is nearby, watching you. He can see you haven't been driven off and is highly agitated. The wind is decreasing. The boy appears exhausted. Could he be out of jhorun?

I don't think we'd be that lucky. What's he doing now?

He's fleeing again. He's near the ravine I mentioned earlier. I am almost there.

Right on cue, Mikal and Lissa heard a commotion in the distance. Something large was moving through the trees. Limbs were broken, trunks were snapped in two, and quite a few trees toppled to the ground, felled by the dragon's bite.

If he couldn't hear Peanut, he can certainly hear you. Be careful. He might be exhausted but he can clearly defend himself.

Understood.

Mikal rose to his feet, prompting Lissa to do the same.

"Gareth has fled," he told her. "He's definitely headed home. That's Pravara. She is going to try and slow him down."

"You tell her to be careful," Lissa exclaimed, rounding on him. "I don't want her to get hurt."

"I already did."

Noticing that the ratty black nylon leash was still trailing off behind Peanut, Mikal slid his hand through the loop end of the leash and resumed their pursuit. The three of them only made it a dozen steps before they heard an ear-splitting roar. The two teenagers nervously eyed each other.

Pravara? Tell me that was you.

That was me.

Are you okay?

I am.

And Gareth?

He is trying to invoke some type of enchantment but I do not think he has enough jhorun to properly invoke it. I decided to break his concentration.

We're almost there.

I would advise you to hurry.

Peanut took off, heading in the general direction he had been running. Deciding the corgi's nose must be guiding her to Pravara, Mikal let the dog lead. Checking to see that Lissa was following, he broke through a line of trees and would have fallen straight down into a thirty-foot-deep ravine that stretched at least that many feet across. Lissa appeared almost instantly behind him and threw her arms around him to prevent him from tumbling down.

Mikal glanced irritably at Peanut, who had wisely veered to the left to walk along the ravine's edge. She had reached the end of her leash and was looking back at him as if wondering why he wasn't following.

"You could have barked, yipped, come to a stop, anything. Some watchdog you are."

They detected movement on their left. As one, both humans and the one dog turned to look at Pravara. She was crouched, wings partially extended, fangs bared, as she stared at a spot on the ground before her. Mikal slowly approached and held up an arm to indicate Lissa and Peanut needed to stay back.

Mikal stepped around a large stump and caught his first glimpse of the wizard that had been making his father's life a living hell for years. The boy was shorter than he was, skinnier, had dark, nearly black hair. His sides were heaving. Blood dripped from a cut above his elbow, directly on the bicep. He was murmuring something under his breath, a chant perhaps.

Mikal took a step forward. Gareth's head whipped around

and he stared, wild-eyed, directly at him. Mikal raised both palms to adopt a non-threatening stance.

"You must be Gareth. I've been looking for you."

The teen's wild eyes jumped to the dragon and then back to him.

"I'm not going to hurt you. No one here is."

"Oh, yeah?" Gareth sneered. "Tell your dragon to stand down or else!"

"Or else what?" Mikal asked, trying valiantly not to lose his temper with the ill-tempered brat.

"You know who I am. You've seen what I can do. I'm warning you. Make him go away or I'll make you sorry."

"First of all, that's a girl dragon. *Her* name is Pravara. Pravara, say hello to Gareth."

When Mikal didn't hear anything, he glanced over his shoulder at the dragon. Pravara hadn't budged an inch, nor had she stopped baring her fangs at the boy.

Gareth's lips began moving again as he resumed his chanting. Mikal snapped his fingers a few times. "Look, enough is enough. Why don't you let Lissa look at your arm? That looks like a nasty cut."

"I can fix it myself," Gareth haughtily snapped, although his bright blue eyes did briefly flicker over to Lissa's before shyly turning away.

Mikal turned back to Lissa and nodded in Gareth's direction.

"That is a nasty laceration," Lissa began as she stared at Gareth's bloody arm. "I know all about herbs and healing. If you don't let me treat that cut then it could become infected. It won't take long. Would you let me help you?"

Gareth wouldn't meet her eyes, but at least he didn't back away from her.

What's wrong with him?

Mikal glanced over at Pravara. *I'd say he's shy. Painfully shy. Especially around girls.*

Like you are?

Excuse me? I am not.

"We're not here to hurt you, Gareth."

"You're lying," Gareth spat back. "You just want my

treasure, like everyone else."

"No, I don't," Lissa argued, shaking her head. "I didn't even know you had a treasure."

Gareth's gaze dropped to the ground. "Oh."

"You have a treasure?" Mikal asked, a bit too eagerly.

Lissa stomped on his foot as she passed by him, handing him Peanut's leash in the process.

"Which he doesn't care about," Lissa quipped, giving Mikal a look that any male in a committed relationship was familiar with.

What treasure?

Mikal looked over at Pravara as she slowly folded her wings. She relaxed her posture and allowed her fangs to disappear from sight.

If I can't ask about the treasure then neither can you.

Spoilsport.

That's something Steve would say.

Where do you think I originally heard it?

"Here, let's be civil about this. My name is Lissa." She turned to point at Mikal. "I'm sure you know who he is, but if you don't, let me introduce Kre'Mikal, son of the king and queen. Over there is Pravara, daughter of Kahvel, the Dragon Lord. And sitting at Mikal's feet is Peanut."

For the first time they saw a fleeting smile appear on Gareth's face, and that was only when he looked at Peanut. The corgi had noticed the newcomer and was anxious for a proper introduction. She gave an exasperated bark and looked up at Mikal, expecting him to release her.

"Peanut is looking forward to meeting you in the proper corgi fashion," Mikal explained, dropping to one knee and draping an arm around the dog. "I'd let her, too, but we need to take care of you first. That arm looks pretty bad. Will you let Lissa look at it? She's an excellent healer. In fact, you may be interested to know Shardwyn had to consult her yesterday when he couldn't solve some fever outbreak in Donlari, I think."

Gareth's eyes dropped.

Lissa timidly approached the boy and held out her hand. "It's nice to meet you, Gareth."

Gareth warily shook her hand. Lissa gently rotated the arm; the cut was about two inches long, with a lot of coagulated blood. It would undoubtedly become infected if not treated soon. She gently released Gareth's hand and looked around the area.

"What are you looking for?" Mikal asked.

"I need some type of disinfectant. And water to wash the wound."

"I have a water bag inside Peanut's sack. It's not much but I thought we should have it in case Peanut gets thirsty."

"Perfect. Get the water and I'm going to see about finding something to cleanse the wound."

After Lissa wandered off Mikal eyed Gareth. "I can only imagine you had a reason why you've done all the things you've done. Creating that nasty curse, bewitching dragons, and even starting fires. You've covered it all, haven't you?"

Gareth hung his head and refused to meet his eyes.

Mikal sighed. This wasn't going how he had envisioned. Maybe if he got him talking?

"You mentioned you had a treasure? Trust me when I say no one at the castle cares. We're more concerned about your exploits. I will say that on many an occasion you've left Shardwyn scratching his head in frustration. Although, if you want to know the truth, it doesn't take much to confuse him anymore."

Gareth briefly smiled again. He wandered over to an overturned log and sat down.

"So, you're Mikal. I always wondered when someone would come looking for me. I never imagined it would be you."

"You wondered if someone would come looking? You've caused quite a few headaches over the years. Of course, we'd come looking. I volunteered to find you. Lissa and I figured out who you are."

The boy yawned and gazed at him with a neutral expression. "Why would you volunteer to find me? Weren't you afraid of me? I worked so hard to make everyone think I was the most dastardly wizard this kingdom has ever seen."

"You certainly didn't make any friends," Mikal admitted

with a laugh. "My foster father certainly isn't any fan of yours."

Gareth blinked a few times. "Your foster father?"

"Aye. Steve. You may know him as the fire thrower. He's the one who figured you out."

"The fire thrower. Of course. I had forgotten you lived off world for a number of years. Wait. Figured me out? What does that mean?"

Pravara settled onto the ground but kept her head lifted high. She was staring straight at the wizard with unblinking eyes.

"Do you remember when you switched their minds and their bodies? While Steve was in Pryllan's body he told me he had a conversation with you. You encouraged him to stay a dragon. Do you remember?"

Gareth nodded. "Aye. That was a few years ago."

"He noticed something then. You were making their lives difficult, sure, but you didn't hurt any of them, despite ample opportunity. That told us back then you had a strong sense of morals."

Gareth scoffed. "And what about now?"

"After you shrunk us, you stirred up the griffins to try and kill us, didn't you? Up until that time you had been classified as an annoyance. As soon as my father learned about the attack on my life, you were reclassified a threat."

Gareth's head fell in shame. "I'm sorry about shrinking you. I don't know if you'll believe me, but I was on my way back to nullify the potion. I felt horrible about it. I only wanted to scare you off. I never dreamt you'd find your way to my house. Imagine my surprise when I came home to find you talking with my mother and my aunt. I panicked. I followed you back to the valley. Once you had rejoined your dragon friend, I released the potion into a gust of wind and sent it your way."

"Well, it worked," Mikal told him. "I never want to be that small again. Hey, I have to ask you something. How are you able to work so many spells? You're ten times better than Shardwyn will ever be and a hundred times younger than he is!"

Gareth let out a short bark of laughter, the first time anyone had heard him laugh. He suddenly sobered, remembering he was supposed to be hiding his feelings.

"It's just something I could always do," the young wizard confided. "I can see the inner workings of spells and enchantments in my head. In order to cast a proper spell, you have to be thinking about what you want it to do. You have to make sure you include the correct words, cover loopholes, and so on, or else you'll get lousy results. I…"

Gareth trailed off as Lissa returned with some black turnip-like roots and a dozen broad hairy leaves.

"Alright. We need a fire. I need to slice these roots up and mash them into paste. Ideally these leaves need to be bruised and dried, but for now I'll settle for just bruised. Pravara, would you take those and crush them in your hand? Mikal, look for a couple of flat rocks. Do either of you have a knife?"

Gareth produced a tiny boot knife and presented it to her, handle first. "Will this do?"

Lissa took the proffered dagger. "It's perfect. Thanks. I have a dozen or so comfrey leaves, but they weren't ready to be picked. In case they're not strong enough the roots should make a passable poultice that will ensure Gareth's arm doesn't become infected."

Gareth felt one of the hairy leaves as Lissa walked by him to give the bundle to Pravara.

"I will confess my knowledge of herbology is severely lacking."

Mikal nodded. "Join the club."

Fifteen minutes later Lissa was finished. She had expertly rinsed the wound, dried it, and smeared a thick paste made from the chopped comfrey roots and crushed leaves. She bound Gareth's arm with pieces of cloth cut from Mikal's undershirt. Gareth had watched, bemused, as Lissa had used his little dagger to slice the prince's undershirt into strips.

"Uh, sorry about your shirt," Gareth quietly muttered once Lissa had her back to them.

"Don't worry about it," Mikal told him.

Peanut barked, causing everyone to jump. Mikal squatted

down to the playful corgi but her eyes were fixed on Gareth and she was patiently waiting to be released so she could properly greet their newest companion. Mikal eyed the boy only a few years younger than he was, sitting quietly on the log and watching them both with solemn eyes.

"Do you like dogs?"

"I haven't met many. I don't have any problems with them, if that's what you're asking."

"She's very friendly. She'll be in your face in no time flat."

Gareth looked down at the corgi and gave the dog a friendly smile. "It's alright. You can let her go. I don't mind."

"I'm only going to ask this once. Are you sure?"

Intrigued, Gareth nodded. "Aye."

Mikal unclipped Peanut's leash and gave the corgi an encouraging pat. "Okay, Peanut. Are you ready? *Release!*"

The corgi bolted, covering the distance to Gareth in three giant leaps. In the blink of an eye Peanut had leapt into Gareth's lap and shoved her face up next to his, plastering the young wizard's face with doggie kisses.

"Ack-pbthh!" Gareth started to laugh, which only encouraged the friendly dog to double her efforts. "I—mmmmph! Wow, this is a strong dog. Maybe we could—ugh! That one landed in my mouth!"

Mikal chuckled while Lissa giggled.

"Sorry."

"My mouth was open."

Mikal snorted. "I know what that's like. She's done that to me a few times."

"On purpose?" Lissa murmured. "I'd just as soon not kiss you after Peanut has, thank you very much."

Mikal flushed with embarrassment. "No, not on purpose. Really? Sheesh!"

Peanut reared up on her hind legs and nuzzled her face next to Gareth's. He wrapped his arms around the dog and began sobbing. Peanut, sensing a friend in distress, whined in empathy and wiggled closer. Mikal and Lissa were speechless.

Mikal looked over at his girlfriend and mouthed *what do we do now?* Lissa's eyes filled with sympathetic tears. She joined Gareth on the overturned log and waited with him.

After a few moments of awkward silence, Mikal sat down on Gareth's other side. Pravara finally relaxed her stance but continued to watch the proceedings.

Lissa put a friendly hand on Gareth's shoulder. "Why are you doing this, Gareth? For over two years you've been quiet. That came to a stop once you had those dragons burn your mark in the forest. Why now? It seems like a desperate ploy for attention. Is everything alright?"

Gareth shook his head. He lifted his tear-stained face and returned Lissa's frank stare. He took a deep breath.

"Two years ago, my father disappeared. Someone out there must know where he is. I'd trade all my treasure if I could just get my father back."

Mikal looked helplessly at Lissa. Before either of them could think of a proper response, Gareth, who was still holding Peanut to his chest, looked over at Mikal.

"You're the prince. Do you think you could find out what happened to my father? Please. I'll do anything!"

Chapter 7 — Cat's Out of the Bag

You want me to tell my mother? What part of 'she'll kill me' did you not understand? All the jhorun in the kingdom won't protect me if she finds out what I've done."

"You did say that you'd do anything, remember?" Mikal reminded him.

"You could always tell her you were just acting out," Lissa suggested. She and Mikal were walking, hand-in-hand, beside Gareth as they made their way back to Delythia's house. "You've taken your father's disappearance badly and didn't know how to handle all the emotions that you've been bottling up inside you."

Thunder rumbled overhead. The sky was rapidly turning dark as ominous-looking storm clouds rolled in from the western horizon. Lissa nudged Mikal on the shoulder and eyed Gareth. Their new companion had his head down, his hands were shoved in his trouser pockets, and he was scowling. Mikal laid a friendly hand on the boy's shoulder to get his attention and then looked back up at the darkening sky.

"Are you doing this? If so, please stop it. It looks as though it will start raining at any time."

Gareth glanced up and frowned. "You think I'm responsible for this storm? I may know my way around a spell, but not once have I ever messed with the weather. There are way too many ramifications."

"Like what?" Lissa wanted to know.

Gareth was silent for a few moments as he considered. "Let's say I noticed that some nearby fields are looking dry and the farmer is going to lose his crops. I could easily write a spell that would summon an enormous rain cloud."

"So, what's wrong with that?" Mikal asked. "You're helping a farmer feed his family and provide food for the village. How could that be a bad thing?"

Gareth sighed. "You can't conjure a physical object from nothing. It has to come from somewhere. So, if I summon that rain cloud, I'm pulling the cloud away from where it was originally intended to go. Whoever gets the rain benefits, but whoever loses the cloud suffers."

Mikal slowly nodded his head. "I understand. The rain you're summoning has to come from somewhere."

Gareth nodded. "Exactly. Years ago, I would have summoned that cloud and damned the consequences."

"And now?" Mikal pressed.

"Contrary to what everyone might think, I really don't want to hurt anybody."

"You certainly could have fooled me yesterday."

Gareth raised his arms in a *what can you do gesture*. "I'll admit you didn't catch me at my best, alright? Two people show up, asking questions, accompanied by a dragon? I panicked. I didn't want to worry my mother."

Peanut, trotting out in front of their little group, perked up her ears and started pulling on the leash. They could see Gareth's house in the distance. The young wizard groaned and started walking slower. Much slower. Peanut turned to give him such a look of disgust that Mikal burst out laughing.

"It's not funny. You don't understand. I'm dead. Once my mother finds out what I've been up to, she's going to punish me so badly that I won't see the light of day until I'm old enough to become a grandfather."

"You told us you were relieved this day had finally come," Mikal reminded him. "No more hiding and no more lying. You've done some pretty bad things, Gareth. It's time to atone for them. The first step is to level with your mother. She deserves to know, don't you think?"

Gareth sulked. "That's not necessarily a topic that's easy to bring up."

Mikal snapped his fingers as a thought occurred to him. "You did say you have a treasure, right?"

Gareth's eyes lifted from the ground and found Mikal's. "Aye. What of it?"

"Have you considered bribery?"

Gareth snorted. "Bribery? You want me to bribe my own mother?"

Mikal shrugged. "I don't know. How about something like, 'Mother, you look tired. Why don't we all go into the village and let someone else worry about doing the cooking tonight? While you're at it, I think you would look lovely in this new dress with this tiara set in your hair.' Take it from someone who's been in a lot of trouble, Gareth. This could work."

Lissa was shaking her head. "I disagree. She doesn't need a tiara to lessen the blow. Just tell her. Be honest with her. I'm sure she'll appreciate that more than any tiara. By the way, if you do have a tiara, I'd be more than happy to give you a girl's opinion on it. I'm just saying."

Mikal was staring at her with a bemused expression. He turned to Gareth and laid his arm companionably across the boy's shoulders. "Come on. We'll help you through this."

Gareth turned to his new friend with a look of surprise. "You will?"

"Aye. It's what friends do."

"You really don't know me," Gareth protested. "How can you claim to be a friend?"

Mikal pointed at Peanut. "Because she trusts you. I trust whoever Peanut trusts. If Peanut didn't like you then she'd show it. As it is, she won't leave your side. I think she knows you're not feeling well."

Gareth clutched his stomach. "I am feeling ill," he admitted.

"You'll feel better once everything is out in the open," Lissa assured him.

"Remember," Mikal whispered as the three of them watched the house's front door open, "no more lies. Your mother deserves to know. Be honest with her."

"Easy for you to say," Gareth muttered, watching his mother's smile slowly dissolve.

Mikal turned to Adyna and bowed. "Hello again. I'll bet you didn't think you'd see us again this soon, did you?"

Adyna stared at Mikal for a few moments, before shifting her eyes to Lissa, and then finally down at Peanut. Her face softened. Then she looked at her son and noticed he was unable to meet her eyes. "Gareth. I see you've met the prince. I ... look at me, boy. What's the matter with you?"

"May we come in?" Lissa hesitantly asked. "Gareth has a few things he needs to get off his chest."

"Does he now?" Adyna took a step back from the doorway and looked to her right. "Del, I think you need to come here."

"What is it?" a second voice asked. Delythia appeared, wiping her hands on her apron as she moved into view.

Adyna stepped out of the doorway and held out an arm. "Please. Come in. Make yourselves comfortable."

Mikal and Lissa were ushered into the house's living room and sank down onto the same worn but comfortable sofa as before. Peanut settled to the floor by Mikal's feet, but angled herself in such a way that she could watch Gareth, who had just taken the chair closest to Mikal.

"What's going on, Gareth? Is there something you need to tell me?"

"I, uh…" Gareth let out a loud breath. "I don't think I can do this."

"Yes, you can," Mikal told him in as patient a tone as he could muster. "You can do this. Tell them."

"Tell us what?" Delythia wanted to know. She had taken a seat next to her nephew and was now giving the boy a concerned look.

"Mother. Aunt Del. I, uh, well, for the past two years I have been searching for some sign of Father."

"That's no secret," Delythia softly told Gareth. "Dinna and I already knew this."

"You did? How long have you known?"

Adyna and her sister shared a conspiratorial smile. "For over a year now. I know you took your father's disappearance very hard, Gareth. It would only make sense that you would go out to look for him. I can't tell you how many times I had hoped you'd return with news that would either explain his disappearance or prove confirmation of his death."

Gareth was appalled. "You want my father to be dead?"

"That's not what she's saying," Mikal cut in, before either of the women could say anything. "She's saying that she wants there to be closure once and for all. If your father is alive, that's great."

"Provided he has a reason for disappearing," Lissa added.

Mikal nodded.

"Exactly. But if you found confirmation that your father is dead, regardless of how it happened, at least you'd be able to stop searching. You're dwelling on his disappearance, and that, in turn, is why I think you were acting up."

"Acting up?" Adyna repeated, frowning. She glanced at her son, who immediately dropped his eyes to the floor. "Gareth, what have you done?"

Gareth's eyes lifted, but only enough to look at Lissa, who nodded her encouragement.

"I was feeling bad," Gareth began. "I missed my father."

"Tell me something I don't know," Adyna responded, folding her arms across her chest.

"I'm the wizard everyone is looking for."

Adyna's eyebrows shot up in surprise. She glanced at Delythia, whose own shock mirrored her own. "What? You're the renegade wizard? You can't be. Your jhorun isn't that strong!"

Gareth sprang to his feet and began pacing. "How would you know? You never talk to me anymore! All you do is bake, day in and day out. You only ever talk to her!" Gareth pointed at his aunt. Delythia's eyes filled with tears.

"I talk to you all the time!" Adyna snapped back, growing angry. "Every single day, Gareth. Where are these accusations coming from?"

"No, you don't, Dinna," Delythia softly told her. "You might say hello, or ask how his day was going, but you don't really *talk* to him."

Adyna's face reddened. "I will not sit here and be accused of—"

Mikal put two fingers in his mouth and whistled, silencing everyone. Peanut was on her feet in a flash and jumped up onto his lap. Mikal gave her ears a tickle before he lowered her to the floor.

"I know what it's like to not have your father around," Mikal began.

"Oh, please," Adyna scoffed. "You're the prince. Your father is alive and well."

"That's right," Mikal agreed, "but for five years I had to live on another world away from him. Both of my parents. Your son has a remarkable talent. He has to be one of the strongest wizards I have ever—"

"Stop calling him a wizard," Adyna scolded. "This is my son we're talking about. He's no wizard. And if he was, I'm sure I'd know about it."

"Did you ever wonder why Shardwyn kept coming to your house and asking you all those questions about your jhorun?" Mikal asked her. "He was looking for the renegade wizard. He had the right house but was focused on the wrong person. Gareth was the one he was looking for but didn't realize it since he thought Gareth was too young."

"He *is* too young to be a wizard," Adyna stubbornly declared. "You still have the wrong person. Besides, his jhorun is the ability to remove the odor from dung. That's why our barn always smells so nice no matter how warm it is outside."

Gareth shook his head. "It smells that way because I hate the smell of dung, Mother. That was one of the first spells I ever cast. It's still active, to this day. That's why the barn doesn't smell like anything, even on a hot day."

"So you say. I'm still not convinced, son."

Mikal glanced over at Gareth, who had now closed his eyes and was softly chanting. Recognizing that he was about to cast some type of spell, Mikal smiled. He sat back on the sofa and waited. Lissa, catching sight of what Gareth was doing, reached out to take Mikal's hand. Together they waited for the demonstration Gareth was concocting.

"This won't be too thrilling as I've used up most of my jhorun today," Gareth softly announced, "but I do believe it will do."

He opened his right hand. A dancing ball of white light appeared on his open palm. He gave it a gentle toss into the air where it remained, hovering near the house's exposed rafters. Peanut, thinking it was a toy ball, barked enthusiastically at the ball of light. The ball circled around the room. As it passed over each person, a small section of the white ball broke off. Ten seconds later each person, including Peanut, had a small white ball of light gently pulsating over their heads, almost like misshapen halos.

Mikal opened his mouth to ask a question but before he could, each ball expanded in size and became a ghostly apparition of the person it was hovering over. Mikal gasped and stared at his own image, which was giving him a creepy smile. Even Peanut was watching her own doppelganger bound, upside down, around the ceiling, jumping over rafters, and silently barking at the other ghostly images.

"There's something you don't see every day," Mikal felt Lissa's grip on his hand tighten.

Adyna was rendered speechless. She was staring, open mouthed, up at the ceiling as her own twin had taken a seat directly above her. Adyna's doppelganger waved at her.

"I can tell you right now that Shardwyn could do something like that," Mikal told the group, "but not without a lot of time to do it. That took you what, one, maybe two minutes, tops?"

Gareth shrugged. He blinked twice at the images on the ceiling and they simultaneously winked out. A few seconds later Gareth morphed into the visage of an old man with a long flowing beard. Adyna and Delythia both gasped with alarm and leapt off the sofa.

Peanut, who had never cared for sudden movement, started barking.

"Shush, Peanut," Mikal quickly told the dog.

"This is one of the forms I have adopted when dealing with adults," the old man said as he addressed the room. "Shifting forms comes quite easily to me."

"That's impressive," Mikal breathed. "I'll be honest, Gareth. I'm jealous."

The form of the old man switched back to Gareth. A few moments later, he rose off the floor and slowly gazed around the room. Each person he looked at floated upward until only Peanut remained. She cocked her head both ways, watching Mikal waving his arms through the air.

Once they were all safely back on the floor, Gareth waved a hand at the fireplace. A mass of smoke floated across the room. After a few moments, the cloud slowly condensed itself until it resembled a griffin. The smoke griffin extended its wings and began flying around the room. After a few passes above their heads, the teenager sent the smoke back to the fireplace and allowed it to join the other smoke and vent safely outside through the chimney.

"I could have given the griffin more detail, but that's about all the jhorun I can muster for right now."

Adyna slowly stood. She stared at her son in silence for a full minute before she timidly approached him. She raised an arm and reached for him. Gareth nodded, figuring his mother finally believed him.

"Aye, Mother. That was really me. I've been able to do—hey!"

Instead of reaching for her son, Adyna grabbed a cushion from the sofa and had smacked Gareth across the face with it, as though they were in the middle of a pillow fight.

"Are you kidding me?" she shouted. She pulled her arm back and walloped Gareth a second time with the pillow. "All this time! The renegade wizard was you? You have caused so many problems, Gareth. Why? Why would you do this?"

Gareth's gaze returned to the floor. "I don't know."

"You don't know? You need to do better than that, young man."

"I was bored?"

"Bored children do not almost take down the entire wyverian population! I heard about that, Gareth. That curse you created for the zweigelans almost destroyed every wyverian there was! The valley is nearby, Gareth. The dragons are our neighbors! What did they ever do to you?"

"I made the curse but I didn't invoke it!" Gareth protested, throwing his arms up against the relentless pounding from his mother's pillow. "It was nothing personal. I was asked to create a curse, and in return, I'd receive…"

Gareth trailed off. He looked sheepishly at his new friends before closing his mouth with an audible snap.

"You'd receive what?" his mother inquired, curious.

"Umm…"

"Gareth, spill. What were you promised? Better yet, what were you given?"

Gareth quietly whispered something under his breath, completely forgetting his mother's excellent hearing.

"Treasure? You were given a treasure for that curse? Do you know how many dragons suffered?"

Gareth's head fell. His eyes filled.

Mikal cleared his throat. "Gareth, you're trying to make amends, is that right? Were you serious about that?"

Gareth slowly nodded.

"How serious?" Mikal wanted to know.

The young wizard's head lifted. "Why do you want to know?"

"Because I just thought of a way for you to take the first step."

Adyna was definitely interested. "He'll do it. I can promise you that."

Mikal noticed a defiant look creep onto Gareth's young face.

"Hold up. This is something we can't force him to do."

"The heck I can't," Adyna disagreed. "He's my son and if I say…"

"Gareth is a young man now," Mikal interrupted. "Let us see if he'll willingly atone for the things he's done."

"What do you want me to do?" Gareth sullenly asked.

"Return the treasure to its rightful owners."

Nice.

Pravara? Have you been listening again?

Of course. If he agrees to return the treasure then he's going to make three zweigelans extremely happy.

I'll see what I can do.

"What?" Gareth demanded, outraged. "I worked very hard on that spell. It was some of my best work! It took me a full week to compose it and two months to imbue that metal fang with it. I provided a service. Shouldn't I be paid for my work?"

"If you're worried about work," Mikal began, "I can assure you that we can find some useful things for you to do. Perhaps you could give Shardwyn a few pointers. He's always blowing stuff up."

"You want me to give up my treasure," Gareth accused, growing angry. He rounded on Mikal. "I thought you were my friend."

"I am. I'm here to help you make amends with your family. And to help you find out what happened to your father. That's why I'm here, Gareth. However, you need to prove to me your intentions are noble. Do the right thing. Give the treasure back to its rightful owners. I'm told you'll make three zweigelans very happy."

Gareth paced the room as he considered.

"Would it be that bad to give it all back?" Lissa gently inquired.

Gareth scoffed. "You're asking me to give up a lot."

Lissa gazed at him with an unreadable expression. "Do you feel comfortable with all that treasure knowing you caused harm to a lot of people? Dragons, too?"

That drew Gareth up short.

"You told me you really didn't want to hurt anyone, but that's what happened," Lissa continued. "You're a better person than that, Gareth. Show them. Show us. You'll do it, won't you?"

Gareth sighed and sank back down onto his chair. Half a heartbeat later Peanut jumped up onto his chair and snuggled on his lap. The young wizard gave the friendly corgi a few scratches behind her ears.

"Alright. I'll do it. It's just that… I was planning on buying them a new house, only…"

"Only you didn't know how to pay for it using dragon gold?" Mikal guessed.

"It's mostly jewels," Gareth confessed, "but aye. There's no one in the village I can trust. Presenting jewels larger than my fist would generate a question or two."

"You were going to buy us a new house?" his mother softly asked, her temper diminishing. "That's so sweet of you!"

"That'll never happen now," Gareth sullenly told her. "With my treasure gone we're back to having no money."

The zweigelans have been notified but there's a problem.

What?

Each zweigelan is unwilling to agree on how much each contributed. They are now bickering amongst themselves, like dragonlets.

What do we have to do? Get your father involved?

Indubitably. He will not be thrilled.

Why?

My father doesn't like to deal with petty affairs. If he's forced to arbitrate this, he's more than likely going to split the treasure between all wyverians.

They've all suffered, Mikal agreed. *Perhaps they should.*

I will suggest it. Do not say anything to the boy. This is not his problem.

You got it.

Mikal stretched and sat up straight in his chair. "Gareth, may I make a proposal?"

The teenager glanced irritably his way, as though Mikal alone was responsible for the loss of his beloved treasure. "Go on."

"You're a wizard. You no doubt possess a strong jhorun. Have you noticed anything different about it lately?"

Gareth's face darkened. "Why? What have you heard?"

Mikal blinked a few times. That wasn't what he had expected to hear.

"The only thing I'm referring to," Mikal carefully said, "is the fact that your jhorun probably isn't as strong as it used to be."

Gareth crossed his arms defiantly across his chest. "There's *nothing* wrong with my jhorun."

"Have you ever depleted your jhorun before?" Lissa asked. When Gareth didn't say anything, she continued. "I'm willing to bet you've been wondering why your jhorun's stamina has been decreasing."

All eyes turned to Gareth.

"Maybe. It doesn't mean anything."

"Gareth, I believe you're stronger than Shardwyn. Actually, I don't think there'd be anyone who could refute that. Do you realize you're the strongest wizard in Lentari!"

Gareth shrugged. "Shardwyn can't be as bad as you say. Crafting a spell is so easy. Anyone could do it."

Mikal grinned. "I'm going to have to disagree with you on that one."

"Why? Because Shardwyn has trouble composing a spell?"

"Gareth, I've seen him blow up his tower, on more than one occasion. In fact, the last time was about three months ago. It scared all of us. My father thought we were under attack and ordered the castle to be sealed. We should have known it was a faulty spell."

Gareth snickered.

"Don't get me started about his potions," Mikal continued. "He typically burns every other potion he attempts, has his completed potions mislabeled, and all of his potion ingredients are probably stale."

Gareth elected to keep quiet but at least he was smiling.

"Don't get me wrong, Gareth. Shardwyn is a powerful wizard. He's done a lot of good for my father. It's just that … he's … hmmm. How do I put this without sounding ungrateful?"

"He's a nincompoop?" Adyna suggested, eliciting giggles and chuckles from everyone.

Mikal smiled. "He's a bit unorthodox at times but at least his heart is in the right place. What I'm trying to get at is we could use Gareth's help in dealing with a problem that, uh, we are facing right now."

"You want to know why our jhorun is weaker than it normally is," Gareth guessed.

Mikal gave the teenager a triumphant look. Gareth scowled. "That doesn't mean that I ... blast. Fine. I have felt the effects on my jhorun, too. I just attributed it to mental stress."

"I've noticed it, too," Delythia added. "I used to be able to predict what the weather would be like for the next week and now I can only accurately predict the next two days. I miss my jhorun. It isn't much, as far as jhoruns go, but I would like it back to the same levels as it used to be."

"That's what we're working on right now," Mikal told her. "My father is aware of the problem. In fact, he's meeting with the Dragon Lord today to address this very problem."

"He's probably already done with his meeting," Lissa reminded him. "It's past midday."

The meeting continues.

"Pravara says they are still in their meeting," Mikal announced.

Gareth gave him a quizzical look. "How do you know this?"

Mikal grinned. "Can you keep a secret?"

The teenage wizard gave him an incredulous look. "Obviously."

"I'm chatting with Pravara. She just told me her father is still talking with my father."

"That dark green dragon is the daughter of Kahvel, the Dragon Lord?" Gareth asked, shocked. "Wizards be damned. Every dragon out there will be out for my blood after what happened yesterday."

"What happened yesterday?" his mother inquired, frowning.

"It's in the past," Mikal hurriedly assured her. "Gareth, help us with our, er, predicament and I'll put in a good word for you with my father. What do you say? Do we have a deal?"

And I will speak to my father about him as soon as he becomes available.

"Pravara will do the same with hers. I'm sure you'd like to go outside again, wouldn't you? The dragons now know what you look like, and through their Collective every dragon knows who you are and where you live."

Gareth paled. He worriedly looked over at his mother and aunt. "I really don't have a choice here, do I?"

Adyna fixed Mikal with a stare. "Are you serious? Could Gareth truly help solve whatever crisis is affecting our jhoruns?"

"I don't know," Mikal admitted. "Honestly, it couldn't hurt to try. The more people we have working on this the better our chances to figure it out."

Gareth leaned forward and gently set Peanut back upon the ground. In less than a second she was back in Gareth's lap. He wrapped his arms around the dog and held her tight for a few moments. He gently set the dog back on the ground for a second time and then hastily stood before the dog could get back on his lap. Gareth slowly approached Mikal and crossed his arms.

"You probably can't guarantee that if I do this then my record will be wiped clean, can you?"

Mikal shook his head, "I wish I had the power to make that deal, Gareth, but that is something my father must approve. I'm sorry."

"Very well. I have my own deal."

"Gareth ..." Mikal rose to his feet, "you're really not in a position to make deals."

Lissa stood. She took Mikal's hand. "Let's hear what he has to say. Gareth, what do you propose?"

Gareth looked back at his mother and aunt and smiled tenderly at them. He turned to look at Mikal. "If I help you solve this jhorun problem then I want them to have a new house. Something nicer than this. No offense, Delythia."

"How many times have I told you to call me Del?" his aunt chastised. "And fear not. No offense is taken. Well, maybe a little."

Mikal nodded. "I was expecting worse. I think I should be able to arrange that."

"One last thing," Gareth continued. "You also agree to

help me find my father or at least find out what happened to him." He held out an arm. "Do we have a deal?"

Mikal grasped Gareth's forearm and gave it a friendly shake.

"We have a deal."

Chapter 8 — Misplaced Affection

I f he gives you any problems, you have my permission to physically knock some sense into him," Adyna informed Mikal as she pushed her son out the door after him. "To think you're responsible for this mess, Gareth. What would your father think?"

"You don't understand. That's what I'm trying…"

"Hush," Adyna snapped. Both she and her sister had folded their arms across their chests and were frowning at the boy. "You will mind your manners at all times. Do you hear me?"

"Yes, ma'am," Gareth sullenly responded.

"I don't care if you're told to go jump in a lake," his mother continued. "You will do it with no questions asked and with a smile on your face. Is that clear?"

Gareth refused to look his mother in the eye. "Aye."

"Good." Adyna turned to Mikal and smiled. She gave him a tiny curtsy and promptly closed the door in his face.

Mikal turned to Gareth as they walked into the forest,

"You're lucky to have a caring mother like her."

Gareth stared incredulously at him, "Are you kidding? She's the most overbearing person I've ever met. She is always telling me what to do. I can't stand it."

"She wouldn't do that if she didn't care for you," Lissa pointed out. She was holding on to Peanut's leash and was constantly pulling the inquisitive corgi back to her side, as Peanut was more interested in exploring the surrounding countryside than listening to their boring conversation.

"Says you," Gareth muttered. "I'll bet your mother doesn't badger you on a daily basis."

"Better let this one go," Mikal quietly advised, loud enough for Gareth to hear but soft enough so that there was a chance Lissa couldn't. The youngster, unfortunately, wasn't paying attention.

"I wish my mother would remind me to brush my hair, or to pick up my room, or to simply tell me she loves me," Lissa answered. Her eyes went wistful for a few seconds before she turned to Gareth and sighed. "I'd wish that more than anything."

Gareth, intent on staring at his feet and not at the warning signs Mikal was trying to give him, scoffed loudly. "Then you're lucky. You don't know how cumbersome an overbearing parent can be."

"Shut *up*," Mikal hissed at him.

Gareth finally looked up. "What? Did you just tell me to shut up?"

Lissa placed a restraining hand on Mikal's shoulder and faced their new friend. "Gareth, my mother is dead. I never knew her. I grew up an only child with just my father to raise me."

Gareth's shoulders slumped. "Oh. I didn't know. Uh, sorry?"

Lissa shook her head. "You didn't know, Gareth. Besides, it isn't your fault. It's just the way it is."

"You don't have a mother and I don't have a father," Gareth quietly observed. "We'd make a good pair."

Mikal coughed loudly and quickly stepped between his girlfriend and the young wizard. He put a protective arm

162   Jeffrey Poole

around Lissa's shoulders and shot Gareth a warning look. "She's taken, pal."

Lissa turned to give Mikal a patronizing look, "Stop worrying. That's not what Gareth was doing. It wasn't, was it?"

Before Gareth could respond, the earth suddenly shook so hard that it knocked everyone off their feet. Even Peanut was thrown off balance, stumbling backward until she sat. It was over in less than two seconds. Everyone hesitantly looked around the forest. Several trees were now leaning precariously against one another. As they watched, one of the two leaning trees fell noisily to the ground, taking out several branches of a few neighboring trees along the way.

"What was that?" Lissa whispered as she cautiously rose to her knees.

Mikal shrugged. "It's hard to say. It could…"

Two huge green forelegs appeared and grabbed two trees, jerking them in the opposite direction, snapping each off at the trunk. The broken trees were discarded, much like two large pieces of trash.

"I trusted you!" an angry female voice roared out. "You assured me these pointless examples of your ire were a thing of the past! What have you to say for yourself?"

It was Pravara. Her fangs were bared, she hadn't stopped growling, and she was glaring at Gareth. Wide-eyed, Mikal looked at his companions. He hadn't ever seen Pravara that angry before. What had set her off? What was this about 'pointless examples of ire'?

Mikal nervously cleared his throat. "Umm, what was that?"

"Not you. YOU!"

Pravara extended a heavily scaled foreleg and pointed one of her two-foot-long talons at Gareth. Twin trails of smoke were rising from her nostrils, an unfortunate indicator that her internal furnace had been stoked and she was ready to spit fire.

Mikal threw up his hands and jumped in front of Gareth. "Whoa! Pravara, take it easy. What's the matter? What's happened?"

Pravara roared again and advanced on their small party, forcing everyone but the corgi to retreat a few steps. Unperturbed, Peanut looked up at her large wyverian packmate before glancing back at her human ones. She cocked her head, uncertain which side she should be taking.

"Another dragon has fallen under your spell! I saw it with my own eyes!"

Mikal and Lissa turned to Gareth with shock written all over their features.

"Tell me that wasn't you," Mikal softly asked. "You promised you were done with all these dastardly acts."

Gareth jerked his hands up into the air. "It wasn't me! I've been with you two. I haven't done anything!"

Lissa tapped Mikal on the shoulder. "I hate to be the one to bring this up, but is there any chance that we have the wrong person?"

Mikal turned to look at Gareth and waited, expectantly, for an answer. "I already admitted I was the one who bewitched the other dragons," Gareth reminded them. "I'm the wizard you're looking for."

"Could there be another wizard?" Lissa asked.

When no one answered, Mikal nudged Gareth in the ribs. "Well? If there's another wizard, would you be able to tell?"

Gareth shrugged. "It's not an easy task, bewitching a dragon. It took me some time to master the process. It's easy for me now, sure, but ... but I have no intention of ever doing it again," Gareth hastily finished as he eyed Pravara's menacing jaws.

"One of my brethren has become bewitched," Pravara growled. She looked pointedly down at the small group of humans. She singled out Gareth. "Do you know who my father is, human?"

"Er, your father is the Dragon Lord, right?"

"Correct. Do you know what he's going to do to you once I announce to the Collective who the wizard responsible for these attacks are?"

Gareth paled. "I swear, this time it wasn't me!"

"Then who?" Mikal demanded. "If you're not the one who did this then we need to find out who did, and quick. If

Kahvel learns about this I guarantee you it isn't going to end well. Heck, if *my* father learns about this—"

"Look, I get it," Gareth interrupted. "I'm going to be in more trouble than I already am."

"Gareth, how did you bewitch the other dragons?" Lissa asked. "It's not like you could go jumping up on their backs. Or could you?"

Gareth shook his head. "Of course not. It's easy, really. I took ordinary rocks and submersed them in a potion of my own creation. I let the stones dry, then all I have to do is drop them into the hands of a dragon. Keep the stones small enough and I can use a gust of wind to blow the stone into a dragon's hand. As soon as contact is made, the dragon falls into a trance and becomes highly susceptible to commands."

"How many of those stones did you prepare?" Mikal asked. "Are they all accounted for?"

Gareth smiled sheepishly. "Come to think of it … all but one."

Mikal and Lissa shared a look. "All but one? You lost one?"

Gareth shrugged. "I always carry a stone with me. You never know when you might need it. Anyway, it happened right after I created the rock golem. I was running for home when I heard your dog barking. I panicked. I must have dropped it in the wind storm. The wind must have carried it out into the valley."

Mikal grunted. He looked up at Pravara. "There's your answer. I'd say the missing stone was found."

Pravara growled. "One of my brethren has fallen into a trance and will not snap out of it. How do we rectify the situation?"

"What happens if a dragon enters the trance and no one is there to issue a directive?" Lissa wanted to know.

Gareth was silent as he considered. "I really don't know. It's never happened before."

"Well, congratulations," Mikal glumly announced. "We're about to find out." He glared at their new companion and hooked a thumb back at Pravara. "This is your doing, Gareth. You are going to help us fix this before her father finds out."

"Or yours," Lissa reminded him.

"Right. Mine, too. You made this potion. How can we nullify it?"

"If I could place my hands on the dragon's head then I could give it a jolt strong enough to break the enchantment. Otherwise, it would have to receive the jolt some other way. A splash of water would do it. A blast of fire would, too, but you'd have to aim it at the head. The rest of a dragon's body is too fully armored."

"Pravara, could you place Gareth on ... hey, who was bewitched, anyway? Do we know?"

"Cylandria. She's young. Younger than I."

Mikal groaned softly. A young dragon had found Gareth's missing trance-inducing stone. This was not good.

"So, what do we do?" Mikal wanted to know. "Can you get Gareth on Cylandria's back?"

"I've already tried to approach," Pravara informed them. She continued to growl at Gareth. "She tried to attack me."

Gareth eyed Pravara's talons and shivered.

"No offense, but I'd rather not go for a ride. Do you think you can force her to land?"

"I wasn't offering to let you ride me," Pravara coldly informed him. "And no, not without doing irreparable harm to her."

"We need to distract her," Mikal mused. "Then when she isn't paying attention, someone can swoop in and drop Gareth on her back."

Pravara stared at him as though she had just heard someone say she had sprouted another tail.

"You may have noticed that there is only one dragon here," she reminded him. "I cannot be in two places at the same time. If I call for assistance then *his* involvement will become known." Pravara again looked at Gareth and growled.

"Isn't there anyone that can help us without giving us away?" Lissa asked helplessly. "There must be someone!"

"I have an idea," Gareth quietly announced. He looked over at Mikal. "Do you trust me?"

Mikal shook his head. "Sorry. Trust is earned, not bestowed. It's going to take some time."

Gareth shrugged and waved his hands in the air, drawing several intricate symbols known only to him. "It'll have to do."

An unknown force slammed into Mikal, causing him to fall to his knees, gasping in shock. Before anyone could ask what had happened, Mikal's body began to swell. His skin darkened, thickened, and sprouted scales. Two dark, leathery wings sprouted out of his back, ripping off what was left of his clothes. Mikal's neck lengthened and his torso stretched to three times its normal size.

Mikal stared uncomprehendingly at one of his arms. It had become heavily muscled. He clenched his hand and felt the power ripple through his muscles. Wait. His hand! He had lost a finger. In fact, it looked as though one of the fingers had merged with another to become a thicker digit. Fingers were now tipped with talons at least two feet long. Then he caught sight of his skin color. He was purple.

Gareth had turned him into a purple dragon.

His long neck twisted, attempting to locate his so-called friend. "Purple? You turned me into a purple dragon? Are you kidding? Why couldn't it be black?"

Gareth shrugged. "It's my mother's favorite color."

Pravara studied Mikal's new form. She gave the young wizard a skeptical look.

"This is your idea? I'm willing to bet Mikal has had no experience in that form, which means he'll be a novice flyer. This plan is doomed to fail."

"Give it a chance," Gareth told her. He looked up at Mikal's dragon-sized form and grinned. "Do you have any idea how difficult it was to learn how to change one form to another?"

Lissa approached Mikal's purple wyverian body and craned her head to look up into Mikal's eyes. "You make a handsome dragon; do you know that?"

The purple dragon's nose jerked down. Mikal eyed his girlfriend and grunted once, which in his wyverian form came out as a growl.

"Do you know how to fly, Mikal?" Lissa wanted to know.

Mikal bent his long neck behind him to inspect his newest

set of appendages. His wings were gigantic! Each must have measured at least thirty feet long and was tipped by a foot long wing talon. He experimentally flapped his wings a few times and then grunted again, satisfied he could handle the mundane task of flying.

"No."

"This will not be easy for you," Pravara warned as she prepared herself to launch into the air. "You are in a new form now. I would encourage you to get used to your new body as quickly as possible."

Mikal's purple visage frowned. "Easy for you to say. You've been a dragon all your life. We should see if Gareth can turn you into a human and see how you like it."

"No, thanks. My mother was a human once and she didn't care for it at all. All you have to remember is…" Pravara's head jerked up and she stared at the sky. "Time's up. She's near. We must hurry!"

"What? You can't leave me now! What were you going to say? What's the most important thing to remember?"

It was too late. Pravara had already leapt into the air, spread her wings, and disappeared from sight. Moments later a bright blue dragon with white jagged stripes running across its torso appeared. It flew directly over them, looking to attack. Pravara swooped low, fired a blast which struck Cylandria's hind quarters, and then ascended high into the clouds. Fortunately for everyone involved, Cylandria took off after Pravara.

"We'd better be going," Gareth advised. "She's going to need our help."

Mikal extended a wing and inspected it skeptically. "Do you really think I can do this?"

Gareth nodded. "I've changed my form a few times. What I've learned is that each body already knows how to move. It knows what to do. You just have to tell it where you want to go, without actually telling it. Trust me, flying is a breeze."

"Huh? What's that supposed to mean?"

"I think he means you shouldn't overthink what you need to do," Lissa guessed. "You don't need to figure out which muscle to move if you want to take a step. Look at us. When we walk do we need to consciously order each of our legs to move?"

"No, I guess not," Mikal admitted. He extended both wings and then looked straight up.

Gareth raised a hand. "Do you want me to climb up on your back or do you want to carry me in a claw?"

"There's no way you're going on my back," Mikal crossly told him.

Gareth sulked. "You're not a real dragon. Why would you be concerned with taking a rider?"

"Listen, I'm more worried about tipping over once I'm in the air. The last thing I want to do is worry about you falling off my back. I have enough things on my mind right now, thank you very much."

Mikal turned to look back at the tiny figure of his girlfriend, who was still holding Peanut's leash. He lowered his neck so that his head was less than ten feet from Lissa and the dog. Peanut, thinking he wanted to sniff noses, inched forward and waited for him to touch his nose to hers. Mikal smiled and decided to humor the dog. Satisfied, the corgi settled back into the grass. Lissa approached and laid a soft hand on the side of his jaw.

"Be safe up there. Gareth, if you hurt him, I will personally feed you to Pravara. Is that clear?"

Gareth gulped nervously. "Perfectly. I'll take good care of him."

Dragon and human eyed each other.

"How do you want to do this?" Mikal hesitantly asked. "I have no idea how to take off."

"Remember what we told you. You don't have to order each wing to flap. You want to take off into the air. Just do it and see what happens. Open your claw. I'll hop on. Just don't squish me."

Mikal opened the claws on his left foreleg and eyed the sky one more time. *Don't overthink it.* All he had to do was tell his body where he wanted to go. Fine. He wanted to go up.

Mikal waited expectantly on the ground, unmoving. Nothing was happening.

Gareth stuck his head through two of his wyverian fingers and tsked loudly. "You have to put in a little more effort than that."

Mikal growled. Gareth jerked his head inside as Mikal clenched his dragon hands. He decided to mimic Pravara's takeoff. Lissa guided Peanut over to a large tree, and together the two of them silently watched the newly formed dragon.

Mikal bunched his muscles and leapt into the air. However, he still thought of himself as a human, not as a dragon. His two massive hind legs gave a tremendous shove against the ground, only his two front legs didn't get the message. The resulting half-jump spun Mikal three-quarters of the way around. His wings flapped impotently as he scrambled to figure out what went wrong.

Lissa giggled with laughter. "I don't think I've ever seen a dragon do a half-jump like that!" she called out. "Did you do that on purpose?"

Mikal glared at his own hind end before turning irritably to face Lissa. "No, of course not. I tried to jump, but only half of me decided to pay attention."

"Think like a dragon," Gareth advised. "You're walking around on four legs, not two. Remember you have to get all four legs off the ground."

Mikal growled and tried again. This time he propelled himself about twenty feet up into the air. His wings snapped open and began flapping. He grinned, realizing he was able to keep himself off the ground. His smile quickly deteriorated into a frown as he realized he wasn't making any additional progress.

"What are you waiting for?" Gareth called out from his hand. "Get going!"

"I'm trying!" Mikal snapped. He rotated his head until he was staring back at the length of his body. His wings were flapping furiously and he also saw that his tail was swishing back and forth, like a long ribbon caught in a breeze. He caught sight of the small flap of skin on the tip of his tail and briefly wondered what it was for.

Mikal felt his body respond, as if it was answering his question. His tail stopped whipping through the air and the flap of skin opened. Suddenly he felt as though he had more control.

Higher. I want to go higher.

He rose steadily higher. Mikal opened his jaws to let out a victorious shout when his ascent faltered and he almost tipped over. He roared his frustration and flapped harder.

"Stop fighting it!" Gareth shouted. "Just relax! Stay focused on what you want to do. If you lose your concentration, you and I are both in trouble."

Mikal ordered his mind to ignore the unusual sensations his wyverian body was reporting back to him. He knew he wanted to go higher and thankfully his body complied. He saw that he had drifted away from the valley and was now over the forest. There would be no landing down there if he had some type of emergency. He needed to get back to open grassland.

Gradually his body listened. A few minutes later he soared out over Lake Raehón's valley. Mikal grunted with satisfaction. Gareth was right. Flying wasn't too terribly bad.

"Look out!"

Gareth's warning forced him to jerk his head up. He saw that Pravara had circled about and was now heading straight for him. Where was Cylandria? Had Pravara managed to elude her?

Mikal, get out of the way! Pravara urgently thought to him. **You're supposed to be following her from behind. Be careful! I have her fixated on me but that doesn't mean she won't come after you!**

Mikal hurriedly flapped out of the way just as Pravara rocketed by. Cylandria's blue form streaked by a split second later. Unfortunately, thanks to his newfound, vastly improved visual abilities, Mikal could see the blue dragon's head swivel about and stare straight at him. Cylandria veered away from Pravara and executed a sharp turn, coming about in a matter of seconds until she was barreling straight toward him.

"Wizards be damned," Mikal cursed angrily. "Gareth, we have a problem!"

"Yeah, I see it. You need to get going! Hurry!"

Mikal twisted in midair until he was facing north, toward the lake. He frantically pumped his wings in an attempt to gain as much velocity as he could. He risked a quick glance backwards. His eyes widened with disbelief. Cylandria was already so close that she was within biting range. In fact, she had opened her jaws and was preparing to take a bite out of his long purple tail.

Tuck your tail and dive! Now!

Mikal didn't argue. He quickly glanced down at the ground far below and wished he was much closer to it. His body responded automatically. His wings drew in and tightened. His tail pushed down and suddenly he was pointing, nose first, toward the ground and falling like a stone.

Excellent! Do not open your wings until I tell you to. I'm going to try and attract her attention.

Whatever you're going to do you'd better do it fast!

"Hold on, Gareth!" Mikal roared. They were now falling so fast he was certain they couldn't pull out of the steep dive.

Yes, you will. You must trust me. We're almost there.

Almost where? The ground is approaching at a sickening pace, Pravara! When do I open my wings?

Now!

Mikal could only hope his body knew what to do. He stared at the ground rushing up toward him. He was going to strike it! There was no way—!

His body jerked. His wings snapped back open at the last possible second. If he didn't know any better, he'd say he could feel the grass passing underneath him as he sailed out over the valley floor and quickly rose up to a more comfortable altitude.

Mikal twisted to look behind. What had happened to Cylandria? He saw Pravara whiz by with the blue dragon hot on her tail. Pravara must have flown close enough to present a more appealing target.

Thankfully it worked.

Mikal homed in on Cylandria's fleeing form and urged his body to pursue. He felt his wings extend slightly and his tail change position. He decided it wasn't worth the risk of falling out of the sky to check to see what his dragon body was doing so he ignored the details. Instead, he focused all his energy on catching up to Pravara and her attacker.

Where are you?

I'm following the two of you.

Are you close enough to get the wizard onto Cylandria's back?

Not unless I throw him.

Hmmm.

I don't think I should do that, Pravara.

You suggested it.

I was joking.

Ah. Please hurry.

I'm trying. Stop zigzagging about. Fly in a straight line and I can catch up easier.

Flying in a straight line will allow Cylandria to catch up, too.

You're bigger than she is. Can't you outfly her?

No. I've tried. It must have something to do with the wizard's potion.

I'll ask.

"Gareth, does your potion make the dragon fly faster than they normally could?"

"Umm, aye. I should have mentioned that. I'm sorry."

"Is there anything else you'd like to mention as long as you're at it?"

"I would hurry. The potion draws upon the dragon's natural abilities. If the dragon overextends themselves, it could hurt them."

"How long does she have?"

"We haven't been up here for fifteen minutes yet, have we?"

"I don't think so. Why?"

"You're sure?"

Mikal growled with frustration. "I'm not sure, Gareth. Why? What happens after fifteen minutes? Are you saying after fifteen minutes the blue dragon is going to be in danger?"

"Aye."

Pravara?

I heard. Remind me to pound him into the ground once this is over.

Gladly. Get ready. When I tell you to, bank right. I'm going to see if I can fly directly over her. I'll drop Gareth onto her back. Then make

sure you still have her attention.
Any suggestions?
I'm sure you'll come up with something. Ready?
Aye.
"Gareth, are you ready? I'm about to drop you on her back."

"I'm ready. Get me as close as you can so I don't drop too far!"

"I'll try."
Go, Pravara!
Pravara's dark green form angled sharply to the right, closing the gap to Mikal rapidly. Cylandria immediately banked right. Mikal urged his body on, anxious to put an end to this horrible ordeal. He didn't even want to think about how they'd keep this from his father.

Mikal saw that he had about five seconds before he'd pass over Cylandria's body so he readied himself. He stretched out his left foreleg and prepared to open his claws.

"I hope you're ready!" Mikal called out. He let Gareth fall just as he flew over the bewitched dragon.

Unfortunately, even in her bewitched state of mind, Cylandria heard the warning he had given Gareth. She executed a flawless barrel roll just as the teenager's feet made contact with her back. Gareth was flicked off like a pesky insect. Mikal's eyes widened with disbelief.

Damn! Damndamndamndamndamndamn!

Mikal drew in his wings and plummeted straight down in an effort to catch up to Gareth's wildly flailing body. The young wizard must have noticed Mikal gaining on him, as he suddenly thrust out his arms and legs in an attempt to slow his descent. Mikal caught him, less than fifty feet from the treetops.

He pumped his wings and gained altitude.
Where are you now, Pravara?
Near the northern border of the forest. Are you nearby? I am trying to avoid the valley as much as possible.
Why?
Sooner or later our activity is going to be detected.

I'm trying to prolong the inevitable.

You don't want to be around when your father finds out?

Precisely.

I see you. Keep zigzagging. I'll be there momentarily.

Were you able to save Gareth?

Aye. I have him.

Nicely done.

Thanks. I didn't really have time to think. I had to go after him.

Is he uninjured?

I do not know. I didn't ask. "Gareth, are you alright?"

"I've just realized how much I hate flying."

Mikal chuckled, which sounded an awful lot like a growl. "You hate flying or you hate falling from high places?"

"Both. Where's Pravara?"

"Up ahead. We're closing on them now."

Mikal heard Gareth sigh loudly. He dropped his neck down so he could look at the boy within his talons. Gareth was sitting with his back up against the palm of his hand, his knees drawn up, his arms wrapped around his legs to hold them in place. He looked miserable.

"What's the matter?" Mikal asked. "Don't like flying?"

"Falling to one's death tends to have that effect on people."

"I caught you, didn't I?"

"Barely."

"Fine. You don't like the present situation, switch places with me. You be the dragon and I'll be the one hopping on its back."

"Yeah, right," Gareth scoffed. "You wouldn't be able to wake the blue dragon up."

"And you can, right?"

Gareth eyed Mikal's purple head. "I told you that I can, remember?"

"So, we're stuck in our present roles until this is over, is that it?"

"Yes," Gareth glumly agreed.

"Then stop complaining. I'm doing this to help you out. Do you realize that?"

Gareth was silent.

"Pravara and I could have just as easily turned you in to the proper authorities. Gareth, I won't lie to you. My father wants to throw you in the dungeon. Care to guess what Pravara's father wants to do to you?"

"Not really."

"Good. Stop complaining."

"I'm not feeling very well."

"What? Are you nauseous? You had better not get sick on my hand. Think about something else."

"Like what?" Gareth moaned. He took several deep gulps of air.

"Well, what can we expect once Cylandria awakens? Is it an instantaneous transition or is she going to be disoriented?"

"There's usually some disorientation involved," Gareth admitted.

Mikal growled. "What purpose do you have for doing this? What do you have against the dragons?"

"What do you mean?"

"Why is it always the dragons? I've never heard about anything else becoming bewitched. Why not the griffins? What about a malwern? Why bother the wyverians?"

Gareth was silent for a full minute before he responded. "I've always admired the dragons. They're regal, majestic. I resent their history, their culture, and even their honor."

"What? Why? What did they ever do to you?"

"The dragons have their Collective. They are never alone. They always have someone to turn to in times of distress. I never had that. I wish I did."

"You mean to tell me you're jealous?"

"Aye, I guess so," Gareth sighed.

I heard that.

"Pravara heard you."

"The dragons are better than us at everything. They have better eyesight, better hearing, and a more highly developed sense of smell."

"If you like the dragons so much then why don't you turn yourself into one and go live with them?"

No dragon would have him. They'd know he's not a true dragon the moment he tried to access the Collective.

How? How would they know?

They just would.

Ah.

"Disrupting the lives of the dragons was fun at first," Gareth hesitantly began, "but lately it has lost its appeal."

"Really? Why would you expect me to believe that, Gareth? You've been doing this stuff so long now; I find myself doubting your motives."

"I wouldn't want someone to make me do things I would never do, the way I've been doing to them."

Mikal grunted. "Fair enough. Look. There's Pravara. Cylandria is still on her tail. We've definitely passed that fifteen-minute mark. This has got to be hurting her now. We need to snap her out of this. Pravara, are you ready?"

I am. What would you like me to do?

At that moment the three dragons shot out over Lake Raehón and rapidly left the shoreline behind. Mikal turned his huge head and surveyed the wide-open water. He received another surprise when, after staring at a specific point for longer than a few seconds, the image increased in size and leapt into fine detail. He twisted his long neck around to stare at the receding shore. He singled out a tree and watched it leap into focus. If he wanted to, he could count the needles on the branch!

He tried the trick several other times and was rewarded with an enhanced view each time. He targeted Pravara and watched her expertly twist and turn through the air as she avoided the ever-pursuing blue dragon on her tail. On and on they all flew, heading out over the open expanse of the great lake. At the rate they were flying they'd be back over solid land in less than ten minutes.

Pravara, get ready to bank left. Wait about five seconds then turn sharply to your right. Wait another five seconds and then repeat that until we catch up. Hopefully it'll keep Cylandria occupied.

Understood.

"Gareth, are you ready? It's time for you to prove you're here to make things right."

"About your hand…"

"Hmm? What about it?"

"It'll wash off. I told you I wasn't feeling well."

"What? Are you serious? Did you get sick in my hand?"

"Umm, no. I didn't get sick."

"What did you do?"

"Well…"

"Gareth," Mikal growled, "tell me what you did. Did you pee on me?"

"I'm just kidding. I didn't do anything."

"Do you see how far away the ground is?"

"Aye. What about it?"

"It's a long way down. Remember that the next time you try and joke around with me."

They caught up to Pravara as she pulled a sharp right turn and started flying toward them. Cylandria followed. Mikal steeled himself. It was now or never.

Mikal opened his claws just as he passed over the bewitched form of the young blue dragon. Gareth dropped a few feet down to Cylandria's scaly back and crouched low. His hands sought out the closest scale and he instinctively gripped it as tightly as possible. Mikal could see him looking anxiously about. He knew what the boy was thinking. Had the dragon detected his presence? After a few more moments Mikal could give a loud sigh of relief. He had made it! Now all he had to do was to make his way across Cylandria's back and up her long, graceful neck.

It took Gareth much longer than anyone expected. Then again, Mikal was sure it was less than a minute. However, that was a full minute of watching Pravara continue to evade her pursuer. Mikal paled. He didn't want to know what this was probably doing to the young dragon. They had to break her out of this trance as quickly as possible.

He has reached her head.

Mikal blinked a few times and refocused his attention on Cylandria's head. There was Gareth, crouched low between the blue dragon's spiraled horns. He had placed both hands directly on her head, palms down, and was chanting. After a few moments he stopped and pointedly looked back at him. He mouthed something but Mikal couldn't hear it.

Your aural abilities are strong enough to be able to

hear what he said.

So you say. The fact is I didn't hear anything. What'd he say?

He said it wasn't working.

What! Why not?

He didn't say. He's trying again.

Mikal watched Gareth begin chanting again. He still couldn't tune his hearing to it. Gareth suddenly stopped, looked back at him, and sat back on his haunches. He helplessly held up his hands. Clearly his second attempt had been just as unsuccessful as his first.

He can't bring her out of it. Now what do we do?

We're still over the lake. Didn't Gareth say a splash of water should be able to break one of his trances?

Mikal eyed the passing water far below. *That'd work, if you could get her to dive in. Somehow, I don't think she will, not even if we both go diving into the water.*

Gareth waved his arms to get Mikal's attention. He clasped both hands in a pleading gesture and then jumped off Cylandria's head. Mikal was ready. This time he had a much easier time retrieving his companion.

"I'm sorry. I tried. I really tried. She wouldn't come out of the spell."

"Why not?" Mikal demanded. "I thought you said you could wake her up if we could just get you to her head."

"I don't know what the problem is," Gareth confessed. "I knew I was good but I didn't think I was that good."

"Modesty doesn't become you," Mikal harrumphed. Once more it came out as a growl. "What do we do? We have to wake her up before the Dragon Lord catches on to what we've been doing. I don't think our luck will hold out much longer."

In answer to Mikal's question, several things happened at the same time. First, Pravara cried out a warning, folded her wings tight against her back, and dropped away as quickly as she could. Next, a new voice sounded, which rose above the others:

Someone better catch him.

And lastly, a large red form appeared out of nowhere and dropped straight down on Cylandria, completely concealing the much smaller blue dragon from sight. It was Rhamalli. The gigantic dragon easily forced the two of them straight down, falling several hundred feet, to splash noisily into the lake. Mikal saw a small, hurtling form also dropping toward the lake. Pravara caught Pheron, Rhamalli's rider, before he could join his dragon in the water.

Rhamalli surfaced first. "I cannot begin to tell you how much I didn't want to do that."

"I'm glad you did," Mikal called down to him. "Thanks!"

Rhamalli lifted his great head out of the water to stare at him. "Who are you? I do not recognize you. Pravara, who is this? And where is your rider?"

"We'll explain later," Pravara assured him. "Where is Cylandria? Why hasn't she surfaced?"

Rhamalli frantically flapped his wings in a valiant attempt to launch himself out of the water, but to no avail without a firm surface to push from. He grew more agitated by the second.

"I've always hated the water," Rhamalli grumped. He eyed Mikal and Pravara circling high above his head. "Were you able to retrieve my rider?"

"I have him here," Pravara assured him. "He's safe."

"Good. I'd hate to think tha…" Rhamalli trailed off as he peered intently at the water and then gave his immediate surroundings a quick check.

"What is it?" Pravara asked. She passed directly overhead to see if there was something amiss.

"I get the distinct impression that I'm not alone in the water."

"An oskorlisk?" Mikal guessed.

Rhamalli gazed up at him. "Who are you? I've never seen a dragon your shade before. And what human are you holding? Pravara, what's going on? Explain to me why there's a dragon present who thinks an oskorlisk might live in this lake."

Mikal looked worriedly over at Pravara. *What's the matter? Couldn't it be an oskorlisk? Steve told me they live in the water.*

In the eastern sea, aye. Not in the lake. Be silent. I will handle this.

"He is a friend. He saw me trying to awaken Cylandria and came to my aid."

Rhamalli tried again to lift off from the lake's surface. Twenty seconds later he gave up and gazed again at Mikal.

"What is your name? Who is your human?"

I don't like lying, Pravara.

Let me think.

It's going to look suspicious if I don't answer. I could say ... wait, what's that?

What?

Mikal pointed a claw down at the water.

"You can see that, too, right?" Gareth asked, from Mikal's hand.

"Rhamalli," Pravara snapped. "Get out of the water. There is some type of disturbance behind you."

"It's probably Cylandria," Rhamalli stated, twisting about. He watched ripples forming on the lake's surface less than three hundred feet away. "I would still like to know how she became bewitched. Was it that accursed human wizard again? The Dragon Lord will not stand for this. He'll—"

Cylandria surfaced, sputtering, less than fifty feet away from Rhamalli. Confused, everyone turned to look back at the ring of ripples that were growing increasingly larger on Rhamalli's other side.

"What am I doing in the water?" Cylandria asked. She shook the water out of her eyes and tried to launch into the air, without success.

"You had become bewitched," Rhamalli informed the young dragon. "I don't think it'd be too difficult to ascertain who's responsible."

Cylandria raised her head up until she had spotted Pravara and Mikal circling high above her.

"You two need to get out of the water!" Mikal called down to them. "That thing next to Rhamalli is starting to move closer!"

"It's moving closer?" Rhamalli repeated, incredulous. He eyed the approaching ripples and bared his fangs. "There is nothing living in the lake that would dare challenge a single wyverian."

Cylandria turned to face the approaching ripples. "There are two wyverians here. I stand by your side."

Rhamalli grunted acknowledgement.

"There are four wyverians here," Pravara corrected. "We stand together."

A stream of bubbles erupted from within the center of the ripples. For close to four minutes the water churned and bubbled, as though there was a heat source directly beneath the surface. Just as suddenly as the ripples appeared, they vanished. The bubbles disappeared next. A thin, wispy black mist began erupting from that exact point. Instead of dissipating it started to coalesce along the surface of the water, twisting and undulating.

"Get out of the water," Mikal repeated, worried.

"I agree," Pravara added. "I don't like this nor do I trust it. Get out. Now!"

Rhamalli redoubled his efforts. Finally, after ten seconds of frantic flapping, Rhamalli rose, dripping water, from the surface of the lake. He turned to look back at Cylandria.

"You must move, young one. Now! I do not know what approaches us. Pravara is right. I don't trust this at all."

Cylandria tried again but right away Mikal could see that downward thrusts of her wings would not lift her from the water. He eyed the swirling black mist. It was now the size of a small fog bank and growing. He came to a rapid conclusion.

"Pravara, come on. We need to help her."

"What can we do?"

"We have to pull her up."

"From the water? While we're airborne?"

"Aye."

"I do not think that's possible."

"Well, we're going to find out. Hurry! That mist is getting closer to her."

"I might be able to do something," a soft voice muttered from beneath his belly.

"Not now, Gareth," Mikal quietly answered back. "We don't want to reveal your identity to them. At all."

"At the expense of what? That black cloud thing doing something to them? If it gets too close, I will help them.

They're here because of me, Mikal."

"I know. I appreciate it. If we can't get Cylandria out of the water in time, we'll have to take you up on your offer. Until then, don't say anything."

"Very well. I understand."

Mikal swooped as low as he was able. He saw that Cylandria was watching him closely, no doubt trying to figure out how he was going to get her airborne again. Pravara appeared next to him. Together they studied the prone dragon in the water.

"Here's what you need to do," Mikal told the exhausted dragon. "Pravara and I will circle around and come at you from the west. As soon as we get close, fold your wings flat and stretch your forelegs as high as you can. Pravara and I will each grab a leg. Do you understand?"

Cylandria nodded. Mikal cast a look at the swirling mist. It was no longer bubbling up from beneath the water, but it did look as though it was now coming together to form a strange shape. They were out of time. Whatever that black cloud was, Mikal wanted nothing to do with it.

He and Pravara flew west, circled about, and then picked up speed as they approached Cylandria's still form. Mikal briefly thought the young blue dragon had given up and slipped underwater when she suddenly broke the surface, kicking her legs frantically. She was only able to raise herself a dozen feet, but it was enough. Pravara swooped in from the left while Mikal took the right. They each grabbed a leg and furiously beat their wings in an effort to distance themselves from the strange dark cloud.

It didn't work. The best they were able to do was pull her through the water. Mikal and Pravara were simply too close together. He ended up smacking his wings into hers while she threatened to tip him over by the sheer power of her own beating wings. Pravara looked over at Rhamalli, who was staring at the black cloud that was slowly changing its shape.

"Rhamalli! We need your help. Hurry!"

Rhamalli blinked once and hurriedly approached. He eyed the three of them before sighing dejectedly. He reached into the water and pulled Cylandria's tail up, lifting her hind quarters completely out of the water. Together the three of them dragged Cylandria north, angling toward the closest shore. Ten minutes later all four dragons were standing on solid ground, collectively gasping for breath.

"Word of this deed must never be repeated," Rhamalli grimly told the group. "It must never be known that I carried another dragon by her tail."

"Nor do I wish it to be known that I was carried by my tail," Cylandria dryly added. "You have my silence."

"Did anyone else see it?" Rhamalli asked. He rose to his feet and looked back out at the lake. The black cloud was gone. "Did you see what it became?"

Pravara shook her head. "No, I did not. Mikal, did you?"

Rhamalli's head jerked back to their group. He stared at Mikal's purple face and blinked a few times.

"The human prince? You're the human prince? How is this possible? No, we'll deal with that later. Did anyone see what the black mist turned into? Pheron, did you?"

Pheron, back on his perch on Rhamalli's back, shook his head. "No, I'm sorry, my friend. What did you see?"

"The black cloud became a figure."

Pravara was interested. "Oh? What did it look like?"

Displaying a rare bout of nervousness, Rhamalli shook his head with disgust. "It formed a humanoid figure, but with the head of an equine and a claw that resembled a malwern's, but much larger. It was beckoning to us."

"The cloud," Mikal breathed. "Of course. The black mist. That must have been the Athanaus!"

Chapter 9 — Hello, Ugly!

What's an Athanaus?" Rhamalli wanted to know. He shook himself vigorously for several seconds. "Is that another name for a disquieting black cloud? And would someone please explain to me why I'm looking at a purple dragon?"

"Why *are* you here, Kre'Mikal?" Pheron asked, sliding down Rhamalli's flank. He approached the large purple dragon resting on the grass and looked up into Mikal's eyes. "What happened to you? Who is responsible for this? Does your father know what has happened?"

Mikal nervously cleared his throat. "I am here trying to keep the peace, Captain. I did not want my father to learn another dragon had become bewitched, so here I am. Pravara is doing the exact same thing. She needed help so I volunteered." Mikal cast a dark look down at Gareth, who chose that moment to count the number of leaves on the ground. "With Pravara providing a distraction I was able to sneak up on Cylandria."

"Rhamalli landing on her forced her into the water," Pheron reminded him. "That's what woke her up. That was my idea, by the way."

"And now I am drenched because of you."

Pheron grinned. "It worked, didn't it? My only concern is, how do we know this damned wizard hasn't bewitched a dozen more?"

"Oh, he hasn't," Gareth murmured, thinking his voice was quiet enough to not be overheard. He was wrong. Pheron rounded on him at once.

"What did you say? Who are you? Identify yourself."

Gareth, who had been sitting cross-legged on the ground, looked up at Mikal. A speck had appeared to the south and was rapidly growing larger. It was Pravara, returning from retrieving Lissa and Peanut. The corgi, overjoyed at being able to include other dragons in her pack, eagerly trotted from dragon to dragon, sniffing noses with each of them, as soon as her four stubby legs hit the ground.

"I really do like your dog," Gareth announced, dropping his eyes down to the frolicking corgi and patting her.

"Answer the question," Pheron demanded. "Identify yourself."

Gareth looked at the angry soldier and smiled helplessly. "I'm not supposed to say. I'm sorry."

"You will answer the question or you will suffer the consequences."

"Pheron, he's alright," Mikal interjected. "He's with me."

"Your Highness, why would he conceal his identity from us? He's untrustworthy. You can see it in his eyes."

Gareth frowned and his shoulders stiffened. He looked up at Mikal. "Are you tired of being a dragon?"

The hefty purple head nodded. "As a matter of fact, I am."

"Good. I've just decided I'm tired of hiding."

Gareth closed his eyes and started chanting. He drew a complex pattern in the air and snapped his fingers twice. Mikal groaned once and immediately began shrinking. His wings folded flat against his back and vanished. His arms and legs shrank back to proper human size while his skin lightened and reverted back to its healthy pink color.

The whole process took less than ten seconds. Mikal rolled unsteadily to his feet and sighed peacefully. He was human again and, truth be told, he wouldn't have it any other way.

Pheron coughed loudly and whipped his tunic off. He hurried over to Mikal's side and handed it to him. "You'd better put this on, Your Highness."

"Hmm? What's the matter?"

"You're wearing naught but your skin, Your Highness."

Mikal glanced down at himself and blushed bright red. With a look of abject horror on his face he glanced over at his girlfriend, who was returning his frank stare. The corners of Lissa's mouth had turned up in the beginnings of a smile.

Mikal hastily donned the captain's shirt. Thankfully the large tunic hung down to his bare knees. He glanced irritably at Gareth, who was trying his best not to laugh.

"I don't suppose the ability to conjure clothing is hiding somewhere in your bag of tricks, is it?"

Gareth chanted a few more lines. Tunic, pants, and boots appeared in the grass before them.

"They're mine," Gareth explained. "We're almost the same size so they should fit reasonably well."

While Mikal changed into his new set of clothes, Pheron approached Gareth and stared suspiciously at him. "I don't know how, because you're awfully young, but you're the wizard we've been looking for, aren't you?"

Rhamalli rose to his full height and growled menacingly. He looked threateningly down his nose at Gareth. Cylandria, exhausted as she was, also looked as though she was ready to take a bite out of him.

After a few seconds of silence Gareth nodded. "I am."

"You're the one who bewitched me?" Cylandria asked. "And you *dare* to show up here under false pretenses? I should bite you in half. You do know this, do you not?"

Gareth nodded again. "You'd be well within your right to do so."

Cylandria's eyes opened wide. She growled nervously and began inching away from him. "I trust this not. He's going to bewitch me again. I wish to leave!"

"The Dragon Lord must be informed," Rhamalli announced. "I assume you've already told your father, Pravara?"

Pravara shook her head no. "Not yet."

Rhamalli huffed out his chest to look intimidating, and Mikal had to agree that he did. "It matters not. This is a problem that can be easily rectified."

Pravara roared her anger. "The only one here who will inform my father will be me, Rhamalli. Is that understood?"

"Then do so, young one. Tell him. Right now."

"I will, but only in person," Pravara coldly responded. "I will *not* use the Collective to relay such important information."

Pheron cleared his throat and approached Mikal. "Kre'Mikal? Can I assume the human king, er, your father, doesn't know about this, either?"

"He knows we've identified the wizard but does not know we've found him. Captain, trust me on this. Gareth has pledged his support in dealing with the Athanaus. He's on our side now."

"And you believe that?" Pheron asked. He cast a disparaging look at the young teenager before turning back to Mikal. "He can tell you whatever you want to hear, Your Highness."

"You're right," Mikal agreed, drawing a scoff from Gareth, "he could have, only he didn't."

"I hope you're right, Your Highness."

"I'll tell my father just as soon as we tell Pravara's. We're closer to her father than mine at the moment."

"Actually, you're not," Rhamalli disagreed. "The Dragon Lord is still in R'Tal."

Mikal was shocked. "But sundown is less than two hours away! He's been talking with my father since sunrise?"

Rhamalli nodded. "Aye."

"That's right," Mikal nodded. "That being, the Athanaus, is what my father and Pravara's father are talking about. The fact that they're still talking tells me they have no answers."

"They need to know it has been sighted here in our valley," Rhamalli decided.

"How fast can you get us to R'Tal?" Mikal asked as he turned to look back at their large green friend.

"We'll be there before the sun sets," Pravara vowed.

* * *

"Tell me something, Gareth," Mikal said as they all walked across the drawbridge leading into the castle's western gate, "have you ever been a dragon before?"

Gareth nodded. "Just once."

"Why only once?" Lissa wanted to know.

"I could never master flying," the young wizard admitted with a smile. "It was too difficult."

"What?" Mikal sputtered. "You told me that it was easy and I just had to trust my wyverian body to know what to do. Were you lying?"

"I, uh, may have been exaggerating a teensy bit. What are you worried about? You did great! You're going to have to give *me* some pointers so I can try again later. Hey, listen, you aren't mad about that, are you?"

"What, turning me into a dragon without asking me first?" Mikal dryly asked.

"Yeah, that."

"Wow. You don't do sarcasm well, do you?"

And you do?

Hush, Pravara. No one asked you.

Mikal heard Pravara's laughter and chuckled. She did have a point. He wasn't the best at detecting sarcasm, either.

"I was, at first," Mikal admitted, frowning at the young wizard. Then he laughed out loud. "But you know what? That was probably the coolest thing I've ever done. I was flying!"

Lissa stopped walking and pulled Gareth to a stop. "Wait a minute. You just said that you had a hard time flying as a dragon. Is that why you kept bewitching them? Were you riding them?"

Gareth's face reddened. He dropped his gaze and refused to say anything.

"I'll take that as a yes." She handed Peanut's leash to Gareth. "Peanut seems to like you. Would you like to hold her leash for a while?"

Gareth's face lit up. "Sure. Thanks. Hey, little Peanut. Are you a good dog?"

Peanut had watched as possession of her leash switched hands. She yipped excitedly, turned around, and pulled on her leash. A plethora of interesting scents were beckoning her forward.

Mikal was lost in his own thoughts. He swallowed nervously. What would Pravara think about Gareth riding a bewitched dragon? What if ... Mikal suddenly cocked his head. He didn't know how, but he just *knew* that Pravara was smirking.

Of course, I am. Your wizard now owes me a favor, and a large favor at that.

What? Why?

Because if my father knew that Gareth had bewitched dragons just so he could ride them against their will, he would lose his mind.

"Pravara says that you owe her," Mikal quietly told Gareth as he led them into the castle.

"What for?" Gareth sullenly asked.

"It's probably for her to maintain her silence," Lissa guessed.

You are correct, Lissa.

Mikal slipped his hand into Lissa's and gave it a gentle squeeze, relaying Pravara's message. Lissa beamed a smile that could illuminate the darkest of rooms.

"Why would Pravara need to keep silent?" Gareth asked, genuinely confused.

"Because if the Dragon Lord ever found out you broke their rule about no dragon riders, and that you did so intentionally, then the consequences would be dire."

Extremely dire.

Gareth scuffed his feet along the floor. "I wasn't hurting anyone."

"What about today?" Mikal pressed. "Cylandria became bewitched and almost hurt Pravara. In turn, Rhamalli had to dunk both Cylandria and himself into the lake to snap her out of it. That's three dragons in one day, Gareth."

Gareth sighed and fell silent.

A burly man in his mid-forties appeared directly in front of them. He was nearly six feet tall, had thinning brown hair, and a bushy mustache starting to show a dusting of gray. "Lissa! What are you doing here? Shouldn't you be at home?"

Lissa hurried forward and threw her arms around him, giving him a fierce hug. "Father! You're never going to believe what happened to us today."

Fensham faced Mikal and bowed. "Your Highness. It is a pleasure to see you again. I am here, along with the other village constables, to request help from the castle, the loss of jhorun, you know. And now I can't help but wonder what my daughter is referring to. Would you care to enlighten me?"

"Oh, it's nothing, really," Mikal told him. "We just happened to identify the renegade wizard (Fensham gasped), found out where he lived (the constable gasped again), and we decided to bring him here. In fact, here he is. Gareth, meet Fensham, constable of Capily and father of Lissa."

Fensham's eyes widened with sheer terror. He took one look at the young boy, grabbed Lissa's hand, and yanked her toward him.

"Ouch! What are you doing?" She pulled her hand free from her father's and rubbed her wrist. "We're in no danger. Gareth is a friend now. He's here to help us."

Fensham eyed the boy, distrust evident in his eyes. "We'll see about that. Boy, you are the one responsible for all the mayhem?"

Gareth shrugged. "You could say that."

"I did say that. The question is, would *you* say that?"

"Aye. I didn't mean to hurt anyone."

Fensham turned to Mikal. "Your father needs to be informed at once."

"That's why we're here. Do you know if my father is still in the dragon cave? I was rather hoping he'd be done by now."

Fensham nodded. "Aye. The king, his senior advisers, and three dragons are all inside that cave. Ugghh. I wouldn't want to be down there."

"Why not?" Mikal inquired.

"My father is claustrophobic," Lissa whispered in his ear.

Mikal chuckled, "Oh." Then, in a louder voice, "I would have thought their meeting would have ended."

"They have much to discuss," Fensham said, sighing heavily. "How much do you know about the jhorun situation?"

Mikal pretended to nod thoughtfully. "Quite a bit, actually."

Lissa stifled a giggle.

"We asked the king what could be done. The last I heard was that he still didn't have an answer."

Mikal looked at his friends and nodded his head toward the door. He returned his gaze to Lissa's father and smiled. "Thank you, constable."

"I told you before that you may call me Fensham, son."

"Fensham. Right. I'll try to remember."

"Take good care of my Lissa."

Mikal looked back at the constable as he followed Lissa outside. "You can count on it, sir."

The entrance to the dragon cavern was located in the northern orchards. There, nestled amid groves of fruit trees was a large, almost perfectly circular clearing. The eastern side of the round hill dropped thirty feet before leveling off and extending another fifty feet before the groves of fruit trees resumed.

Pravara was there, talking with a dragon Mikal didn't recognize. This new dragon was roughly the same size as Pravara and was completely white. Everything was white, from the long-curved horns, to his wings, to the wing flap on the tip of his tail. He stood out in stark contrast to Pravara's dark green coloring. Also present were two squadrons of armed soldiers, standing stiffly at attention.

Pravara watched their small procession approach. "Mikal, Lissa, Gareth, this is Lorofer. He is one of my father's consultants."

Lorofer nodded politely to each of them. Peanut, never one to be ignored, gave a loud, piercing bark. Gareth quickly handed the leash back to Lissa. Startled, Lorofer looked down at the small creature and then back at Pravara. "You were not jesting. I never would have imagined a being so small could have emitted a noise so loud."

"Indeed," Pravara agreed. "She's quite harmless. The little creature is intelligent. She knows we have just completed introductions and she also knows she wasn't included."

Lorofer lowered his head and gently inched closer to the corgi. Peanut bounded forward, stopped less than a foot from Lorofer's massive jaws, and dropped into playful dog pose. The white snout slowly crept forward. Mikal could hear the white dragon inhaling, no doubt sampling Peanut's scent in an attempt to figure out what manner of creature she was. Just as soon as they were close enough, Peanut licked Lorofer's nose. Startled, Lorofer jerked his head away. The white dragon shifted his weight to one leg and used the other to run it along his nose.

"That was unusual," Lorofer decided. "However, not altogether unpleasant."

"Peanut is fond of dragons," Mikal helpfully explained. "She just welcomed you as a new member to her pack."

Lorofer nodded sagely, as if he knew all along. "Of course."

"We need to talk to my father," Mikal told the white dragon. "Actually, both Pravara and I need to talk to our fathers. Can we go down?"

"While spacious, the cavern will not hold another dragon," Lorofer explained, "which is why I am up here. Another will have to join me. A moment, please."

Thirty seconds later they felt the ground tremble. Several seconds after that, the second dragon emerged into the sunlight. This one, Mikal noted, was the same vibrant yellow found on local pontal. Mikal briefly hoped the dragon was female.

She is. That's Kalendra. She is liaison to the dwarves. Just for the record, you should know that there are several male yellow dragons, too.

Duly noted. Wait. Kalendra is the liaison to the dwarves? Then why is she here? There aren't any dwarves present.

Have you ever negotiated with the dwarves? As a people they are incredibly stubborn, highly temperamental, and quick to jump to conclusions. Kalendra's talent is defusing hostile situations.

However, it appears her skills are not needed here, so at the moment she is a bystander.

What about Lorofer? What's his role?

You may think of him as security.

Why isn't he down there protecting Kahvel?

Protecting my father from what? It's an enclosed cavern. Lorofer has already inspected the cavern and pronounced it safe. His skills are best suited up here, where he can guard the tunnel.

Oh. That makes sense. Shall we go?

Aye. After you.

Mikal took Lissa's hand and started down the tunnel. He kept an eye on Gareth, as if he expected their new friend to have a change of heart and vanish from sight, as wizards were wont to do. True to his word, Gareth remained by their side. His breathing was ragged, he had drops of perspiration trickling down his face, and he looked pale.

"Hey, we're right here with you," Mikal assured him. "I told you I'd put in a good word with my father. You've upheld your end of the arrangement so far. I will do the same."

"Thanks," Gareth whispered softly. "I don't think it matters. I think I'm going to be sick."

Lissa reached into one of her pockets and pulled out a plant. She pressed it into Gareth's hand. "Here. It's a type of spearmint. I was going to make a tea with this but I think you need it more. Chewing the leaves can help relieve nausea."

Gareth eyed Lissa's gift. The plant had square stems, opposite crinkly leaves, and emitted a slight menthol smell. He brought the harvested plant up for a closer inspection. "This will keep me from getting sick?"

"That's right. If you…"

Lissa trailed off, watching Gareth shove the whole plant into his mouth, roots and all. "Um, you only need a few leaves."

Gareth grunted and continued to chew.

They emerged into the subterranean cavern. Mikal blinked with surprise. Lorofer was right. There wasn't room for four dragons. Kahvel and a second dragon, one that was a deep maroon color, were on the far side of the cavern. They were each resting on the ground and facing the small group of humans. Mikal spotted his father, Commander Rhenyon, and three other high ranking castle officials sitting at a table that had been erected in front of the dragons. Mikal assumed they were in the middle of a debate since each side was talking at the same time.

"It felled three dragons without lifting a hand!" Kahvel growled. His fangs were bared and his eyes had narrowed to slits. "Every drop of jhorun had been drained from their bodies."

"What is it, you use the jh…" Kri'Entu trailed off as the newcomers entered the cavern. The entire cave fell silent.

Kahvel's great golden head turned toward the new arrivals. "Pravara. I'm assuming you have a significant reason for this interruption?"

Pravara nodded. "I do, father. However, my news correlates with Mikal's, so I think he should be allowed to go first."

If a dragon had an eyebrow to raise, then Kahvel would have done just that. The Dragon Lord looked at Kri'Entu and inclined his head. The king slowly stood, prompting the rest of men at the table to follow suit.

"Son, what is it? Has something happened?"

Mikal took several steps forward and nodded. "Aye. I'd like to introduce you to someone. Father, this is Gareth, my new friend. Gareth, this is my father, Kri'Entu. Standing next to him is Commander Rhenyon, followed by three of his closest advisors, Aleric, Ondo, and Jacobi."

His father's bloodshot eyes flicked momentarily over to Gareth's before settling back on his.

"You made a new friend. That's nice, Son. Is there anything else?"

Mikal frowned.

"I thought you'd be more excited than that."

"That you made a friend? You're not a child any more, Son."

"You shouldn't tease your father," Lissa quietly scolded. "It isn't nice."

Kri'Entu heard her. "You're teasing me? Is there

something I should know about this boy?"

Mikal put a reassuring hand on Gareth's shoulder and pushed him forward a few steps. "I thought you'd like to meet the renegade wizard you've been looking for."

The air went utterly silent. Kahvel reacted first. In less than a second, he whipped his long neck around and brought his head to within three feet of Gareth's. "You? You are the one responsible for attacking my dragons?"

Mikal quickly stepped in front of Gareth and held up both hands. "I know what you're thinking. You need to hear the whole story before you leap to conclusions."

"Conclusions?" Kahvel snapped. "There are no conclusions, only facts."

The king approached and stared hard at the trembling youth, then looked back at Mikal.

"You're sure, son? This is the wizard?"

"Pretty sure," Mikal conceded. "He turned me into a dragon a few hours ago."

"What?" His father looked angrily at Gareth. "You turned my son into a dragon?"

"We needed to do it," Mikal explained. "Pravara needed help to break Cylandria out of her trance."

"What?" Kahvel snapped, stepping forward again. "Another of my brethren has fallen victim to this wizard, this *boy*?"

This isn't going well.

Tell me about it.

"Cylandria has already been taken care of," Pravara told her father.

"Gareth is only the partial reason why we're here," Mikal told his father. "You don't need to worry about him. What we need to worry about is the Athanaus. Father, we saw it."

A collective gasp went up. Everyone, including the dragons, were on their feet and staring as if the Athanaus had just joined the meeting. Mikal was about ready to ask them to calm down when his father pulled him into a hug. "Tell me you are alright. Tell me it didn't touch you, son."

"I'd like to tell you that I wasn't close enough to be worried, but I was."

His father's expression became stern. "Mikal, what were you … how did you escape?"

"It was easy. I happened to have a set of wings on me when I saw it."

"You were a dragon then."

"Aye."

The king looked over at Gareth, who had been silently observing them. As soon as Gareth knew he was the one being watched, he dropped his gaze to the floor.

"We made a deal, Father," Mikal quietly explained. "His father is missing. We're all guessing that he's dead but I told him that I would look into it if he'd help us figure out what to do about this Athanaus."

"He's just a boy, Son," his father pointed out. "What could he possibly do to help?"

"Just a boy? Father, he turned me into a dragon. He created a wind storm strong enough to uproot trees and prevent an aerial attack. He created a rock golem in less time it takes for me to put on a pair of boots. And this was all done earlier today, by the way. He's way more powerful than Shardwyn will ever be."

"And more reckless," his father quietly observed.

Mikal grunted. "Probably. We need his help, Father, just as he needs ours. Oh, and I, er, made one other concession to him."

"Oh? Why do I get the impression that I am not going to like this?"

"Because you probably won't. He wants a new house."

His father's eyebrows shot up. "Does he now? Why in the world would you agree to that, Mikal?"

"He's trying to look out for his family. He and his mother live with his aunt. They don't have a house of their own."

"Oh."

"It could be any house, Father. Just make sure it has glass in the windows."

"What?"

"Their windows don't have any glass in them."

"Ah. I see. I will consider it."

"I don't need you to consider it, Father. I need you to

agree to it. For me."

His father was silent as he considered.

"You wanted me to take more responsibility," Mikal persisted. "That's what I'm doing."

"Very well," the king said, raising his voice for all to hear. "His past transgressions will be overlooked."

Gareth smiled with relief.

"Provisionally," Kri'Entu added.

Gareth's smile melted away.

"My son is right, Mister Gareth. We do need your help. If you are as powerful as he says, you could be a tremendous help."

"Will you assist me in finding my father?" Gareth timidly asked.

"I will honor my son's deal. You help us deal with the Athanaus and I will exercise every power at my disposal to attempt to locate your father, be he alive or dead. Once this Athanaus creature has been dealt with, then we'll talk about your new house. Do we have an accord, Mister Gareth?"

Gareth took a deep breath and nodded once. "We do."

"You are more trusting than I," Kahvel dryly observed, once Kri'Entu looked up at him. The Dragon Lord lowered his head, looking Gareth straight in the eye. "You may have made your peace with the human king, young wizard, but you have yet to deal with me."

Gareth swallowed nervously. "I know. I'm sorry for everything I did."

"You wish to atone for your actions, human?"

I smell a trap.

Mikal looked over at Pravara. She was staring straight at him.

What was that?

My father is up to something.

"Aye." Gareth's quiet answer could barely be considered a response. He cleared his throat and tried again. "Aye. I don't want anyone mad at me."

"Then this will be our accord. You will work with my dragons to teach them how to resist being overcome by spells such as yours. Is that understood?"

"But it doesn't work that way," Gareth stammered. "I used a potion before."

"Are you saying there is no precaution against a trance?" Lissa asked, coming to Kahvel's aid. "There isn't anything that could negate the effects of a potion?"

Gareth thought for a moment. "Well, I guess it's possible. There are a few methods, but they would have never known how."

Lissa smiled and placed a hand on each of Gareth's shoulders. She gave him a firm shake. "That's what he's talking about. He wants your help in making sure it doesn't ever happen again."

Kahvel gazed appraisingly at her. "Correct, young Lissa. That is precisely what I said."

Mikal noticed the flush creeping back into his girlfriend's face. He looked over at Gareth and nudged him in his ribs.

Gareth finally nodded. "I accept. I'll teach you what I can."

Satisfied, Kahvel grunted. "We have an accord. Now, tell us what you know about the Athanaus. What did you see?"

Mikal recounted the events earlier in the day, starting with their discovery of the loophole in the census and finishing when he explained how they had dunked Cylandria in Lake Raehón.

"This mist emerged from within the lake," Kahvel mused. "Interesting. That's the second reference to water. Could it be hiding within the water?"

"Possibly," Kri'Entu decided. "However, if it's now living or hiding within Lake Raehón it would explain why Verdayn is experiencing the increased loss of jhorun. I do not like knowing how near it is to that village. I do not want a repeat of what happened in Capily."

"My dragons are closer and more at risk," Kahvel pointed out. "So what do we do? We have sighted the creature only twice, and each time my dragons had all the jhorun drained from their bodies when they tried to attack."

"Will it regenerate?" Lissa asked, forgetting she was addressing the Dragon Lord. "Will a dragon's jhorun regenerate like a human's?"

Kahvel nodded. "Aye, only it takes far longer to completely recharge."

"How long?" Kri'Entu asked.

"Nearly a month, if not longer."

Kri'Entu turned to Gareth. "Mister Gareth, you're the wizard here. Do you have anything to contribute?"

Gareth shoved his hands into his trouser pockets and slowly paced in front of the dragons. He was softly mumbling to himself as he walked the length of the cavern.

"Where's Shardwyn?" Mikal whispered to his father. "Shouldn't he be here?"

"Shardwyn is indisposed."

Mikal groaned softly. "What did he do this time?"

"A little accident in his tower. He turned his beard blue and grew another set of arms. He's a little self-conscious about his appearance at the moment."

Lissa stifled a giggle. Mikal stared at his father with wide, unblinking eyes. "Tell me you're kidding."

"I wish I could, Son. Shardwyn told me he was trying to replicate a shifting potion, which would have transformed himself into an ant. Apparently, he's lost something important and feels it may have slipped down inside a crack in the floor."

Gareth walked by. "Turned part of himself blue? Grew an extra set of appendages? He mixed up the dosage of zuneik and mistook cedell for theerest. It's a common mistake."

Kri'Entu gave Gareth an appraising look before turning back to his son. His eyebrows had lifted and he actually smiled. Relief washed over Mikal. Thankfully his father's reaction to the renegade wizard was finally starting to look favorable.

"This Athanaus can't be killed?" Gareth asked, passing by again.

"Correct," Kri'Entu answered.

"And we know it escaped from some type of prison?"

"Correct again."

"Where?"

"Somewhere off the coast of Capily," the king answered.

"Where *specifically*? If we can't kill it, we must get it back inside its prison. Then we have to figure out how it got out so it doesn't do it again."

"And how would you propose we do that?" Kahvel asked, bemused. He had already posed this question several hours before.

"I say we go inspect the dungeon where this thing was held."

Kahvel's mouth snapped audibly shut. Whatever he was expecting to hear, that wasn't it.

"We don't know where that was." Kri'Entu turned to the wyverian leader. "Didn't you say the original source of information was the water dragons?"

Kahvel nodded. "It was. What's your point?"

"The first village to report the loss of jhorun was Capily, on our western shore. Water dragons must live in the area. That's where we look."

Kahvel reluctantly nodded. "There are about eighty water dragons living in that area," the Dragon Lord quietly acknowledged. "Please keep that to ourselves. They would never forgive me if they knew I revealed their numbers and location."

"It stays with us," Kri'Entu vowed.

"How does this knowledge help us?" Kahvel asked. "What are you planning? The answers you seek lay hundreds of feet below the surface."

Kri'Entu sank back down in his chair and reached for a piece of parchment. He opened a bottle of ink and began to write. "I will task Shardwyn with finding some way to communicate with the water dragons. If he's going to stay cooped up in his tower, then the least he can do is something useful. There must be a way."

Gareth stopped his pacing and looked over at Mikal. He mouthed something to Mikal, who instantly nodded. "Father? We have an idea."

Kri'Entu looked up. "Oh? Go ahead."

Mikal nodded at Gareth, giving him permission to speak. "Wouldn't it be easier to go down there and take a look for ourselves?" the young wizard asked.

The king stared at Gareth as though he had lost his mind. "And how would you propose we do that? We believe the floor of the Erudian Ocean to be anywhere from four hundred feet deep to well over five thousand."

Gareth looked over at Mikal and grinned. "It's easy. We become water dragons ourselves."

Chapter 10 — A Whole New World

"That? That's your big idea? You want to turn me into a water dragon? Didn't you have enough fun at my expense the last time you turned me into a dragon?"

"We need to know where that mist thing was held and how it got out," Gareth explained, raising his voice and looking around the room as if daring someone to challenge him. "This would be the most logical thing to do."

"By turning my son into a dragon?" the king sputtered. "I like this not, Mister Gareth."

The young wizard turned to Mikal's father and shrugged. "I'm just trying to help. You wanted my opinion, remember? Well, that's my answer."

"Have you turned someone into a water dragon before?" Mikal hesitantly asked. He looked at his newest friend and saw an eager gleam in his eyes. Mikal sighed. "I'd like to think that you have, but something tells me you haven't."

Gareth shook his head. "I haven't, no. But I will say that I've always wanted to try."

"Try what? Turning someone into a dragon?" Mikal groaned aloud. "If you're going to experiment on somebody then it really ought to be you first."

Gareth was silent as he considered. He eventually nodded, "I see your point. Very well. I'll go with you."

"My son isn't going anywhere," Kri'Entu flatly decreed. "Especially not as an aquatic dragon. It's out of the question. I'm sure Shardwyn will be able to come up with something."

Mikal surged to his feet, "Shardwyn? Father, we don't have that kind of time!"

"I know his credibility is waning," Kri'Entu began, "but I'm confident that, if given enough time, he will prevail."

Mikal shook his head. "Time is a luxury we don't have, Father. We need to see what's down there, how the Athanaus was imprisoned the first time. That could tell us how to imprison it again. We need information. This would seem to be our only viable option. I'm sorry to say we can't wait for Shardwyn. I will agree to go."

"Mikal, no!" Lissa exclaimed, pulling him to face her. "You're going to let him turn you into a water dragon? Are you insane? You don't know what's out there. For all we know, the Athanaus could be waiting out there to ambush you. No, it's way too dangerous."

"I forbid this, Son," Kri'Entu proclaimed, agreeing with Lissa. "The risks are too great. A journey into the depths of the Erudian Ocean would be fraught with peril. You would be on your own. We will have to think of something else."

"I know of no other option," Kahvel confided. "The longer we wait, we give the Athanaus more time to lay siege to our people. We must act swiftly before another settlement is targeted, be it human or wyverian."

Kri'Entu leveled a gaze at the Dragon Lord, "That's easy for you to say. How would you feel if Pravara wanted to put herself in that kind of danger?"

Kahvel gave the approximation of a wyverian shrug, "I concede the point. However, I'd like to think that if the situation were reversed and it was Pravara volunteering to place herself in danger, then I do believe I would be more open minded than you are."

The king folded his arms across his chest and tried to stare down the immense golden dragon, "Oh, really?"

"Well, I'm sure I can include her if she really wants to go," Gareth helpfully added.

Everyone turned to the young wizard.

"If I can turn a human into a water dragon then I know I can turn a winged dragon into the water variety. Actually, come to think of it, I think it'd be easier."

All eyes swiveled to the Dragon Lord's. Kahvel was staring hard at Gareth. Twin tendrils of smoke drifted up from each nostril.

Smiling, Kri'Entu looked up at the leader of the wyverians, "You were saying?"

Kahvel stared, unblinking, at Gareth for a few moments longer before finally looking back at the king. A growl formed but was quickly quelled.

"There's no proof that this simple human boy has the power to change one form into that of another."

Gareth's eyes traveled up Kahvel's long golden neck until he had locked eyes with the Dragon Lord. He cleared his throat. "And if I could? It sounds like you wouldn't have any objection to her joining us, would you?"

The entire group waited with bated breath for Kahvel's answer. "Very well. I did say I would be more open minded than Kri'Entu. I agree. If the human king agrees to allow his son to be transformed into a water dragon, provided it can be done, I will allow Pravara to do the same."

Why in the world was my name dragged into this?

Mikal stifled a smile. *Don't blame me, blame our fathers. My father isn't pleased about me being changed into a water dragon, and...*

And you think mine is?

That's the point. Look at your father. It looks as though he's ready to bite Gareth's head off, and I don't mean that figuratively.

I'm inclined to let him.

Anyway, to answer your question, I think my father would secretly like you to accompany me in order to keep watch over me, as annoying as that is.

What did I ever do to him?

Nothing. I think he was trying to make a point.

And that point is to allow the two of us to be shifted into water dragons?

And Gareth, too. I think he wants to go. In fact, he has to. He's the one who needs to see where the Athanaus was held prisoner.

Be advised. Your father just asked you a question.

Mikal's head snapped up. "Did you say something, Father?"

"Aye. Mister Gareth says he can have the shifting potion ready by tomorrow morning. We will now return to the castle so you can prepare yourself for tomorrow."

"I understand."

I guess I'm going to be a water dragon tomorrow.

My father just broke the news to my mother, Pravara admitted. **We are indeed going together.**

Has he even asked if this was okay with you?

It was more of an offhand 'are you okay with this' question. I told him I was.

Thank you. I'm glad you'll be there.

You're welcome. Just so you know, I didn't do it for you.

You didn't? Why did you agree to go?

To earn my father's approval.

What did your mother say about all this?

She wasn't thrilled about placing me in danger but she does understand the severity of the situation.

Well, until tomorrow!

Until tomorrow.

* * *

"I still don't think it is a good idea," Lissa said the following morning.

A small crowd had gathered at one of the many piers scattered across Capily's waterfront. Two giant three-masted galleons floated serenely on the calm waters while several dozen much smaller vessels were mired nearby. There was room for dozens more vessels, of all shapes and sizes, but thanks to the cooperation of the weather, most were in use. Fensham was there, holding his daughter's hand. Peanut was also there, whining, as she pulled at the leash in Lissa's other hand.

"There, there, Peanut," Lissa soothed, squatting down to drape an arm over the corgi. "Mikal will be back before you know it."

Unconvinced, Peanut shot Mikal an imploring look and continued to pull on her leash. Mikal dropped to one knee and stooped low in order to draw a hand through the water. He stared up at Gareth, who was silently watching him. "I sure hope you know what you're doing."

Gareth waved off his concerns. "You worry too much. All I had to do was modify my shifting spell by changing the destination environment. Then I had to—"

Mikal tuned the boy out as he described all the aspects of the spell that had to be changed. To him it wasn't worth the hassle, but to Gareth, who assured him he could see the changes in his head, it was. True to his word, it had only taken the young wizard two hours to modify the spell.

Shardwyn, intent on watching the young wizard at work, had wandered by Gareth's temporary quarters no fewer than ten times, lingering in the doorway, moving off only when the young boy glanced up. Each time, Gareth caught a glimpse of an elderly man wearing a hooded cloak. Growing concerned, Gareth had contacted Mikal, who tried to pull Shardwyn into the room but was only able to grab a handful of puffy white smoke following the elderly wizard's rapid departure.

"It was Shardwyn," Mikal had explained. "I think he's curious about what you're doing."

"Then why hide?"

"He probably hasn't figured out how to lose the extra arms he grew during his latest botched potion attempt."

"Ah."

Having concluded his elaborate explanation about his shifting spell, Gareth looked around. "We seem to be missing a dragon."

"You seem to be just as unobservant as ever," Pravara's dry response came.

Gareth whirled around. Behind the crowd of people was Pravara, both wings folded flat, she was resting comfortably on the ground. At the sound of her voice every person turned to look back toward the village. Every human, except for Mikal and Lissa, gasped with shock.

"Do all you dragons move about this quietly?" Gareth asked, amazed.

"When we want to. Do you know how you're going to change us into water dragons? Do not be concerned if you cannot. No one will think less of you for trying."

"Trying? Please. I have it ready right here. And it's a spell, not a potion. There will be no chance of us reverting to our air-breathing forms until I invoke the counter-spell."

Mikal nodded. "Smart. I hadn't even thought of that."

"My shrinking potion wore off once Pravara washed herself in the water. The last thing I wanted was to be hundreds of feet below the surface and suddenly find that we have lungs instead of gills."

"Gills?" Mikal repeated, frowning. "You're giving us gills?"

"How else are you going to breathe underwater?" Lissa asked, trying valiantly not to smile. "Your body will need oxygen. You have to get it somehow."

"I didn't think that far ahead, okay?" Mikal grumped.

Gareth stepped to the pier's edge and looked down at the murky water. Mikal joined him, and they watched a half dozen kytes floating languidly on the surface. Alerted by the presence of the dragon, the fluffy birds rose into the air, several of them relieving themselves on the way up. Mikal eyed the small floating piles of kyte excrement as they slowly dissolved.

"That's nasty."

Gareth shrugged.

"Doesn't that bother you? We're going to be swimming in that."

"They pooped on the top. We're going down below."

"Gareth, look at it. It's dissolving."

"So?"

"It means it's mixing with the water. That's gross!"

"If you go swimming, you have to be willing to look the other way," Lissa told him as she appeared on his left. "I usually choose a secluded spot to swim. I know what's in the water, but I choose to not let it bother me."

Mikal paled and swallowed nervously. This was not his idea of fun. Gareth grinned and looked back at Pravara, who was silently watching.

"Is everyone ready? Who wants to go first?"

Mikal glanced back at Pravara, who inclined her head as if to say *be my guest*.

"I may as well get this over with," Mikal remarked. "What do I have to do?"

Gareth pulled three small clay figurines from one of his pockets. There were two small humans and one larger figure of a dragon.

"Sorry. These figures aren't modeled to scale but I think you'll see where I was going with this."

Mikal picked up one of the small human figurines and studied it. It was about two inches high and had incredibly realistic details carved onto its features. Hair, facial features, crude outfit, they all looked like him! He looked at the other figure. This one had longer hair, was thinner, and had a knapsack slung over his right shoulder. Just like Gareth did now.

"These represent us?" he asked the wizard.

Gareth nodded, "Sorry. They aren't very good. I was in a rush last night."

"You carved this last night, in addition to creating the shifting spell?"

"Carving time was included in the two hours. Be quiet. I'm trying to concentrate."

Gareth's eyes closed and he fell silent. He picked up the figurine resembling Mikal. His lips began to move as he silently chanted. Mikal looked at the third figure. It was a dragon, and clearly had been carved to resemble Pravara. The figure was standing majestically on all fours and had both wings slightly extended, as if she was in the process of either folding her wings against her back or else was preparing to take off. Two spiraled horns protruded from her brow while the dragon's tail was wrapped protectively around its feet.

"I never stand like that," Pravara noted.

Mikal turned to see that the large dark green dragon had moved up quietly behind him. He held the small figure of the dragon up so that its much larger counterpart could get a better look. "It's not bad, is it? He's a pretty good carver."

Pravara grunted noncommittally. Mikal turned to hand the dragon figurine back to Gareth when he caught sight of his own hand. It had started swelling, just like a balloon. He turned to Pravara and opened his mouth to ask a question when all of a sudden, he began having difficulty breathing. It was happening!

Mikal clawed at his neck, trying to fight off the frightening feeling. His body continued to swell as large bumps formed all over his skin and rapidly grew into scales. His clothes peeled away as his torso lengthened, thickened, and then lengthened some more.

Mikal gasped for air. He couldn't breathe. He tried to stand but found that his body refused to cooperate. He made another gasping noise and instinctively reached for his throat. This time he tried to clear any obstacles away from his neck but got the distinct impression that his throat was now much farther away than his hand and it would never be able to reach it. He tried twisting to see for himself what the problem was. Off balance, Mikal toppled onto his side and flailed about helplessly. His eyes stung terribly so he closed them.

"Get him into the water!" Gareth snapped. "Hurry!"

Something rammed into his stomach, propelling him off the pier and into the cold murky saltwater of the Erudian Ocean. He quickly sank out of sight.

Deeper and deeper he fell until, at once, his senses recovered. He opened his eyes and blinked a few times. He took a deep breath and felt a cool tingling sensation near where he thought his stomach should be. He blinked again. What he saw had him gaping with astonishment.

Everything was crystal clear.

A school of fish zoomed by, swimming in circles above his head. Each tiny fish sparkled radiantly as it swam in and out of the sunlight filtering down from the surface. The playful school of fish pulsed and throbbed, as if it were alive. A grouper, easily the size of a normal human man, entered his peripheral vision and lazily swam by, small in comparison to himself. Mikal stirred, stretching his unfamiliar muscles. The grouper flicked its tail and disappeared in a swirl of phosphorescent algae. Mikal could actually trace the path of the grouper by simply following the glowing line. It reminded him of the huge mechanical birds high up in the sky, back in Steve and Sarah's home world. He reached for the glowing blue trail but frowned when he realized his arm was so short that it could barely extend far enough to scratch his other arm.

A loud thump caught his attention. He craned his neck to view the water's surface. It was churning and bubbling. He should investigate. His first instinct was to kick with his back legs, but discovered they were disproportionately small, of no use to swim. Remembering what Gareth had said the first time he became a dragon, he instructed his body where he wanted to go.

Mikal felt as though he had begun swaying from side to side, yet his tiny arms and legs remained inert. He was undulating back and forth, as serpents do in water. Mikal shrugged. If this is how water dragons swim, then so be it.

As he ascended, Mikal discovered that the neck of a water dragon was similar to its airborne brethren. He was able to bend his neck completely around and inspect his own body. Mikal grinned. Water dragons were incredibly cool!

This wingless body was smaller than the winged version, much more like a serpent than any other dragon he had ever seen, including the rare two-headed zweigelans. At least the winged dragon Gareth had turned him into when they were trying to break Cylandria out of her trance actually looked like a dragon. This one looked more like a snake.

What color was he? A deep ocean blue? No, more of a dark sea-green. It was difficult to tell in the dim light. Granted, it was getting brighter and brighter the higher he swam, so maybe he should wait to address that question as soon as he broke the surface.

His long, serpentine neck rose gracefully out of the water

and he stared at the silent spectacle before him. There were people lining the shoreline. There was Pravara. He blinked a few times and noticed his vision began to blur.

Mikal? Are you well?

Pravara sounded concerned.

I'm fine, Pravara. This is weird. Much weirder than being a winged dragon, but you know what? I think I'm enjoying it. I don't know what's wrong with my eyes. The longer I'm up here the blurrier everything becomes.

Dip below the surface. Your eyes are drying out. After all, you are a water dragon now.

Ah. Got it.

Mikal dunked back into the water and felt his stinging eyes clear. He extended his neck and again looked at Pravara.

I think this is the coolest thing that I've ever done. Promise me you won't tell Gareth I said that.

Your secret is safe with me. Speaking of which, Gareth's about ready to change me, too. Do you have any advice?

You'll be swimming just like a serpent. Don't fight it. Tell your body what to do and it'll do it.

Understood.

How is it that I'm able to stick my head out of the water? Shouldn't I be suffocating, like I was earlier?

Pravara leaned her head out over the water's edge and inspected Mikal's new form.

No. As long as you don't extend your neck any farther out than you already have, you should be fine. Do you see those slits on either side of your abdomen? They are three feet long and there are two on either side. Those are your gills.

So, that's what that feeling was earlier. I thought I felt something tingle down there. It must have been when I breathed in water for the first time.

Mikal noticed that Lissa had tapped on one of Pravara's claws to get her attention. He wasn't able to tell what she said as his vision had become too blurry again. He quickly submerged back into the water to clear his eyes and surfaced once more.

Did she say something to you?

Your mate wanted to know if you were alright. I assured her that you were. She says she'll wait in the village for you at her father's office.

Perfect.

She says that you are very brave for doing this. How would you like me to respond?

Oh, uh, I don't know. Tell her that I'm doing this for her. Girls usually like it when their boyfriends do something heroic.

Pravara mouthed something to Lissa, who then turned to face him with a look of sheer adulation in her eyes. She looked back at Pravara and said something else.

What did you tell her?

Exactly what you asked me to tell her.

Did she say something else?

Aye. She said she loves you.

Mikal paled. His jaw fell open, revealing a nasty set of wicked fangs.

Pravara turned to Lissa and said something else. Lissa looked back up at the huge dragon Mikal had become and blew him a kiss. Gripping Peanut's leash tightly in her hand, she turned to walk with her father back to his office.

What did you say to her?

You didn't ask me to say anything else to her.

Yet you said something. What was it?

Just that you loved her back.

What? I never said that!

But you do, don't you?

Even if I did, I'd want to say that to her myself.

Have you?

Have I what?

Told her you loved her?

What? Pravara, what business is that of yours?

I may not be proficient on human customs, but typically if the human female says those particular words to a human male, shouldn't the human male say it in return?

We'll talk about this later. Are you ready to get in here or not?

Aye.

At a sign from Pravara, Gareth picked up the tiny dragon figurine and nodded his readiness. Pravara immediately launched herself high into the air, tucked her wings, and dove headfirst into the dark blue water. By the time she surfaced her transformation was complete.

A second serpentine neck appeared in the water and gently swayed beside his own. Mikal eyed Pravara's new form. She was yellow. It wasn't a bright shade of yellow but rather a diffused softened shade, like a yellow shirt that had been left out in the sun for too long. Her chest, Mikal noted, was a salmon color. Pravara saw that she was being watched. Her lips moved as she said something to him. The soft trills he heard had an elegant grace about them. What startled him the most was that he could understand her.

I miss my wings, Pravara said.

Mikal snorted. *Trust me when I say you won't miss 'em in here.*

A splash sounded nearby. Both Mikal and Pravara whipped their heads around to stare at a rapidly disappearing trail of bubbles. A moment later, a third serpentine neck rose gracefully out of the water. This one was covered in shiny black scales from top to bottom. Even the scales on its chest matched the rest of its body, making it resemble a long black tentacle. Mikal scoffed. His new body responded by growling.

Really? You make yourself jet black while we have to be blue and yellow?

I couldn't help it, Gareth sheepishly answered. *Black is my favorite color.*

How's it possible that we're able to talk to each other? Mikal asked. *I didn't know I could speak 'water dragon.'*

Gareth gave him a condescending look. *We are water dragons now. We're speaking a language that only they can understand. Look at Lissa and her father. They cannot understand us just as we cannot understand them right now.*

Will we be able to speak to each other once we dive underwater? Mikal asked.

I'm not going to dignify that with a response.

If we are done comparing scale colors, may we go? Pravara dryly asked. Her vision must have become blurred because she had started to rapidly blink her eyes. All of them had.

Mikal pulled his neck underwater and twisted about until he was facing straight down. Even with his heightened vision he was unable to see the ocean's floor. The color of the water faded from azure blue to inky blackness.

How far down does it go? Mikal wondered.

Unknown, Pravara answered. *Let us be off.*

The three companions warily eyed each other and dove straight down. Almost immediately they swam straight into each other and became entangled. Their heads smacked together. Twice.

Whoa, watch what you're doing, Mikal growled, noticing his tail had become entwined with Gareth's.

You first, Gareth countered. *I was swimming in a straight line.*

You couldn't be. That's what I was doing.

Pravara managed to disentangle herself first. *Getting used to these new bodies will take some time. We must learn the nuances of water dragon locomotion if we expect to be successful with this quest.*

You swam into us, too, Mikal reminded her.

I am aware. Mikal, you take the right, I'll swim in the center, and Gareth will take the left. Are we agreed?

Mikal swam over to Pravara and settled in on her right while Gareth took the left. Pravara nodded approvingly. *Shall we try this again?*

Side-by-side the three newly shifted water dragons slowly descended into the murky depths of the open ocean. Mikal was amazed. Of all the places he had visited across the kingdom, and there were many, nowhere did he see more wildlife than during their descent.

A school of medium-sized bright red fish zipped by and stopped nearly a hundred feet away. The writhing mass of fish paused, as if giving Mikal a cursory glance. A few moments later it darted off, leaving a trail of bubbles as the only indication it had been there.

The deeper they went, the darker it became, yet the water was teeming with life. Ahead, there appeared a massive cloud of sediment, but on approach they were startled to learn that it was a gathering of thousands of tiny silver minnows. As they reached the border of the cloud, the school of fish practically exploded. Thousands of tiny fish went in thousands of different directions, leaving the water as clear as Mikal had ever seen it.

I guess they don't like water dragons, he mused.

Water dragons are probably the top predator in this area, Pravara answered. She had quickly perfected the side-to-side swimming technique and was making it look as though she had been doing it for years. *It's no wonder the native wildlife is giving us a wide berth.*

Is anyone else worried about the lack of light? Mikal wanted to know. *I'd say in about ten minutes it's going to be too dark to see.*

Pravara's head turned as she noted the levels of light in the water.

I assumed that this form would be able to see in the darkness. Every dragon I know can, although I will admit that I do not know any of our cousins in the water.

And if we can't? Gareth asked. *What then?*

What are you asking us for? Mikal demanded. *You're the wizard here. Can't you conjure some light for us to see by? Wouldn't that work?*

I can easily conjure a fireball but that wouldn't work too well down here, would it?

I'm not talking about a fireball, Mikal argued. *I'm talking about anything else that would give off light.*

Let me think about it.

Think fast, Mikal pleaded. He eyed the inky blackness he and the others were heading toward and swallowed nervously. He took a deep breath, which brought a rush of water flowing over his gills. He sighed with contentment. The ice-cold water was both soothing and refreshing.

Even if Gareth wasn't able to conjure light and they had to explore the depths of the ocean in darkness, Mikal wouldn't complain. This was the adventure of a lifetime. He couldn't wait to tell Steve and Sarah about his experiences as an aquatic dragon. He looked back where the water was lighter, and above, toward the surface. Lissa was up there. She was waiting for him.

She had said she loved him. Those simple three words had originally filled him with panic, but as he swam with his two companions, in utter silence, he realized that being loved by a girl wasn't that bad at all. In fact, not that he'd ever admit it, he was glad Pravara had relayed the messages.

He took another deep breath and felt more of the cool, refreshing water flow across his gills, sending tingles up and down the length of his body. Invigorated, he urged his body to swim faster, propelling himself ahead of his companions. Just then a dark brown rotund fish about the same size as his water dragon hand rose up from within the heart of the blackness and swam straight toward his open jaws. Mikal was certain the stupid thing was going to swim right into his mouth. At the last moment it veered away.

Mikal flinched, closing his eyes and bracing for the worst. A series of lights danced before his eyes. Surprised, he snapped them open and was greeted by the growing blackness. What was it he had seen?

Mikal closed his eyes once more. Nothing happened at first, but after a few seconds the lights returned. There were tiny sparkles of light everywhere! Sarah would have loved it. Mikal remembered Sarah had a fondness for the sparkly dust she called glitter. So, was this underwater glitter? Why couldn't he see it when his eyes were open?

Mikal cracked an eye open and was met with an inky blackness so complete that he could barely perceive his two companions swimming next to him. He closed his eyes and waited for the lights to return. There they were! He glanced over at Gareth. Gareth's serpentine form could easily be discerned swimming amongst the swirling specks of light.

That is so cool! You guys gotta try this!

He described the view. Gareth protested for a moment, then tried it.

I see your point, Pravara said, after a few seconds passed in silence. *I did not think this form had a parietal eye but clearly it does.*

A what? Mikal asked.

A parietal eye. It's a concealed third eye used in the absence of ambient lighting. It is highly sensitive and can detect the tiniest traces of light, even when you think none are present. That's how we dragons can see so well in our caves.

Pravara and Mikal both felt Gareth's mirth. Then he felt Pravara's ire. She didn't like being laughed at.

Dragons have three eyes? Gareth asked, still mentally

chuckling. *Is that what you're telling me?*

Until this moment I would have said only winged dragons possessed the hidden eye. Thanks to this experience I now know water dragons have it, too. Makes me think land dragons might also possess a parietal eye.

Whatever it is, Mikal began, *and however we got it, I don't care. I'm glad it's there. I was starting to worry.*

Not me, Gareth haughtily informed them. *I knew we'd be able to see.*

You did not!

Did so.

No way.

It's true!

You wish.

That's enough you two, Pravara scolded. *There's no need to argue. Does it really matter who believed what, and when?*

Aye, Gareth and Mikal said in unison.

You may argue to your heart's content just as soon as we are all finished, Pravara grumped. *And I don't have to listen to it.*

Satisfied he had got the last word in, Mikal glanced over at his new friend. The black form Gareth had become blended almost perfectly with the water. Without the help of the parietal eye, as Pravara had called it, he wouldn't be able to see him at all.

Mikal looked down at himself and watched his body move rhythmically through the water. He couldn't begin to imagine the power necessary to create a spell which could shift a person's form from one to the other. How had Gareth learned how to do it?

Gareth, can I ask you something?

Sure. About what?

Spells.

Alright. What do you want to know?

I always thought spells were spoken out loud.

They usually are, the wizard agreed.

Then what was with those carved figurines? Weren't those talismans?

Talismans? No. Those were spells, too.

Are they different types of spells?

The figurine performs the exact same spell as if I spoke it aloud.

How?

I think I see where you're going with this. A spell is an incantation that the caster says out loud.

Mikal nodded. *Right. That's what I've always thought.*

The carved figurines are just objects I imbue with the power and properties of the spell.

Now you lost me.

A spell can be a word, or phrase, or a combination of words that utilizes jhorun to make something happen.

Mikal grunted once by way of acknowledgment.

In this case, once I created the shifting spells, I then tailored each one for our own personal use. One for me, one for you, and one for Pravara. However, that was last night. We weren't ready to go last night. So, I carved those figurines and imbued the properties of the spell into the figurines so then all I had to do to activate the spell was invoke the figurine. Think of it like creating the arrow to be fired by the bow.

Oh! I get it now. I just thought the spell had to be spoken in order for it to work.

Gareth gave him a piteous look. *What did you think those figurines were? Toys?*

Don't look at me like that. I don't know much about your jhorun or how it works, alright?

They swam in silence for another twenty minutes until Mikal noticed a temperature drop in the water. He looked at his two companions to see if either of them noticed. If they had, they gave no indication that they cared.

Does anyone else think that using gills to breathe is better than using lungs? Mikal asked companionably as they dropped deeper into the depths of the ocean. *I can feel the water flowing through my gills. I can feel the water getting colder, and it doesn't bother me. I can taste the water getting saltier, and it doesn't bother me, either. I'm not sure why some water tastes saltier than others but it just does.*

Salinity, a new voice answered. **The deeper you go, the more the pressure builds, therefore the salt content increases.**

Who's there? Mikal looked left, then right, and then back behind them. *Who speaks?*

What are two humans and a winged dragon doing in my realm?

Pravara stopped swimming and looked suspiciously about. *You know our true nature? How? Who are you?*

There was a disturbance directly in front of them. Something was coming up from the depths of the ocean, and it was enormous. Judging from the amount of sediment this creature was kicking up, Mikal guessed the owner of the voice was easily three times their size.

It was a water dragon, an actual denizen of the deep. He was a deep violet color, almost black, but not as dark as Gareth. Thanks to the iridescent shimmer sparkling all across the water dragon's sleek form, Mikal knew this new dragon looked way cooler than they ever would.

As Mikal stared at the large form, he was startled to see that the water dragon was missing scales here and there. There was also a twenty-foot section on his torso just under his front left leg where the scales didn't line up properly. Was it a scar? Had he been injured in some type of battle?

Yes, to both questions, human.

I'm not a human at the moment, alright? How could you tell I'm not a real water dragon?

Would you have any difficulty spotting a newly transformed griffin trying to pass itself as a human?

Probably not, Mikal admitted.

It is the same here.

Who are you? Mikal wanted to know.

Are you friend or foe? Gareth cautiously asked.

I am Fernius. I will be your guide for the duration of your visit.

Mikal was incredulous. He shared a look with Gareth. *We've been assigned a guide? How did you even know we were coming?*

Fernius looked straight at Pravara. **I was notified by a winged cousin. Perhaps you've heard of him? Kahvel?**

That's my father! Pravara stammered. *He asked you to look out for us?*

Look out for you? Fernius repeated, confused. **No, my duties are only to guide. Your *father?* Your father is the aerial king?**

He is known as the Dragon Lord, Pravara corrected.

Whatever, daughter of the aerial king. Two humans

masquerading as one of us. Are you still curious why you have a guide?

Tell me something, Mikal began, hoping to change the subject. *Are all water dragons as big as you are?*

Big? I like you, human. I have never been called 'big' before.

You mean there are others larger than you?

You may find this disturbing, but the three of you are the smallest shealk I have ever seen.

Shealk?

Aye. Shealk. You probably refer to us as simply water dragons. Calling one of us a water dragon would be the same as one of the shealk referring to a human as a biped.

Surprised, Mikal nodded, *Got it. You call yourselves 'shealk'. I'll make sure I tell my father.*

Your father? Are you son of the human king?

Aye. I thought you knew?

Fernius' eyes shifted and they pinned Gareth. **And you? Who are you?**

I'm Gareth. I am, um…

He's a friend of mine, Mikal finished quickly. *He's here to help me figure out how the Athanaus escaped its prison.*

Ah. I was wondering when you surface dwellers would come inquiring about that creature.

What do you know about it? Mikal asked their shealk guide. *We saw it briefly when we flew over Lake Raehón.*

It emerged from within the water like a cloud of black mist? Perhaps it took a form of some sort?

Aye! Mikal answered excitedly. *I saw a horse head and a large claw.*

I saw almost exactly the same, human prince.

Where was it held? Gareth asked. *Was it somewhere close?*

No. The prison is located far from here, in waters much deeper than this. Should you choose to follow me, there are a few things you must know.

Mikal and Gareth nervously eyed each other before looking over at Pravara.

Go on, Pravara urged.

In waters that deep, you three will feel the effects of the immense pressure and cold. Your parietal eye will be of little use.

Gareth needs to see where this thing was held. We're hoping to get an idea how to get it back in there.

Your plan is doomed to failure.

Mikal scowled. *I'm really starting to hate it when people tell me that.*

Why is it doomed to failure? Gareth asked.

Because it took twenty of our strongest warriors, and three shealk wizards, to seal that abomination in its prison in the first place.

What! Mikal breathed, shocked. *The shealk are responsible for capturing the Athanaus the first time?*

AYE.

Wizards? Gareth repeated, homing in on the one word that had caught his attention. *The shealk have wizards?*

Now Gareth had Pravara's attention. *The shealk had wizards?* she repeated, amazed. *My father never told me that.*

***Have** wizards,* Fernius corrected. **How else do you think we drove the creature into its prison?**

I thought I heard that the Athanaus predates the wyverians, Mikal recalled. *Does that mean the shealk came before the aerial dragons?*

Of course. Those who grew tired of living in the sea crawled out of the water and acquired lungs. And wings.

How? Gareth demanded.

Using jhorun. How else?

So, if I understand you right, the shealk imprisoned the Athanaus the first time. Couldn't they do it again?

No.

Why not?

Because there is only one shealk wizard left, and he was the first victim of the thriper after it escaped.

Chapter 11 — Didn't See That Coming

Mikal remembered the passage his father had read from the thin book from the Archives. A thriper was a formidable enemy. *That's just great*, Mikal grumped, inadvertently baring his considerable fangs. *The only one with a chance of recapturing the monster has been incapacitated.*

Can you tell us what happened to the shealk wizard? Pravara gently asked. *Is there any hope of recovery?*

Fernius shook his head, **No. The thriper drained every last drop of jhorun out of his body. Only recently has he started to physically recover. His jhorun, I am sorry to report, has been lost forever.**

Thriper? Gareth repeated, confused. *Do the shealk call this monster a thriper?*

That's what this monster is, Mikal answered. *I heard my father call it by that name.*

Pravara swam close and nudged Mikal with her tail. *Will*

your jhorun work on a shealk?

Mikal tried several times to shrug but ended up looking like he was suffering from a nervous tick. *I wish I could say, Pravara. I've never met any shealk before today so I have no idea.*

Mikal started to turn back to the much larger shealk when Pravara nudged him again. *Does it work on non-humans?*

I really don't know, Mikal confessed.

What is your jhorun? Gareth asked. *Is it something powerful?*

My jhorun has been the subject of debate for years, Mikal answered. *I always thought it was the ability to enhance other jhoruns. I could take someone's jhorun and amplify it greatly.*

That isn't the case now? Gareth asked, intrigued.

Well, a few years back a new aspect of my jhorun manifested. I learned that I could give jhorun to someone who didn't have any.

Fernius blinked with surprise and faced Mikal.

A moment, if you please. You said that you're able to bestow jhorun to whomever you want?

Only if they don't presently have any. I've given jhorun back to a few people who had theirs stripped from them by hostile enemies.

And it worked? the shealk excitedly asked.

Well, aye. It just wasn't the same jhorun as before.

Clarify, Fernius demanded, growing suspicious. **What do you mean by that?**

The jhorun I can give isn't the same because every example of jhorun is different from every other. My mother had her jhorun taken from her when she was abducted, a number of years ago. I applied my own to hers, and she was much happier with her new one.

Are you saying you could return our wizard's jhorun but it might be different than what he's used to?

Mikal gave his large sea-green head a violent shake. *Absolutely not. I never said that it would work. What I'm trying to tell you is that I'm willing to give it a try.*

Satisfied with Mikal's answer, Fernius began swimming straight down. He looked expectantly at the three of them. **Based on what you told me before, I assume you'll be following me?**

Are you taking us to where the Athanaus was held?

Correct. Call it a thriper. To give it a different name suggests it should be feared.

Well, I'm afraid of it, Mikal admitted. *You said it yourself. It sucked every last drop of your wizard's jhorun. That's reason enough to be scared.*

Such a human thing to say.

Then it's a good thing we're human, Gareth mumbled under his breath.

How long will it take us to get there? Mikal asked.

At least an hour, perhaps longer.

Great, Mikal grumbled.

* * *

You're sure?

Aye, I'm sure.

There can be no doubt, Gareth. I need to know.

Mikal, I already told you. There's no chance the spell will wear off. Remember what I said just before we shifted? I'll have to invoke a counter-spell before we can shift back to our normal forms.

You can't fault me for being nervous, Mikal explained. *I'm used to unorthodox work ethics and unreliable results.*

Allow me to venture a guess, Gareth began.

No, he gets that enough without my help.

Gareth snorted while Pravara ignored them. She had caught up to Fernius.

You did say that you are our guide, right?

Aye.

Then talk to us. Tell us about our present location. How is it you can see in the total absence of light? What's your secret? How is it you can see so clearly?

Jhorun.

Aren't you worried about attracting the Athanaus?

Stop calling it that. It's a thriper, nothing more. And no, I'm not.

Why not?

If the thriper appears, all I have to do is to outswim the three of you.

Gareth and Mikal joined Pravara and stared uncomprehendingly at the huge shealk. Mikal frowned. *You'd really leave us out here to fend for ourselves if the Ath... the thriper appears?*

It was a joke, human. I made it to lessen your discomfort. You should really learn how to relax.

Lissa tells me that all the time.

Who is Lissa?

She's —

...his mate, Pravara interrupted.

Why is everyone so eager to call her my mate? Mikal asked in a fit of exasperation. *There's no purpose to it.*

I'd say if the purpose of it is to make you blush and feel uncomfortable, Gareth nonchalantly remarked, *then it's working.*

Shut up.

Gareth laughed, but his laughter died off as the last of the glowing algae vanished from the water. Even with their third eye it was now so dark that they were effectively swimming blind.

The three newly christened shealk came to a stop. Their shealk guide grudgingly halted his descent and waited for them to catch up.

We're close. Don't stop now.

But we can't see anything, Fernius, Mikal told him.

Fear not. I can.

But we can't see you, either! Wizards be damned, Gareth. And I do mean that. Are you not a wizard? Can't you do something?

Let me think about this.

Why not gift yourself with nocturnal vision? Pravara suggested. *If I were to venture a guess, I'd say that's how Fernius can see where he's going.*

Nocturnal vision, Gareth muttered. *Let's see. It's not nighttime, but if I alter the active time and substitute the current time, and then omit the part about the absence of the sun since the sun is out, then I should be able to do it.*

The sun isn't out down here, Mikal pointed out.

But it is out, Gareth contradicted. *Be quiet. I need to concentrate.*

What is he doing?

Our friend is an aspiring wizard, Mikal told their shealk companion. *If anyone can figure out how to help us see down here it will be him.*

Gareth looked over at Mikal and nodded his head.

Thanks.

Don't prove me wrong.

He is a wizard? A shealk wizard?

I realize that's how it looks at the moment, Fernius. Just remember he's a human, not a shealk. A human wizard.

Another shealk wizard. How remarkable.

I just said he isn't a shealk wizard, Mikal argued. *Stop addressing him like he is.*

The large shealk swam close and pointed a small claw at Gareth's prone form, forgetting that Mikal wouldn't see the gesture.

He is a wizard and right now, he is a shealk. That would make him a ...?

Human wizard, Mikal stubbornly insisted.

One second he was swimming in absolute darkness and in the next it was as though someone had opened the drapes on a sunny day. Mikal turned to look at his companions. Both Pravara and Gareth were studying their surroundings, as though they were seeing the watery environment for the first time. Mikal shook his head. In this case, it was true.

Mikal looked down. The ocean bed was less than a hundred feet away. A thick blanket of seaweed and marine plant life covered every square inch of the ocean floor. Mikal was also surprised to see that the ocean floor wasn't flat. In fact, there were valleys and hills everywhere. Further out, he could see a chain of underwater mountains.

Directly below him was a gently swaying sea of thick green plants spreading out in all directions. It reminded Mikal of the dragons' valley. However, it was very easy to spot any irregularities as one's eyes skimmed over the tops of the plants. He had instantly noted a tall, slender object projecting almost straight up from the floor, rising to a height of at least thirty feet. A dozen feet away in opposite directions were a second and third, only these two spires were somewhat shorter than the one in the middle.

They're masts! Mikal excitedly told the others. *It's a shipwreck!*

I wonder how long it's been down there, Gareth wondered aloud.

Fernius swam to the closest mast and struck it with his thick, powerful tail. It trembled under the assault but didn't move.

I'd say a year or two. Had it been here longer than that, it would have splintered and broken.

Where was the thriper's prison? Mikal asked.

Fernius swam over to a nearby mound of rocks and circled to the opposite side, facing due south.

It is here.

Mikal swam toward the hill when he noticed he was the only one doing so. He turned to look back at Pravara who, in turn, was looking back at Gareth.

What's the matter? Pravara was asking. She started swimming back to Gareth. As she neared the black shealk, Gareth sank lower and started nosing about on the ocean floor.

What are you doing? Mikal called. *We're here. The prison is right over there. We've come all this way. Don't you want to check it out now?*

There's something here, Gareth told them, surprising them all. *I'm feeling a pull coming from somewhere around here. Don't ask me how I can do it. I can just sense whenever jhorun is nearby.*

The three other shealk joined Gareth as they stared down at the seaweed-covered ocean floor.

If there is, how do you propose you find what you're searching for? Trying to find an object lost on the ocean floor is virtually impossible. It could be covered by seaweed, or sediment, or possibly resting underneath another object.

Gareth continued to gaze down at the swaying green floor when he flicked his tail to move closer, reached down with one of his front claws, and sank it into the soft soil the tall seaweed was growing in. When his claw came back up his companions saw that he was clutching something. Even though the object was covered in a brown and green film, Mikal could tell that it was a shield.

It probably came from the ship, Mikal guessed. *It's just a shield, Gareth. What's the big deal?*

Gareth studied the shield in his webbed claw. As delicately as he could, he wiped the back of his other claw across the shield's surface, clearing away layers of accumulated grime.

I've seen this shield before.

Mikal looked over at Pravara and held her gaze a few moments before he turned back to his friend. *You have? When?*

I'm not sure. I just know I've seen it before.

Maybe it'll come back to you. Come on. We've come this far. Let's see where the Athanaus was held.

Thriper.

Whatever.

Gareth dropped the shield and joined his companions as they swam toward the small hill that Fernius had pointed out. On the southern side of the hill was a jagged gouge in the ocean floor— twenty feet long and perhaps ten feet wide. A closer examination suggested something had desperately clawed its way out. They could see large pieces of the ocean floor, which had been the roof of the prison, were brutally ripped apart.

Pravara swam up to the jagged hole and peered inside. *This is where it came from, no doubt about it. There's a large cave inside. I see broken rock littering the floor.*

Mikal and Gareth joined Pravara and looked inside the Athanaus' former prison.

Are you ready? Mikal asked their wizard companion.

You first.

You're the wizard. It should be you!

You're older.

Fine. I'll go.

If you two are done bickering, may I point out your companion has already entered?

Mikal and Gareth stared. Sure enough, they could see Pravara's long tail quickly disappearing into the darkness.

There's only room for one other in here, she reported back.

Two shealks, one dark green and the other jet black, lunged for the opening at the same time. Both became wedged inside the small opening.

I'm the wizard, Gareth protested. *It should be me!*

Trying to conceal his victorious smirk, Mikal wriggled his tail for several minutes before he came to an unpleasant realization. He had no idea how to make his shealk body move in reverse.

What are you doing? Gareth demanded. *Get out of the way! You go back and I'll go forward.*

Easier said than done. I can't make myself go backwards.

What are you talking about? Gareth sputtered. *Of course, you can.*

Oh, yeah? Let's see you do it.

Watch and learn.

Gareth gave it a full five minutes before he admitted he was just as helpless as Mikal. Fernius approached and took the tip of Mikal's tail in his teeth.

You are the most pathetic excuses of shealk I have ever seen.

He gave Mikal's tail a quick tug, yanking him out of the hole.

Now, get going. I do not wish to linger around here.

Mikal watched as Gareth ducked into the opening and vanished.

You have a most unusual companion.

True, Mikal admitted.

Is he really a wizard?

Well, I'm really a human. That should answer your question.

Is he young by human standards?

Aye. He's a few years younger than me. He's fifteen.

Who are his parents?

What? Why do you want to know that?

His gift is atypically strong.

How would you know? Have you met many human wizards?

Fernius settled to the ground and studied Mikal. **If I have, would you be surprised?**

Mikal eyed the huge purple shealk and nodded. *Aye. I would. You'd have some explaining to do.*

Not to you, I wouldn't.

Have you?

Have I what?

Met many human wizards?

One or two.

How? When?

That does not concern you, human prince.

Gareth and Pravara reappeared.

It isn't that big, Gareth began, as soon as Pravara had exited the cave. *There's no real sign of anything ever having been in there, except for some serious clawing at the entrance.*

It appears to be a natural cave, Pravara added.

That's right, Gareth confirmed. *I couldn't find any evidence of enchantments or spells.*

What does that tell us? Mikal wanted to know.

That perhaps the Athan ... I mean the thriper was asleep and something woke it up. Once it did, it wanted out.

Fernius, from his position nearby, grunted once. The three smaller shealk looked over at him and waited, wondering if Fernius was going to say something. When he didn't, Mikal and Pravara turned back to the jagged opening in the ocean floor.

Perhaps we should...

Your wizard companion is leaving.

What?

It would appear that Gareth is going back for the shield, Pravara explained. *Come. I wish to see what he's doing.*

They followed Gareth back to the spot where he had dropped the shield. He had picked it up once more and was silently studying it. Mikal tried to cough in order to clear his throat but the only thing he heard was a quiet rumble coming from deep within his chest.

Fine. I'll ask. Gareth, what's with the shield? Is there something we're missing?

The answer is here, Gareth told them. *This shield has been enchanted. I can sense the jhorun within it. Will you come with me? I want to explore that sunken ship. It's the only logical place this shield could have come from.*

The four of them swam over to the remains of the ship. Surprisingly, it was resting upright, having apparently sunk in calm waters. The ship's hull, while mostly intact, was covered with barnacles. A huge gouge stretched almost the length of the boat, and well below the water line, suggesting the boat had run afoul of rocks. Mikal figured it must have sunk amazingly fast to have dropped straight down without tipping over, as sunken ships typically did.

Gareth swam over to the huge gouge and looked inside at the boat's interior. He stretched out a foreleg as much as he could and felt around inside the jagged hole before pulling his leg back out.

Did you feel anything?
Not a thing. This arm is too small.
Use your tail. It's much longer.
My tail? You think I can grab something with my tail and figure out what it is?
What are you searching for?
I don't know. There's something in there that's emanating jhorun. I can sense it, just like I did with the shield.

Fernius swam over to the side of the ship and placed his eye next to the serrated opening so he could see within the ship's hold. With a grunt he spun around and carefully inserted his long supple tail into the hole. Not to be undone, Gareth did the same.

Can you feel anything? Mikal asked.

No, Gareth automatically answered.

Aye, was Fernius' response.

Mikal moved closer. *You found something? Already? What is it?*

Fernius withdrew his tail from within the ship's bowels. The tip of his long flexible tail had coiled around a two-handed broadsword. The large shealk deposited the sword at Mikal's feet and reinserted his tail into the ship. Twenty seconds later he withdrew it once more, bringing out a small sack.

What's in there? Gareth asked, giving up on getting his tail to replicate what he had seen Fernius' tail do.

Mikal poked a talon at the sack and gave it a quick jerk, ripping it to shreds. A stream of gold coins flowed out, sinking into the thick bed of seaweed.

Do you think it's a treasure ship? Mikal guessed.

Can you tell us anything about that weapon? Pravara asked.

Gareth nodded. *This weapon has been enchanted, just like the shield.*

Enchanted to do what? Mikal asked.

How do you know this? Pravara pointedly asked, at the same time.

Because I'm the one who enchanted them, Gareth quietly answered. *I remember now. This was from a group of weapons I was asked to enchant several years ago. Those men paid well, so I made certain that the swords wouldn't break, the shields couldn't be pierced, and so on.*

So, what happened to them? Mikal wanted to know. *How'd they end up down here?*

More than likely the vessel was caught in a storm, Pravara guessed.

I'm responsible for this, Gareth whispered. His jet black shealk body sank slowly to the ocean floor. *I'm the reason the Athanaus escaped.*

How? Mikal countered. *Did you see any of those weapons in the cave? Did it look as though the Athanaus—*

Thriper, Fernius gently corrected.

…used one of those shields to dig himself out? Mikal continued, ignoring Fernius' constant corrections. *No. Why? Because he escaped on his own.*

I believe your wizard companion. He is responsible.

Gareth groaned as Mikal rounded on the much larger shealk.

You don't know that for certain.

Look at the facts. The thriper is attracted to jhorun. A ship sinks nearby, carrying enchanted weapons. Enchanted with jhorun. It's easy to see what happened. The proximity of those weapons awakened the thriper and, once it was awake, it escaped.

Why in the world would you enchant weapons for a bunch of strangers? Mikal asked as he turned back to look at the black form of the wizard.

They paid me well, Gareth recalled. *My aunt's house needed work. The roof leaked. The chimney needed new mortar. Neither my aunt nor my mother could afford the price for the labor and materials. That job paid two hundred gold grifs. I took care of all the details, allowing my aunt to think she had won some type of lottery and therefore had the funds to fix our home. Not all of us are born into luxury, Mikal. I had to do what needed to be done to help my family.*

That's the first thing you've told me that I could relate to, Mikal confided. *No one thinks less of you for doing what you did.*

Good, because I'm not sorry.

However, Mikal continued, *if Fernius is right, the presence of those weapons woke up the thriper. The question is, how do we get it back in there?*

The better question would be how we are expected to keep it in there, Pravara added.

Luring the creature back into the prison will be easy. It's attracted to jhorun. We have a wizard amongst us. It'll come looking for him.

Are you talking about me or your own wizard who has lost all his jhorun? Gareth asked.

You, young wizard. Our wizard is bereft of jhorun. You, however, will be too tempting a target to ignore.

That's just swell, Gareth grumped.

Can't we just kill this thing? Mikal suddenly asked. *Wouldn't it be easier than trying to trap it and seal it back up?*

That would be my suggestion, too, only …

Only what? Gareth prompted. *Finish that sentence, please.*

… I don't think it's possible.

Why not? Mikal asked.

Think about it. That thriper has been imprisoned for a very long time. Long before I was hatched, I might add. The fact that it was imprisoned, rather than destroyed, suggests it either cannot be done or it is more difficult than anyone expected.

So now what? Mikal looked at his companions. *There has to be a way to take care of this once and for all.*

I agree. I would recommend we consult Lord Phaedren.

Who's Lord Phaedren? Mikal asked. *Is he your king?*

Fernius nodded. **Phaedren is lord over the water as Kahvel is lord over the air.**

Does he live far away? Pravara asked, growing nervous. *Do you think Lord Phaedren will see us?*

I should think so. Follow me.

The three companions held back to converse privately.

Did you think there would be a chance we would meet their Dragon Lord? Pravara asked, casting a worried glance at Fernius. *What if we say the wrong thing and anger the shealk? What if we end up ruining relations between our two species?*

Hey, I have just as much at stake here as you do, Mikal pointed out. *Your father is the Dragon Lord, so you're the representative for all aerial dragons. I, on the other hand, am the son of the human king, so I get to speak for all humans. I really wish my father was here. He'd know what to do and would be able to say all the appropriate things.*

Well, he isn't, Gareth haughtily informed him. *You're the prince, Mikal. Haven't you ever watched your father conduct official business as king?*

Well, yeah.

And you've seen what he does when there's a visiting dignitary, right?

Yeah, I guess.

No, there's no guessing. You already know what to do. Make your father proud. And that goes for you, too, Pravara. You've no doubt seen your father in action. Stop worrying about what to do or say and let it flow naturally.

That's easy for you to say, Mikal growled, hurrying to catch up to their large shealk guide, who was threatening to leave them behind if they didn't pick up the pace. *You don't have to worry about screwing up and embarrassing your family.*

Every time I cast a spell, or create an enchantment, I pretend my father is with me, by my side. Just once I'd like him to look straight at me and tell me he's proud of me.

I promised I'd help you find out what happened to your father, Mikal reminded him. *I meant it.*

Thanks, Mikal.

Thirty minutes later they encountered a second shealk. Mikal had lost all sense of direction. This new shealk was slightly larger than Fernius, had thin, somewhat curved horns that angled straight out from his skull, and was several shades of blue. The top half of his body was a deep dark blue which gradually brightened as it approached the lower half of his body.

Who's that? Mikal whispered to Pravara.

Unknown, she answered. *I didn't see him approach.*

Neither did I, Gareth confessed.

I must leave you now. I have been called away. You are in good company. He will see you the rest of the way.

You're leaving? Mikal asked. *How come?*

As much as I'd like to see the outcome of this particular meeting, I have been assigned duties

elsewhere. Farewell.

Fernius flicked his tail and zipped away. Mikal had no idea a shealk could swim that fast. Could he do that if he tried? It sure didn't feel like it. He was rapidly tiring and it was becoming increasingly difficult to keep up with their guide.

How much farther is it? As I'm sure Fernius told you, we're not really shealk, and weren't prepared for a long journey. I don't know how much farther I can go. Pravara and Gareth are probably as tired as I am.

Their guide had briefly slowed as Mikal explained their plight, then quickly picked up the pace.

I know we're in a rush, Gareth grumped, *but I was really hoping to have a chance to rest my tail.*

You're over exaggerating your movements, Pravara informed him. *That's why you're tiring too soon.*

You're telling me you're not tired? Gareth asked incredulously. *You've been swimming as long as we have.*

No, I'm not tired. I would not say no to a brief pause, for your sake, but I can continue.

We are almost there, their guide's brusque voice cut in. **You may rest when we arrive.**

Do the shealk have their own city? Mikal quickly asked, anxious to see where and how a shealk lived.

Do the aerial dragons?

That is a good point, Pravara admitted. *We don't, so that must mean the shealk do not, either.*

What's your name? Mikal asked, adopting the friendliest manner he could muster.

Their guide remained quiet, aside from a low hum that almost felt like a growl.

I never would have thought Fernius would be the talkative one in the bunch, Mikal whispered to Gareth. Pravara overheard and suppressed a chuckle.

Sometime later Mikal tasted a difference in the water. He looked all around. Several hundred feet above his head he could see the surface of the water. He hadn't realized they had been ascending. He nudged Gareth and indicated he should look up.

I was wondering about that, Gareth whispered. *I think it might be time to cancel my nocturnal vision spell. Are you ready?*

Mikal and Pravara both nodded. The ambient light faded. Mikal closed his eyes and waited for his vision to switch to his parietal eye. As before, he started seeing tiny swirls of light. It was enough to adequately see where he was going. He looked over at his companions and saw that they, too, were looking around with renewed wonder.

Have I told you how glad I am you're here?

Gareth turned to look at him. *Are you talking to me or Pravara?*

Both. I'm glad you're both here.

Gareth's black head nodded once in acknowledgement.

As long as we're being honest, I am glad both of you are here as well, Pravara confided.

Would you three like a minute alone so that you may profess your love for each other?

Their guide had stopped swimming and was now in what could be considered an underwater mesa. It was ringed with rugged rocks and had small subterranean mountains on all sides except where they'd come from. Mikal looked up and saw that several of the rock formations jutted up out of the water. Perhaps the explanation for the wrecked ship below. He also noticed that it was now bright enough so that he could resume normal vision.

There, waiting for them in the direct center of the small underwater valley, was a shealk of such a dazzlingly bright red color that Mikal briefly wondered if he might have been a shealk-shaped ruby. Each scale sparkled in the filtered sunlight as the shealk's body gently swayed back and forth, as though it was swimming in place. Mikal saw the glittering red head shift as it watched their procession approach.

Do you think that is Lord Phaedren? Pravara quietly asked.

If not, then I say he could be a damn fine candidate, Mikal decided.

Of course, it is Lord Phaedren. Do not speak unless spoken to.

Their guide stopped far short of the ruby shealk's location and indicated that the three of them should continue on. As Mikal, Gareth, and Pravara settled into place directly in front of the silent red shealk, Mikal sensed there were others nearby. Mikal glanced once at the cool, calculating eyes that were studying him intently, before he lifted his head and scanned the area.

As if on cue, four more shealk swam into view. Several of them were the same sea-green color as Mikal, while a third was completely white and a fourth was a deep, rich blue.

Greetings, humans. Greetings, cousin. I am Lord Phaedren, master of all you see. Who are you? Why are you here?

Mikal's head lifted. *I am Mikal, son of Entu and Callé.*

The human prince. I know of you. You are welcome here, Mikal.

Mikal nodded as Pravara gently inclined her head.

I am Pravara, daughter of Kahvel, aerial Dragon Lord, as I've heard him called here.

I know of you as well. The great deeds of your father have reached even my ears, young Pravara. You are welcome here.

Gareth inched forward. He fixed Lord Phaedren with a neutral stare and gently bowed his head, as he had seen Mikal and Pravara do.

I am Gareth, son of…

At the mention of Gareth's name, Lord Phaedren immediately growled and looked over at their uncommunicative guide, who was resting nearby on the mesa floor.

How is it this human has your name, Gareth?

Mikal, Pravara, and Gareth exchanged shocked looks before all three of them, as one, turned to stare at the blue shealk resting quietly a hundred feet behind them. He refused to meet any of their eyes.

Because, My Lord, he is my son.

Chapter 12 — Shealk Shock

Would you like to run that by me again? That can't possibly be right. There's no way that my father is a shealk. He's a human, as is my mother. Do you know what that makes me? A human, plain and simple.

The large blue shealk who had guided them in pushed off the ground and drifted closer.

Except you're not, my son. I always knew we'd see each other again; however, I never thought it would be under these circumstances.

Gareth placed himself directly in front of their guide and gave him a long, hard look.

If you're my father then you'd know what happened to me three years ago at the start of summer.

Are you referring to your period of depression after your defeat at the hands of the fire thrower? Or are you referring to the blacksmith's daughter and your fascination with her? If memory serves, that was the year she gave you your first kiss.

Gareth stared at the shealk with shock written all over his features.

Oh, yes. I knew of your competition between yourself and the fire thrower.

You did? How? When did you know?

I knew from the moment you were born that you inherited the same strength of jhorun that I once possessed.

You're this shealk wizard we've heard about? Why didn't you tell me? Does mother know?

The blue shealk sank to the mesa floor and shook his head. **I wanted to tell her. Many times. I lacked the courage. I thought if I told her, then she'd take you from me and I'd never see you again.**

But you left anyway! Gareth sputtered, his anger rising. *I thought something I did might have driven you away!*

Son, you could never drive me away.

Then why did you leave? You broke Mother's heart! She thinks you're dead. I thought you were dead, too! Why didn't you come back?

It's complicated, son.

You ought to give it a try, Mikal suggested. *He's pretty smart.*

Very well. My Lord, would you permit me to speak with my son in private?

I require you to explain yourself to me. You will stay here.

But what about the others? This is a personal matter.

YOU *brought your human son here, Gareth. Proceed.*

As you command, My Lord, Gareth the elder grumbled.

Thanks, Gareth the younger said at the same time.

We need a way to refer to each of them without calling them the same name, Pravara noted.

What about just using 'senior and junior'? Mikal suggested. *That'd work, wouldn't it?*

Gareth frowned, which resulted in him baring his fangs. *I don't want to be called 'junior'.*

Nor do I wish to be called 'senior', the elder Gareth added.

Everyone present turned to Lord Phaedren, who had settled himself to the ground and was watching the proceedings with a bemused expression. He turned his glittering red head to regard both father and son.

I would suggest the two of you work this out. Otherwise, I will assign names I am quite certain neither of you will like.

Can you just use a different name? Pravara asked Gareth's father. *Is there any other name you've used before?*

Why should I give up my name? Gareth the elder demanded. **I've had mine longer than my son has had his.**

I haven't heard anything from you in over two years, the younger Gareth reminded his father. *This is the least you can do for me. Allow me to keep my name.*

So be it. On land, in my human form, I was called Balthor. I can use that again.

Lord Phaedren stirred. ***As in, 'Balthor the Wanderer'?***

Everyone turned toward Balthor, and Gareth spoke: *I'd like to know why I'm talking to my father, under water, in the middle of the ocean, and he's a shealk. Does that mean I'm able to change my form to shealk whenever I want?*

No. When I met your mother I was in a human form. When you were conceived, I was still in my human form. That makes you fully human.

Except my father is a shealk, Gareth reminded him.

Aye.

Why did you turn yourself into a human?

That's a difficult question to answer, my son.

You should give it a try. I'm all ears.

Balthor sighed. **I learned how to change my form many years ago.**

How old are you? Gareth interrupted, as his father was taking a breath.

In your years? Seven hundred eighty-two. That's nearly eight centuries, Son. I started yearning for something else. I was tired of the water. I wanted to see dry land for myself, and I wanted to do it without scales or wings.

During those travels I met Adyna. Over time, we fell in love, and for the first time in centuries I was truly happy. Then we learned we were expecting a baby and I became concerned. I had the same questions as you, my son. Would you be covered in scales? Would you have gills instead of lungs? The day you were born I sighed with relief. You were happy, healthy, and completely human.

For five years, I was able to sneak away and spend several months at a time with you and your mother. Unfortunately, my previous life caught up with me. I heard that two shealk were spotted off the shores of Capily. We rarely venture to the surface, and if we do, we are exceedingly careful not to be seen. So, when I heard of the sightings, I knew they were looking for me.

I told your mother I had received word that a family member had grown sick, and I was needed in Capily to care for them. I'm sorry to say that I presented myself as a very convincing liar. She never suspected anything. I traveled to Capily, shifted back to my original form, and intercepted those who were looking for me.

What did you tell them you were doing? Gareth wanted to know.

I decided to tell the truth, only I omitted a few details.

A few details? Lord Phaedren growled.

I explained I had been traveling, I'd made some new friends, and had been eager to learn more about their culture.

But you're a wizard. Mikal asked. *Didn't you have responsibilities?* Lord Phaedren growled. ***Indeed, he did.***

I confided with Amentharias and convinced her to take over my duties whenever I was away.

Who's Amentharias? Pravara asked.

Our other wizard.

She was my only friend. She alone knew what I was going through. She agreed to help. I owed her everything.

Amentharias was killed. Our community needed our wizard back.

What does that mean? Mikal asked, looking from face to face. He settled on Balthor's as Gareth's father met his eyes.

It means they had me followed. They knew I was swimming to the surface, but thankfully that's all they knew. It had become increasingly difficult to sneak away to be with you and your mother. Every opportunity I

could, I would spend with the two of you.

So, what happened two years ago? Gareth demanded, growing angry again. *You're telling me that for two years you were unable to come see us? To be with your wife and your son?*

Balthor growled. **Two years ago, my life changed forever, and it wasn't a good thing.**

Can you tell us what happened? Pravara gently asked.

I was in such a rush to return to my son and my wife that I accidentally stumbled into a smoker. I instantly recognized it for what it was and invoked a number of spells.

Excuse me, Mikal interrupted, comically raising one of his disproportionately small forelegs as though he were still in his human form and wanted to ask a question, *but what is a 'smoker'?*

A smoker is a hydrothermal vent, Balthor explained. **An area of the seabed opened and there was a vein of molten rock directly below. Can you imagine what happens when ice cold sea water makes contact with hot molten rock?**

Well, I now know what to avoid, Mikal casually remarked.

So you say. Most vents have a tall, chimney-like structure around it and are easy to locate. Fresh smokers are much more dangerous. There is no indication until the vent opens and begins expelling its poisons. They are silent killers.

What did you do? Gareth asked in a worried voice.

I cast every protection spell I could think of, in order to stay safe. Water purification, scale strengthener, and containment spells. I couldn't leave you and your mother alone in the world so I vowed to stay alive. What I didn't know, however, was the thriper's prison was nearby. The massive amounts of jhorun I expelled wakened the creature. It escaped because of me.

No, it didn't, Gareth argued. *It escaped because of me. That ship with all the enchanted weapons sank nearby. That's what woke it up.*

Balthor stared at his son and cocked his head slightly to the left. **That ship? Son, that ship sank less than a year ago.**

That's right. It sank and scattered enchanted weapons everywhere. One of them woke up the Athanaus and it escaped.

Are you telling me you think you are responsible for awakening the thriper, my son?

Gareth nodded.

Then rest at ease because it escaped over two years ago. I was there when it happened. The trance on the thriper couldn't have been very strong since it escaped its prison almost immediately. It emerged, starving for jhorun. I, unfortunately, was the first being it saw. I had exhausted my jhorun trying to protect myself from the smoker. I was no match for the thriper. It depleted my jhorun so badly that there was nothing left to regenerate the next day.

Didn't I hear that the Athanaus only escaped last year? Mikal turned to look at Pravara for confirmation. *My father said they started noticing the drain on people's jhorun at the end of last year. We just assumed that was when the creature escaped.*

Balthor shook his head. **It depleted its available jhorun and began actively seeking other sources. You must trust me on this. There is only one shealk responsible for the thriper's escape, and that is me.**

So that's why you were unable to return to Gareth and his mother, Mikal deduced. *With your jhorun gone you were unable to shift back to a human, is that it?*

Correct. I wanted nothing more than to return to my human family, but that dream had been taken from me. I felt like an extreme failure.

Gareth stared at his father with a sympathetic look. *All this time. You were stuck here because you couldn't switch back to a human. I should have known you wouldn't have deserted Mother and me.*

Deserted you? Never, my son.

Mikal glanced over at the shealk Dragon Lord. Phaedren was strangely quiescent as he sat there, watching the father and son. Sensing he was being watched, Phaedren turned to Mikal.

You have something to say, human?

Do you know who I am?

If you don't like to be called 'human', say so.

Sorry, that's not what I mean. What I meant to say was, do you know what my jhorun is?

No. How would you expect me to know that?

Wow. Let me try that again. My jhorun is very unique. It's been defined as the enhancement of other jhoruns, if you presently have a jhorun to be enhanced, and—

This helps us how, exactly? Lord Phaedren asked.

You didn't let me finish. Not only can I enhance an existing jhorun but I can also give jhorun to those who don't have any.

What? Lord Phaedren sputtered, rising several feet from the mesa floor. *You can?*

Would you mind saying that again? Balthor slowly asked

Mikal explained, focusing on how critically important it was for the recipient to accurately describe their jhorun. Balthor looked excitedly at Mikal before turning to look at his son. Turning to Lord Phaedren, he reverently bowed his head.

My Lord, please, would you permit young Mikal to apply his jhorun to me?

So, you can shirk your duties once more by hiding on dry land?

I've never hidden from my duties, My Lord.

I will permit the human prince to heal you. With regards to your desire to see your human family again, that remains to be seen.

I cannot abandon my family, My Lord. Please, have mercy.

We will discuss your life as a human once the thriper has been contained.

Is that why you're allowing me to have my jhorun back? So I can try to solve yet another problem when no one else can?

What's that supposed to mean?

My Lord, I do not think you have any idea what we wizards go through on a daily basis. Healing, communication, protection. We're responsible for it all. Why do you think I was sneaking away? There has to be

more to life than work.

Can you train another?

To become a wizard? No. That level of jhorun is something you have to be born with.

Like your offspring?

Don't even think it. He will *not* have the same life I did. I want him to be free to do whatever he wants. He is a human, My Lord, not a shealk.

I will consider your words. Young Mikal, would you please see if you can restore our wizard's jhorun?

Mikal swallowed noisily and looked at Gareth's father, who was now giving him an imploring look in return.

I'll do what I can. Do you have someplace quiet where we can go?

Behind me is a cavern. You may use that.

Balthor swam off. Mikal cast a quick look at his friends and then followed. Lord Phaedren was right. Near the far ring of jagged rocks was a rather large outcropping of stone that was extending in to the underwater mesa. Swimming around the outcropping revealed a mouth to a tunnel that curved in and to the right, depositing them inside a large empty cavern.

What do you need me to do? Balthor anxiously asked.

I need you to tell me about your jhorun. How does it work? What do you typically do with it? What are your triggers?

My triggers? I don't know what you mean by that. My jhorun is the ability to work with spells. I can see the inner components of a spell in my head. I can determine which …

You can determine which components are needed to make an accurate spell, Mikal interrupted, hearing enough of a description of Balthor's jhorun to trigger a recent memory. *You can work complex spells in your head without having to speak them out loud. You can—*

Explain yourself. How do you know this?

Because Gareth told me. That's his jhorun, too, Balthor. You share the same jhorun. This will be easier than I thought.

How does this help us?

It helps us because I already know how your jhorun works. Now be quiet. I need to concentrate.

Mikal closed his eyes and ordered his parietal eye to

remain closed, too. He wanted total darkness for this. He felt his jhorun tingle throughout his body and he cast it out at Balthor. He was right. His jhorun did not encounter any jhorun within his friend's father. The Athanaus had drained it all.

Switching tactics, Mikal focused on what he knew about Gareth's jhorun. Now, he had to transfer enough of his own jhorun to Balthor so that it would start regenerating, and then he had to give the jhorun a set of instructions which would define its tasks.

Clearing his mind of all random thoughts, Mikal pictured an empty room, much like the cavern. He focused his jhorun and siphoned off a tiny amount and pictured it as a small, dancing ball of light.

A spark of light appeared in his imaginary room. Whether or not it appeared in the cavern with them was unknown; he was unwilling to open his eyes and break his concentration. Once the spark was burning bright enough, he brought up all his memories of Gareth telling him how his jhorun worked, and all the mundane explanations of what he did to modify a spell. Mikal applied it to the spark of light.

The spark turned light green. It had accepted the instructions. In his mind he pictured Balthor waiting quietly in the empty room. His large blue shealk body was resting comfortably on the floor, unmoving. Mikal ordered the spark to move over to the prone form and to sink into the water dragon's chest.

He waited a few moments to make sure the shealk had accepted the jhorun. He sent his own jhorun to investigate. He felt the spark and knew it was there. After a few moments, he withdrew his jhorun and allowed himself to open his eyes. Balthor was still there, staring expectantly at him.

Well?

It's done.

It is? I didn't feel anything.

Try to do something. Remember, your jhorun is going to be weak. It needs rest and time to regenerate.

Balthor's mouth began moving, only Mikal couldn't hear anything. Was he chanting?

It's working! I don't know how you did it, but I can feel it. It's faint, but it's there. Thank you! Thank you very much!

You're welcome.

Balthor hurried outside to inform the others, giddy with excitement. Lord Phaedren gave Mikal an appraising stare as he rejoined his friends.

Well done, young Mikal. You have my thanks.

And mine! Balthor cried, unable to contain his excitement. He was now swimming in circles around the small mesa, coming dangerously close to the jagged rocks reaching high up out of the water.

You have my thanks, too, Mikal. That was my father you just helped.

I know. I told you I'd help you find him.

Yes, you certainly did. I owe you. Big.

Well, let's put our heads together and figure out what we're going to do about the Ath… er, the thriper.

I agree. I must prevent the rest of my shealk from suffering the loss of their jhorun.

Do you have any ideas how we're going to contain it? Pravara asked. She ducked low as Balthor zipped by, causing ripples in the water that threatened to pull them closer to the rocks.

The answer is simple. The thriper is attracted to jhorun. We now have two shealk wizards in our midst. It should seek us out. All we have to do is locate a suitable cave to hold it.

You already have a cave, Mikal pointed out. *Use the one it broke out of.*

Do you not think it would recognize its former prison? Do you not think it would avoid the area?

Hmm, good point.

Gareth cut in. *Find another cave. I'll go in there and expel enough jhorun to attract the thriper. Once it goes in, I'll sneak out and then we seal it up.*

You're forgetting the part about the Athanaus being awake, Mikal reminded him. *We have to knock it out before that happens or else it'll just escape again.*

Balthor stopped his mad sprint around the mesa perimeter

and joined the meeting.

Have you something to add, Balthor?

My Lord, there isn't any way I'm letting my son enter a small cave with that thriper at the same time. Leave the creature to me. Now that I know what we're dealing with, I'll be better prepared. I can render the thriper unconscious. You, my son, will be ready to seal that cave. Do you think you can do that?

Gareth solemnly nodded. *You can count on me, Father.*

Lord Phaedren lifted his head and emitted an electrical pulse. A bright blue flash appeared briefly above the Dragon Lord's head, and no fewer than two dozen shealk arrived.

The time to end the terror of the thriper is nigh. Go. Report back here once an acceptable cave has been found in which to imprison it.

The shealk all nodded and flicked their tails, zipping out of sight at frightening speeds.

Gareth turned to his father and nudged his tail with his own, *So, mother doesn't have any idea that her husband is a water dragon?*

Balthor's head dropped. **No.**

Were you ever going to tell her?

Someday, my son.

Well, guess what? That day is now. When this is done you and I are going to pay mother a visit where you will tell her everything.

We will deal with the thriper first. Once it has been incapacitated, we'll discuss the possibility of Balthor leaving these waters again.

No. He needs my help to take care of the thriper. Do you want it? Well, it comes with a price.

A word of caution, my son. He is My Lord. He does not bargain.

Wisely spoken.

Then figure this mess out on your own. Mikal, Pravara, we're leaving.

What? Balthor gasped. **You can't. I need your help!**

You know it, Father, and I know it. But apparently, he doesn't. Lord Phaedren is going to grant my request to allow you home or else I don't cooperate. Do you hear me, Lord Phaedren? I am not one of your subjects. You cannot order me around.

I can hold you here, arrogant human.

Gareth pointed at Mikal and Pravara. *Do you plan on holding them, too? He's a prince. She's the daughter of Kahvel, winged Dragon Lord.*

Lord Phaedren growled as he tried to stare Gareth down. *Look, this isn't open for negotiation. I lost my father two years ago. Now I find out that he's alive and well, and wants to return home to us.*

He is a wizard. There are no others to take his place. That cannot be allowed, no matter how hard you champion his cause.

How about a compromise? Pravara suggested.

What compromise? Speak, Pravara.

Allow him to continue living as he has done in the past. Half of the year he can live with his human family, and the other half he can live among the shealk to fulfill his obligations as wizard.

But I don't want him to stay here, Gareth protested.

Gareth, Mikal slowly said, *couldn't you visit him here? Like you're doing now?*

Gareth's mouth snapped shut. *I hadn't considered that.*

You want your father to be with you at all times, Pravara soothingly said. *Lord Phaedren is looking out for the welfare of all shealk under his protection. His people need a wizard. Your father is that wizard. You cannot be selfish, Gareth.*

Gareth sighed as he looked at his father. He slowly rotated until he was facing the ruby countenance of Lord Phaedren. *Very well. I would agree to that if you will.*

I will consider it. That is the only answer I can give you right now.

Seeing that Gareth was about ready to protest, Mikal flicked his tail to get his attention, figuring a light nudge wouldn't hurt anything. A split second later, he was horrified to learn that his tail was much stronger than he had thought possible. He had knocked Gareth completely over and his friend was now lying, face first on the ground, directly in front of the sparkling leader of the shealk.

Lord Phaedren suppressed a chuckle. **That really isn't necessary. I do not require anyone to bow that low in my presence.**

Gareth slowly lifted himself up and angrily looked at Mikal. *What was that for?*

I apologize. I just wanted to get your attention. I had no idea my tail was that strong.

Congratulations. It worked. What did you want?

Lord Phaedren told you he'd consider the compromise. I wanted to remind you that what you're asking has never been done before. He has a lot to consider. The fact that he's willing to consider it is a good thing.

What if he doesn't? Gareth asked.

You do realize that I am right here, don't you?

If he doesn't, at least you'll know how to find your father and spend time with him. You can get to know your shealk heritage a little bit better.

If we get that thriper locked back up then he'd better agree, Gareth scowled.

And I can still hear you.

Has something like this ever happened before? Pravara asked, mistakenly believing the shealk Dragon Lord was about ready to lose his temper.

Elaborate. Has what **happened before?**

Have there been any other shealk wizards that have had problems like this before?

No.

Of course, Balthor said at the same time.

Lord Phaedren turned expectantly to Balthor and waited for an explanation.

I'm assuming you'd like me to expand on that.

You assume correctly. I have never known of any discourse amongst the wizards before.

With all due respect, My Lord, you should pay better attention.

Explain.

Wizards have been known to change their forms and escape to dry land for years. Whether they choose to join their aerial cousins in the sky or their wingless brethren on land was unknown. My former mentor informed me that he used to become a griffin whenever the stress threatened to overwhelm him. Flying through the open sky, as a griffin, was the only way he could find in order to relieve that stress. His absences became so frequent that I found myself increasingly taking over his duties.

These unapproved absences will cease!

On the contrary, My Lord, I would recommend you increase our downtime in order to avoid situations like this in the future. Do you think the wizards are the only caste that have freely risked their lives in order to regain their sanity? We are a hard-working species, My Lord. Every shealk would follow you into the depths of the Zarut Smoker if necessary. However, you need to realize that there are physical limits. Concealing ourselves from the rest of the world taxes our abilities. Protection, concealment, healing, and memory modification. Those are just a few of the spells I administer daily. Well, when I had jhorun, that is.

For two years I haven't been able to practice any jhorun. What was the result? We have been sighted on more than one occasion by the surface dwellers. We have to rely on what I remember of archaic medicine and healing. Plants, poultices, salves, and so on.

What are you trying to say, Balthor?

Your decision to live, privately, deep beneath the surface is costing us, as a species. Shealk are abandoning the water in greater numbers than ever before.

You allowed our fellow shealk to desert our community?

Of course not, My Lord. Have I aided those that truly needed a break? Aye. But, before you lose your temper, I want to add that I have always added a time limit to each of my spells. That was their incentive to return to the water. To be caught up on the surface, in shealk form, would be a fatal mistake.

You have given me much to think about.

I have only the highest respect for you, My Lord. I am a shealk, and I am fiercely proud of that. It's time everyone felt the same way again.

Noted. I will call on you and we will discuss our options.

Surprised, Balthor nodded. It would be an honor, My Lord.

Less than half an hour later, they received the first bit

of good news Mikal could remember hearing in a long time. A dark blue shealk, much darker than Balthor, reported that he had found a cave similar in size to the Athanaus' former prison. It was northwest of their present location and at a depth of over twenty-five hundred feet.

Mikal eagerly looked over at the leader of the shealk. *That's good news, right? Is it far enough away from here to work?*

Phaedren shook his red, iridescent head.

No. The water is too deep. Only the most gifted shealk dare venture that deep.

What? What does that mean? What difference does it make if it's a little deeper than we are now?

The depth of that cave is three times the depth of the original thriper cave. You felt the water pressing in on your body before? That would be nothing compared to this.

I had wondered about that. The water was colder and it was harder to breathe. I never would have imagined being a shealk, living in the ocean, could be so dangerous.

Is it not as dangerous as a human on dry land?
Huh? Of course not.

Will the air not thin at the top of a mountain?
What does a mountain have to do with anything?

More than you realize. I'm talking about the altitude. If you ascend into the clouds, then the air becomes thin. For the shealk, the deeper you swim, the greater the chance of damaging your body.

Oh. Mikal felt all the blood drain from his face. He briefly wondered what that must look like, as a shealk. *I think I'm beginning to see your point. How did that blue shealk survive so deep?*

He is strong. Swimming at those depths requires great skill.

Mikal nodded, impressed.

You ask if that cave will work? No, it won't.
Ah.

Five sightings later, they reported finding a suitable location, a cave slightly larger and deeper than the thriper's former prison, and it was up against the base of a large rock formation. The new cave could easily be sealed by a simple terra tremor, since it wouldn't take much to move a few of

the large boulders over the cave opening. Balthor promised
to teach his son the necessary spell to accomplish it. Gareth
insisted he already knew one that would work.

My Lord!

Mikal turned to see a gray and white shealk practically
appear out of thin air. Or water. Whatever. A powerful blast
of water slammed him against Pravara, and the two of them
were flung aside like the tiniest fish in the sea.

I have news, My Lord! announced the newcomer.

Speak.

The thriper! It is on the move!

How do you know this?

**Kahvel sends word. His subjects engaged the thriper.
They reported that it abandoned the fight and fled.**

The thriper fled? Are you sure?

**That's what Kahvel originally thought, My Lord.
Several of his subjects tried attacking as it fled but...**

But what? Speak!

**They claim it stopped and stared at a fixed point in
the distance. Kahvel suspects it located more desirable
prey. Then it began moving. Fast.**

What prey? Where is it going?

**Us, My Lord. It's heading straight toward us. It will
be here in three hours.**

Chapter 13 — Out of Time

The shocking announcement was met with silence. All eyes turned expectantly to Lord Phaedren, who continued to rest his considerable bulk on the canyon floor. A brief spark of blue light appeared above the messenger shealk's head, drawing everyone's attention to him.

My Lord, perhaps you didn't hear me. The creature is heading toward us. What are your orders?

I heard you the first time.

What are we to do, My Lord?

The only thing that has changed is the time table. Balthor, you said that you alone will find a way to render the thriper unconscious.

Correct, My Lord.

Prepare yourself.

I will be ready, My Lord. Son, would you help me prepare, please?

Gareth nodded. *Of course.*

Father and son departed in a flurry of bubbles, leaving

Mikal, Pravara, Lord Phaedren, and the messenger. Mikal watched a white shealk swim by the southern entrance to their enclosed canyon at least three times. Were they Lord Phaedren's guards? Were they doing the same thing he had seen his father's human guards do countless times throughout the castle?

Lord Phaedren turned to the messenger shealk. *Vinarth, how reliable is your information?*

My Lord?

If our winged cousins observed the thriper heading west, how do they know it hasn't veered to intercept some other prey?

Because our winged cousins are in pursuit. Sadly, they have learned they must follow from a discreet distance. They have already lost a number of their own as they tried to vanquish the thriper in three separate encounters.

'Lost a number of their own'? Pravara repeated, shocked. *Did they say who? Or how many? Are they still alive?*

Vinarth turned to Pravara and gave her a neutral look. *Unknown. I was only told they were unsuccessful.*

Pravara looked worriedly at Mikal. *What if my father is one of those?*

We'll deal with that as soon as we're able, Mikal assured her. *If he's had his jhorun drained, like Balthor had, then I'll personally restore it myself. In fact, I will help any winged dragon that suffers from an encounter with the Athanaus.*

Thriper.

Would you please stop doing that? Mikal sighed, turning to look at the shealk leader. *You can call it thriper if you'd like. I first heard it called Athanaus. It means the same thing, okay?*

Pravara? Are you there? Are you safe?

Mikal watched Pravara give a visible jerk and fall silent. *Are you okay?*

It's my father! Pravara told him. *He's using the Collective!*

Surprised, Lord Phaedren turned to Pravara. *You are speaking with Kahvel?*

Aye. Just a moment, please. Pravara concentrated on the faint presence of her father and immediately felt his concern. *Father? I am here.*

Are you safe? Kahvel mentally repeated.

For the time being. We were just notified the thriper is on its way here.

The what?

The thriper. It's what the shealk call the Athanaus. Lord Phaedren knows he has less than three hours to transform the cave they found into its next prison.

Three hours? Are you jesting? Pravara, I sent that message nearly two hours ago!

Are you telling me we have less than an hour to prepare for the thriper's arrival? Father, that's not enough time!

I have tried to slow it down. We have been rendered useless. Five of our brethren have tried, and failed.

Are they still alive? Pravara hesitantly asked.

Their eyes are open, and they are breathing, but they are mentally absent.

It's their jhorun, Father. The thriper has drained all of it. It happened to one of the shealk, too.

That would suggest we wyverians use jhorun much the same way as the humans. I do not accept this.

Believe it, Father. The shealk have opened my eyes about a great many things. If we restore jhorun to our fallen brethren, they will be fine.

Do you hear yourself, Pravara? There is no way to restore jhorun that has been completely depleted.

I watched Mikal do it to Balthor, Gareth's father. He's already volunteered to help as soon as we shift back to our regular forms.

In that case, I would owe the humans?

Yes.

Damn. Very well. He has my utmost appreciation. Lord Phaedren emitted another blue pulse from the top of his head, and suddenly there were shealk everywhere.

We must evacuate the shealk! The thriper will be here in less than an hour, not three as we originally told. Go!

The shealk scattered. Lord Phaedren glanced once at Mikal and Pravara and swam back toward the cavern that had been used to restore Balthor's jhorun. They followed and then gasped as they noticed the cavern was empty. Phaedren had vanished!

Alright, you saw him swim in here, right? Mikal asked, looking around in amazement.

Pravara nodded. *Aye. There must be a false wall or a concealed tunnel. We must find it. I do not want to be left behind.*

That goes for both of us, Mikal agreed.

Thirty seconds later, Pravara found the concealed tunnel against the back wall of the cave. Mikal thought it looked natural, formed by volcanic activity. What was remarkable, however, was how well the tunnel opening blended with the surrounding walls.

If I didn't know any better, I'd say a dwarf did that.

Pravara ushered him through the tunnel and hurried to catch up to Lord Phaedren. Nearly five minutes later they emerged into a much larger, better illuminated domed cavern that stretched upward for several hundred feet. Smaller cave openings dotted the smooth gray walls, stopping at least fifty feet from the top of the cavern. A soft, bluish glow was emanating from each of the small caves. Mikal could tell that something was moving about in each one. Were there shealk in each cave? Was this where the shealk community lived?

The huge dome was bustling with activity. Lord Phaedren had settled in the center of the dome floor, turning and issuing orders.

Each cave will be checked. Every occupant is to evacuate to the Gian Fields. If you see a youngling that needs help, offer it. If the elderly are struggling, help them. We will be abandoning this cavern in less than five minutes.

Lord Phaedren, Mikal called. *Where's Gareth?*

I'll take you there myself. I must speak with Balthor immediately.

They followed the shealk leader into a cave that looked as though it was no different from any of the dozens of others all scattered across the dome's interior. This tunnel led into a smaller cavern that had only two shealk in it. One was black and the other was blue.

I mean, look at this, Gareth was saying. *Look at our arms. I can barely use one to scratch the other. Why are they so freakishly small?*

Balthor turned around. He was holding a glowing indigo crystal in his mouth. He deposited the glowing stone on a slab of flat rock that must have served as a workspace. He suppressed a chuckle.

To a shealk, our legs are considered vestigial.

What does that mean?

As the shealk evolve, those organs or appendages that do us the least amount of good will eventually shrivel up and disappear.

Excuse me? I do not want anything to shrivel up and disappear! Nothing!

Enhance your calm, son. It is a process that takes many generations. What you see now started many thousands of years ago and it will probably take that many more before our arms and legs completely disappear.

Look at us! We already look like serpents. Is this what the shealk want to happen?

We can discuss this later, son. We must work quickly. Balthor coiled his tail around a large rock and smashed it down on the glowing crystal. He inspected the shattered stone before gathering several larger pieces in his mouth. He spat them out at Gareth's feet.

Lord Phaedren's voice startled them. ***I come with grim news. You have less than one hour to be ready.***

What happened? Balthor demanded. **Is the thriper traveling faster than we originally anticipated?**

There was an unknown delay in getting the message to us. Tell me what I can do. How can I help?

You are offering to help us prepare?

Aye. I think we would all help, if we can.

We were just discussing options for sealing the prison. I say we use levitation to move nearby rocks and boulders to seal the thriper in its prison. My son seems to think creating an actual terra tremor would work better.

And I still say levitation will work, just not as fast, Gareth argued. *You need to move those rocks as quickly as possible, right? A terra tremor will do just that.*

What happens if your terra tremor is too powerful and ends up knocking a boulder or two on top of the thriper? It would awaken it, son. Why take the chance when you don't have to?

Father, you're out of practice. I could create a terra tremor which could level one of these mountains or a tremor weak enough to move only a simple stone. The point I'm trying to make, Father, is that terra tremors can be tricky if you don't know what you're doing. Lucky for you I do.

I have been practicing jhorun long before you were ever born, young one. Do not even try to lecture me about the nuances of terra tremors.

That's exactly my point, Father. Perhaps you're a little too old to accomplish something like this.

Mikal's eyes widened with surprise. He saw Balthor silently regarding his son. Lord Phaedren grunted once.

You are your father's son, young Gareth. Arrogance in a shealk wizard is a good thing. Now, pushing aside who is right and who is wrong, the thriper grows ever nearer. Tell me of the plan to immobilize this creature.

Would you like to do the honors, son?

Gareth nodded enthusiastically. *You bet. Here's what we're going to do. We're going to use a layered spell.*

Elaborate.

This spell will have multiple parts, Gareth translated. *The results of the first layer will dictate how the second layer behaves, and so on.*

Very well. Go on.

The reason we haven't been able to battle the thriper is that this monster is essentially nothing more than mist. We either need to fight the mist or to change the thriper into something that we can vanquish.

Change the thriper? Mikal repeated, intrigued. *How? Into what?*

I'm getting to that. The first layer is a shifting spell, making the thriper into something substantial, something physical we can touch.

Go on.

The second layer, Gareth continued, *will be an isolation spell, to lock the thriper into that form.*

So that it cannot change back, Pravara surmised. *Excellent.*

The third layer is one of the most important and will set loose a barrage of stimuli. Sights, sounds, smells. The more we can incorporate, the better.

Elucidate.

If the thriper is now in a physical form, Balthor

explained, coming to his son's aid, **and in a form that can experience sensations and emotions, we can render it unconscious by simple sensory overload.**

Then what? Mikal wanted to know.

The fourth layer is levitation, Gareth continued, frowning. *I still say there must be a better way to do this but for now, it'll have to do. This part of the spell will gently pick up the thriper and suspend it in the direct center of the cave. That way if there's a terra tremor, or something else in the area that might create a noticeable vibration, the thriper should not be able to detect it.*

Excellent. Proceed with extreme haste.

There's more, Balthor added. **Once the thriper has been lowered into the cave and suspended to the floor, the final layer will render the surrounding area mute. No noise, no nothing. It's another way to keep the thriper immobilized.**

I'm handling the last part, Gareth proudly announced. *Once I get the signal, I'll create a terra tremor that will seal the prison. Then all you would need to do is post warning signs so that in the years to come you don't forget about what's buried out there.*

Can you create the spell in the time allotted?

Balthor ducked low and came up with two of the glowing crystal shards Mikal had seen earlier. He gingerly set the shards on the stone dais before them.

We already have it here, My Lord. Once my son and I agreed upon the spells to use, it was relatively easy to assemble. We are ready.

Most impressive.

That sounds like a very complex spell, Pravara noted. *What are the chances of the spell not working the way it should?*

Don't worry, Gareth confidently told his friend. *I'm the one who made the spell so it'll work just fine.*

Balthor emitted a long, low growl.

With my father's guidance, Gareth quickly amended. *His jhorun isn't strong enough yet to manipulate the spells, but thankfully mine is.*

Are you inferring that my spells are no less superior than yours? You have much to learn, my son. Pravara, there is no chance this spell will not work as it should.

We are two of the strongest wizards who have ever lived. This spell is a masterpiece.

Mikal thumped his tail on the ground once and inadvertently tipped himself over. After a brief struggle to right himself, he looked sheepishly at his friends.

Sorry. Um, I have a question. If you're so certain your spell is going to work properly the first time, why do you have two of them?

Everyone turned to regard the stone dais and the two glowing shards. In unison, all eyes swiveled to Balthor's.

Would you believe the crystal provided two suitable shards?

No. Keep both shards at the ready.

Mikal thumped his tail again, but this time much softer. He was able to remain upright.

I have another question. What happens if, after being inundated with all these stimuli, the thriper isn't overcome and isn't rendered unconscious?

Gareth looked over at his father and shook his head. He didn't know. Balthor returned the blank look. He didn't have an answer, either.

It's the best we could come up with in such a short amount of time. Do we know how far away the thriper is now?

No. We should leave. The closest source of jhorun must be out at the new site.

Mikal followed the shealk leader out into the main dome. Whereas before the shealk community was bustling with activity, in the short fifteen minutes they had been talking with Balthor and Gareth, the entire dome had been deserted. The five of them retraced their way to the small secluded underwater canyon, and then into the open ocean. A dozen shealk rose silently up from their positions near the mesa's entrance and circled their leader. The entire group swam to the east.

They were, Mikal noted, angling back toward the dark clear waters of the deep ocean. The light was fading rapidly, forcing him to switch back to his parietal eye. For nearly ten minutes Mikal followed the shealk leader and his entourage out toward the icy blackness of the Erudian Ocean. They crossed over deep trenches spanning hundreds of feet. A tall, twenty-foot cylindrical structure belched out dark smoke— they gave the smoker a wide berth.

They approached a line of underwater hills, ranging from several dozen feet high to well over a hundred. Lord Phaedren singled out a spot on a tiny hill far to the left. There, at the base of the hill, was a dark opening. The shealk leader swam over and peered anxiously inside.

This is it. Balthor, commence preparations at once.

Mikal peered inside. It was dark, covered with small black stalactites that looked as though they had formed when hot magma had been forced through tiny cracks in the cave's ceiling. Mikal looked to see if Pravara was nearby. She was engrossed in a conversation with the shealk leader. Mikal saw Balthor swim up and go into the cave. Mikal angled himself so he could see what his friend's father was doing.

Aren't you supposed to be waiting for Gareth?

No.

Where is he, anyway? I don't see him anywhere.

My son became separated from the group and is on his way. Too bad he won't arrive here in time.

What? Why wouldn't he make it here in time?

Because Lord Phaedren has agreed to keep him distracted. I do believe my son has been purposely diverted to the Gian fields. Fear not. A dozen of our fiercest warriors are with him.

Gareth isn't going to like that one bit, Mikal observed.

No, he won't.

How are you going to lure the Athanaus inside the cave?

Thriper.

Whatever, Mikal growled.

All the shealk have been evacuated. We are now all that lay between the thriper and the shealk. It will be famished. It will see me and will pursue me into this cave. Once inside I will invoke the spell.

How long will the spell take to render it unconscious? What if there's a delay and it goes after you? There won't be any room to flee in there. You'll be trapped!

The spell will take some time to be fully deployed,

Balthor admitted. His long neck jerked up and he nervously scanned the area, as if sensing the thriper was nearby. **However, the first layer will be instantaneous. The thriper must be made solid. The second layer will not engage until it does.**

So, there's a chance the spell won't work if the first spell, er, first layer doesn't successfully shift its form?

Correct.

What form is it going to take?

We decided to give it a form it has taken many times before. Hopefully, once it sees its new form, it won't panic and try to resist.

What form? Mikal repeated.

A horse.

A horse? A horse cannot survive underwater. Wouldn't its appearance down here do the job for us and kill it?

Once the equine form is locked into place, thanks to the second layer, then the third layer should render it unconscious in seconds. Selecting a non-aquatic form is just another way to keep it in its cave, where it will be safe.

I still don't like you going in there by yourself.

I am the wizard. The protection and safekeeping of the shealk is my responsibility. It is an honor to serve.

What would Gareth say about all of this?

Young Gareth has not been told of the true plan. Understandably, Balthor fears what his son would do.

The thriper is near! Pravara reported. *I am in contact with the winged dragons that have been in pursuit. The thriper just disappeared into the water. It will be here in a matter of minutes!*

Everyone but Balthor should be behind the western ridge. No exceptions!

Mikal wished Balthor good luck and followed Pravara. They allowed themselves to sink to the ocean floor, dropping down below the rock outcropping. Half a dozen shealk heads peered anxiously over the ridge and waited.

How long do you think we'll have to wait? Mikal whispered to Pravara.

The thriper approaches! Everyone, remain concealed!

Mikal looked back toward the direction they had come and scanned the dark water. He couldn't see anything. The thriper was out there? How would they know? The thriper could sneak right up to them and no one would be the wiser.

I don't see it.

It's moving fast, Pravara told him. *It must favor the equine form as it looks as though a dark immobile horse is heading straight for us.*

Where? I don't see it!

Cast your eyes much lower. It is less than a foot off the ocean floor.

Mikal stared at the bed of the ocean for a few seconds before he finally spotted it. Pravara was right. The thriper was mostly in equine form. It had the head, neck, chest, and front forelegs of a horse. Then it drifted sideways a bit. The front half may look like a horse, Mikal decided, but the back half was a swirling cloud of mist. The mist tapered, forming a tight curlicue where the tail should be, before fading into the cold depths of the icy waters. The thriper's head turned. Mikal just knew it was staring straight at him.

This isn't going to work. His tail began undulating, pushing up and away from their hiding place. He started to drift upward. Lord Phaedren hooked his tail through Mikal's and instantly jerked him back down.

Stay down and stay silent. We have not been detected. Yet.

Balthor appeared in front of the cave, right on cue. He was glowing! An eerie blue glow bathed the shealk wizard's body from the tip of his nose all the way down to the farthest reaches of his tail. Gareth's father must have been using every scrap of jhorun he could muster in order to look as appealing as possible to the thriper.

It's working! Pravara hissed excitedly. *It's heading toward the cave!*

They watched, mesmerized, as the eerie horse figure moved unerringly toward Balthor. The thriper's front legs fizzed out and were replaced by a disproportionately large claw. The large avian claw looked completely out of place on the horse, although Mikal recognized it.

That's what we saw above the water the other day, Pravara reminded him. *I can only fathom the claw must have formed in*

anticipation of feeding. I certainly hope Balthor knows what he's doing.
We have a problem.

Mikal and Pravara glanced at each other before turning to look at the shealk leader.

What is it? Mikal hesitantly asked. They hadn't even invoked the complex layer-spell yet.

Balthor's jhorun is failing. It simply hadn't enough time to regenerate after you restored it.

What? Oh, no! Mikal peered over the stone ridge. Lord Phaedren was right. Balthor had lost the blue glow and was now casting anxious looks to judge the distance to the cave. Unfortunately, the thriper was still far enough away from the cave to hesitate. It rotated its horse head, appearing uncertain. Then, surprising everyone, the thriper turned its back on both Balthor and the ridge. Something was approaching, and that something was moving fast.

It was Gareth!

The jet black shealk zipped by the thriper just as it was reaching for him with the large claw. Gareth arrived at his father's side and cast him a disparaging look.

Did you really think that I would let you face this thing by yourself?
You shouldn't be here, son. You're supposed to be a long way away by now.

The thriper regained its bearings and drifted closer.

The worst covert operation I have ever seen. I was on to the shealk guards right away, but it took me a few minutes to come up with a spell so I could escape.

They heard the shrill screech of the approaching thriper. It was less than ten seconds away.

Father, get inside!
And leave you to face this abomination? I left you once. I won't do it again.

From behind the ridge Mikal saw Gareth chanting! What could he ... Balthor grunted with surprise as an unknown force pushed him into the cave. Gareth ducked inside at the last possible moment to avoid the swipe of the thriper's claw.

You had better know what you're doing, son. Balthor opened his jaws, displaying the two glowing crystal shards. He spat them both out and caught one with the tip of his tail.

Take the other. Hurry! Be ready in case we need it.

Father and son huddled together in mock terror as the thriper arrived at the cave entrance and looked inside. It paused for a moment, as if it might have sensed something amiss. After a few seconds, it fully entered the cave and extended its abnormally large claw. Balthor leveraged his tail up and brought it alongside the closest cave wall.

By the power of the shealk who have imprisoned you once before, I banish you back to the depths of hell from whence you came!

Balthor cracked his tail against the inside of the cave. Both he and Gareth heard the crystal shard crack. Gareth sighed with relief. His father had done it! He had invoked the spell! It was over!

The thriper was writhing in pain and lost its equine characteristics. Instead, it reverted back to a swirling cloud of black mist. The dark cloud shrank, drawing in on itself. After a few moments it began swelling and changing. A shape was beginning to form. The spell was working!

The mist reversed direction and fled the cave.

Mikal growled with dismay at the sight of the thriper speeding away from its new prison. The thriper's new form was not quite complete but everyone could see that it wasn't a horse that had fled the scene.

Mikal could see the creature thrashing wildly about. He stared at the receding cloud of mist. Even from a distance Mikal could see what the Athanaus was changing into. Both he and Pravara gasped with alarm.

The thriper had become a winged dragon and was desperately clawing its way to the surface.

Chapter 14 — Sealing the Deal

For several seconds no one said a word. Gareth looked back at his father and then at the receding form of the thriper. He pointed his tail at the rapidly dissipating trail of bubbles the enemy had left behind.

What happened? Did we miss a step somewhere?

Mikal might not have figured out how to execute a shrug in shealk form, but Gareth's father didn't have any problems. Balthor looked at the second shard still clutched in the tip of Gareth's tail.

Not that I'm aware.

Well, it wasn't exactly how we planned but the spell did work. Father, the thriper is gone! The shealk are safe!

Mikal swam over to his friend and stared incredulously at him. *What are you talking about? The spell didn't work. Far from it! It just turned the thriper into a dragon and it fled. It fled, Gareth! Do you know what that means?*

It means the shealk are safe.

What about the rest of the kingdom? Mikal angrily protested.

Do you have any idea what will happen if we let that thing loose on the kingdom?

Gareth's black shealk head looked up at the faint shimmer of light that was the surface.

Your friend is right, Balthor told his son. **The thriper must be pursued and eliminated once and for all. I would gladly stand by your side, but until my jhorun has a chance to properly regenerate, I am unable to shift. You will have to do this on your own, my son.**

No, he won't, Mikal disagreed. *I'll be with him.*

I, too, will be there, Pravara added.

The spell failed, Lord Phaedren pointed out. ***How do you three plan to defeat the thriper? You will be no match for it.***

Gareth's head snapped up. He craned his long neck to look up and then looked excitedly back at his friends.

That's it!

What's it? What are you talking about, son? Balthor wanted to know.

The thriper! Father, that's how we'll beat him! The way I see it, the spell partially worked. The first layer succeeded, although I will admit it's not how we had originally planned it. Then the second layer was triggered, locking the thriper in that form so it'd be unable to change back. If it could have changed, then it would have. That's why it took off for the surface. It no longer had gills!

There's a good chance the third layer was triggered.

Gareth turned to his father and shook his head. *There's no way of knowing for sure.*

Did you see the way it took off from here? Something scared it.

Or else it knew the form it had been shifted into had lungs and needed air. It would have drowned if it didn't reach the surface!

Comprehension flooded into Mikal. He looked back at Gareth and nodded approvingly.

Either way you look at it, the meaning is clear: the thriper is mortal. It knew it was going to drown unless it did something about it. As long as it's locked in its physical body, it should be able to be killed.

Exactly! Gareth beamed a victorious smile. He handed the second crystal shard to his father. *We have to go. Mikal, Pravara, are you ready? Race you to the surface!*

Without waiting for a response, Gareth took off, heading straight toward the flickering sunlight. Mikal looked over at Lord Phaedren and then at Balthor.

Please keep an eye on my son. Tell him I will be with him just as soon as I can.

Mikal cast a quick glance back at the shealk leader to see if he was going to refute Balthor's statement. When he didn't answer, Mikal angled his head toward the surface of the water and gave his tail a mighty flick. He soared straight up. Pravara was right beside him, matching his speed.

I think you should let your father know.

Pravara nodded. *I just told him. The problem was, he asked me questions about the thriper-dragon. What color? How big? What is the orientation of its horns? He was displeased to learn I didn't have any answers to give him. All I could tell him was that it was large, winged, and struggling to make it to the surface.*

What if it didn't? Mikal asked. *What if it drowned before it got there?*

Do you really think we'd be that lucky? Pravara challenged.

You have a point.

Gareth was waiting for them just below the surface. Mikal could see the bright blue sky and fluffy white clouds. The tips of the underwater mountains surrounding the shealk canyon were nearby.

You two sure took your time. Are you ready? We are all going to jump out of the water at the same time. I would encourage the two of you to jump up as high as you can.

Why? Mikal asked suspiciously. *Can't you shift us back as we are now?*

Gareth shook his head.

I'm told winged dragons don't like the water too much. It can be incredibly difficult to return to the air when your wings have become water-logged.

He's not wrong, Pravara agreed. *I'll be ready.*

Mikal, are you ready? Gareth asked. *You and I will have the most difficult time. We are going to need some space to get used to being a winged dragon again.*

You're turning us into winged dragons now?

How else were you planning on pursuing the thriper? Gareth asked.

Fine. I see your point. Do what you have to do.

I need you to get out of the water first. I've triggered my counter spell to activate as soon as your tail clears the water. The higher you can get the more time you will have to get re-acclimated to being a wyverian again. Pravara, be ready.

I will be ready, Pravara assured him.

Mikal smiled. He had enjoyed being a water dragon. He couldn't wait to share his adventures, but he was looking forward to having the vast blue skies above his head again. He wanted to be able to take a deep breath of fresh, clean air. He wanted to see his parents again.

And, most importantly, he wanted to see Lissa. He sighed. There was no point denying it. He missed her. He missed spending time with her. He missed seeing her face brighten every time she looked his way. He missed the way she could brighten his mood, regardless of the day he was having. He sighed again and shook his head. It felt as though they had been apart for weeks, even though he knew they had been separated for less than a day.

He dove to a depth of a hundred feet, turned about, and surged forward, traveling as fast as his tail could propel him. His shealk body breeched the surface of the water and was instantly blinded by the intense sunshine. Almost immediately his eyes began to burn, but then a myriad of new sensations caught his attention. He felt his body changing. His arms and legs expanded. Muscles sprouted, wings appeared, and the scales covering his body thickened and turned jet black.

A searing flash of pain engulfed his body. Shifting spells weren't meant to be painful, but this one had to hurry. His entire body stung, like getting a scab ripped off. Fortunately for him, the entire process was over in less than two seconds. Mikal grunted with surprise. He had become a winged dragon in less time than it took to get out of bed in the morning.

Pravara's newly restored dark green body soared past him, rising steadily into the air on powerful wings. Mikal chuckled. Apparently, she had been just as anxious as he to get out of the water.

Mikal started pumping his large leathery wings. His wing talons skimmed the surface of the water as he fervently tried to keep himself from going for another swim. Gareth was right. The last thing he wanted to do was get this body wet.

Mikal's long black serpentine neck turned to look down at the ocean falling steadily away below him. Where was Gareth? Had he made it? Mikal cast his gaze to each side. Land was nowhere in sight. How far out to sea had the shealk taken him?

A deep blue dragon with jagged stripes of yellow appeared. It flew perilously close to Mikal before rising into the sky. Its long, polychromatic neck twisted to the right and studied him, as though he was the one that looked absurd.

"You've *got* to be kidding. Gareth? Is that you?"

"Were you expecting someone else?" the strangely hued dragon answered.

"I have never seen a dragon with markings like those," Mikal admitted. "Why did you choose blue and yellow? You do know those colors aren't natural, don't you?"

"So what? I wanted something different. You can be the boring black dragon this time."

Mikal regarded the oddly colored dragon before glancing down at his own chest. Shiny jet-black scales covered his torso and extended all the way down to his belly. He looked at his wyverian forelegs. Huge muscles rippled beneath the skin. Each hand had four claws tipped with talons that were two feet long. His wings looked to be over a hundred feet long from tip to tip and his long powerful tail made up at least half his body length. This body had power, Mikal thought excitedly. Who in their right mind would want to a challenge a dragon that looked like he did?

Mikal smiled approvingly at Gareth.

"I don't know why you gave me the black dragon this time," he started, "but I am glad. This is really cool. No offense to your shealk heritage, Gareth, but I think I prefer being a winged dragon instead."

"No offense taken," the young wizard assured him. They had finally caught up with Pravara, who was presently cruising through the air without moving her wings. "Are you glad to be a winged dragon again?"

Pravara turned her dark green head and watched them

approach. "I will never complain about my wyverian species again, not that I ever did in the first place."

"Do you know where we're headed?" Gareth asked, fighting to use the same air currents that Pravara handled so effortlessly.

"I just informed my father that we are now in pursuit of the Athanaus. I have asked for help since none of us knows what the thriper looks like now. My father informed me he has made apprehending or destroying the thriper his top priority."

"That really doesn't help us that much," Gareth commented. He was still fighting the currents, beating his wings much more than necessary.

"Don't fight the currents," Pravara advised. "Use them. Raise your wingtips up. Let the wind flow under your wings instead of pushing them down. Trust me, I had that same problem when I was young."

"You still *are* young," Mikal countered.

"As I was saying," Pravara continued, ignoring Mikal's quip, "this helps us, in that my father has tasked every dragon with searching. Do you understand? Every available dragon is now airborne and searching for the thriper."

"We don't know what it looks like," Mikal reminded her.

"It doesn't matter. All wyverians use the Collective. We just have to find out who isn't using it. Once the thriper is identified, we can and *will* destroy it."

"And how are we going to do that?" Gareth wanted to know. He was now cruising through the air much like the other two.

"We're working on that," Pravara answered.

"There's Capily!" Mikal exclaimed, twisting his head around to stare down at the seaside village. "I can see Constable Fensham's office. Look! There's Lissa! I need to talk to her."

"We are otherwise preoccupied," Pravara curtly told him. "Your love life will have to wait until the thriper has been located and dealt with."

Mikal longingly looked down at his girlfriend, who was staring speculatively up at the three passing dragons. He could see that Lissa had recognized Pravara and was frantically gesturing to her father, who had just joined her outside his office. He knew she was wondering if the other two dragons might be he and Gareth. If only he could talk with her, even if it was only for a few moments.

"You're a wyverian now," Pravara told him, correctly guessing what was running through his mind. "You have the ability to telepathically communicate with anyone you choose. Talk to her, Mikal."

"How? I've always been on the receiving end of one of our mental chats. I've never instigated one before."

"Concentrate on who you're trying to contact," Pravara gently explained. "Think about her. Focus. Allow yourself to share your thoughts. I believe you will find that she will welcome the contact."

Mikal kept his head trained on Lissa as long as he was able. Just then they passed through a thick gray cloudbank and she was lost from sight. He sighed. If Pravara said he was capable of talking with her, then he certainly wanted to learn how to do it.

Thoughts of his girlfriend swam through his mind. Her smile. Her touch. The many walks he had taken with her while she demonstrated her vast knowledge of medicinal herbs and plants. He thought of the day he had finally told his parents that he was interested in a girl and wanted their blessing, which they had immediately given him. Mikal thought of the hushed conversation his parents had when they thought he was out of hearing range. He knew they had been happy for him since he had heard his mother's voice repeatedly raise in pitch and giggle uncontrollably.

Lissa? Are you there? Can you hear me?

When she didn't respond, he despaired. Clearly a more experienced dragon would have succeeded. Pravara could talk to him halfway across the kingdom and he couldn't even reach someone less than two leagues away. Mikal sighed. What if something happened to him? He wanted to tell Lissa that he loved her, even though he hadn't ever said it before.

What? Mikal, is that you? Did you say you loved me?

Mikal closed his eyes and shook his head. He stilled his

thoughts and smiled. Lissa's soothing presence appeared in his mind.

Lissa? Is that really you?

Aye. It's me! You were one of those dragons, weren't you? I knew it!

Aye. I am the black one. Gareth chose blue and yellow this time around.

Mikal, you said you loved me. Is that true?

Mikal hesitated. If ever there was a time to reveal his true feelings, then this would be it. He took a deep breath and focused on Lissa's presence in his mind.

I guess I did.

You guess? Either you do or you don't, Mikal.

You know that I do, Lissa.

Then tell me. Say it to me right now.

You think I'm afraid to say it? I love you, Lissa. I love you more than I would have thought possible. I cannot begin to imagine living my life without you in it.

Several seconds of silence passed.

Lissa? Did I lose you? Can you hear me?

You said it! You actually said it!

Of course I did. You heard me, didn't you?

Do you mean it?

Every word.

You have no idea how you've made me feel, Mikal. I want you to know that I am yours, always and forever.

Did we just get engaged?

He felt Lissa giggle with excitement.

I think we just did. Isn't that fantastic?

You know what? It really is. I don't even care if my parents don't agree.

Why wouldn't they? They love me. I'm a delight!

Mikal snorted, causing Gareth to give him a side-long look.

What are you doing? Where are you going?

He explained the situation. **Either way, we know at the moment it can be hurt, even killed.**

Mikal, I'm impressed. That's very commendable of you three. Your father would be proud. You already know how proud I am of you.

Several seconds of silence followed before Lissa began

speaking again.

I just told my father about the Athanaus. He said that only a true prince would put the safety of the kingdom above his own.

Wow. I don't know what to say to that. You didn't tell him about us, did you?

About being engaged? No. I think we should tell him together.

Agreed. Hey, I don't suppose you have seen any other dragons fly by?

Aye, about ten minutes ago. We rushed outside just as it flew into the clouds.

Can you tell me what it looked like? What color was it?

It was brown. Solid brown.

Are you sure?

Aye. I remember telling my father that particular dragon reminded me of a flying horse.

It must have been the thriper! Lissa, you have no idea how much help you are. Thank you! I'll be in touch!

A feeling of warmth spread throughout his body. Mikal was concerned at first but then realized that he must be sharing Lissa's emotions, the love she was feeling for him. If so, he could get used to it.

Oh, so you approve, huh?

Uh, did you hear all that?

Aye. And I love you, too. Please be safe, Mikal.

I will. I look forward to telling our parents.

That same warm sensation appeared again.

As do I, my love.

Mikal severed the mental connection and reeled in shock. Had he really just become engaged? All he had wanted to do was talk with her. What would his parents say when he broke the news? Was he really as unconcerned as he had led Lissa to believe? Mikal grunted once. As a matter of fact, he was.

"Pravara, I have some great news for you."

"Oh?"

"Lissa thinks she saw the thriper." He repeated her description.

Gareth flew close. "That must be the right one."

"We need to know for sure," Pravara pointed out. "At least

this gives us a starting point. I am relaying the information to my father."

"I hope we hear something soon," Mikal said to Gareth. He turned to look down at the passing countryside far below them. The western coast had disappeared and now there was nothing but leagues and leagues of leafy green treetops as far as the eye could see. Mikal looked north. The distant peaks of the Bohani Mountains were just becoming visible. "I say we head toward R'Tal. If the thriper is looking for jhorun, that would be the most likely target."

"It's not heading toward R'Tal," Pravara promptly answered. She had started growling. "A solid brown dragon has been spotted heading northeast, toward the human settlement of Verdayn."

Mikal groaned. That should have been his first guess, the village where this quest had begun. Pravara had dipped a wing and turned northeast. He hurriedly mimicked her movements.

"Could it be heading toward the valley where my mother and aunt live?" Gareth asked worriedly. "It's in the same direction as Verdayn."

"All the more reason we find this thing as soon as possible," Mikal told his friend. "We'll find it and stop it before it has a chance to terrorize anyone else."

Fifteen minutes later Lissa proved him wrong.

Mikal? Are you there? Can you hear me?

Lissa? What are you … is everything alright? I can sense your distress.

My father just heard from the constable. Verdayn is under attack! There's a dragon wreaking havoc all across the village.

We're almost there.

Mikal, I don't want you anywhere near that thing. What happens if you are hurt? I won't be there to help you.

Nothing is going to happen to me.

But what if something does? Mikal, you can't say for certain you won't get hurt.

You're right, Lissa. I can't promise you that. What I will promise you is that I will do everything I can to make sure this thing doesn't hurt anyone else.

Please be safe.

I will. I … wizards be damned!

What? What is it?

We can see the village. There are fires everywhere. Lissa, I have to go. I love you. Don't ever forget it.

Mikal severed the connection before Lissa could respond and focused on the tiny brown figure that was circling around the village. It was a dragon, and it fit Lissa's description perfectly. It swung low and belched out a stream of fire, engulfing another half dozen homes.

"Why's it doing this?" Mikal asked, confused. "Doesn't it still need jhorun? What's the point of burning everything down?"

Pravara roared a challenge. The thriper's head instantly jerked up and scanned the area. It located the three of them and roared its defiance. The thriper spat a huge fireball straight toward them. Mikal barely had time to duck out of the way.

"Whether or not it needs jhorun is irrelevant," Pravara snapped. Her chest expanded as she gulped air. Within moments the scales on her abdomen were glowing. She targeted the thriper and let loose a single, powerful blast.

Mikal watched, envious, as Pravara's shot, from at least fifteen hundred feet away, raced unerringly toward the creature. The thriper tried to flee, but ended up jumping directly into the path of the oncoming fireball. It roared in pain as its sensitive wings were burned.

"How did you know it was going to jump to its left?" Mikal asked, bewildered.

"I have been a dragon my entire life. Longer than you, longer than Gareth, and certainly longer than it has. It's now a wyverian, and I know how a wyverian will behave."

The thriper was able to strafe the village a final time before the three of them were close enough to be considered a threat. Mikal saw that each of its blasts had generated powerful explosions that had completely decimated homes and small buildings. He growled as his gaze shifted back to lock on the thriper. It was gaining altitude and circling around the village in ever increasing loops. What was it doing now?

Mikal felt an intense hatred rise up within his chest. This being has caused more than its fair share of mischief and terror. If only there was something he could do to bring the accursed creature down and end its reign of fear. He hesitated as he felt his stomach grow warm, as though he had fallen asleep basking in the sun. A quick check of the sun confirmed that it was, at present moment, hiding behind a cloud. Confused, he lowered his neck to see if he could see for himself what was going on with his abdomen.

It was glowing, much like Pravara's. Did that mean he was preparing to spit fire? How was he supposed to aim?

His wyverian body gave a tremendous cough. A jet of fire erupted from his mouth and blasted harmlessly into the air, missing the thriper completely. Mikal frowned. The sensation had been disturbingly like vomiting. Surely there was a better way for a dragon to spit fire without feeling nauseated?

Mikal tried another cough. A tiny burst of fire escaped through his jaws. The fireball fell harmlessly away from him before petering out a few seconds later. How had Pravara done it? What was the trick?

A flash of light caught his attention. He glanced to his right and saw that Gareth was having just as little success in trying to spit fire at the thriper. His last shot came through his nostrils, and now his wizard friend was holding his nose in pain with a look of sheer disbelief on his reptilian features.

Mikal focused his attention on Pravara, who was edging closer and closer to the circling thriper. She raised her neck up, opened her jaws, and blasted another shot. This one streaked straight toward their foe and slammed into its tail. It roared in pain. Mikal's eyes narrowed. He had seen Pravara's chest inflate and then rapidly deflate, almost like a sneeze. Was that how it was done?

Mikal took a deep breath, locked his gaze on the thriper, and coughed as hard as he could. The cough stopped halfway through and the jet of fire spiraled out of control, heading toward absolutely nothing. Mikal growled with frustration. He wouldn't be able to hit the broadside of a barn, as his foster father Steve would have described it.

Mikal beat his wings and ascended. Clearly, the best use of his time was to keep watch and make certain it didn't slip away.

He checked the area. Pravara was quite effectively hitting the thriper with blast after blast of white-hot fire. The brown dragon's wings had become black. Scales were missing in several places on its chest. Yet for whatever reason it remained. What was it trying to do? Sooner or later Pravara was going to score a fatal blow. Why wouldn't it flee?

Something stung his right rear leg, like the prick of a thorn bush.

"That was my fault," Gareth said.

"Looks like your aim is just as bad as mine."

Gareth nodded. "I never imagined being a dragon would be this difficult."

"Don't be too hard on yourself. I can't hit it, either."

"At least you didn't hit me. Mikal, I was aiming for *it* and I hit *you*."

"Since we're both useless at hitting it, the least we can do is to make sure we don't lose it again. Come on, we need to follow Pravara."

Both dragons rose steadily higher. Pravara, still firing blast after blast, had just scored another hit on one of the thriper's already blackened wings. It roared in pain and suddenly banked sharply to the east. It fell like a stone and disappeared into a nearby cloud bank.

"Follow it!" Pravara called. She tucked her wings and dropped straight down, vanishing into the clouds seconds after the thriper.

Mikal and Gareth followed.

"We're being followed," Gareth quietly told him as soon as they were free of the clouds.

Mikal glanced behind him. Two other dragons were trailing behind them. One was a brilliant white dragon and the other was a deep blood red color. In fact, Mikal could see a rider on the red dragon. It was Pheron! That meant the red dragon was Rhamalli.

Mikal sighed with relief. That meant Kahvel, Pravara's father, knew where they were and had sent backup to help deal with the thriper. Ten seconds later the number had grown to six, and in less than a minute had increased to more than two dozen.

"It has to know that there's nowhere to go," Mikal quietly observed.

Gareth nodded.

"I was thinking the same thing. There's no place for it to hide. We've got dozens of dragons trailing behind us."

Mikal turned to look back at the ever-increasing mass of wyverians following behind them. The distinctive gold dragon at the front of the procession was Kahvel. Mikal turned back to their adversary. They weren't gaining on it. In fact, no one was.

Mikal groaned. He suddenly realized why the thriper had been able to stay ahead of them. It wasn't suffering from a loss of jhorun. Every single dragon pursuing it was, which meant no one was at full strength. Mikal detected movement in his peripheral vision and automatically looked over at Gareth. His friend was chanting!

"What are you going to do?" Mikal anxiously asked the wizard.

"Stop interrupting! I need to concentrate."

Chastised, Mikal fell silent.

"For your information, I'm summoning a storm. We are nearing the Sea of Koralis, and I can sense there's a nasty thunderstorm off the southeastern coast. I'm going to try and put it directly in the thriper's path."

"Um, Gareth? You may have noticed, but *we* would also be in its path. Do you really want to do that?"

Gareth stopped chanting and shared a look with his friend. "You have a point. I should probably rethink that."

"What else could you do to slow the thing down? None of us have the strength to overtake it."

Gareth was silent as he considered.

"What about the wind?" Mikal asked, growing excited. "Remember those powerful winds you created when we were following you earlier? Could you do something like that again?"

"Same problem," Gareth answered. "I could do that but it'd affect us just as much as it'd affect the thriper."

The number of dragons trailing the thriper now numbered well over fifty and more were joining the chase every minute.

Mikal watched as they tried to overtake the thriper but ended up falling well short. In fact, it almost looked as though the thriper was pulling away from them.

"Do something!" Mikal urged. "It's going to get away. You're the wizard. Think of something!"

"No pressure there," Gareth scowled.

The skies cleared and they could see that they were rapidly approaching the gentle curve of Lentari's eastern coast. The great sea stretched out endlessly to the east, while the coast curved northeast on their left and southeast on their right. The passing countryside quickly transitioned from trees to open grassland as they approached the cliffs bordering the Sea of Koralis. Without the ample clouds to provide cover, the thriper dropped low, descending to an altitude of less than one hundred feet.

Mikal watched the thriper barely skimming above the ground. He watched it pass over several large boulders. Gareth was chanting once more. As Mikal watched, three boulders, each more than adequate to inflict serious damage, hurled into the air and sped straight toward the thriper. The brown dragon, sensing movement, swerved to avoid the formidable projectiles.

They passed over a farm that was situated near the cliffs, complete with a barn, livestock, and several hay stacks. One of the stacks lifted from the ground and was flung straight up. The thriper collided with the hay, causing the stack to explode. Undeterred, the brown dragon flew on.

"Might I suggest something a little firmer than a pile of hay?"

"Like what? One of that flock of bolgers? Dragons eat bolgers. The last thing I'm gonna do is feed that thing. I didn't see anything else to throw. Besides, I don't see you doing anything to stop it."

The thriper jetted out over the cliff's edge and dropped out of sight as it fell toward the water. Mikal, Gareth, and the rest of their wyverian posse followed as closely as they could, determined not to let the evil creature out of their sight.

The thriper leveled off and headed out to sea. The huge group of dragons following behind growled with exasperation. None of them had their full strength and no one, not even Kahvel the Dragon Lord, wanted to risk trying to fly too far over the great sea, should they need to turn back. The dragons all knew that there was at least ten hours of solid flying before they would encounter the desolate western shores of Culargel. Game was scarce and there was a severe lack of fresh water. All wyverians viewed the great sea as the eastern boundary to their natural territory and rarely, if ever, ventured farther.

"Someone needs to get out in front of it," Pravara announced, being the closest dragon to the thriper. "Maybe we can force it into the water."

"How?" Mikal demanded. He and Gareth were the next closest wyverians. "Gareth and I are nowhere near strong enough flyers to pull that off."

But I am.

"Who said that?" Gareth wanted to know.

"That's my father," Pravara answered. She was now continuously beating her wings in an attempt to pace the thriper. Unfortunately, the brown dragon was slowly, but steadily, inching away.

"Your father?" Gareth repeated. "You mean that's the Dragon Lord?"

"Aye."

You mustn't overextend yourself, Pravara warned her father. **There is nothing but water below. You would lack the strength to extricate yourself from the sea.**

I know what I am capable of, young one.

My Lord will not be alone, a new voice mentally added. Mikal and Gareth looked back. Rhamalli and his rider were now flying side-by-side with Kahvel.

We can do this, My Lord.

Agreed. Are you prepared?

Aye. We will go on your command. We ... wait a moment. My rider has given a suggestion. If we are able to push ourselves a little bit harder, then it stands to reason the thriper would be able to, too.

You are implying that the thriper will still be able to avoid us?

Rhamalli nodded. **Aye. We need a diversion.**

Agreed. To all those pursuing and in range, give it everything you have. Now!

Over five dozen dragons let loose with huge bouts of flame, fireballs, and anything else they had in their arsenal. The thriper, having already sensed the impending attack, tucked its wings, executed spins and rolls, and easily avoided the vast majority of the strikes. A few fireballs managed to make contact on its abdomen but bounced harmlessly away.

Mikal swallowed nervously. Dozens and dozens of speeding fireballs whizzed by frighteningly close. One false move on his part would no doubt end up with him getting struck and, knowing his luck, get the one part of his wyverian body burned that wasn't protected by scales. His wings.

Mikal pulled his wings a little closer to his body and struggled to keep up. Gareth, he noticed, was trying to match Kahvel and Rhamalli's pace but was failing miserably. His wizard friend had now fallen behind him and was continuing to drop away.

"Stop trying to catch up to them," Mikal scolded. "Look at the Dragon Lord. He and Rhamalli are gaining on the thriper."

"It destroyed my village," Gareth groaned miserably. "I want to make it pay for what it did."

The thriper dropped even lower. Mikal decided to try another blast. His fireball, while significant, spiraled harmlessly away from the thriper and slammed into the surface of the sea. Sprays of water flew in all directions. A second fireball made contact with the sea a few seconds later, sending up more sprays of water.

Mikal eyed Gareth. The wizard was still just as bad a shot as he was. He was about ready to crack a joke when he detected movement in his peripheral vision. The surface of the sea had turned choppy. Mikal's jaws snapped closed. He cast a quick glance at the thriper. If only they could somehow force the thriper closer to the surface.

"That could work," Mikal whispered.

Gareth struggled to catch up.

"What? What did you say?"

"Gareth, we need to get the thriper to fly lower and we need to do it right now. Where's Pravara?"

Pravara's sleek dark green form appeared by his side.

"I am here. What is it?"

"Pravara, get word to your father. We need to get the thriper lower, by at least another fifty feet. Hurry! I don't know how much time we're going to have!"

Confused, Pravara relayed the request. Kahvel and Rhamalli immediately struggled to get closer and rise above the creature. Their adversary seemed to match their moves.

Mikal looked down at the churning waters and growled with frustration. The churning, roiling waves were becoming gradually less so. They were running out of time!

He fired off another shot at the water. And another. Gareth, unsure what Mikal was doing, followed suit.

"What are you two doing?" Pravara asked, bewildered.

"Shoot at the water!" Mikal cried. "Don't argue. Just do it!"

Pravara added her shots to those of Mikal's and Gareth's.

"We're trying to buy them some time," Mikal explained between shots.

"Time for what?" Pravara wanted to know.

Before Mikal could answer, they heard a deafening roar. The skies darkened. A cloud? Mikal looked up and gasped. A dragon, larger than he had ever seen before, was directly overhead. It was descending fast. Mikal watched the thriper try to evade, but the gargantuan dragon was quicker. It folded its wings flat against its back and it plunged straight down.

The huge dragon landed directly on the thriper and together the two of them fell toward the surface of the water. Mikal was finally able to get a good look at the new dragon. It was easily three times the size of him, was a lighter shade of green than Pravara, but had black stripes all across its abdomen and wings.

"It's Rinbok Intherer!" Pravara exclaimed, shocked. "He's the former Dragon Lord!"

"Pull up!" Mikal cried out, hoping the big dragon could hear him. "Don't go near the water!"

At the last possible moment, Rinbok Intherer snapped

his wings open and sailed out over open water. He lazily beat his great wings as he steadily rose higher into the air. The thriper, Mikal saw, had somehow managed to avoid splashing down. It was flapping like mad and was struggling to remain airborne. Its wings dragged along the surface half a dozen times before it was finally able to rise slightly into the air.

Mikal groaned. It didn't work. He was so certain that there was an osk...

Something erupted out of the depths of the water. Something huge, even larger than Rinbok. It was dark, it was long, and it moved impossibly fast. The front of the ridiculously large creature emerged from the water and they could see it.

It was an oskorlisk, a great sea serpent.

As Mikal had surmised, the huge serpent had been attracted by the lights from the numerous blasts of fire. The wyverians might have been the top predator in Lentari, but the one disclaimer to that fact was that it didn't apply to the sea. Not where the oskorlisk were concerned.

The thriper made a last-ditch effort to escape but simply wasn't fast enough. The oskorlisk clamped its jaws down on the thriper and pulled it, still struggling, into the sea. Then the water started frothing even more angrily than before.

The dragons hastily returned to the safety of the skies. Mikal watched, transfixed, as not one but three different oskorlisk appeared and fought with the first great serpent for a piece of the prey. They fought, they shrieked, they hissed angrily, and just as quickly as they had appeared, it was over.

The thriper was no more.

Epilogue

How did you know that the former Dragon Lord was in the area?" Lissa asked, raising her voice to be heard over the howling wind. "How did you know that he'd appear when you needed him most?"

"I didn't," Mikal answered, turning his long serpentine neck back so that he was looking directly at his fiancée.

This time Lissa was wearing the cinch sack. He could only see the back of Peanut's head. Gareth was flying nearby, earning himself a few warning woofs, as Peanut hadn't decided whether or not to invite the colorful dragon to be a member of her pack. Gareth turned his blue head to smile at Peanut. In his wyverian body, it looked like he was growling. Peanut growled right back.

"You're telling me that the thriper was destroyed because of a bit of good luck?"

Mikal shrugged, nearly dislodging Lissa from her place on his back.

"Rinbok Intherer told me why he was there," Mikal said,

angling south to avoid flying through a large bank of clouds. Dipping below the fluffy cumulus clouds, he spotted the large castle he called home in the distance. "He was trying to protect Valkira."

"Who's Valkira?" Gareth asked, coming up beside them. Peanut switched back to her warning woofs.

"Rinbok Intherer's only daughter. Didn't you hear what Pravara said? This is the first time Rinbok Intherer has made an appearance since he abdicated the position of Dragon Lord a few years ago. Apparently, he still didn't want to surface, but he is very protective of Valkira and was trying to stop her from joining the pursuit. I guess she is just as stubborn as her father."

"Which one was she?" Gareth asked. "Did we see her?"

"He wouldn't say. However, I did catch him watching a green and tan dragon longer than any other. That had to be her. Anyway, once we flew out over the water and saw how low the thriper was flying, he suspected we might try to get an oskorlisk to attack. His jhorun, while still affected somewhat by the thriper, was nowhere near as diminished as the rest of the dragons. He was able to overtake the thriper, descend from above, and force it down to the water. That's where the oskorlisks were waiting and they took care of the thriper for us."

Lissa's brow furrowed. "Rinbok's daughter is green and tan? I don't think I've seen that combination before on a dragon."

"Think of it like this. If she were lying flat on her stomach, and if viewed from above, you'd see only green scales. However, if viewed from directly beneath then you'd see only the tan."

Lissa nodded. "Got it."

"And that huge dragon used to be the Dragon Lord?" Gareth wanted to know. "I'll bet he never had any problems getting his subjects to behave."

Mikal's head nodded. "I would agree. Quite frankly I was surprised he was willing to talk to me at all. I don't recall ever meeting him before."

"Then why did he talk to you?" Gareth asked, bewildered.

"He must have had a reason. I still can't believe dragons can get that big."

"He's friends with my father and my foster parents. I can only assume he knew who I was because of that."

"He knew who I was, too," Gareth glumly added. "Although he wasn't as impressed with me as he was with you."

"And whose fault is that?" Mikal asked, suppressing a chuckle. "You have gained some notoriety, that's for sure. It'll take time to undo."

"I said I was sorry, didn't I?"

"We know you're sorry, Gareth," Lissa acknowledged with a smile. "Mikal is just teasing you."

They touched down at the dragon cavern just outside the castle. Lissa scurried off Mikal's back in time to see Gareth shift back to his human form. Before the transformation was complete the wizard had already cast a second spell, outfitting himself entirely in black. Tunic, trousers, boots, everything. The young wizard tugged his tunic into place and smoothed a few wrinkles from his pants. He glanced over at Mikal and nodded once. In the blink of an eye Mikal was back in his human form, too. Gareth chanted a final time and Mikal became attired in a matching outfit, only his was buttercup yellow.

Mikal groaned. "Really? Yellow? Was that really necessary?"

"I could have chosen pink."

Lissa giggled, drawing Mikal's attention. He immediately spun in place and pulled her in for a hug. He gently held her face in his hands and gave her a tender kiss.

"I've been wanting to do that for a while now."

Lissa wrapped her arms around him and held him tight. "You're absolutely certain your parents are going to be alright with this?"

"Alright with what?" Gareth wanted to know.

"Aye. I'm positive."

"*Who* is alright with *what*?" Gareth repeated, frowning. "What do you two know that I don't?"

Mikal hooked an arm around his friend's shoulders and

pulled him toward the castle.

"Come, my friend. You can hear it the same time we tell it to my parents. They're going to love this!"

* * *

"Father. Mother. Lissa and I have something we'd like to share with you."

Both of his parents sat back on their thrones and clasped their hands together. Mirroring each other's movements, his mother and father placed their hands on their laps and silently regarded him.

"As you know," Mikal slowly began, fervently wishing that they were alone in the Antechamber without a room full of people watching, "Lissa and I have been seeing each other."

Constable Fensham, standing beside Commander Rhenyon, was staring, unblinking, at him. Mikal swallowed nervously.

"I have asked Lissa to be my bride and to always be by my side. It is with great joy that I can say that she has accepted."

No one moved. No one spoke. Lissa stared at her father and frowned. "Father? Isn't there something you'd like to say to me?"

Fensham smiled at her and clasped his hands behind his back, but elected to keep quiet. He looked, deferentially, at the king and nodded his head. Lissa glanced quickly at the king before dropping her eyes to the ground.

Mikal couldn't ever recall hearing the Great Hall this quiet before. With a startled look on his face, he slowly spun in place and saw that everyone, including his parents, were staring expectantly at him. Lissa quietly took off the cinch sack on her back and let Peanut out, who instantly bolted straight toward the queen. Ny'Callé stared at the energetic corgi sprinting across the room, held up a hand, and gave her a quiet command.

"*Wait.*"

Peanut slammed on the brakes and slid the remaining few feet over to the queen's throne. Ny'Callé casually reached down to retrieve the leash that was trailing behind her, but not before ruffling the fur on Peanut's head.

"This isn't what I had envisioned," Mikal murmured softly, as his eyes shifted back to his father's. He took Lissa's hand and held it tightly. His mother drew his eyes. He watched, confused, as his mother held out her empty hand.

The silence continued. Ny'Callé cleared her throat and tapped her husband's shoulder with her waiting hand. His father sighed, reached into his robes, and pulled out a small leather pouch, which jingled as he handed it to the queen.

"Very well, dear. You win this round."

The Great Hall erupted into cheers. More confused than ever, Mikal stared at his parents. What had happened? Why had his father given a money pouch to his mother?

"Your mother informed me that before this mission was over, you and young Lissa would be betrothed to one another," his father explained.

Lissa gasped aloud, while Mikal's mouth fell open. His mother knew? How? When?

Ny'Callé rose from her seat and embraced Lissa with a fierce hug.

"It was only a matter of time. I could see the way the two of you looked at each other. A woman knows these things. I told your father of my suspicions. He doubted me. Yours, too, Lissa. In fact…"

She held out another hand. This time it was directed at Fensham, who grudgingly handed over another small pouch. Smiling triumphantly, the queen pocketed her winnings and beamed her approval at both her son and his fiancée.

"Mister Gareth," the king formally said as he rose to his feet. "Step forward."

Gareth swallowed nervously and took a few tentative steps toward Mikal's father.

"You are impetuous, young Gareth," the king began. "Impetuous and reckless."

Gareth's head fell.

"Yet you did the right thing. You aided my son and helped save the kingdom from the clutches of the thriper. You alone were able to vanquish an ancient creature long thought to be invincible."

"I didn't do it by myself," Gareth hastily corrected. "My friends helped me. Without them I don't know where I'd be."

"I would imagine," Kri'Entu casually said, "you'd still be investigating your surprising shealk heritage, am I right?"

The three companions were once more rendered speechless. Mikal stared at his father in utter shock, while Lissa glanced over at the queen, who failed to hide her smile in time.

"How do you know that?" Gareth asked in a subdued voice. "How could you have known?"

"Perhaps someone told him?" a new voice said.

A man in his late thirties appeared next to the queen. For someone so young, his black hair was streaked with premature gray. He was taller than the king, lean and muscular, and had piercing green eyes. He wore a serious expression on his face and he only had eyes for the young teen, who was staring suspiciously back at him.

"Who is it?" Mikal softly whispered to Lissa.

His fiancée placed a soft finger on his lips. "It can only be Balthor. Hush."

"Father?" Gareth tremulously asked. "Is it really you?"

The strange man finally smiled. "It's been a long time since I've been in this form, son. Much too long."

"What ... when ... how did you get here? You said your jhorun was too weak to shift! And wasn't Lord Phaedren against your returning to the surface?"

"My jhorun has regenerated enough to allow me to shift. I won't be able to shift back to shealk for quite some time. Thankfully, Lord Phaedren has accepted my compromise. I can only hope you meant what you said earlier, my son. I hope you will come visit me beneath the sea."

Gareth nodded fervently. "I will, Father. I will! I promise. Does mother know you're back?"

Balthor shook his head. He quickly glanced around the room as though he was embarrassed that there were so many witnesses to the private conversation he was trying to have with his son.

"She does not. Perhaps we could go see her? Together?"

"I'd like that, Father."

"I will be sending along a team of builders," Kri'Entu formally announced. "I believe that was our arrangement, wasn't it, Mister Gareth?"

Mikal watched as his friend's eyes filled. Gareth hastily swiped the back of an arm across his face.

"May I inquire as to the nature of this arrangement?" Balthor asked curiously. He turned to look up at the king and bowed. "Why would you send builders along with us?"

Kri'Entu looked over at Mikal and nodded his head.

"It was part of the deal I made with Gareth," Mikal explained, drawing Balthor's full attention. "He agreed to help me deal with the thriper if we would provide him and his mother a new house."

"A new house?" Balthor repeated, puzzled. "What was wrong with the last one?"

Still overwhelmed with emotion, Gareth stared at the floor.

"Gareth and his mother moved in with his aunt after you disappeared," Mikal answered quietly. "Gareth took your disappearance badly and his mother decided a change of scenery was in order."

Balthor nodded. He placed his hands on Gareth's shoulders and squeezed them affectionately. Balthor turned to look back at the king.

"I appreciate what you are willing to do, Your Majesty, but I do not think that will be necessary. I will build my family another house. Besides, I have no intention of living with my wife's sister any longer than duly necessary."

"Your position is commendable," the king told him. After a few moments of silent contemplation, he looked back at father and son and clasped his hands behind his back. "It's truly unfortunate that I cannot honor that request."

Balthor, who had just taken a step toward the exit in the opposite direction, turned and regarded the king with a neutral stare.

"I had an accord with your son. I promised him a new house and a new house he will receive. A team of builders will be dispatched to Verdayn to build that house. Now, if you'd like to assist the builders so that you can say you helped construct your new home that would be fine. Or, you could simply sit back and let others do the work. It matters not to me. That's my offer, Mister Balthor."

Balthor gazed at the king with a bemused expression on his face. "May I propose a counter offer? I will design the house and provide the building materials. If you'd like to send a few laborers to help me build it, I would accept the help."

Kri'Entu cocked his head and pretended to think. "And here's my counter offer. I provide the building materials and you can select a team of laborers. Their fee will be covered by me."

Warming up to the game, Balthor smiled. "Am I in charge of the laborers?"

"If you so desire."

"Then I accept."

"Excellent. Pick a plot of vacant land and select your team. I will expect to hear frequent updates."

Dismissing the matter, Kri'Entu took the queen's hand and faced the assembled guests in the Great Hall. He held out a hand and indicated Mikal should take his place on his right. Mikal, in turn, pulled his very reluctant fiancée up to the podium next to his father. Right on cue, Lissa's face blushed crimson.

"Friends and guests, we have cause to celebrate! Kre'Mikal has finally chosen his bride. May I present the soon-to-be Kre'Lissa, daughter of Fensham, the kingdom of Lentari's future princess!"

"Princess?" Lissa squeaked with embarrassment as the Great Hall erupted into cheers.

Mikal turned to his fiancée and smiled. "You cannot tell me that you didn't see this coming. I am a prince, after all."

Balthor and Gareth smiled and bowed in front of the royal family.

"With your leave, Your Majesty," Balthor began, "I'd like to see my wife. It's been too long. My son and I would like to return home."

Kri'Entu nodded and turned to Mikal. "May I assume you still have Verdayn's portal key?"

Mikal nodded. He reached into one of his trouser pockets

and produced the key.

"Perhaps you'd like to personally see to it that Mister Balthor and his son reach their home successfully?" the king asked.

Mikal took Lissa's hand. "I would, Father."

* * *

"That? That's where you've been living, son? I had no idea."

Gareth bristled with annoyance. "Aunt Delythia's house may not be the nicest but it has been home for the last two years."

Balthor was instantly contrite. "I am so sorry I was gone for so long. Damn that thriper."

"You don't have to say that anymore," Mikal reminded him. "It became a tasty treat for a pack of oskorlisks."

"I wish I could have seen it," Balthor wistfully said.

The front door to the house banged open. Adyna appeared, wearing her worn flannel dress and her apron. She stared at the procession gradually walking toward her. She was about ready to call for her sister when she noticed the man walking silently next to her son. Her eyes widened. She slowly exited the house and began walking toward them. Her speed increased with each step until she was running at a sprint.

"Balthor! You've come back! Oh, Balthor! I thought you were dead! Where have you been?"

Delythia appeared in the doorway, smiling. She nodded at Mikal and Lissa and then dabbed a worn handkerchief at the corner of her eyes.

Ignoring the questions being fired at him, Balthor pulled his wife into a hug and held her tight. He noticed Gareth approaching and pulled his son into the hug, too. Together again, the family slowly rocked back and forth in their embrace, sobbing hysterically.

Mikal pulled Lissa away from the newly reunited family and clasped her hand tightly in his. He leaned down to grab Peanut's leash and guided them back toward Capily.

"Come on, Peanut. Let's go home."

Author's Note

Book #8. Wow. I was getting ready to say that I was floored I had published so many but the simple fact that this book makes the third I've released in the same year speaks volumes. Several years ago, that would have been unheard of. I was envious of those authors who could release new titles that quickly. I even felt bad for the readers. Imagine reading the second book of a trilogy and then learning you were going to have to wait a full year before you could find out what happened.

Thankfully I'm managing my time a teensy bit more effectively now, so it has helped with my release schedule. So, let's address the million-dollar question: what's next? Well, the sixth book in the Tales of Lentari series has already been plotted, outlined, and started. Using my same timeline as I used for Thoughts for a Portal and Wizard in the Woods, this one should be done and released by the end of this year. My wife cautions me that it might take longer than that, since she wants a hand in the writing, but I continue to be optimistic. We'll make it by the end of the year.

I have gone on record a few times mentioning that I was thinking about starting a new series. I've written eight books about Lentari, and this next one will make nine. I'm kinda curious as to try something new. Don't get me wrong, I will continue the Tales of Lentari series. Thanks to my increased number of titles I release each year, I'll be able to keep the Lentarian fans happy, but I would like to try something else. Something in fantasy? Sci-fi? Maybe a mystery? Or possibly a combination of all three? I'm not sure. I have so many ideas bouncing around in my head that it is difficult to single out just one.

Regardless of the direction I end up taking, rest assured that Tales of Lentari isn't going anywhere anytime soon. I'd be foolish to alienate the fans and trust me, they're everywhere. The last time I looked I had made sales and fans in over sixty different countries. For me, that's mind blowing. The last thing I want is to have a horde of angry fans cyber-stalk me. :)

Are you looking for something to read while you're waiting for the next Lentarian title to be released? It surprises me how often I'm asked for recommendations on other titles/series to check out, so I've started including some suggestions in here. So, we'll call this the "if you liked mine, then you ought to check out theirs" segment. I've read all of these titles and have loved every single one of 'em. Without further ado, here's my list of books that are worth checking out:

The War of the Blade series, by J.D. Hallowell.

The Blue Moon Detectives series by JH Sked

The Klondaeg series, by Steve Thomas

The Martian, by Andy Weir

Ready Player One, by Ernest Cline

I've read them all and would heartily recommend them (which I have many times) to anyone.

I would also like to mention that I enjoy chatting with the fans, so if you ever have a question you'd like answered, or would like a little more insight into certain characters or plot points, feel free to look me up on my blog, www. AuthorJMPoole.com. If you stop by and say hello, then you will get a hello back! I'm also on Facebook and will entertain all friend requests. The only thing I ask is that you don't spam me. Keep it civil!

Also, as an author, I'd again like to remind you, the reader, of the importance of reviews. Nothing will help an author out more than by leaving a review wherever you purchased the book. Loved it? Liked it? Hated it? Let me know! I would greatly appreciate it.

If you'd like to follow the progress on the latest book I'm working on, then I would encourage you to sign up for my newsletter so you'll never miss another book release, or contest, or any other bit of news that I pass along to the readers. You'll even get a free short story for signing up!

The Daily Scroll: https://mailchi.mp/892eb3929891/authorjmpoole

Hear that? The portal is chiming. I'm overdue to return to Lentari for a spell. A certain teleporter has just been asked for help. Of course, she said yes. Together with the help of her fire thrower husband they hurry to save a kingdom they didn't know existed.

J.
August 2015

Fan Submissions

As many of you know, I will oftentimes see if any of the fans would like to name a fictional character. I asked for quite a few this time. Here's what I used:

Human names

Brikon, Andra, Adyna, & Jamien — Kantami
Gareth, Alwyn, Catrin, & Delythia — Nicki Jones
Bresk, Valtor, & Jasmyre — Andy Florek
Aleric — Tamara Newman
Ondo — John Monk
Jacobi — Toni Trick

Dragon names

Selendran, Malthryp — Brett Gable
Kalith — Christina Dean Carr
Amentharias — Amber Leigh
Sorahono — Kantami
Falgoth, Balthor — Jason Harvill
Lorofer — Freddy Gandolfi
Vinarth — Linda Palantino
Kalendra — Tamara Newman
Fornius — John Monk

Jhoruns

Split wood w/o using tools — David E. Ratcliffe
Water location & purification — Caroline Craven
Removing foul smells from barn, levitating rocks from fields — Charla Hinkle

ABOUT THE AUTHOR

Jeffrey M. Poole is a professional writer who writes in both the fantasy and mystery genres. His series are listed below. Jeffrey lives in picturesque Southern Oregon, with his wife, Giliane, and their Welsh Corgi, Kinsey. His interests include archery, astronomy, archaeology, scuba diving, collecting movies, collecting swords, and tinkering with any electronic gadget he can get his hands on.

In March, 2015, Jeffrey became a proud member of SFWA, the Science Fiction & Fantasy Writers of America! Jeffrey encourages readers to connect with him on Facebook (facebook.com/bakkianchronicles). Fans can also follow him online at: www.AuthorJMPoole.com.

BOOKS BY JEFFREY POOLE

Mystery
CORGI CASE FILES
Case of the One-Eyed Tiger
Case of the Fleet-Footed Mummy
Case of the Holiday Hijinks
Case of the Pilfered Pooches
Case of the Muffin Murders
Case of the Chatty Roadrunner
Case of the Highland House Haunting
Case of the Ostentatious Otters
Case of the Dysfunctional Daredevils
Case of the Abandoned Bones
Case of the Great Cranberry Caper
Case of the Shady Shamrock
Case of the Ragin' Cajun
Case of the Missing Marine
Case of the Stuttering Parrot
Case of the Rusty Sword
Case of the Secret Staircase (short story)
Case of the Unlucky Emperor
Case of the Ice Cream Crime

Scan the QR code to sign up for his free newsletter!

www.ingramcontent.com/pod-product-compliance
Lightning Source LLC
Chambersburg PA
CBHW050141120726
47903CB00002B/449